PARTICLES AND LUCK

Also by Louis B. Jones

Ordinary Money

PARTICLES
AND LUCK

When one begins to count, one begins to err.
—old Latin saying

Louis B. Jones

Pantheon Books · New York

For my mother

All rights reserved under International and Pan-American Copyright Conventions. Published in the United States by Pantheon Books, a division of Random House, Inc., New York, and simultaneously in Canada by Random House of Canada Limited, Toronto.

Library of Congress Cataloging-in-Publication Data

Jones, Louis B.
Particles and luck / Louis B. Jones.
p.   cm.
ISBN 0-679-42285-4
I. Title.
PS3560.0516P37 1993
813'.54—dc20   92-29816
CIP

Book Design by M. Kristen Bearse

Manufactured in the United States of America
First Edition
987654321

For their technical help, the author wishes to thank John Burnett of Harvard's McKay Laboratory and Nick Herbert, author of *Quantum Reality,* neither of whom is to blame for any inaccuracies; the Marin Arts Council for its support; Betsy for the hideout; Nick for the even better hideout; Dr. Theodor Geisel for his edifying stories, here slightly changed; *il miglior fabbro* Oakley Hall and his wife, Barbara, for their discerning reading; and Brett; Brett for many things, large and now small.

The fundamental structure of matter involves a certain something material and a certain something non-material. Maybe modern quantum mechanics has provided some mathematics for discussing these two mysterious elements, but they remain quite ill-defined. Still, all you need to make a given universe is particles and luck.

—*J. H. Burnett*

PARTICLES AND LUCK

1
Putting Signs on Everything

Say there is a very fortunate young newlywed, a theoretical physicist named Mark Perdue, who has just purchased a deluxe semidetached unit in the Cobblestone Hearth Village Estates development—across from the Paradise Mall in Terra Linda—at the edge of the new-built Phase III section where the lawns and driveways aren't installed yet but where all the foundations meet new seismic code requirements and everybody is guaranteed a Mount Tamalpais view. Suppose also that, at the age of twenty-seven, he occupies a prestigious chair in the physics department at Berkeley: four years ago, when he was only twenty-three, he published a now-famous article on the subatomic constituents of matter, which set him up for life; and since then it hasn't mattered what he does. People treat him like "a genius," and probably always will, despite his more objective private pessimism—yet a somewhat emancipating pessimism—that he won't be having any more inspirations, that he's had his one great idea and is therefore retiring, if a bit gladly, into the sort of Einsteinian irrelevancy that celebrity seems to raise scientists to.

Then suppose further that his wife—whom he just married this month—is a beautiful, prosperous patent lawyer from Palo Alto, in Intellectual Property, named Audrey Field, who, four years ago in Boston, started out strictly as his roommate, much too improbably beautiful for him, but, across the safe barrier of that improbability, grew into his friend, and thence, by their not paying attention, into his destined wife, with the time-lapse indetectability of inertial slow motion, making last month's marriage ceremony finally inevitable—and who, lying beside him in the new condominium's bare bedroom on this particular morning, braces her back against the wall, pulls her knees up, sets the soles of her feet against his spine, and with her legs begins pushing him off the edge of the bed. "Do you remember what happens tonight?" His face is cemented into sleep, and he can't answer, unable to open his eyes in the surfeit of light in the empty condominium. It was only twenty-one days ago that he and Audrey—on the same afternoon!—took possession of their unfurnished Cobblestone Hearth unit and "got married," and now he wakes every day in this new condition as if in a strange new aquarium, his motions displaced prismatically. "Tonight," she says, "I'll be in Los Angeles, and you're on your own."

In response he gives up a phlegmy segment of a hum,

guilty only of absentmindedness, but brought thereby into contact with the usual, dimly moral, headache—of non-specific morning doom—which always looms larger and truer in the solitary moment of judgment before you've lifted your head from the pillow into the atmosphere of forgetful vanity in the world. This morning in particular it seems obvious that the success of his famous *subatomic-deconstruction* essay (so called) was only a matter of luck, or professional fad, which washed him up onto this rather boring pinnacle, permanently, too young. The essay merely pointed out something obvious (involving the sub-atomic commas and periods and asterisks everything is made of; and showing that the words we use for them will determine their character and destiny), which, at the time, no one else happened to be self-absorbed enough, or lost enough, to think of. Now he can get all the beam he wants at the highest-luminosity colliders at Stanford. He doesn't have to teach *any* undergraduate courses. They tried to give him a personal secretary, devising activities for whom, every day, would have been a constant source of embarrassment. Conversations in the corridor, when he approaches, fall quiet and open out genially—conversations among older, more eminent physicists who better deserve an appointment to the Potts Chair and who do have to teach undergraduate courses—and who probably observe his present apathy with malicious amusement. The tone of everything changed slightly when, in connection with book publicity on the popularized version of his work, his photograph appeared in *People* magazine, his arms folded, a Luciferian glower on his face and, actually, a fake lightning bolt in the background, made of tinfoil wrapped around a cardboard zig-zag.

Audrey starts pushing harder with her legs, half his body already sticking out from beneath the covers. "Audrey, don't." He tries to put some command into his voice. His knees are slipping over the edge of the bed. "Audrey— my allergies." On a final great push, the rest of his body spills over naked onto the carpet—a carpet still waxy with the new-car smell of a fresh California condo but deeply impregnated with powdery allergens like dust and pollen and dried rug-shampoo surfactants that, on contact, alter the acidity and electrolyte balance of the mucous membranes. The whole of California is allergenic, breaking up in the dry heat into a pernicious hay dust.

"I won't be back till super late."

"Why?"

"The pope the pope the pope the pope," she sings in a descending scale as she casts off the blanket and bounces. "You'll be all alone by yourself." Her legs, kept perpetually hard and tanned as forearms by her lucky resolution never to have children, swing off the bed above his head, scissoring him briefly in that sweeping field of pleasure whose vertex is the somber grave. Where play always becomes surprisingly deliberate. In a forbidden peek, he fails to blind himself against seeing the white string that, incredibly, emerges from within, the seal of the female's incalculable lunar sabbath. It repels thought. Her legs—the legs he is married to!—a little bit knock-kneed, rope-tendoned behind the knee, flat-footed balletically, wonkily—stride with happy force across the floor to the Closet Suite that was a prized option of the Cobblestone Hearth Mini-Deluxe package, and whose doorjambs the pale, copper-haired Buyer's Tour Rep fondled and clung to during their buyer's tour, so that Mark—newly famous and very respectably employed, flirting obviously with the Buyer's Tour Rep in his fiancée's presence—felt like a stud.

Audrey says, her voice in the closet strangled by the

NIKE T-shirt she pulls off every morning, ". . . Licensing negotiations for the pope's-visit theme properties."

"Children's lunch boxes," he tells her, to show he really had been listening when she told him about it last night at dinner. She suspects him of never hearing a word she says. "Pinball machines," he adds.

"I doubt anybody'll want to market a pope pinball machine. Do you know why pinball is sinful?" Her voice is muffled by clothes in the closet and by her motion deeper—into the attached bathroom, where the click of her OrthoNovum dispenser is audible, its beige plastic zodiacal wheel against the tile countertop. Then the bang of the metal wastebasket: the used-up OrthoNovum wheel landing on its floor. She knows the last few pills in the cycle are placebos, but she always takes them anyway, just in case, superstitiously. "This begins my month without birth-control pills. So we have to be careful, starting now. Do you know why pinball is sinful?"

"Is it?" says Mark. He gathers himself closer together on the floor, trying to pool his body heat.

"This is theology we got from the Vatican lawyers yesterday. Pinball is sinful because it's random. It's chance." She leaves, going downstairs to the kitchen in her bathrobe, theologizing. He's pitiful, forsaken now naked on the floor where only his *utter* motionlessness will keep the muff of warm air from wafting away from him, and protecting a slight, miscellaneous erection, now subsiding, of mixed motives, perhaps having to do with the thought of adultery, axiomatic to the thought of new marriedness. ". . . Pinball is like card games and horse races. It's wicked. Because wherever random chance is in the universe, the devil is there. Even God doesn't know where that pinball will bounce. The devil's hand grabs it and moves it around."

Which would imply that all the particles of matter in the universal vacuum are not in grace, they're in hell, colliding meanly. When, at Stanford, the photo plates come out of the accelerator chamber and he looks at the skittering white tracks against the black background, he's watching the evil spell that drives the ultimate specks of matter into madness, the madness of separation from God, from pure spirit. One of the more controversial, if accidental, results of his famous essay was the annoying idea that matter can never be intelligible, matter and consciousness being a powder and an ether that may never mix, except mysteriously.

". . . Are you moving?" Audrey's voice is acoustically shaped by the kitchen cupboards downstairs, and it seems to echo down the empty hallway of their future marriage together, growing more distant as he lies there trying not to stir, to keep the pool of body warmth. He's guilty of having let marriage be *her* idea all along. On a trip to China for a series of conferences last spring, they were advised to register in all Asian hotels as Mr. and Mrs. Perdue; and being addressed as Mrs. Perdue seemed to make her sleeker, disconcertingly. On the plane home, she tilted her head uncharacteristically and said—her voice pitched at an odd new insertion slant—that she rather liked the way marriage felt after all these years, and after all it's only words on paper in a document somewhere. He had learned over time that Audrey's feelings are magnetically correct— that she feels *for* him, according to a sort of marital division of labor. And so they were married at city hall, in an errand. Her most persuasive argument at the time was *Besides, it won't change anything anyway,* which seems still to be true.

"We're out of molasses," she says matter-of-factly, fully knowing that molasses is necessary to his oatmeal every morning, fully knowing, even though it's never mentioned, that setting a nickel of brown syrup at the north, south, east, and west quadrants of his oatmeal is the only way he can begin his day. This is a manipulative new way of getting him out of bed in the morning, by panicking him. "Ope, there's a message on the tape," she says cheerfully, as if the loss of molasses were the most trivial thing in the world. The Record-a-Call makes a mechanical slurp as it rewinds the tape, and she turns up the volume to broadcast the message upstairs:

"Hello? Hi, this is Roger Hoberman, your next-door neighbor, the old pot-walloper, remember? With the Olde Fashion Pizza? Well, I got this thing, and I guess you probably got one, too, and I thought we should figure out what to do about it. I want to protect my investment here, and something like this would be a real pardon-the-expression pisser. So my number is 499-3889. You may recall I met you a couple times by the dumpsters, and I pointed out that you should drop by the Olde Fashion, and I'll cut you a free one. Be that as it may, we ought to do something about this. And it looks like tonight is a deadline, so we might have to do it tonight. Hey, I'm a businessman, I don't need this. So whatever." He hangs up.

Mark shouts into the nap of the carpet, "I'm not doing that. You have to do that."

"I'm going to Los Angeles, honey," Audrey sings in a rising and falling tune. He doesn't reply. There's something about Roger Hoberman's sheer size, football player–like, that makes him want to forget about the whole thing. Their Buyer's Tour Rep, on their tour of the condominium, paused to look out the west window at the adjoining unit, and said, "I suppose I should mention. You have a neighbor. But he'll be leaving soon. He's . . .," her mind sought the right expression, ". . . divorced."

The television downstairs is warming up, and the

"Today Show" theme music, commercially redolent of sunrise and coffee, fills the condo. Audrey's feet are on the steps. "I'm getting the squirt gun," she warns as she climbs the stairs.

"I'm coming," says Mark without moving, his eyes fixed open now upon the polyester yarn of the carpet, whose regular molecular chains broadcast a shine. "Do you realize I don't even have books in my office? People stop talking when I come down the corridor?"

"They respect you." Looking for something on the night table, she steps over him.

"These aren't ordinary people, Audrey. These are like Heidi Martinger and Chuang Tzu. And like Shem Sefirah. I'm *half* some of their ages."

"You'll feel better after oatmeal."

"Sefirah was *with* the quantum chromodynamics group. And Chuang Tzu *did* the Bell Inequality. There are thirty-three Nobels at that school. Don't you think they wonder what I'm doing with the Potts Chair in Theory?"

She efficiently hoists her robe around her hips as she goes into the bathroom to make her vigorous gushing mare tinkle. "And now honey? You'll be all alone by yourself, but I'm going to make it foolproof. There'll be cream chipped beef in the microwave. And I'm putting signs on everything. . . ."

Instead of the sound of the toilet seat comes the rush and slap of water in the shower. "Bye," she says, closing the door, leaving him forlornly rearranged. He is the more beloved member of the marriage, but the marriage doesn't seem therefore unjust, a lucky belovedness having been the spell cast over his whole life. And the infinitely complex bargain that is marriage, not to be too closely audited, adjusts the balance of justice by many secret leaks and siphons. Downstairs he can hear the post–commercial break theme music of the "Today Show," and, yielding to a new appetite, he climbs up against the bed and goes to the closet, where his terry-cloth bathrobe is lying on the floor.

His feet are stiff. The staircase, its thick carpeting and smooth fresh-stuccoed walls enclosing a big wedge of air-space, continues to seem an ideal architect's rendering, abstract and rather pleasantly alienating to a groggy new-comer to California, where even one's dearest old values are immediately refracted in the clear air. It turns out, though he hadn't expected it, that he loves California, completely, amnesiacally. On the "Today Show" as on a daily morality play, the handsome black anchorman, the intelligent but replaceable young woman, and the fat weatherman buffoon stand for three model ways of stick-ing yourself into the world on this weekday morning: there's valor, there's beauty, and there's the desperate clowning of those who have neither—which must be Mark's group. Barefoot and terry cloth robed, he feels cozily backstage in life as he walks on stiff feet to the counter and wrenches the lever on the cappuccino machine that releases the sieved metal cup, which he bangs on the waste basket's rubber rim to dislodge the black plug of yesterday's coffee grounds, toxic-looking.

He turns on the faucet, but clumsily, halfway, and a perfectly smooth column of water stands on the floor of the sink like a glass-blower's strand. Still sleepy enough yet to be tender and clearheaded, he rests his weight on his el-bows on the sink's threshold, and he falls into a lucid stupor over the tube of falling water, which imprisons a filament of cold daylight. Its base is like a wineglass foot that pushes outward an encircling lip of trembling water, which always threatens to close over. It's beautiful. It's impossible to imagine the whole thing could be time reversible—as if you could run the movie backward, provided you could also reverse particle charge and particle parity, and, in a mirror-reversed universe composed of antimatter, watch the water swarm together up the drain into a column and thrust itself up into the faucet—resulting in the identical apparition: a tube of water.

Of course it's too large-scale an event to be time reversible. Yet ever since his first thermodynamics course as a sophomore, Mark has been bothered by the, certainly babyish, question: how "big" does a thing have to be to suffer "time"? He was always so literal minded; it was his fortunate defect. You're supposed to be happy with the textbook dogma, that "time" begins to "move forward" exactly at the point where subatomic events are large enough and general enough that statistical mechanics become relevant and entropy is possible. Only the very tiniest interactions go either direction in history. Making "time" a mere subjectivity of mortal humans—clumsy, giant, entropic humans, with their immense dull fingerprints and their gauge-misting breath and crushing rubber shoe heels as big as planets, and their smell of death. Only humans, as they rot, go around thinking they see "causes" in "sequential" events.

"Honey, the machine," says Audrey, coming down the stairs damp in her absorbent robe. He seems to have accidentally turned on the cappuccino maker.

"Oops." He goes near the explosive machine to flick the on-off switch. Two weeks ago the first cappuccino machine blew up because he had left it on, embedding cast-iron shrapnel from its steam chamber all over the kitchen walls, but fortunately he wasn't home. "Did we ever get another timer?" he says as he scans around for a coffee scoop. Everything in the house is equipped with timers that automatically shut off. Before they bought an electric kettle that turns itself off, Mark melted three teakettles. Coming home, they would discover ingots of aluminum pooled and hardened under the burner, or oval drips of copper like unspendable pence on the floor of the oven—with, interestingly, bright beads of some alloy that had been sweated out of the copper, silver BBs with a perfect sphericity as if produced in a gravity-free environment. He'd thought at the time it might be molybdenum.

"Here, I'll do that," she says, taking the coffee scoop from him, which is hanging on the end of his arm in his hand.

With a click, the Record-a-Call machine starts to hum, indicating that it's receiving a message. The bell had been turned off on the phone. *"Hi. I guess you guys are still in bed. This is your neighbor Roger Hoberman. I left a message for you last night. So I'm over here, and I just noticed both you guyses' cars are still in the carport, so I thought I'd give you a try. But hey, I guess you're still sleeping, like I say. So anyway, I'm going to do some stuff. Call me when you get up. My number is 499-3889. Because it looks like we have to do this tonight."* He hangs up.

"Can he see us?" Audrey says, edging toward a window.

"From over there? Probably. It's right over there."

Maybe it will be possible to avoid Roger Hoberman during their entire residency here, which feels temporary because of the general but nonspecific feeling that they'll soon move on to a real house more befitting their prosperity. And temporary because of the absence of furniture. All they have is a card table and two folding lawn chairs. In the dining area, the suspended lamp fixture hangs low over the place where a dining-room table would go. The only inhabitants of the second bedroom are Audrey's snow skis, the same Day-Glo colors as boxes of laundry detergent, lying in the middle of the floor forbidding entry. The fireplace bricks will never be dirty, except for whatever dust settles under the andirons. The fireplace was thrown in free as a promotional gimmick, because they were among the first fifty buyers in Phase III. But Mark just isn't the type to buy a cord of firewood. Or even to know where to buy firewood, or to associate with the kind of person who buys firewood. Whereas that Roger Hoberman has a huge mound of it stacked beside his back door. *With* an expensive blue tarp to keep it dry. He's the kind of guy that will have lots of expensive new furniture he's proud of. He's always washing his purple van in the carport; suds run down the gutter every weekend.

"I'll start the oatmeal," Mark says, not meaning it. "Where's the little pot?"

"It's right where it always is." Audrey, to get across the room, must pass a window, so she drops down on her knees to dip beneath the level of the sill. "Just watch. *I'll* be the one ending up dealing with *that*." Her tone indicates that the merchandising agreements surrounding the pope's visit are, themselves alone, a big enough job for one person to handle. "I take such good care of you."

"Fuff . . .," Mark says, with a gesture of dismissal toward the west, toward Roger's adjoining unit, ". . . some things"—meaning that Roger Hoberman represents a category of trivial encroachments in life that are best combatted by ignoring them, unrealistically. Opening the refrigerator, he concludes his defiance vaguely: "—You know?"

Her back is turned. It seems now an attitude he's trying out, like an actor on a set, in this acoustically odd condominium, in this acoustically odd new marriage. Sometimes, like now, when he's testing her boundaries, he is as if suspended within her, secure and small and vaguely discontented. "You know what I mean?"

She has two fresh yellow Post-it notes, a butterfly on her fingertips. On the face of the toaster, she sticks one of the yellow squares, with the word "toast" written in her script. She says, "See? You'll be fine."

2
You'll Be Fine

hen imagine this same physicist sitting alone at his desk at work with the door closed, running his fingers over the artificial wood-grain surface on his desktop, thinking aimlessly about the process by which the wood grain is photographed and printed onto the polyvinyl medium. There is no reason for his being on campus today, but he shaved and dressed and turned off the TV halfway through "The Brady Bunch" and got into his new car in the carport and came in here saying hello to the usual people and going into his office. A certain painful lighter-than-air feeling, related to impatience, has been ballooning in his chest on this warm autumn day with its thin, valedictory

October sunshine on the eternal campus lawns. The Potts Chair professorship is a newly endowed "perpetual chair" in the department.

When the phone rings (arriving exactly at its predestined moral lull in his office), he picks up the receiver with the familiar disappointed-in-advance feeling of being rescued, that a ringing phone always inspires—though it's logical to suppose that this will only be another newspaper reporter inquiring about the Z-zero particle that was recently created at Stanford. There has been some excitement in the halls this week, some of the champagne in Handicups perfunctory at big experimental successes, followed now by the bleakness of the apparently inevitable realization that, at prevailing energy levels, there are no more particles to be found. The Z-zero, which had been predicted theoretically, was the missing apex of the pyramid, and so the quarks, the leptons, and the gluons are supposedly the last, fundamental, indivisible granules to be discovered— or at least that's what the reporter will want to hear. That's how the event has been misconstrued by the press. And now on the phone he'll have to explain it all again "in layman's terms," fighting the reporter's barely disguised joy in uncovering scientific futility, his nosy search for some millenial despondency among the scientists in having vainly predicted and found the Last Particle.

"Professor Perdue?" says the voice of the departmental work-study assistant Shubie Behejdi, and sweet remorse enters his life again. Her voluptuous double chin, her forearms on her desk blotter so angelic, her eye whites unmarred by a single thread of red, her expectant spine as she sits in her secretarial chair poised always to sustain the most heartbreaking curve from her shoulders to her hips— today is Shubie's last day in the department before her voyage to the Middle East with her family. When she started in the front office last spring, as a math major privileged to be on work-study, at first Mark didn't notice her, hazing her over in the blind spot that floats to protect him from beauty. But he began to realize that she grew uncomfortable and confused in his presence, her gaze unfocused. Which made him then start mirroring her behavior exactly, their eyes always swerving apart like two positive-poled magnets. And finally when he married Audrey three weeks ago, Shubie told him (in his office but with the door *open*) in a peculiar heart-stopping moment of eye aversion, *I am not jealous. Now you are safe for me.* When he responded that he didn't know what she meant (though his ears rang with the knowledge that he knew exactly what she was saying), she answered, *Now you are a married man, you are safer for flirting,* and she left the office groping as if blinded by a joke blown up in her face, swatting toward him with a manila envelope.

"I have call for you," she says over the phone. Her voice is rendered vulnerable by her postnasal drip, a slight laughing rawness in the throat that makes him want to enfold her. An allergy joins them.

"Shubie, I'm bored," he tells her for some reason, meaning it more than he had intended. His good luck has been piling up so uselessly unspent, this is how you start spending it, by simply starting to throw out a few uncharacteristic remarks.

"I have a call for you. Maybe it will be exciting."

"What do people do for fun, Shubie?"

"Me?" At this moment she would be leaning back in her secretarial chair tilting her head in that earring-guarding way she has on the phone. "I'm going to the Art Club tonight to see a band with a disgusting name I won't even say. And I will dance."

"You're going with the guy with the red Dodge Charger."

"Marco? Are you spying on me?"

"You can't fool me, Shubie." The Art Club—more properly the Art and Artifice Club—is one of those crowded new nightclubs on nethermost San Pablo Avenue where the rooms are so dark and the music is so deafening that a sort of stunnedness, a sort of namelessness, allows touch. Mark hasn't been to any such club in his life—these days they all have concrete floors and no furniture, which perhaps may deter any serious touching—but he imagines the place as tumbling glimpses of body parts in the green glow of an occasional EXIT sign. He had, until this minute, thought of Shubie very differently. Why is she going out dancing on the very eve of her long trip?

"Professor, you are spying on me. You should be ashamed."

"I'm jealous," he declares. She was right. His being married makes their flirting more frontal.

"Of Marco? I don't want Marco. He has no education, he's just a superficial American boy."

"He's got you. He's got a great car. He can do what he likes. Tell Marco Professor Perdue'll kick his butt."

"Gosh, I think physicists would be dull." Her English grammar is always winsomely damaged on her full lips.

"Shubie, I'm capable of anything at this moment." Just saying it lightens his limbs. He had thought he was harmlessly joking, but the feeling of not caring about anything fills him like helium and makes him want to grab something and fling it, except that his office is empty and nothing is within reach. "You shouldn't be out dancing anyway. You'll have jet lag in Israel."

"This person is waiting on the other line. He is Mr. Hoberman."

"Shit. Okay, whatever. I'll be good."

"I'm putting you on hold now . . . Professor Perdue."

"Yes, okay. Shit."

The silence of "hold" stops his ear as Shubie leaves him, declining to comfort him, maybe reproaching him for such easy reckless profanity on the phone, alone in his empty office without books or wall decorations or writing implements or even shelves, with just three broken type-writers—old IBM Selectrics that got stacked in here and forgotten, with *Property of the University of California* stenciled in military-looking letters on their sides. It's fitting: all that's in here is a clean desktop, and if he has been "doing" anything lately it's been thinking about surfaces, the physical structure of surfaces, especially the molecular and subatomic border that defines the "edge" of some-thing, which looks to the human eye like solidity. The atoms on an edge, where liquid air begins, must have a different kind of job from the atoms in the middle. For one thing, there's the sizzle of light—and perhaps therefore an increased number of crazy time-reversed positrons in the knit making a millimeter-long stitch backward in time. But, as always, he can't help but resort to the childish idea that space is structured like dot-matrix pictures: as the table's edge moves through the grid of space, it illuminates new dots of "solidity" as it travels, in Gauge space. So matter is to be pictured as a kind of unsolid shimmering special effect, as if one stood in the midst of a rainbow.

"Go ahead," says Shubie's public voice. "Go ahead, Professor," she adds—saying, too, by the insertion of an extra calorie of warmth in her tone, tactfully, shamefully, goodbye to Mark: her leave of absence from the depart-ment is to be indefinite, which means forever.

"Mark Perdue?"

"Yes. Speaking."

"Hi there. This is Roger Hoberman, your next-door neighbor at Cobblestone Hearth Village Estates."

"Yes, hi," says Mark, drawing air deep into the shallows of his lungs, seeing that he'll have to be patient today. He and Roger have never spoken, only greeting each other evasively if they chance to cross paths in the carport or at the dumpster: he seems to be in his forties, with big soft shoulders, large face, janitorial gravity in his gait. But actually Mark has hardly noticed; in his general effort to avoid neighborliness, he fairly sneaks through Cobblestone Hearth Village Estates, which continues to feel like graduate student dorms. At the mailboxes, he immediately throws out the Apple-computer-printed flyers inviting him to Cobblestone Hearth Exclusives, like wine tastings, and he has never once visited the Cobblestone Hearth Upper Class Club, from which in the evenings you sometimes hear the sounds of neighbors' hilarious voices in the large broth of a shared Jacuzzi.

"Listen, did you get one of these things?" Roger says.

"What things?"

"Okay. I'm sorry to be getting to know you under these circumstances, but I got this thing. You probably got one, too, because your property is involved. I'll read it to you. Are you ready?"

"I'm ready."

"As I say, it's pretty weird. There's some other stuff, but I'll just read this part: *Be it known unto all men by these presents, that the Acquisition Systems Company of America claims to be, and has for five years claimed to be, in possession in fee simple of that certain body of land described as follows: the once and former Domain of the Tamalpais Land and Water Company, described as granted by His Excellency Governor Pio Pico to Abraham Albert Valdez Gutierrez, on that certain map entitled 'Holdings in Eternity of the Mexican Empire, July 6, 1846,' which domain extends from the north watershed of Mount Tamalpais between the boundary of the Rancho de Corte Madera del Presidio and the boundary of the Rancho Sausalito until an east-west line three hundred feet beyond the Corte Madera Creek—''* Roger pauses *''—which is marked forever by the Dog Tooth Stone; that the Acquisition Systems Company of America surveys and improves that land annually unto its boundaries; that on November 1, 1992, it will have kept these boundaries intact for a continuous period of five years and may thereafter exercise all rights and privileges of ownership, ad coelum ad usque; and that furthermore its possession of these lands is open, notorious, and hostile. Cordially, blah blah blah.* . . . So you see. Tomorrow is November first.''

"What happens November first? Maybe I wasn't listening."

"November first it becomes *theirs.*"

"Who is Abraham Valdez . . . Albert . . . ?"

"That part almost makes it seem like a joke, doesn't it?"

"Who is he?"

"This old guy. He *died* like probably at least forty years ago. You're not from around here . . ."

". . . No, I'm not from around here," Mark repeats with irritation. The words were oddly extorted from him by Roger's pause.

"There used to be a bar in Sausalito with Abraham's picture on the wall. He was the Sausalito Greeter, in the 1920s. He stood by the roadside waving at everybody. He was an Indian or something. He was crazy. Anyway, listen. I haven't been in my unit a complete year, but I *suppose* they've been sending these letters for five years. At the top it says, *The State of California requires us to publish annually the following document.*"

"Is any of this our property? Supposedly?" Mark is pushing his palm softly into the desktop, where pellets of energy are always exploding into matter as violently as Niagara Falls but silently and tinily, always in the process of knitting themselves into a quiet desktop rather than, say, a nuclear explosion or a quasar or a roaring black hole in space; and he feels he is saying farewell to it: the silent, polymeric-vinyl surface is a shore he's pushing off from this morning.

Roger continues, "They're talking about some of the most expensive real estate in the I-don't-know *state*, maybe? *Country*, maybe? I think it goes all the way to that little ridge behind where there's a big tree."

"But it crosses our property?"

"You know where the minishop has that little playground in the parking lot? It's all made out of railroad ties and old rubber tires?"

"This east-west line runs through our yard, you're saying."

"I've been out here all morning with a tape measure and a clothesline."

In a moment when neither says anything, the predicament mounds up around them. At last Mark speaks. "Despite the fact that he was, as you say, crazy. This Abraham."

"Yes, this corporation is basing their claim on *that*. On *that*. Which maybe they can get away with. Who knows."

"Do they have an address?"

"The letterhead gives the San Francisco address of the Acquisition Systems real estate division. And it has a number to call, which I called, but the guy wasn't in his office. It's like a big corporate *thing*."

"Did you reach anybody?"

"The one guy's secretary said he would be out all day because he had to check on some property in Marin County. Don't you see? We might have to do something about this today. Because tomorrow is November first, and they have to survey and improve their boundaries."

"You know what?" says Mark. "Something I noticed, in fact?" In fact, this morning he had been taking out the garbage and had seen a new gleam in the rough weedy dirt beyond the dumpsters and had risked his loafers to go out and look at it: a bronze plaque set deep in fresh-dug earth. "You know those bronze plaques they put in the ground that say, *Private Property—Permission to Pass Revocable at Any Time?*"

"You saw one of these?"

"On the other side of the carport."

"You have to show me where. Was it always there, or did it just appear?"

"I've never seen this stone. Does it resemble a big dog tooth?"

"The stone? I don't know, everybody calls it Dog Tooth Stone. Or my kids do. Kids are always onto Indian shit, down at their level. But listen, Mark. As I say, I'm sorry about the circumstances, but maybe we should just *ask* a lawyer. Like just *ask*. There might be some letter we have to send before November first, legally."

"How far into the property does this new boundary run?"

"Okay. All I have is this Mickey Mouse tape measure because the True Value wasn't open yet—but as far as I can tell, the boundary goes right under your house *and* my house. It goes all the way to the Vietnamese people on the other side. I mean, it slants, so it cuts off more of my house because I'm a corner unit. With you, it just cuts off your breakfast nook, but with me it's right the hell under my entertainment room. Do you think you could meet me at work? I'm the owner-manager of the pizza place across from the old Holiday Inn. I think I mentioned."

"If it does look like a tooth, would it be a canine?" It seems unlikely that a stone should remain uneroded in any shape like a tooth, given the local blue shale of the Northern California Coast Range, which crumbles into stacked chips under the heel.

"The stone?"

"Is it literally a canine? Or a molar, or an incisor?"

Roger pauses. "Well, listen, Mark? Listen, *I'll* find a lawyer. You don't bother. And then you come into Terra Linda and meet me at my place. You know where the Holiday Inn used to be? Across from there? I'll bring this letter from Acquisition Systems, and maybe you should bring your Cobblestone contract, because obviously we have to show we're property owners. We paid money for these places. Actual cash money. Which, doesn't that give us some rights?"

"I'm not sure. Possibly not."

"How soon can you make it?"

"Roger, it may not be such an emergency. After all, we *live* there."

"Yeah, but look what it *says*. We have to go by what it says on the document, and it *says* they'll exercise all the rights and privileges of ownership. Those are the *words*. I'll tell you something I've discovered. The new style these days is *Go for it*. You know? People say, *'Be smart.'* It's whatever you can get away with. Especially in the new generation coming along, complete nonintegrity is pretty much the norm. Everybody says, 'Don't be stupid, go for it.' "

Mark—perhaps a member of the new generation coming along—says, "I hardly think we're going to be thrown out onto Hearthside Lane with all our belongings in Hefty bags."

"I think we should be serious about this, Mark."

"Well, of course, Roger. Let's be serious."

"It says right here in black and white. And if they want to be assholes about it, then fine."

"By all means, let's be serious. I think I can get away from my many onerous responsibilities here, just for a while. I'll meet you at your pizza parlor."

"Okay, fine. In the meantime, I'll find a lawyer."

"That sounds efficient."

He hangs up to discover himself irresponsibly pleased by the prospect of trouble, and while the hung-up phone is still reverberating he springs out of his chair and leaves his office, and he heads down the corridor toward an EXIT, traversing the sixteen steps to the door, keeping his footfalls on the checkerboard linoleum's black tiles and avoiding the reds—apparently deciding that, without having considered it, he will be walking in the *opposite* direction from his parked car, maybe delaying his meeting with Roger a little, maybe making the trouble a little worse. Why not. It's unweighting, having your property jeopardized. He will insist on paying for the lawyer himself: Roger seems a hardworking, unlucky man who doesn't have a lot of money to spare. The brass bar at waist height on the EXIT door yields to his momentum, with a clank, and he is freed from the old floor-polish smell of the physics corridor, into the grove of eucalyptus at the back of the campus. A holy scent of Vick's Vap-O-Rub inhabits this grove.

By breathing very deep, he can make his breastbone tick, once. His *body* wasn't meant for academic life, for breathing the chalk dust of corridors, or the refrigerant smell of sweaty pipes at Stanford where the liquid hydrogen is squeezed down to its boiling point. Being out in the stinging cleansing air straightens his shoulders, makes him a few centimeters taller as his vertebrae unclench from the habitual spinal curve of incubation that characterizes all the physicists in their offices along the corridor like separately floating babies decaying. Finally they die in suspension—like Professor Sourcil, who gave up the lease on his apartment in 1981 and has been living in his office ever since, with his stacks of paper plates and his cans of Campbell's Chunky Soup and Lean Cuisine and his bank passbook and his suits hanging in dry cleaners' plastic bags—and his senile determination never to read anything new in his field, but simply to go on teaching Newtonian mechanics. By semiannually redescribing "reality" for a new group of easily impressed freshmen, he has diagrammed himself magnificently in isolation from it. To Mark Perdue (the generalist! blessed by a superficial education!), this eucalyptus grove itself feels like "reality," like freshly *experimental* reality, with its thousands of vertical tree trunks floating past all around, a ghost army, illustrating again the obvious old mystery: "spatial-ness," "three-dimensionality," which more and more can be construed in Gauge theory only as a series of mathematical models, in disbelief of the story the eyes and fingers tell. You become habituated to the conventional idea that you're always swimming and wading through space; yet you can't microscopically tweeze your way into the idea of three dimensions without discovering only further two-dimensional maps, abstractions, layer upon layer, "space" itself being merely a tantalizing legend we live within, an immense presumption, an axiom—physics itself being only a constellation of supposedly zero-dimensional points, held together by superstitions like gravity and mass and momentum, conventional words to muffle our nerves and protect us from electrocution by *instantaneity*. Which isn't an idea you'd want to publish, for fear of opening yourself up to accusations of being metaphysical, in a department poised to ridicule. Even now walking through the pathless grove, he stretches out a visible "hand" "toward" the "obviously" moving, drifting "trees," and tries to imagine it looming namelessly as an alien pre-metaphysical abstraction, to project himself back into that innocent garden before things were given names.

At which point—as if he had planned it this way or somehow anticipated it—Shubie Behejdi herself revolves into view among the trees, a manila folder clutched to her breast to provide a pretext for following him out here. In her walk, as she moves toward crossing paths with him, he sees deliberateness, against which he is powerless. Or at least the sidewise deliberateness of which a shy person is capable. This being her last day in the office, some sort of physical contact is predestined, especially now that she has committed herself to intersecting with him out here behind the building. Already he tastes guilt. It will be the first extramarital touch of his marriage, to be begun in the innocent experimental assumption that such brief errors are not abnormal even in the best of marriages. The only way to go through with it is to shut his eyes and turn off his mind and press his face through an impossible curtain to "kiss" such an unasked-for girl as Shubie Behejdi, a girl much too sexy, and thus to invite a spell of bad luck the way most men do all the time without thinking. Mark has always been exempt from unfairly attractive women, protected by a speck in his eye. Audrey (his wife!) is surely good-looking, blonde and thin, but she meets his gaze directly, without the disguise of art. The prenuptial contract she drew up actually turned out to favor *him* in every article. During the four years of living together, orbiting routinely in various apartments' kitchens or lying down together in unconscious hip contact while she falls asleep recounting her day, they've come to share a numbness that must be trust, the real thing, under the spell of the two chrome-framed art posters that she hangs prominently in every apartment they move into, a Frida Kahlo self-portrait in traction and a Georgia O'Keeffe anatomy of an iris incapable of fragrance.

"Hi there," Shubie says from a distance, with a cheerful, brave sniff. Her eyes are reddened by the chronic postnasal tenderness that marks her for him. "I'm on my way to Duplicating." And then for a minute there is a sustained press of the eyes, conveying real regret and, scarily, a fresh cunning. Once in the spring semester, he asked her why she was taking classes at the school, and she said—looking him in the eye, holding his gaze with hers—*Only because I have no green card. And I prefer California to Paris;* the remark seemed unmistakably erotic, almost obscene, and his mind in its snug-fitting casket was so helplessly magnetized that he couldn't do anything but stand there facing her—they were talking by the faculty mailboxes—while Shubie smiled and held his gaze too long, showing her beautiful eyes rimmed in black. Then she turned away. At nineteen, everything is easy, inconsequential. The same look—of a withheld joke—fills her eyes now. What will he gain by beginning an affair with a nineteen-year-old, except perhaps, foolishly, the thrill of taking poison in intoxicating doses, the rejuvenation of being reborn into risk and mistakenness.

Yet even now—his eyes glazing over as he faces her in greeting—he can feel the necessary novocaine spreading in his soul, over his face like a smile. He's going to regret this. "Hello, Shubie," he says in a tone of voice intended to imply all the complexity of the situation. As she nears, he breathes deeply of the clear, dust-flavored air of October, which he forsook when he decided as a sophomore to get out of the forestry program and major in physics. Now he will never live among all those silent, sequoia-rimmed canyons amid glacial air from the ice age, having chosen instead the breath-deprived euphoria of mathematical abstractions (for he does indeed habitually hold his breath in mid-equation), in offices and laboratories, his pencil poised in leaping above paper. As she nears, Shubie's cushiony plump body seems to move more consideringly. She lowers the covering manila folder, revealing her body. He makes eye contact with her across a closing distance of about ten feet, with a tree trunk momentarily intervening.

He says, "Duplicating?"

She smiles.

And suddenly the very idea of duplication is loaded with infinite promiscuity. The dark-eyed girl bends a corner of her smile and makes the rather mild, obscure witticism, "I'm going to duplicate," then holds out both arms to show her body like any other pretty nineteen-year-old's body, her chest in a fresh blouse, her hips tented neatly by the pleated skirtlike shorts all the girls are wearing these days. His gaze would foam all over her if he didn't lower his eyes to the ground and fix on a leaf, wishing for an escape from this pathless wood while at the same time unable to move. It's a lot easier to be bold on the telephone, where one's breath in the plastic sieve, one's lip on the plastic rim, simulate intimacy. Here, facing her flesh, there is something uncomfortably contractual about merely flirting.

She says, "Today is my last day," and stretches both arms out gladly to stir the idea of liberty—but not quite—because self-consciousness tags her and she draws them in. She folds her arms across her chest. He won't have to kiss her. They're both too self-restrained. In fact, they're both terrified by this encounter. Fate will take her away before he'd had a chance to sin. In his relief, he realizes that his one shoulder had floated upward toward his ear. He stretches it down. His thumbs, too, hidden in his pockets, have been symmetrically tapping his four fingertips in a repeated descending scale.

"Well? How long will you be gone?"

"Nobody knows. The disputation over property, it could take forever. My aunt will call my uncle insane, for the legal advantage. He is very rich." Shubie's uncle, whom she describes as a powerful landowner in the Palestinian neighborhoods of Jerusalem, is losing his wife by divorce, for the strangest of reasons: his right arm, severed from his body by a sheet of glass in an explosion, had been surgically reattached to his shoulder. And now, three years later, though the operation was a success in every other way, he has lost his love for his wife because of his own increasing neurotic delusion that his touch is no longer authentic, his right arm no longer genuine. He can't sleep with her any more, and gradually a detachment has cut him off from his business activities. Now that the wife is asking for a divorce, long battles over property will ensue—at which, for some reason perhaps peculiar to Moslem law, whole families must be present, even distant relations.

"When's your plane?"

"My plane? Early tomorrow morning. Very early."

Yet she's going dancing tonight at a club. "I suppose . . . I suppose you're all packed and everything."

In answer, she tilts her head toward the residential side of Berkeley and says, "I have an apartment here. Is very easy to get to." Meaning what? Having glanced at him, she looks wildly away, shifts her weight, and her forearms cinch to a tighter knot over her breasts, crimping the manila folder.

"Shubie"—his eyes are fixed on her shoe, whose lip

reveals a between-toe crevice; he looks away to the trees—"something has come up, and I think I may have to go home for the rest of the day." (The remark means *I'm married*.)

"Yes, okay," she says, chastened. Her lower lip swells. Mark begins to consider objectively the distance between them, and the weird, actual possibility of leaning across space and kissing the work-study secretary Shubie Behejdi.

"Of course my wife," he says—letting the word out of his mouth all unwillingly in a moment of schizoid dissociation, insulting Shubie, and raising himself to middle age, when naturally he ought to embrace her or something—". . . would probably get sick of me . . . if I just started staying home and hanging around the house."

A stupid jest—it was a sentence he didn't know how to finish, and it feels now like a non sequitur.

But the word has flown to her and done its damage; her hip has ticked a little bit inward, her smile frozen in anesthesia, her eyes withdrawn in slight dilation. He joshes his way hopelessly further into the logic of his insult, "I mean if I stopped coming into campus. She'd have to keep moving me around. Like the credenza. So I won't leave depressions in the carpet."

So there it all is. Custodial wife. A fictitious piece of huge furniture. Even a carpet he seems to cherish. He is so weightily married that his claim to his real estate will be unchallengeable today.

Shubie makes a tossing gesture, and she squints sheepishly aloft, as if to admit she has been wicked and doesn't really regret it—Allah is up there, probably more indulgent than "God"—and Mark remembers with a pang of further loss that she isn't stupid.

"But Shubie," he says, "I hope things go well for you over there. I hope you have a good trip. I do."

And then he decides impulsively that, having restrained himself from administering the contractual ''embrace,'' he is free now to throw everything away and actually embrace her. Which he does, taking the step toward her with the stiffness of being bandaged.

And which he discovers her prepared for, her smile wincing in anticipation, her arms rising mannequin-like, his ''I do'' hanging maritally in the air among the trees all around them, where steam is rising from dew-moistened bark as the late morning sun strikes it. Her hands, and the manila folder, touch his spine. Their kiss misses, but his lips brush her cheek, and then their cheeks marry, his nose in her hair, and he looks over her shoulder for spectators, witnesses. Her face makes a burrowing motion, and together they loosen their embrace to revise it, and actually bring their lips together to kiss, eyes closed, now planets in tangency.

Now he's in trouble. He had always been a homely man, sharp nosed and wild haired. All his young life his features, when glimpsed in mirrors or windows, seemed focused angrily around a theoretical quark invisible to others. But since his accidental elevation to fame, he has perhaps begun to seem intellectually magnetic or powerful or something. There's a fashionable new seriousness in this Republican decade that makes his type seem more attractive. Or maybe it's something as simple as the new glasses frames that the receptionist at the optometrist talked him into. Shubie's mouth mutates under his, baring gentle teeth that imply a light grip on his lower lip, jestingly. Her breasts, harder than Audrey's, and apparently oddly wider-spaced, are pressing up against his narrow physicist's chest—which however is broadened slightly by his being now a married man. Her hips adjust on a mysterious fulcrum. She has a different center of gravity than Audrey.

Embracing a strange woman's body, the foreignness is exciting, the bizarre transcendence. His hand slips down to the curve of her girl's hip. His fingers hold the rough beige fabric that, ten minutes ago under the fluorescent light of the office, defined her untouchability. Now he is an adulterer, married only a few weeks to Audrey Field, the beautiful lawyer with the sexily lifted upper lip who, each morning, having skipped breakfast, sweeps out of the condo on a wind of ambition that makes him jealous, leaving him alone with the rest of the "Today Show." He loves Audrey. He loves her upper lip and her cracked voice and her smart gaze so intense she can almost seem cross-eyed. But somehow it's his love for his wife that makes the whole idea of Shubie Behejdi forgivable. And, too, maybe it's still possible to think of this as nothing more than a goodbye kiss. Her left thigh parts from its mate, lowering her center of gravity. She doesn't know a thing about him. She is kissing her preexistent notion of Professor Mark Perdue. Which is fitting, because he is kissing *his* preexistent notion of Shubie Behejdi the beautiful Parisian Iranian secretary who takes classes only to make her visa legitimate, and who will probably turn out to cause unthinkable trouble in his life. What if she comes back soon from her leave of absence? How would their breakup occur? What if he can't get rid of her? His picture of this apartment she mentioned includes a sink of rusty porcelain, an old refrigerator whose inner plastic partitions are broken and spore stained, a taped-up poster in the bathroom . . .

She severs the kiss by pulling her face to one side, dramatically. Suddenly she seems very young.

He says, "This isn't right, you know."

"I know," she says, drawing back to look at him. His warning came out somehow as an urging. It's a soap opera.

"Things . . ." He makes a rolling motion with his hand,

meaning, *Things have consequences.* Yes, they could have an affair, but it would soon mean they would have to stop kissing and talk, to face the ordinary private people beneath the skin, to rise arduously through the usual ordinary layers of disappointment toward faith, like married people.

But Shubie doesn't see any of that. The moisture on the surface of her eye carries a single gleam of bounced sun, and in that gleam is concentrated the reflected world she sees: vanishing, vaporizing, inconsequential, a rising mist. Why wasn't he this attractive to women when he was younger and more superficial? Now, though hardly an old man, he feels his hands turn to hoofs as he touches her, his breath turn sour like a dentist's. Yes: must this not be, for her, like facing a dentist's looming mug—when one confronts the forehead creases, the dry lips, the hopeless crepe skin of the eyelids, the essential lunar unattractiveness of males?

"And my wife," he adds. "She's out of town tonight . . ." He tosses an eyebrow ruefully upward to indicate the hopelessness of their predicament. Then he draws back from her, realizing he seems to have just proposed a secret meeting, and in fact is morally adrift in the idea. Shubie's glance conveys fear, or a kind of plea. No one is to be seen in the woods around. Even behind him, the forest is empty of witnesses. An awkward space has grown between them as they tip away, separated now by the tingle of self-preservation.

Her eyes fix on the ground and she says, "I'm going to the Art and Artifice Club."

"Ah!"

Her eyes lift momentarily, then fall. She grins, tilts her head. "You have a message from Dean Joaquin. He wants you to fill out a form for the search committee, I put it in your box. Also, Professor Bloom wants to know, can you move your meeting forward to eleven-thirty, because on his lunch hour he must take his daughter to electrolysis.''

He had forgotten. He was supposed to have lunch with Arnold Bloom from Critical Theory. "Is he in his office?" He turns aside on the excuse of checking his watch, though he never wears one, so he studies his bare wrist. "It's probably eleven-thirty now."

"It's eleven-thirty now."

"When did he call?"

"Just now. He said he would go to the Cafe Med right away. You should just meet him there if you can."

"Fine. Thank you, Shubie."

"I am going to Duplicating," she says with a flap of the manila folder.

"Very good." He scowls at the ground.

"Okay." She turns and walks off downhill so fast that small earthquakes grip her flesh with each step.

"Right," he says, and he turns toward the Cafe Med, also walking fast. If that was their farewell, it was abrupt. They seem to be fleeing in opposite directions, neither looking back, having somehow, by an exchange of office business, disturbingly sketched over the kiss and driven themselves apart. He necessarily, as if superstitiously, refrains from looking back over his shoulder. Every object in the woods now—a small boulder, a Haagen-Dazs wrapper, a dusty frisbee—seems jarred up, optically shifted. The *air* is different in the world of infidelity. It's clear.

He bows as he trudges up the steeper incline through the grove toward the sunny edge of the campus where Telegraph Avenue hits Sather Gate, to get to the Cafe Med and meet Arnold—apparently choosing to make Roger Hoberman wait an extra hour at his Olde Fashion Pizza. Why does he apparently enjoy prolonging this real estate problem, letting it ripen? He borrows the necessary confidence from his new sexual magnetism. Yet he quickens his pace in merry panic, climbing the slope toward the sunshine beyond the trees, his hands lifted at his sides as if they held bannisters, playing an invisible melody in which four-note scales descend to the little fingers, as he flees the scene of the crime, whistling breathlessly the Pink Floyd tune that is always flickering somewhere in his mind and comes back especially when he's distracted, ''Wish You Were Here.''

3
I Do

Emerging into the sunlight at the plaza of the Administration Building, he is an unchanged man despite his having just actually kissed Shubie Behejdi, blending into the crowd with a shrug. It was a very strange moment, they both fled so quickly from the spot—after breaking apart for an exchange of routine office business facing each other in the fresh surface chill of damp contact. He may even *look* just kissed, feeling swollen short, or creased, walking blessed through Sather Gate in the crowd of students, predominantly Asians, now that their own tectonic plate is getting crowded, jumping over to ours, driving up property values, driving up the grading curves.

Along Telegraph Avenue the usual caucasian nomads' card tables are set up, vending pottery, tie-dyed clothes, crystals that concentrate spiritual energy. Panhandlers who live in the park come out to sit every morning on doorsteps, or in the bus-stop shelter made of a new aluminum alloy that resists graffiti. Or they stand and talk on street corners in small groups like stockbrokers or seditionists. When the sun hits them in the morning in People's Park, they come out from under their heaps of old tarpaulin, or their cardboard Zenith box, or their piece of plywood on a toppled shopping cart, or whatever, and—luxuriously sleepy, wealthy in proportion to the number of things they don't have to worry about—they emerge from People's Park, the half-acre square of earth historically notable for having been declared sovereign territory in the sixties. With its own domestic policy and foreign policy. It probably still is.

He veers to step on a metal grating that fills two sidewalk squares and always requires four strides to cross, discovering that for the last minute he has been deep into his Counting, an obsessive-compulsive game that has structured his gait since earliest childhood, involving a symmetrical pattern of footfalls and fingertaps and tongue motions. *That* is something Audrey tolerates in him which would scare off a simpler girl like Shubie. Before he sits down anywhere, he has to lift the chair discreetly and tap each of its legs four times—upper left and right, then lower left and right—sixteen taps altogether. And every time he sets down a glass or a coffee cup—even at home in the morning with Audrey, when the predawn TV light illuminates their sleepy angelic ministrations separating coffee filters with a nerveless thumb or measuring coffee grounds, eyes gently dimmed—even then he must start his day touching the cup's underrim to the countertop in a sixteen-

tap pattern: north, south, west, east. It's a way of crystalliz-
ing space around him as he moves, which since childhood
has felt like establishing order and justice, geometrically.
No one ever notices; only a spouse would notice. A girl like
Shubie might even be disturbed, to see him touching his
tongue to sixteen orthogonally gridded points on his upper
lip each morning before setting his spoon in his oatmeal;
or always spooning his oatmeal from the north, south,
west, and east cardinal points and tapping his elbows alternately against his waist; or, when he's deep in the study of
a book, controlling his breath while he works his tongue
like a telegraph key touching, sometimes, sixty-four tiny
subdivided zones of the palate, some on the inhale, some
on the exhale. He's sure Audrey first noticed something
was odd when, in their first apartment together, he always
lingered to step twice, with both feet, on the topmost stair
of their fifteen-step staircase so that his footfalls would add
up to an even sixteen. And there was the time he wouldn't
let her withdraw money from his bank account because he
couldn't explain his indefensible but snug-feeling numeri-
cal system of keeping his bank balance always in exponen-
tial multiples of four. He said, "I just have my own little
system," and she pinched his earlobe saying, "You and
your little systems." She seems to have decided they're
harmless. She even said once that she *liked* his incessant
whistling of "Wish You Were Here," a compulsive habit
that must surely annoy everybody else, like his colleagues
along the physics corridor, who can always hear him
coming.

That he just kissed his secretary is so amazing that he
feels viewed by a hidden camera, a basically nice guy who
can therefore get away with a short unpunished excursion
into sin. Her accent alone, and her Levantine grammatical
mistakes, render her lips irresistible as they form words,

holding the space within her mouth to define the shapes of foreign vowels. His freedom to kiss that mouth seems a sexy new cruelty. He slows his gait. And he relaxes his elbows, which had been nudging the air in tempo with the alternation of his footsteps, negotiating the sacred maze in space around him, which branches all the faster when he isn't paying attention. He should relax. Clearly, his fate is to grow more cruel and attractive as he gets older, like Sean Connery. It was in eighth grade in Boston that he first withdrew from the injustice of love, when he learned that intellectual brilliance is slimy to girls, sitting behind Cynthia Brauback in English in a trance of desire, going deaf to the teacher's voice, his knoblike mind slipping into a sweaty pouch muffling the sounds of the lecture as he contemplated Cynthia Brauback's polleny peach of a shoulder in a sleeveless dress, the numbness of her flesh rendering his soul purely, excruciatingly conscious, a ghost. Which is how he became such a serious person, by repression.

Which must be, too, how he could be attractive to such a glamorous girl as Audrey Field. As roommates in Boston, they grew gradually into the shapes of spouses by habitual mutual rubbing, put off guard by their incompatibility: she much too ambitious and glamorous and superficial, a law student going through a process of unbeautifying herself, avoiding boyfriends; and he an almost invisible graduate teaching fellow, tolerated in the physics department as lost and harmless, before his big essay was published; Harvard has many such bad investments, who continue to orbit the department in postgraduate limbo like NASA debris. It was only because of its complete improbability that he and Audrey began a friendship, more sincere than any other, talking late into the night in the kitchen. And when one night he skipped, naked, into the bathroom and closed the door, to discover Audrey there too—naked too—they found that the landlord's house painters had temporarily removed the doorknob, and they were trapped inside, forced to stand only inches apart, in a bathroom containing nothing but a canvas painting tarp and an A-frame ladder—on a floor area so small that they had always had to keep the bathroom scale outside in the hallway. Audrey had indeed, as a law student, hidden her beauty, so it was a shock to discover the forbidden, supernatural shape of her, which to touch is compulsory. And after that night, they were married by a shared shame, more intense, more binding, than any common intimacy. The next day began the small courtesies, the offer to make coffee, to pick up dinner. Which, still today, provide the only daily evidence of their love.

The usual panhandlers on Telegraph Avenue, for some reason, never pick him to approach for money. Haste Street always requires a perfect sixteen paces to cross, his heels landing in their predestined footprints. The leather soles of his four-hundred-dollar English boots—the one extravagant purchase he let himself get pushed into after he got the paperback book advance and Audrey insensitively threw out his Adidas—leave molecules of leather on the cement surface of the street, big soft loosely bonded organic molecules, the carbon bond so smushy. His sole glides on a surf of particles, an effervescent fizz. Microscopically, the cement could be the surface of the sun, storming. A skin of atoms at the top is bleached and bleached, giving up its binding electrons, crumbling, exploding, sucking energy to create time-space out of the immediate vacuum, where unborn "virtual electrons" flutter between existence and nonexistence. Implying an electrical storm about *any* surface. In most materials, an outer layer is somehow *specialized* as surface. Even in nonmetallic organic materials, a roughly hexagonal packing of atoms must realign itself along the unclean edge. Implying a world of crusts. A world of haloes.

"Perdue."

Arnold Bloom is crossing the street from Cody's toward the Cafe Med carrying an armload of new books. "Saw you in the paper again," he says, his long funny red face a joy to see, the frail parchment of his eyelid a symptom of the intellectual life. Philosophy has been refining him over the years like a disease. "I think it was the Washington Post. You're an icon," he says.

"That would be the work of the paperback publicist," says the smooth voice of Mark Perdue, famous adulterer. "What was it?"

"Fluff. 'Faces in the News,' or something like that. You needed a shave. Another ten thousand dollars in alumni gifts."

Bloom's slower pace is a pleasure to fall in with. Mark had been walking too fast, his hands lifted to slide on imaginary railings, the street a tunnel, his brain a flute, his quick pace whisking troublesome details up to him in a bernoullian wind (cigarette-pack cellophane at the curb; a Finger-Lickin' Good foil packet for a moist towlette; the unrectifiable earthquake-tilt of certain sidewalk squares; the insoluble graffito etched into the Haste Street curbstone: *"ARE est you"*—which he glimpses every day and hates for its meaninglessness.)

Bloom says, "You'll be inflated so big you'll vanish. You'll be a fog. We'll all be groping around in your midst saying 'Where'd Perdue go? He disappeared!' "

"Well, I apologize. Sincerely. It was all my wife's idea. I prefer being compared to Zeno," he says, referring to a more serious article last year that held him up beside Zeno, Parmenides, Heidegger, Bohr. It wasn't simply that his vanity was flattered; he actually agreed with the writer: he, too, thinks his famous expectation that matter should be intelligible is, in the late twentieth century, indeed slightly heroic, pathetic.

"So how are you?" Bloom says. "The annoyances of fame notwithstanding."

Recklessly, only because it happens to be true, and because it's the first thing that pops into his mind, he says, "I just kissed the work-study secretary," in a weak second, a between-synapse second of incredible irresponsibility. Immediately he feels like one of those men who brags of intimacy, like there's *physically* a scum on his skin.

"Excellent," says Bloom, his arm rising to dismiss the whole idea. It's a blackboard-eraser gesture. "Now you have to rent a love nest."

Typical Bloom response. Waft everything away. It almost makes Mark feel insulted—but he says merely, "ARE *est* you."

"What does that mean?"

"Somebody wrote it in the cement back there. Why don't they write meaningfully? It drives me crazy. It actually really bothers me."

"That is its significance then. That's what we would call the author's intention—the author having vanished. I first started thinking about this one time when I was sitting in my backyard and I heard a motorcycle about a mile away. The motorcyclist had no muffler, and I got so angry at having my tranquillity disturbed, I realized that disturbing my tranquillity was the fellow's intention. A mile distant! His aggression was aimed at me particularly, not just any fat old bourgeois on his lawn chair. This is my accidents-are-intentional tape. Stop me if I've already been through this with you."

"I mean I really kissed her."

"Who, Shubie? Like 'kissed'?"

"She's quitting the department." He shrugs. "So." He shrugs again. The danger of his ever being unfaithful is rapidly falling away as he speaks. "However, I must admit, while she worked there I found her exceedingly attractive."

"My goodness, Mark. We're talking about *Shubie*."

The Cafe Med is big and seedy, the air filled with the smell of forty years of coffee grinding, the roar of the milk-steaming nozzle every thirty seconds like always another jet taking off. He feels oddly fugitive as he enters. For some purely emotional reason he has begun to affect a limp now. There's no line at the counter, and Bloom orders a *caffe latte*, with a stoop in his shoulders and a dab of the tongue on his lips which—recognizable to Mark from various similar situations in cafeterias and commissaries from Yale to Hoover—is Bloom's characteristic finickiness around food. Bloom once told him he is glad for his shoulder aches, because he feels that his inspirations live in muscular knots, and that regular massages or saunas would reduce his creativity. Mark drums his fingers on the glass counter-top in time with the silent, mentally fluted "Wish You Were Here." *ARE est you, ARE est you.* "I'll have a regular coffee," he tells the counter man.

"Shubie may not be a good idea," says Bloom. "I'm going to impolitely be your moral counselor on this."

"Don't worry, I know Shubie is not a good idea. The fact is, today is her last day in Physics, and that's all there is to that." Why can't he just touch things *lightly*, without his finger coming away anchored by a sticky strand? He looks around the Cafe Med, narrowing himself in public space.

"First of all, there's Audrey, which is whether you like Shubie much or not. And secondly, do you know Shubie's story? She's rich, for one thing." Bloom gets his coffee in an obviously stinging-hot glass and rushes it bumbling to the nearest table.

"Well, in any case," Mark says.

"Are you limping?"

"Just for today. It's psychosomatic."

"She's rich, for one thing." Bloom seats himself with the regal butt-wiggle of his eager confident pedagogy, beginning a lecture. "She's green-card Eurotrash. She's not an Iranian, she's a *Parisian* Iranian. Basically, she's Eurotrash, but with her there's the complication of unbelievable money. You will find her quote unprincipled unquote. I'm saying you're out of your depth."

"Yup." Mark finishes the hasty job of tapping his chair legs, four taps per leg, and he sits down and presses his shoulders back, especially stretching the teacherly anger that collects in his right shoulder from checking student calculations, pencil poised. How could a muscular knot contain creativity? Shubie's love, even if unconsummated, will improve his self-esteem, make him stand up taller, and soon he could go around as impressive as the conspicuous, self-pleased frat boys who walk around campus looking like big shiny presidential hard-ons.

"Mark, she's in the international elite. You and I are middle class, which is a much nobler thing to be. We're interested in work and culture and ethics—artists, scientists, statesmen, writers—all of which is very fragile. But the elite is just like the lower class. She's off the hook, Mark. She has no values. Not only is she in the elite, but she's young, too. She doesn't even notice who you are, specifically. Why does she even have that job? Why is she taking classes at Cal?"

"To keep her student visa."

"Exactly!"

"Have you ever actually talked to her, Arnold? She's

very . . . sincere." The word, its insufficiency, summons a picture of her deer-caught-in-headlights eyes, appalled by his mention of his wife's absence. "In fact, Arnold, our encounter amounted to more of an agreement *not* to get involved."

"The text of that encounter is capable of deconstruction. Go back and look. That encounter, I'll wager, was *also* a specific agreement *to* get involved. I'm talking subtext. Just go back and look."

Mark gives up. With a lifted shoulder and a lifted eyebrow, he tries to show he is open to such a stupid idea. "Electrolysis?" he says, cleverly, placing a forearm on the table between himself and Bloom.

Bloom is forced back to his *latte,* his forehead freshly corrugated, and Mark is filled with irrelevant affection for him, for the way his children have ruined his priorities, for the passionate attention he devotes to everything in his view. "Ah, my daughter. Actually, it's not electrolysis. That's just what I'm telling people. Actually, she's getting one of those beetles implanted under her skin."

"What beetles?"

"Subcutaneous beetles. This is the new fad."

"Why do they do that?"

"Explanations vary. It makes you sexy. It makes you lazy so you won't be ambitious. It gets you high. The real reason, of course, is, all your little friends are doing it. Jasmine has to have a little bump on her forearm just like all her friends. Actually, girls have it planted on the ankle. Boys on the forearm." He shrugs. "Seventy-five dollars for the operation. And you have to go to Chinatown to buy the live beetle for twenty dollars."

"I think it's weird. Is it safe? A *live* beetle?"

"It dies as soon as it gets under the skin. It's a harmless fad."

"But doesn't it get infected?"

"That's why you need this particular species of beetle."

"Why do *you* have to take her to the appointment?"

"Her driver's license got revoked. This is a phase she's going through, okay? But listen, I'm changing the subject. With Shubie, you can't put yourself in her mind via the usual empathy. You think you can, but you can't. She's what we would call quote soulless unquote. The international rich, like that, aren't morally developed."

Mark sits up straighter, drinks his coffee, sets down the cup, and taps its underside rim against the saucer four times on each cardinal point. "Arnold, how do you know all this about her?"

"Just because I'm an astute observer of the passing human scene. For instance, her mother drops her off in the morning in a dented Bentley. That needn't be cause for deduction, but think of the symbolism. For an Iranian immigrant, a dented Bentley! The grille is all smunched in."

He remembers the moment-of-mass in her hips, a somehow Iranian moment-of-mass, more central and more mobile than his birch, Scandinavian wife's, freed from centuries of grave European theology, freed from practical considerations. He scans the room to fill his eyes, to keep rinsing himself, keep correcting his suspicious slouch. Atop Bloom's stack of new books is his creased old spiral-bound notebook, with a penned notation he has half-noticed before: *If I were Vidal Sassoon I would not live in Watsonville. I do/don't live in Watsonville. Therefore, I am not Vidal Sassoon.*

"So tell me, what are you doing?" says Mark.

"Viruses."

"Any good new viruses?"

"I've got a student who's got something. It kills mainframes on modem. You turn on your computer and try to bring up any text, and it automatically starts replacing it with the entirety of some Kierkegaard book, either *Sickness unto Death* or *Fear and Trembling*. Your monitor starts going, 'The self is a relation that relates itself to its own self. Or, more simply, the relation of the self to its own self is a self-relation consisting in the relation, bah-dah bah-dah bah-dah.' And the other one you'll like. He's got a disk virus that versifies scientific texts, like physics. He calls it Lucretius. It searches for rhymes and dactyls and it puts any text into verse. You come back in the morning and it's all in iambic pentameter."

"I still don't understand any of this, Arnold."

"This is still early."

"All this has big quotation marks around it. You know that."

"No, quote real life unquote has quotation marks around it. Deconstruction is the one thing that doesn't. People have never been outside of quotation marks."

"Does this cup of coffee have quotation marks around it?"

"Well, it would help if it weren't a cup of coffee in California. But I would say yes, every coffee cup in California has quotation marks."

"Whereas a cup of coffee in Brooklyn wouldn't?"

"Mark, you know as well as I," Bloom's tone falls into a tired limerick, "that every cup of coffee has quotation marks around it. And every molecule and neutrino and electron in the coffee has quotation marks around it. Don't be hypocritical; you've been a much more troublesome semioticist than I am. What has your work been *about*? At least I pretended to resist this. At least I came in late, after it was safe. I seem to have even waited till it was out of fashion and in disgrace."

"Do I have quotation marks around me right now?"

"Where'd Perdue go? He was here a minute ago."

"Come on, Arnold. Do I have quotation marks around me now?"

"I swear there used to be a body of information here known collectively under the name Perdue."

"I want things to *not* have quotation marks."

"Have patience. If anything will ever liberate you from quotation marks, a computer virus will." Bloom's clasped hands fly apart. "I'm talking to the famous Mark Perdue. The Mark Perdue who exploded physics."

"That was an accident, Arnold. You know that."

"Still." He makes an elbow-nudging motion, leering.

"I was just trying to be literal."

" 'Literal.' " Bloom winks.

"I was trying to do exactly the opposite, in fact." Mark finds his voice is rising, and he allows it, within limits. "I was trying to show the *impossibility* of Uncertainty. It was supposed to be an epistemological *contribution*, Arnold. Every single one of these articles misunderstands what I was doing. But they figure, since misunderstanding is the whole point of deconstruction, well then fuck it, why not."

"Relax, Mark. The right people don't misunderstand it."

"I believed there's such a thing as reality. All right? I believed that reality exists independently. Or at least I believed that was a meaningful proposition."

"Fine, Mark, fine. You asked. These viruses are only fun if you have a sense of humor about where they're going. Meanwhile, what are you doing?"

Mark sips his coffee, suddenly truly sick of Arnold's good-naturedness, his way of seeping into cracks and widening them. Or rather, sick of himself, his mean impatience. How could he have confided so thoughtlessly—so ignobly!—that he had held Shubie in his arms? He looks around the huge anonymous Cafe Med, phantom lint tickling his lip, or his nostril, but no amount of rubbing it with his knuckle will make it go away.

"Nothing," he says, surprised at the candor of saying it so simply. "I haven't been doing anything since I got here. Thinking about surfaces. But really there's nothing there. I just *feel* good thinking about surfaces."

"I know the feeling. Follow it. Keep thinking about surfaces. Keep limping."

Mark looks around the room. That same ugly mural looks like it's been there for fifty years.

Bloom says, "Weren't you interested in time reversal? That sounded interesting."

"I hate the math. That's all mathematical. It's all in ten dimensions. When you go back in time, space gets all fucked up."

Bloom gasps. "I've *noticed* that!"

"*If* you're a quantum particle," Mark clarifies, annoyed, humorlessly.

"You're making another *Heart of Matter* appearance." He intends this as some sort of consolation.

"Oh." Mark shifts in his chair, starting to feel trapped. "They want me to say some sort of stuff."

"Really? Do they edit *you?*"

"They want me to say the universe is made of nothing. They get a bigger audience that way. They bring me on as the gnome. With secrets of the cosmos. The wizard. People want to hear there's no such thing as matter any more."

"Well, that's true—isn't it?"

"Mm," Mark bows to kiss the trembling black edge of his "coffee," thinking of the producer—George something, a short man—telling him, his head stretched upright with indignation, *You may be a scientist, but I've personally got the highest-rated, most award-winning science show in history. I could get any other eminent scientist to say those words. Would you like to check your contract?* He was referring to the document Audrey herself had drawn up. So that Mark just stood there stupidly feeling checkmated on the vast studio floor, beside a camera taller than he. The producer is a man whose mind closes down as soon as anyone else starts speaking. Which is one straight, sure route to success, of a sort.

"Nothingness is romantic," Arnold says. "But also it's true, isn't it? Everything is made of waves?"

"That's an old theory, now considered simplistic. In fact, one view now is that the vacuum is full of all the 'mass' in the universe. There's no vacuum, there's only a plenum—even between particles."

Arnold looks at him. "How interesting."

"But they won't let me say that."

The new version of his script is supposed to represent a compromise between him and the producer—wherein, however, the producer's crucial words, *Everything is made of perception; nothing is really there!* have been retained. In his last appearance on the show, Mark's tiny cut-out figure, looking xerographically reduced, hovered in the black space between atoms, jiggling. And they put reverb on his voice as he shouted up at the audience from the distance of his shrunkenness, his small arms thrashing in windmills as he drowned in space. Lifting the coffee again to his face, he realizes with a happy twinge of irresponsibility that, because the taping is tomorrow morning, if he should forget absentmindedly to bring the script home now, he would delay the production schedule and annoy everybody. "Anyway, Arnold, you know none of this is literally meaningful."

"You're famous," Bloom offers, and his hand drifts

sideways to indicate the whole world outside the window. "You'll always have a job."

But the impatience has swollen in Mark's chest again— like an urgent sense of immediate waste all around, or like sharp *jealousy* of something, of everything. Having an affair with Shubie Behejdi obviously won't help. Arnold seems to sense his sudden anger, because—great steady hopeless friend that he is—he rushes to draw him back into this easy argument. "Anyway, Mark, about viruses. Everything I'm doing is right there in your own book."

"I gotta go, Arnold."

"All I'm saying is, a virus lets you develop a consciousness that's still innocent. Just think about that."

"I'm out of here." He stands up.

But Bloom stands up, too. "What's your hurry? So. Tell me. How've you been? How's life treating you?"

"See you. Sorry."

Mark is out on the street—almost putting a little skip in his gait to slip across the threshold. The kinder and more considerate Bloom was, the more unworthy Mark felt. Which shouldn't be the case, because Bloom is probably his best friend around here, and a source of warmth and confidence. But he wants some fresh air, that's all. He wants to fan this strange impatience. Today he just wants to replace his usual routine by the substitution of a problem, as big a problem as possible: his own eviction from his bit of real estate at Cobblestone Hearth Village Estates. An attractive problem because it will have a solution of some sort. Unlike the problems a scientist is accustomed to.

There was one scary minute in talking to Shubie, just before they drew apart, when their scalded souls outshone their bodies, and his voice seemed to come ventriloquistically from around a corner behind a tree: *My wife, she's out of town tonight*. But if by chance she thinks of that as an invitation—if, misunderstanding, she actually calls him tonight—he will rebuke her—despite the forward rush he feels in recalling the vulnerable, mistrustful moisture in her momentary gaze. It's peculiar, he lived for four years with Audrey and never once lifted his eyes to another woman. But the marriage ceremony seems to have fenced out a zone of desire he'd never before noticed, and now the world appears to him full of women—bank tellers and grocery cashiers and undergraduate students, their breasts nosing the inner fabric of their blouses, their eyes settling on him, their voices lingering on uninvited personal topics.

Keeping "Roger Hoberman" waiting all the longer, he'll first stop for lunch at the little delicatessen with the funny name—he forgets—on Shattuck Avenue next to Black Oak Books. He feints to one side in sidewalk traffic, to set two footfalls—first left, then right—on a traction-blistered steel plate embedded in the pavement. He has a heartache: Arnold Bloom's linguistic virus rushes in between all the particles of everything and explodes everything; it makes you sick just to think of it. Everything is gripped by the forceps of his quotation marks. By holding each separate word in suspicion, you can atomize the language, atomize thought itself. No spark can cross the gap between words, to string them together into a meaningful sentence. The gap between words is infinite: it *is* the abyss. It is *the* "Abyss." Even immediate experience, transmitted through the Morse code of nerve sparks—the pressure of pavement under the heel or the popcorn-smelling breath of Telegraph Avenue against the face—becomes suspicious like a surrounding mirage, a personal storm of hallucinations. Limited to the speed of light, the eye presses blind through the funnel of time. The only way you can keep on plunging along through ''space'' on Telegraph Avenue is by some kind of faith, faith which keeps all ''clocks'' ''ticking'' in the world, unexamined faith, which anybody, even the most ordinary person, is capable of, swinging a foot forward.

4
Having Forgotten to Stop at the Body and Soul Together Deli

As he rises on the entrance ramp to drive out of Berkeley toward home, gathering speed in pulling out of Shubie's orbit and recovering his own moral heft and agility, he admits the idea that Bloom may be right about her: she's not so simple. He's not imagining it, there *is* some erotic doubleness in her saying she takes classes here because she prefers California to Paris. And the more he thinks about it the more sure he is: when he mentioned his wife's absence tonight, her eyes sharpened for an unguarded moment. The floor of his stomach leaped. They were both falling. They were both, in Bloom's odd phrase, "off the hook." Suddenly it seems certain that he could never sleep with her, that he's a weak man, thankfully. Maybe you become, at last, too *specific* a person to be promiscuous, not general enough any more. In your early twenties, you could still be anybody. He lifts one hip in his seat to tap his back pocket, making sure (as he does on every freeway entrance ramp) that his wallet isn't lost, while, on the curve, his car's momentum is squirted leftward by the tilted concrete ramp, toward the bridge, toward Roger Hoberman's Olde Fashion Pizza, where surely this new danger will catch him like a safety net: a property dispute.

And then, for symmetry's sake, he lifts the other hip and taps the other back pocket. Maybe Shubie didn't plan to kiss him when she came outside into the woods. Maybe she actually did have an errand at Duplicating despite the fact that her manila envelope was empty. Their mannequin embrace in the grove rises before him horribly reconstructed by reinterpretation: she was only being a cheerful pliant employee, she never meant to imply anything, everything was distorted in his vision by the charged field of selfish egotism that surrounds him lately. In fact, she never said anything explicitly inviting. Just that she prefers California to Paris. And "I'm going to duplicate." And like a pervert he thought *that* was sexy. And then he kissed her, her arms lifting as she waded into him.

But her own kiss moved unmistakably beneath his, her mouth revealing almost a snarl, her tongue hooked, her thigh in cute shorts drawing aside to expose the pressure of that other tongueless mouth, her hands with the manila folder gliding on his spine. It was almost predatory. She said, *I'll be at the Art and Artifice Club,* immediately after he said his wife would be gone. Adultery begins to feel strangely like a responsibility, and he regrips the steering wheel and shrugs to relax and grow taller in his seat, letting up on the accelerator pedal to lift and drop the car over the new seismic cracks on the road to the bridge, which, ahead, writhes like a half-emerged brontosaurus across the bay, its back broken. Alongside the right-hand lane, a cassette's disemboweled tape shimmers in the wind, snagged on pavement, a brook of tinsel in the low October sun. A stiff rag is stuck on a chain-link fence. The last stoplight on this road to the bridge, which has always been a permanent detour, turns yellow, then red. The usual billboard facing him at the stoplight—for months a Courvoisier ad involving candlelight and an expanse of silky thigh—has changed this week:

Trick-or-Treating at Shadygrove Mall for the Whole Family

217 Friendly Trustworthy Merchants, IN COSTUME!
No Worries about Automobile Traffic!
Safe Hygienic Candy and Treats!
All Brand-Name in Factory Wrapper!
Bobbing for Apples!
Great Pumpkin Visit!
Safe Traditional Fun in an Ambience of Security!

The light turns green, the race is on again and, as always, his car, resolutely in the slow lane, frustrates the more impatient drivers. Traffic is shunted to the right and to the left by orange rubber traffic cones and big plywood signs with arrows in fluorescent spray paint. This road between the freeway and the bridge is always under construction, paved with jostling rubble and rectangular iron lids, bathed in poisonous dust, illuminated at intervals by immense billboards like windows to heaven. Mark's eye instead rises to rest in the immense hemisphere of sky over the bridge where the grains of air are all chiming to the same wavelength of "blue" above the huge bay—similarly hydrogen-blue—trillions of tons of water resting flat, whose horizon seems slightly distended by its ache for the moon, or perhaps bulged up by the illusion one gets of actually embracing the curvature of the earth within this immense bay. His tires begin their cyclic thump on the bridge surface, and the bridge's spokes begin to slice past his window at regular intervals as the bay revolves slowly beneath him, and he enters under a new constellation: Marin County. Across the water Roger Hoberman has been kept waiting; he's getting angry, waiting in the darkness of his Olde Fashion. At this time of midday, to be out driving around, it feels like the hour of adultery, when most decent souls are at work or at school. A university job provides so many opportunities for truancy, for seeing your own illicit, immature-looking shadow on unfamiliar pavements in midday sunlight, he's in the best possible position to become one of those men who has a mistress. The very idea is arousing, stirring him even now as he drives—the doubleness and deceit, of having "women" on both sides of the bay, the cruelty of treating them as interchangeable under the sun. He is capable of it. He's a scoundrel, cross-ing the bay, pushing back in his seat to straighten and lengthen his back, adjusting the steering wheel to take the swing to the right, after the bridge, through the chrome-glinting car-dealership section of San Rafael, over the over-pass that will deliver him upon Highway 101.

And then Roger Hoberman's pizza place will be beyond the next hill, announced by a sign that towers above all else. He remembers it. The words "Olde Fashion" will be formed in neon ribbons that imitate Gothic script. By the time he gets there, he will have dismissed the stirring in his lap, the inherited secret sensation of carrying a few live ounces of syrup deep in an inner reed. There seems almost some justice in the events of this morning, something Hammurabic: a man kiss his secretary, he lose his house. I take it back, I was only kidding, I want everything to go on as it did before, on earth as it is in heaven, give us this day, et cetera—he sends up the anciently minted old words in a single impatient handful, agnostically, keeping them blurred, in the old hope that, to work, their magic value must remain unknown even to himself. Which must be how the pope himself sends them up, the old sneak. His fingertips are automatically tapping the steering wheel's vinyl knuckles, in order from left to right. Everything is orthogonally arranged within his desk drawers at work, and at home the gas is turned off at the meter, and the electricity is turned off at the fuse box; he's sure because he went back to check twice this morning before leaving home, momentarily distrusting his routine. His car moves along in the slow lane, where the jealous gods won't notice it.

At the top of the next hill, Terra Linda spreads out before him. Where is the big sign for Roger's Olde Fashion? He doesn't see it. The Holiday Inn has been bought by some new hotel chain with a sleeker image. The wonky old jelly-bean-spangled Holiday Inn emblem from the sixties—as badly designed as a banana split stabbed into the ground—has been replaced by a simple green rectangle better fitting this decade: *The Clarion*, it says in script, like a bank note.

There is the Olde Fashion Pizza sign, as big as a truck fifty yards above the ground. And beneath it the window-less building. Or not exactly windowless, but fenestrated by high narrow slots that are tinted dark plastic amber to imitate stained glass, so that the darkness inside will have a minor root-beer glint here and there. He remembers. He may have actually been inside once. Or if not this particular one, he's been inside places like it—the jukebox light illuminating varnished surfaces, the sense that filth prospers in all the unlit spaces with convection-distributed grease fuzz, the red pepper flakes in shakers on every table, and the sticky little napkins in dispensers. He glides off at the exit ramp and enters the frontage road, exactly in pace with all the other cars, maintaining a safe, constant distance among the cars, like the uniform electron wavelength that establishes the quantum. Here is an idea: traffic engineers could use an *electric* (rather than a fluid) model to describe traffic flow, the cars electrons, the freeways the circuits. Different freeways and roads and destinations would be rated for voltage, amperage, wattage. So that a place like Roger's Olde Fashion would be assigned a certain wattage, like forty watts, on, say, a 220-volt freeway. All of which would make urban planning nightmarishly efficient and systematic, in these overvalued California suburbs where already real estate under pressure is breaking up into meaningless fractal parcels (like his own), and cash flow per square foot is the criterion of survival, and all Asia is getting rich and coming over here. How can a dingy, sixties-style place like Roger's pizza parlor be competitive? It looks like it's built in a flood zone, with a film of filth at knee height all around.

And there is Roger Hoberman himself, standing on the roof of his place apocalyptically. Holding a push broom and wearing an apron. He waves as Mark pulls into the parking lot, probably recognizing Mark's car—for, in fact, Mark's car is the only one in the lot—implying there are no customers, even at noontime. And now he remembers having been here before, having eaten a room-temperature salad on Styrofoam, with garbanzo beans stained purple by beet juice—and having been struck by the emptiness of the several forbidding rooms, the stickiness of the tables, the obsolescence of the video games, like Pac Man, and Pong, so that—he now recalls specifically—he opened the door onto the air-conditioned gloom and heard the high blip of the tennislike Pong game, in which two opposing hyphens on a screen batted a period back and forth, going "plik . . . plik . . . plik . . . ," that sound from the lost decade of his life—and immediately he was hit by a steep wave of the sadness that dominated his graduate school years in Illinois, where draft beer was, forlornly, thirty cents a mug, and Three Dog Night songs were being played on jukeboxes. Probably Roger's Olde Fashion still has those same video games.

The edge of the parking lot, in the cold parallelogram of the building's shadow, is a good place to park the car: Roger won't see him quickly popping the hood and disconnecting the battery cables—which he accomplishes with the tidy swiftness of routine, the positive-terminal nut yielding easily under the grace of daily practice—and he goes out to the middle of the lot slapping his thighs to brush off the granules of engine grime. Looking upward, he must shield his eyes: Roger comes to the edge of the roof with his push broom and a length of green garden hose.

With a gesture all around him, he says, "Damn kids!" which must be some sort of explanation for his being on the roof.

"Should I wait inside?" Mark calls upward.

"Get Justin to give you a slice. I'll be right down."

"Okay."

Tapping his back pocket to make sure his wallet isn't lost, he crosses the asphalt to the door recovering the youthful live cushion under his footstep: it feels good to be out in the world, moving on paving, squinting in sunshine. He might have been anything but a physicist.

Actually, perhaps he couldn't have been anything but a

physicist. But it's regrettable that physics keeps him indoors, among blackboards that blindside him, or fiddling endlessly with a bubble chamber waiting for a shy particle to leave a skittering clue on the film like a petite bracelet of bubbles, getting the procedure wrong over and over again while his expensive allotted time elapses. Every day, chalk dust makes his throat velvety. When he gets inside the Olde Fashion, the smell—of refrigeration? of mop water? of old beer spilled under the traction mat behind the counter?—brings back his previous visit, a year ago, when he had a salad here alone. Audrey was supposed to leave work and meet him, for an appointment or something. The air is as cold as a basement's. The innocent eye, fighting the darkness, swims to an emerging white plaque that threatens of birth defects and miscarriages, to women who drink alcoholic beverages, served on the premises.

It turns out Roger has put in new video games. One of the obsolete ones, a Space Invaders, has been unplugged and pushed against the wall unconscious. Across the room "Justin," in a white chef's tunic and a styrofoam straw hat, with lanky hair, is playing one of the new Gene-Deficient Vampire Bunnies machines with a high-resolution screen and an Intel microchip—and obviously he's deep in combat, knees locked, butt sprung, forearm poised to slap the gamma grenades—so Mark decides not to bother him until his game is over. He lifts a chair and quickly, discreetly, taps each of its four legs, four times, on the floor, and then sits down—finding himself at the same table he had on his last visit here.

It still has the same wobble. A few Sweet'n'Low packets are littered on the floor around one leg, where somebody tried unsuccessfully to staunch the wobble. A stack of empty cardboard Olde Fashion Pizza boxes—freshly folded by Justin?—stands three feet high beside the table, and he leans over the top box to read its lid, whereon a cartoon dog, named McGruff, wearing a detective's trench coat, is depicted leaning against a lamppost:

"MCGRUFF SAYS:"

—If friendly neighbors invite you in, don't accept.

—Don't try to make any new friends, especially if they're older. Just stay with the friends you know.

—If anybody gives you anything homemade, immediately throw it away. Then tell an adult.

Roger's heavy footfall on the roof makes the ceiling overhead snap and crunch. The sounds of Justin's video game—explosions of gamma grenades and the occasional strangled cries of predatory KGB Gorillas as they vaporize on contact with a Bunny's force field—are obviously the sounds of an expert player. KGB Gorillas are exploding all over the screen. From where he sits, Mark can see them die, characteristically dissolving in a local shimmer of pixels. Justin doesn't simply scatter the gamma grenades randomly; he aims. There are very few wasted explosions.

"Can I help you?" murmurs Justin entranced, still playing, still facing the screen.

"That's okay, finish your game."

Heavy footsteps trail away, above, and ladder rails clonk against the eave in the back corner. It's a peculiarly sheltering sound, and for some reason Mark has the irrelevant certainty of *liking* Roger Hoberman, despite his being obviously the sort of person you don't want to make a great friend of. Liking, perhaps, his bigness and competence, or his taking responsibility for whatever the problem is on the roof. At the sound of the door, he stands up from his chair to greet him, feeling like Roger's guest, here in the world.

But Roger, as he enters the swinging door, is too busy to shake hands, dragging a green rubber garden hose whose loops multiply on squeezing through the doorjamb and hook on the door handle, strangling his shoulder.

"Professor, hey," he says. "Just a second." He leans into the harness of coils with all his weight, freeing the hose from the pinch of the door as it falls shut. He's wearing blue jeans and a white string-tie apron. As he drags the hose toward a back room, it pees on the floor in a trail. "Any leaks?" he asks Justin, who, after a distracted pause, murmurs, "Hang on," then fires off a volley of gamma grenades with an adolescent rapidity of hand-eye coordination that Mark envies. If Mark could have such fast reflexes on the Vampire Bunnies game in the University Laundromat, he could play easily on into Hyperspace. Justin probably breaks into Hyperspace with every game. Already, Mark can see, he's got his Bunny into a high-speed Combat Puck.

"Hey!" Roger says, dragging his shoulder-yoked hose toward a closet. "You've got a customer!"

But Justin—whose Combat Puck is swinging through an asteroid shoal at the speed of light, almost upon the point of breaking into dreamy, blooming Hyperspace—can't respond.

Roger drops the hose loudly on the floor. "Hey!" he says, frightening Justin. The boy (while his Bunny intersects perfectly with a KGB Gorilla and explodes as the niggling GAME OVER song plays) turns toward Roger with shoulders limp in sincere repentance. Then, to Mark, Roger says, "Just a sec," and he leads the boy behind a partition into an office. "Justin, I don't pay you three dollars an hour to play video games. The way the world works is, you have to stay on the ball. Or else the ball will roll right over you. I'm not kidding. It happens. It frigging rolls right over you. So when a customer comes in, you have to be like that customer is the only thing in your universe. Besides, that damn game is going to rot your brain. So, okay? Are we clear? I'm only telling you this for your own good. I'm trying to tell you things matter. Things don't *not* matter. It's how the world works. Now what I want you to do is check around for leaks. Start in the storeroom and work your way to the other corner of the whole place, and see if you can find any weird puddles of water. Okay? The whole place?"

Roger—a large man, built for responsibility—reappears in the doorway scowling. He says, tossing an elbow back toward Justin. "Kid."

"He did ask, 'May I help you.' He said it as soon as I came in. And I told him, no, go on playing your game."

"Nevertheless." Roger swats toward the room where Justin is. "He's got to learn. *Some*body's got to hold things together."

Gluons hold things together, is Mark's useless thought, infinitesimal fluttering particles that exist in name only, among the illogically suspended powders the universe is made of. But Roger Hoberman seems at this moment convincingly the king of the universe—as irrelevant as a king, as janitorial, holding things together—seating himself in a chair in his Olde Fashion's darkness and pointing toward the opposite chair indicating Mark should sit down, too. He indicates the roof with a toss of his eyes: "Checking for leaks. Just in case. Plan for the worst, hope for the best. That's my motto. But listen, stay put." He lifts himself out of his chair and unties his apron. "I'll get a couple of slices. The Red Baron is decent, it's got sausage and bell pepper. You want beer?"

"No thanks. Just water."

Roger goes behind the kitchen counter wading through

a herd of orange and black balloons loose on the floor. "They give these things these asshole names like the Red Baron and the Gummi Bear Polka and the Slime. But shit," leaning over the counter and pushing his shoulders up, he makes eye contact now for the first time, at this distance, and with the barrier of a counter between them, "it's a franchise. It's all unitized. Everything these days is unitized. Everything is because you don't want to be sued. I have to serve each unit exactly like it comes from Atlanta. I'm supposed to be wearing my straw hat right this minute, it says in the sidework manual. They could probably sue me for that." He taps a styrofoam hat, textured to look like straw, on the counter, then he disappears behind the refrigerator door. "But my view is, it's a franchise but at least the chairs aren't bolted down to the floor. To me that makes the difference. That's the dividing line."

Mark, always awkward, always unable to banter casually, just sits there looking around. This is why he fails at parties, why he studied physics antisocially, why he's lucky a woman like Audrey Field puts up with him. If Shubie Behejdi actually came to his house, would they lie down on the bed? Or on the living room carpet beneath Frida Kahlo's terrible regard?

Roger, clanking about behind the counter, says, "I'll get the letter. I brought it in with me, it's in my office. Just let me get these babies in. Seems like we should see the lawyer first, then you can show me this brass marker you found in the ground. . . . You'd better not fuck up, you fucker," he adds. He's addressing the microwave oven. He slams the oven door and, kicking balloons, he disappears into the back, where his voice is again audible. "Justin. Justin, you're supposed to be checking for puddles. Well, I doubt she needs to talk to you that bad, she comes around here every twenty minutes. And besides, I didn't hear it ring.

No, absolutely not. I would have heard it. I was right out front, and I would have heard it. Just tell her you have to hang up, you're at *work*. And start looking for any water that wouldn't normally be there. Could you do that? I'm not paying you three dollars an hour to talk to *Shandra*."

. . . He can be heard slapping papers around on his desk. Mark would almost like to play Vampire Bunnies meanwhile, but surely if he did he would lose Roger's respect, and, too, he's stuck in his chair by a childish sense of being loyally guilty along with Justin.

Roger comes back with a torn-open envelope and tosses it on the table. "Here. Sure you don't want a beer?"

"No thanks." He had expected the envelope to be large and fat. It's disappointing to find only a single page—of rich impressionable stationery—with the logo of Acquisition Systems embossed at the top (an empty compass, the cardinal points unlabeled, the needle missing).

"Dear Mr. Roger P. Hoberman," it begins, "The State of California requires the Acquisition Systems Company of America to publish annually the following document, also entered at the Office of the Recorder, County of Marin." Mark runs his glance over the page Roger read faithfully on the phone, his eye catching at the capitalized words, ancient proper names, and his thumb glides over the print, which dents the very paper. The letter ends with the signature:

Cordially: Big Adcox
          Communications Coordinator, Real Estate Division
          Acquisition Systems of Northern California

"Is 'Big Adcox' a person?"

Roger comes out of the kitchen. "Big Adcox is who you get when you call the Real Estate Division, but he's never there. I tried calling twice, but they said he won't be in his office all day.''

'' 'Big Adcox' . . . is a name,'' Mark asserts tentatively.

Roger seats himself opposite. "Barons won't take long. Atlanta sends them pre-zapped.''

Mark sets down the page, trying to focus on what Roger just said, and he looks around the room as if to see Atlanta.

It makes Roger remark, ''Specialty fast foods is in a bit of a down cycle just now.''

"I see.''

"I think we should put up a wall.''

"What, a wall around the property?''

"Great big fuckin' wall.''

"Do you really think that's necessary? We *live* there, obviously. Possession is nine tenths of the law. They can hardly kick us off. Even supposing the property does over-lap.''

"Hey, I measured it. You want to measure it? I'll show you.''

"It's just too preposterous, Roger. They're a big multina-tional corporation.''

Roger taps his temple wisely. ''Plan for the worst, hope for the best . . .'' Floating a palm outward, he shrugs around himself at his pizza parlor, to illustrate everything his philosophy has made possible—the wandering bal-loons on the floor, the dead video games, Justin passing through the room putting a cassette in his Walkman, the mountains of empty pizza boxes. ''. . . That's my motto.''

5
Roger Plans for the Worst

Mark buckles his seat belt. Roger guns the engine of his van, revving it too high. "Something like this comes down to physically drawing a line in the dirt," Roger says, and his finger travels like a scalpel over the seat upholstery between them. "Physically." Mark shrinks, smiling filmily. Roger puts the van in gear. "Because what I think is, this is called 'adverse possession,' you know? Where they really *can* take over the land just by being on it long enough. It's like squatter's rights. It's an old law. If you stay on somebody's land and claim it for some number of years, it becomes legally yours. Did you know about this?"

"Uh," says Mark, distracted by the lurch of Roger's van as he almost clips a parked car with casual expertise, swerving out of the parking lot and onto the street. Mark probably should have insisted on driving, but it would have been too much trouble reconnecting his battery cable and then of course explaining to Roger that he disconnects it for the sake of a harmless compulsion rather than for any rational reason.

Whereas Roger hasn't even buckled his seat belt. He arches his back and takes his wallet out of his back pocket to bang it down on the dashboard: a truly venerable wallet, as thick as a bar of soap, fattened by receipts and business cards and five-dollar-rebate coupons and stored yellow Post-it notes with motes and lint stuck on the stickum, all laminated together in the humidity of his back pocket, held together by a girdling rubber band and curved anciently to the shape of his hip. His jeans' back pocket has a bleached-white rectangle atilt scarred into the fabric.

"I'm not saying we have to physically fight with Big Adcox. I'm not saying that. My theory is—I've been thinking about this, and my theory is, Big Adcox is the guy assigned to this. He has to walk the boundaries or something in order for the company to claim it's legally theirs. And tonight is October 31st and he's going to walk the boundaries. Plus, they've probably done some kind of 'improvement,' like put up a post here and there. Because it says in the thing, they survey and improve their land. So you and I have to build a fence and scare him off. I mean, let's wait and see what a lawyer says. But I bet it turns out we have to keep him *physically* off our property."

The van must have a big engine: it accelerates up the exit ramp lifted by Roger's reserves of repressed violence and easily finds a place in swift freeway traffic. Then he cuts, steering with one draped wrist, into the next lane, and he puts the pedal to the floor, blasting up the hill. Mark discovers himself withering in the passenger seat against the door; he had forgotten how people off campus are assholes, how you have to be an asshole in the world off campus, where common courtesy seems meekness. "Well, one thing we might bear in mind, Roger," he says trying to sound like a moderating influence perhaps even braking the car, "I'm not really sure to what extent we can claim any legal ownership of those yards. After all, it is a condominium."

"Didn't they explain that to you?" Roger, at sixty-five miles per hour, is pressing up within six feet of the car ahead, which turns on its blinker to get out of his way. "They explain all that on the model tour. It's written into the sales rep's little script she follows. We each do own a strip, but it isn't a parcel. Who knows what a 'parcel' is, huh? You're a Mini-Deluxe, too, aren't you? Well, there y'are."

"Mm." He shouldn't have let Roger drive. All your good luck doesn't count when your feet aren't in contact with the ground. Tomorrow he'll be safe back at school thinking about surfaces, or perhaps finally going to the library to see what's been done on quantum time reversal in Hilbert spaces—doing something to overcome the paralysis of all the professional honors that were heaped on him, something to show that his ideas are not "mere metaphysics," which is what Karlheinz Pflugsk said in the paper he delivered at last year's Rochester conference. A most destructive insult because it's somewhat accurate. He ought to begin looking into the experimental evidence, especially on materials under stress and fracture. When a new surface is created in a material by breakage, like a Turkish Taffy bar shattering rather than stretching, how must the electron bond adapt along the shining glassy break? Perhaps, like a shortened xylophone-plank, the broken material chimes with a higher-frequency standing wave. Surely the swarm of disturbed electrons on the end are more confused than those in the middle. But, irrelevantly, his heart breaks: how pathetic matter is.

"What options did you get?"

He fills his chest with a breath. "Sorry?"

"I went whole hog. Hobby nook, family entertainment center, gas fireplace, designer drapes, cathedral ceiling, *literally* the whole hog. Central vacuum. Optimism, that's the ticket."

"Sounds wonderful." The houses passing under his sight beside the freeway, as Roger pulls off at the exit, seem rubbed to vanishing by the years of going unnoticed by billions of drivers. Yet solid matter somehow persists, unobserved, a vibrant comb of standing particles, visible to the deluded eye, a singing dust held up in formation by a magic spell as powerful as lightning, undiscoverable. And stuck moving "forward" in "time." If only because each particle is hung in a web of light, moving irreversibly at light speed. The realization that everything a physicist touches will subdivide endlessly into abstract motes always gives Mark the childhood cross-eyed headache of finite limitation, of hating his own mental processes, his own skin. And, too, there's something angry in Roger Hoberman's manner, something merrily aggressive about his way of listing the expensive features of his condominium. And his driving is so vengeful, he has this effect of making Mark physically smaller. On campus, the naming of rumored or fictitious particles can occupy a man's mind legitimately. He could easily get himself slated for the first experiments at a new, higher energy. They'd let him have all the time he wants on the Stanford linear collider, and he would seem to be doing something if he went there and chose an exotic target and smashed up something like a "new" particle. Which he could then name. And then fit it into the growing pyramid of particles under the Z-zero. Like everybody else during the seventies and eighties, using up the alphabets, Greek and Roman, to name new hadrons. "I should have mentioned," he wanders into saying, "I can't really be away from campus too long today."

"So anyway, Mark?" says Roger. "I already bought some bunting and pennants, I hope you'll split the cost with me."

"Why do we want bunting and pennants?"

"To put up at the boundaries. Even if I'm jumping to conclusions, it's a good idea just on general principles. Of course, a real fence is what we want, but even bunting'll provide a temporary *symbolic* barrier. All they had at the store was this orange and black. And the pennants are old Oakland Raiders pennants, but I got them at a discount because they're obsolete. Do you have a decent flashlight? I've got shovels and one flashlight, if you've got some kind of flashlight."

"What do we need shovels for?"

"Wait, that was 740, we're looking for 764." Roger, the heel of his palm grinding on the steering wheel, swings the truck with native recklessness through a U-turn on Lincoln Avenue throwing Mark against the door while a surprised pedestrian watches from the curb holding by the hand a child in a ski mask with a bloody butcher knife. Mark gathers himself away from the upholstery around him; it's a shoe-box-shaped van with *Kustom Kozy Kar* emblazoned on the rear spare-wheel cover and ("options"!) tobacco shag carpeting, tobacco velour seats, electric windows. Painted on the side panels is an airbrushed southwestern desert landscape of mesas and saguaros in purple and fuchsia mists with an unidentifiable cellophane shimmer in the pigments, but all frosted over by carbon monoxide. He has probably gone into debt for this. An embossed plastic strip on the dashboard, imitative of silver, reads *Limited Edition*.

"He said it would be a Victorian house."

"Roger, listen, what exactly do we need shovels for?" He pictures himself and Roger making *clank* sounds in the dark by lantern light like grave robbers.

"Post holes. I already got a post-hole digger. I bought it. But I'll just *eat* that. Because I'll keep it for myself after. But first off, we'll start with bunting and pennants, just as a formal marking. Then we'll dig for fence posts and so forth. There it is—764."

The house is one of the large old Victorians common in Northern California with ornate woodwork painted in ice-cream colors wrongly psychedelic. Roger parks at the curb. On the lawn is a sign of hanging shingles indicating the house is occupied by various professional offices—an accountant, a trio of CPAs—and one that must be their lawyer: "Victor Person Incorporated, A Complete Legal Service." But the house itself is cordoned off by a yellow plastic ribbon reading *dangerdangerdangerdangerdanger*, strung across the pillars of the front porch.

"Earthquake," Roger says, as, with a slap, he gathers his half-pound wallet from the dashboard and opens his door to slip off the saddle. Both their doors slam—making them sound, in the neighborhood acoustics, like a couple of buddies—and they go up the driveway toward the house. Last month's earthquake, violent enough to dislodge a section of the Bay Bridge and shake down houses in the city, was imperceptible to Mark, who, during the fifteen-second interval of sine-wave distribution, was riding in the Livermore office's famously slow main elevator, oblivious of the motion of the earth around him; he got out into the parking lot and drove home, and he noticed only on the drive that traffic was lighter than usual, a few stoplights weren't working, emergency vehicles kept passing, a couple of exits were blocked off. It wasn't until he got home that he learned about it, looking for the six o'clock broadcast of "The Love Connection" on Channel 44 but finding only disaster footage on every channel. There's still an odd blameworthy feeling in his not having noticed it. It's typical of him, to have gotten off lucky, as usual, to be excluded from the, characteristically San Franciscan, gregarious glee of disaster.

"Must be him," Roger murmurs.

A man in a three-piece suit appears on the front porch behind the barrier. "Mr. Hoberman?" he says across the distance. "I'm Victor Person." He pets his necktie.

"Hello, Mr. Person. Roger Hoberman."

The lawyer has been sitting around in his office with nothing to do, wearing a twelve-hundred-dollar suit. Roger, whose size and bulk provide the gravitation of the moment, conducts Mark toward the porch stair to offer handshakes across the yellow ribbon. Mark is suddenly glad for Roger's partnership. It seems logical that he should be compatible with large, uncomplicated, stalwart people. "My neighbor Mark Perdue. Is it safe to be inside there?"

"Oh, this," says Person. "Just ignore it, it doesn't mean anything. We have some litigation going on. Just a moment, I'll be right back. Wait right here." With first an arresting shove of both palms, he vanishes into the house. Roger inclines toward Mark to observe, "I bet we're already paying for his time." Mark, not wanting to give the impression that he and Roger are equally sophisticated, sways to stand aside looking skeptical as the lawyer comes back—with two clipboards holding fine-printed legal-size forms. He offers them across the plastic ribbon. "These are standard waivers," he says. "If you'll just sign them."

He tries, vaguely, to scan over the document despite an obstinate, dreamy resistance to focusing on it, which has something to do with the intensity of repellent sunlight on the page, or something to do with his being truant today, restless, jealous of every passing second, of every inch of space elsewhere . . .

> . . . caused directly or indirectly by any environmental hazard on or adjacent to the premises, or resulting from any consumer product which has been or will be determined to be associated with product-related injuries or syndromes; by enemy attack by armed forces; insurrection; rebellion; nuclear radioactive contamination; or any psychological stress syndrome yet undiscovered . . .

"What is this, basically?" Mark says, the phosphorous-white rectangle filling his eye, the words on the page turning to ants. He'll sign it.

"It doesn't mean anything." Mr. Person gives him a pen, and Mark writes his name on the line. It's probably true that it doesn't mean anything, that a good lawyer can annul any paper you've put your signature on.

"Waiving what kinds of things?" he says as he signs it.

"You haven't been forced to reveal your sex or age or religion; I'm not responsible for acts of God; you entered upon my premises of your own free will." Mr. Person smiles as he accepts the signed waiver. Then he lifts the yellow ribbon and swings back the gate of his arm. "They're getting to be a universal practice, in these litigious times."

"Is the house okay?" says Roger. He ducks under the ribbon and hands back his clipboard. "Is it earthquake damage?"

"Actually, it's an ongoing case. But don't worry, the house is perfectly safe."

"Why is it strung off?"

"It pertains to some litigation we have going on, and so of course I shouldn't talk about it."

Maybe a builder is being sued, or the previous owners of the house. It certainly feels structurally sound. The floorboards resonate solidly under his hard leather heel. Mr. Person leads them into a limited parlor on the right, beyond which is a further room, where his desk is. On the clients' side of the desk, two chairs wait, and Mark, entering, discovers nervousness, a miscellaneous feeling of being arraigned. What is he guilty of?

Roger says—his gaze still drifting as he takes in the situation—"I hate to seem like a cheapskate, but are we paying for your time right now? I know you guys charge for every six minutes, isn't that so?"

Mr. Person doesn't answer until he's standing behind his desk grasping his lapels, and Mark suddenly knows that Victor Person is a recent graduate, and this is a new law practice with few clients. "As I said on the phone, Mr. Hoberman, Mr. Perdue, I have a complete rates-and-remuneration disclosure, which is available to every client for his inspection, and it's automatically furnished to the client as a matter of record upon entering into an agreement." He smiles, a bit hopelessly. Mark returns his smile, while in his mind, in the algae dimness of the Art and Artifice Club, body parts churn into view. In such a place, wouldn't Shubie stand around uncomfortably? In her luminous blouse? Wouldn't she refrain from leaning against walls and avoid bumping into people? It isn't her sort of place. Yet *surely* that was an agreement to meet: when he said his wife would be out of town, her immediate response was that she would be at the Art and Artifice Club tonight.

What could be more clear? And the way she then swal-
lowed a smile, looking down?

Roger says, "Mr. Perdue and I can just sit here while you
read this," and he reaches into his pocket. Mark, startled
by the sound of his own name, realizes more consciously
that in this office a chill makes him aware of a damp sheen:
shame. "I brought it with," Roger says, picking apart the
letter, which he has folded six ways like homework.

"If this is what you read to me, I don't think I need to
read it," says Person, nevertheless accepting it as Roger
passes it across the desk. He looks it over with the utterly
relaxed scalp, the slack eyelids, of complete self-confi-
dence. He is a handsome young man with a recent haircut.
"You read this same letter to me on the phone this morning. And, as I told you, I will want to make a copy of it only
in the event that we enter into an agreement."

"Great, well then, what do you think? Here's what I
think. What Mark and I were just saying is that this is
probably adverse possession. As I told you on the phone?
And the letter says it's been five years, which might be the
amount of time you need to take adverse possession of
land. Is that right? Is five years the time?"

"That's the sort of thing we would determine," Person
says, sitting down, while he gestures toward the two seats
on their side of the desk.

Mark had been standing behind his chair. Having discreetly rocked it forward and back, then side to side—
which, in tight situations, can substitute for the required
leg tapping—he sits down in the spindly old thing. It has
a small white price sticker on its inner arm, freshly pen-
ciled: "$1750.00." Maybe he should have called Audrey
and asked her to recommend a lawyer. The events of the
day have, at this point, gone out of control. He would
somehow have to get rid of Roger Hoberman if, by an

obvious misunderstanding, Shubie does expect him to show up tonight at the Art and Artifice Club. According to Arnold Bloom's theory, people luckily misunderstand each other with maximum efficiency. The more he contemplates the idea of his secretly loving her—the skim-milk-blue whites of her eyes, the downy hair at her hairline, the tendon of her swift ankle strengthened in phys ed, the top-side shadow on her forearms of fine black hair—the more a kind of general stickiness unfits him even for fighting this small real estate war. Looking across the desktop at Victor Person Incorporated, he steels himself to return home tonight and reheat the cream chipped beef in the microwave and finish Jauch's terrible (unbelievably stupid!) book *Are Quanta Real?*, taking occasional breaks to stand in front of the television until his soles ache, flipping from channel to channel, falling always back upon MTV. From now on, this will be his life. Elderly at twenty-seven, he's a Potts Professor, risen to a state of detachment above pleasure. The final disappointment of physical pleasure is that it betrays you at last with a sort of metaphysical sadness. Even orgasm itself, lying there on the mattress splayed like a body crashed through the skylight, is a letdown because it turns out to be so singular, and so finite. Only big Brobdingnagian extinction-bound humans desire the infinite—the infinite which is already in the possession of the smallest subatomic particle at our fingertips. And therefore the frustrating ''moment'' of ''time'' keeps moving along like a pinched seed that squirts ahead out of one's grasp. The human subjective experience of time feels like a *lag*, the lag of ''information,'' which never quite catches up (at the speed of light.) Subatomic particles don't suffer time because they're already complete, immortal, Parmenidean, existing eternally in a state of utter consummation, all symmetries intact. What remains eternally in-complete is the relationship between the "particle" and the rough human picture of a particle laid over it, the ancient repulsion between the physical and the intelligible.

Sensing a lull he's responsible for, he speaks up, "My wife Audrey . . . ," and he looks from Roger to the lawyer and back, ". . . is an attorney."

Both Roger and Victor Person look at him. He has spo-ken out of turn and interrupted. "But she's in patent law. She wouldn't know anything about this kind of thing."

Roger resumes with the lawyer, "Do you know who this Abraham Gutierrez was?"

"I only know what you told me on the telephone. Our office doesn't provide title searches . . ."

"He was crazy. He was the town character. I mean, he's been dead for a long time, but they called him the Greeter, because he hung around the wharf all day and waved to everybody. He was completely mute. He was a homeless person."

"I don't need to know anything about the original claimant."

" 'Original claimant'! He lived outdoors. He wasn't any-body. That's the whole point. He didn't have a residence, he was a nonentity. These people at Acquisition Incorpo-rated are basing their legal claim on a *hobo*."

Person's fingertips move up his necktie to begin palpat-ing the knot. At last he says, "It would be necessary to evaluate his claim."

Roger looks at Mark, then back at the lawyer. "Well, anyway, the point is, if we did something to the land—just anything—like if we just put in a couple of fence posts on the part of our yard that Big Ancox wants—then it's ours again. Is that right?"

"That is the situation I would advise you on." Mr. Person's chair, too, has a price sticker. So does the desk: $11,900.00. It's an ornate square ton of dark wood.

"Like before November 1st," says Roger. "That's tomorrow."

"Why November 1st?"

"That's the date it'll be five years. This is the reason I'm saying we have to do this *tonight*. Because, see, maybe Acquisition Systems has been sending these letters for five years to the previous owners of the land. Or to the Cobblestone Hearth management. Is it five years? Is that the legal amount of time to take adverse possession?"

"All that would be part of the case."

Mark interrupts: "Roger, if it takes five years, then we're okay. We've only lived there for a year." He turns to the lawyer. "Mr. Person? Why don't you call Acquisition Systems' lawyers? They probably have a legal department. Why not call them right now and ask?"

"Well, you're not my clients yet, Mr. Perdue. I'd be happy to prepare a proposal and estimate for you, depending on what desires you have in the matter. Unfortunately, we would have to first enter an agreement formally. That way everybody is protected. And of course I wouldn't be able to reach their attorneys by telephone. They wouldn't be reachable, as a matter of professional protocol. And as a matter of protocol, I wouldn't try to telephone them."

Mark's confusion must be plain on his face: the lawyer says, "I can't act on your behalf until we've entered into an agreement." His hands hold an invisible agreement in thin air, shaped like an accordion expanding and contracting.

"Mark, wait," says Roger, then turning to the lawyer. "When it says 'open, notorious, and hostile,' does that mean like really hostile?"

"That is language." To Mr. Person, *language* is an important word, and his hand's soft encircling grip on his necktie slides up and down. "That is definitely language."

"Because, yeah, okay," Roger stands up to his feet and turns to Mark. "Why don't we quick go back over there and start digging some post holes? We have a lot to do before tonight. Right?" He surreptitiously winks at Mark.

Everyone looks at everyone else.

Disguising any disappointment, the lawyer slaps his chair's armrests and says, "All right then, fine." He stands up, letting his arms rise to hold the air around them and guide them both toward the door again. "I believe I *have* your addresses. Because now if you'd like us to prepare an estimate—"

"No, let's wait," says Roger, with a glance to Mark—and again that corny wink, in which Roger's whole brow labors to hook Mark offstage. "First we have to see if Mister Big shows up tonight. Eh, Mark?"

Person says, "But first . . ." He lifts the two clipboards from his desk and removes the waivers to reveal more forms beneath. "These are affidavits of nonagreement. Again, these are meaningless." He hands Mark the clipboard and the pen. It's a dense page ending in the statement that the above information has been read and understood, which Mark writes his name under.

"They indicate merely that there is no understanding of any kind between us."

"Fine," says Roger, while signing his.

"I bill monthly. My secretary will set up a separate file for each of you, in the event that you two may eventually desire . . . separate representation."

Mark has been looking around the room. As if many pinpricks in a photo were letting daylight through, his eye begins to discover those small white price stickers everywhere—on the fireplace bellows and the copper planter; on the sets of old books, on the bookshelves themselves, on old lamps. It makes him put his hands in his pockets. "Mr. Person, I have a question," he says. "Do you agree that Roger is right in supposing that this is adverse possession? And they're using some old historical technicality as a pretext?"

"Well, then I'd be into the area of advice," he says. His smile is rueful. "It would be necessary for you to read and sign our limitation-and-release material. And then I'd have to prepare a promise of services. And then I'd have to represent to *their* counsel . . . I'm sorry, I don't mean to be mysterious. But in the legal environment . . . ," he shrugs with happy helplessness. His fingers begin again to tickle the very tip of his tie.

"Tell me this," says Mark. "Is there such a law as 'adverse possession'? Is there a law on the books that lets you take over people's property?"

"Yes." Gradually he frowns. "I can say that."

"And it takes five years? And you can do it without even any legal title?"

"According to California law, the claimant must show color of title. But as for your specific situation, I haven't made any remarks." His frown deepens as he grasps his lapels high near the collar: he's Abe Lincoln.

Roger says, "Do these people have 'color of title'?"

Mark says, "Wait, I don't understand the term. What's 'color of title' to land?" Impertinently he pictures the mesas and saguaros illustrated in purple mists on the side of Roger's van, where an airbrush has invented real estate.

Person says, "Well, that would involve my involvement. You understand, I'm not advising or directing you in any way."

Mark says, "Just tell me. Do you think we have something here? Or not?"

Still grasping his lapels, he frowns and says at last, "Yes. I would say you have . . . something."

"Good," says Roger. "Come on, Mark, we've got a lot to do."

"Let us know if you want to pursue this." Oddly happy to be jilted, the lawyer follows them outside where they duck under the yellow *dangerdanger* ribbon. They descend the few steps of the porch. "We'll have you on file, and our monthly file-maintenance fee is nominal."

"Take it easy," Roger says in farewell to Mr. Person, who beams in the archway behind the ribbon, his belly stretching it, his forearm rising to make a tick-tock swing on his elbow. Roger takes Mark's arm to lead him to the van, and Mark acquiesces, the nice guy always yielding to the more self-certain people around. He might as well face it. Tonight he will wait primitively in the dark behind freshly planted pickets at the edge of his property, with "Roger Hoberman." It's absurd.

Then he has a thought. That was a brush-off; the lawyer is happy *not* to get involved. Mark looks back over his shoulder to see him still standing in the archway to wave them away, glad to be safe behind his ribbon. Roger arrives at the truck and unlocks Mark's door for him. "The guy is just a rip-off artist, like all lawyers, like the dickhead that did my bankruptcy for me when I lost this other pizza franchise I used to have. I used to have a Shakey's franchise, but that's a long story."

Mark, for the first time, notices the rash of red specks on Roger's neck where he has apparently been shaving impatiently with an old blade, or without a mirror. And hairs sprouting from within his nostrils. "Roger, you're divorced, aren't you?"

Roger—interrupted just as he was warming to the topic of lawyers in general—tosses his eyes toward the sky and, turning away to walk around to the driver's side, taps his wrist against his forehead. "Sheesh!"

6
Using Up the Alphabets

He doesn't elaborate. "Sheesh" might be an expression of frustration with Mark's perfectly innocent question, or more likely—as his tone implies—it sums up all womankind, their inscrutable way of marrying us and then divorcing us, as, slamming the door and putting the van in gear and pulling away from the curb, he bounces to settle back in his seat into the complacent happy rudeness of men without women. Indeed there does seem something valorous and fraternal in simply having a job to do, and Mark braces himself for the trip back. A scientist's usual activities don't provide the ordinary manly pleasure of certainty. You instead spend your whole life in scrupulous wimpy professional self-doubt, being tentative, being wrong about things, being wrong over and over again in experimental design or in calculation, so that your neck tendons are permanently taut and your collarbone tends to levitate. Or if, for a minute, you seem to be right about something, you then devote months to looking for your own mistakes as if they were pearls, so there's almost a dread associated with *positive* results; there's almost a feeling of security in going on being wrong as usual. And then if you publish, everybody else in the professional community begins disproving your results, and somebody like Karlheinz Pflugsk, from his promontory in Switzerland, murders you with such a perfectly placed quiet lightning bolt as "merely metaphysical."

Which may in fact be motivated by some kind of jealousy, because of Mark's having been awarded, much too young, the Potts Chair in Theoretical Physics at Berkeley, a position possibly even Pflugsk envies, despite his living in the scientific utopia in Switzerland at CERN, where they've got a bubble chamber as big as a house and they drink old French wine in the evening on the patio outside the cafeteria and go hiking in the sparkling air toward Mont Blanc—and where the particles seem to be getting bigger and fatter all the time, and more tender, more lingering, than at the homely old Stanford Linear Accelerator, which is getting to feel increasingly dated, like the cardboard set from "Voyage to the Bottom of the Sea." Their old tin can of a Mark II detector was perhaps merely *lucky* to have come across the first few Z-zero particles last week. At CERN, where they've got the newest calorimeters and scintillation hodoscopes and ring-imaging counters, they'll soon be creating thousands of Z-zeros a day. The essential drops to be pressed from the vacuum, like the heavy gluons or the top quark, will surely be scared up into existence at CERN, never at Stanford. Dimensionless abstractions, for an instant they will cross the semantic boundary from "theoretical" to "virtual"—and "Pflugsk" will be looking on to see the proton decay evidentially and then to pronounce their "existence." And assign them some adjectives.

Roger says, "Actually, I think it all started when I got my first kidney stone."

"What all started."

Or, somebody in Pflugsk's position probably has no choice but to oppose a far-off American physicist's skepticism, if only because Pflugsk and his generation have built the axioms of their epoch by making physicists' *adjectives* glamorous. By being epistemologically sloppy. So that, these days, you can't get through five minutes of social conversation without being asked about quarks and charm and strangeness. When a young American physicist, trying to be as innocent as Einstein, asks for "reality" to be restored to physics, it embarrasses the priests whose magic spell had kept every particle hovering in the blur of Uncertainty, in a mathematician's erasure smudge. Beside the freeway, a chain-link fence whirs past at sixty miles per hour, inches from Mark's window, making a transparent wall. A belch rises in his throat, the nervous, xerox-tasting belch of Berkeley heartburn, which, come to think of it, tastes of Shubie's office coffee, xerox-flavored coffee from the eternal Mister Coffee machine in the departmental mail room.

"I get kidney stones," Roger says. "I'll show you."

"Where?"

"Well, heh, they're not in the car," Roger says humorously.

"Kidney stones?"

"I'm talking about my divorce. I think a kidney stone caused my divorce. Isn't that a kicker?"

"Wow," says Mark unenthusiastically. Patience alone (which is really not patience at all, but just a glaze of fixed anger) will get him through this stupid adventure. Which however is, amazingly, perhaps preferable to being at the physics department, where he goes around blameworthy of the disintegration of matter into semiotic dots and dashes. If he were as accomplished a mathematician as everybody else at Berkeley and Livermore, they might respect him. He never meant any harm. All he did was keep trusting intuition, keep asking that a particle be imaginable, keep asking that a particle "exist" in some human sense.

Roger muses, "Doesn't make sense, does it."

"No, it makes perfect sense," says Mark, fearing to hear the story of Roger's kidney stones. "So are you going to drop me off at my car?"

"Or else possibly the kidney stone just led to deeper problems."

"Roger, are you going to drop me off at my car?"

Roger plainly teeters on the brink of his kidney stone story, then relents, with a misty-eyed look into the next ten minutes: "Yeah, and I guess I'll assign Justin some work for while I'm gone. Then I can meet you at Cobblestone. It's already late. We probably won't get started digging until after five. Do you have any flashlights or lanterns?"

"Well, Roger, you know, he didn't say anything conclusive."

"Sure he did. He said right out. But he's a fucking lawyer, he didn't want to reveal anything without first being paid a shitload. Poor guy. Did you notice the little price tags on everything?"

"Yes. What was that?"

"Who knows? It's probably smart to be a lawyer, but I'm glad I'm not one."

Turning back to the window, Mark decides that he's been trying *not* to be Roger's friend. And that that's an excellent plan of conduct. Life is already complicated enough. You don't have to waste your time trying to find the redeeming qualities in every mediocre guy who comes along, and you needn't feel guilty about it—you can just go ahead and not be a nice person, for once. In the lull after Roger's remark, he responds faintly, noncommitally, insultingly: "Hm."

Roger, apparently feeling encouraged to go on, says, "You know what else I hate?"

"What." The syllable fogs Mark's window glass.

"Rock-and-roll music these days. It's the same thing as lawyers. I never thought the time would come when I'd say I'm too old for rock and roll. But I really don't think it's *my* problem, I truly think the *music* is crummier than the sixties. And you know why? Lawyers. Lawyers and accountants and MTV and big corporations. I truly believe when we were kids it was spontaneous. I believe the real rockers would have been doing it even if they weren't paid for it. Is that naive? Like nowadays, when you listen to the radio, you can tell they *only* do it for money. *Only.* The music is *designed* just to sell the pimple medicine or whatever. You know? Insurance agents, too. Same thing. They want me to put speed bumps in my parking lot. Speed bumps. Which basically only gives the skateboarders something to skazz-jump off of. And *then* watch people get sued. Seems like I'm always out there telling those kids they'll crack their heads . . . Pink Floyd, right? 'Wish You Were Here'?"

"Hm?" Mark hadn't realized he'd been whistling. Deep in his pockets (in further secret evidence that he's unfitted for this excursion and should have stayed on campus) his fingers have been flexing in a symmetrical pattern of alternating octets, while, in synchronization, the soles of his feet have been pressing pedals in the carpet in alternating order. He's a calliope of nervous tics.

Roger bursts into song, banging the steering wheel, *"So . . . so you think you can tell / Blue skies from pain! / Yahdah yah dah dah / Yah dah dah, Can you tell a green field / From a cold steel rail! . . ."* With a sidelong glance at Mark as the truck glides off into the freeway exit ramp, he begins to sing louder, *"Something something something somethi-i-ing / WISH you were HERE!"*

Mark smiles appreciatively, while in his heart a hole opens, which leads to all his life's empty restlessness and mistakenness, which on most days one isn't conscious of. It's just car sickness, expanded to universal proportions. Being around somebody like Roger who has access to all the usual sources of happiness within himself—Mark is so seldom around such people any more, it only makes him feel alien, adolescent again. He remembers Roger's type from school, the type of guy who was able to own and fix a car, flunk classes handsomely, talk to girls as easily as if they were his sisters.

"So!" Roger says. "Physics, huh?"

"No," he says, just to cut things off. "Not really."

"Mass times velocity equals force," Roger tells him. "For every action there's an equal and opposite reaction." Illustratively, Roger's fist collides with his palm, his hands momentarily off the wheel. Steering itself, the truck pulls into the Olde Fashion parking lot and lurches to a halt, and Roger gets out, reaching blindly behind himself to snatch his burnished bronze wallet from the dashboard. Still the lot is empty of cars. Apparently his previous pizza franchise was also a failure. He seems to have a knack for driving away customers. He probably bullies them into ordering food they don't want.

"Hey!" he says joyfully. "When we get home, let's try calling Big Adcock again. Maybe he's got a cellular phone the secretary could try. All those people have car phones."

"Mm," says Mark, and he opens his door to spill out of the van, his sole making contact with the flat earth again.

"Something else I was thinking," Roger says. Standing beside the car door, he turns to loiter—which will delay Mark's leaving all the more, because he doesn't want to pop his car's hood and begin reconnecting the battery terminals while Roger stands around to watch—and be forced, therefore, to explain his habit of disconnecting them, a simple neurotic preference, a nicely *inexplicable* neurotic preference.

"The lawn finally arrived yesterday, did you notice? Did you see the big flatbed parked in Phase II? It looks like it's for Phase II, but they promised they'd put the lawn in Phase III long ago, so I think it must be for us. So what I was thinking is, why don't we just go over and steal a couple rolls and put them in our yards? And then we'll have some real lawn going right up to the borderline. If Big Adcox comes around, the place'll look totally developed out."

"Fine, I'll meet you back there," says Mark, now dizzy with impatience. They are talking across a distance of about ten feet on the asphalt.

Roger makes a gentle fist and slugs affectionately in air at hip height. "Okay, buddy. 'Bout ten minutes." He turns and goes inside, while Mark watches pessimistically to see that he actually does enter. And indeed, his pessimism pays off. Roger stops and spins to say, "Oh! Yeah! You know what? I just remembered. Phase III is supposed to get a spray-on lawn. But what the hell. We don't even have driveways in yet." Then finally he turns and goes through the heavy oak door.

Mark's car—whose license plate declares itself, as always, to be 4BN2338, a cipher that, like his social security number, doesn't admit any numerological analysis, our most intimate numbers belonging always to an infinitely inscrutable cabala—is parked eight paces away across old sun-whitened asphalt; and in his solitude after the trombone of Roger's voice has ceased, he can feel the whole world rising back up to become his again: the freeway surf is pleasantly louder, a circular saw whines and then rings at a construction site somewhere, a distant earth-moving tractor beeps rhythmically as it backs up. A fine suburban smell is in the air—of car exhaust modernly rubber flavored by emission control systems, and the smell of the dry cleaner across the parking lot, and a Dunkin' Donuts' sugar smell. He contacts his car key in his pocket, and the phrase "identity of indiscernibles" pronounces itself in his mind, loose words from old lecture notes, the same phrase (Leibnizian!) that always gets knocked loose when he turns his regard to his car, exactly like every other car on the freeway these days. He pops the hood and lifts it to reveal the basted, tar-sticky engine, which is protected from him by his pure halo of incompetence, his surrounding palsy-blur of compulsive-obsessive habits; and as he works the battery cable onto the terminal, he tells himself again—still testing the idea—that he has nothing else to do today (and that the concept of adverse possession, though it seems ridiculous, might be an actual legal threat, perhaps reducing the eventual resale value of his condominium) and that therefore he really will spend the rest of the evening with Roger Hoberman building a fencelike structure at the border of their property and waiting there for the appearance, before midnight, of this man with the incredible name of

Big. And forgetting about Shubie Behejdi, whose plane leaves at dawn tomorrow. Maybe he's a fool.

But he would like to stand on the actual line in the dirt and look at Roger's measurements. If the property in question is just a matter of a few inches, then a legal quarrel doesn't seem worth the trouble; he should simply *give* it away, it's only dirt, you can't take it with you. Besides, the claim itself is so preposterous, its legal language so archaic, the role of Abraham the crazy man from the woods so cartoonish. He lets the hood slam down, wipes his hands on the rag behind the seat, and gets in behind the wheel, seating himself to drive "home," but as an "adulterer" now, a sort of impersonator, departing Roger's crumbly asphalt parking lot, whose surface is so old that it's decaying in pools into its constituent gravel, in a flood zone still free of speed bumps. Maybe such mistakes as kissing Shubie in the woods are commonplace and forgivable, small nonrecurring phenomena that needn't be united conceptually with the main body of one's life. That is, kissing Shubie Behejdi needn't *mean* anything in particular; it's what the Argonne National Lab types used to call "an event of negligible cross section." It's surprising how inconsequential an illicit kiss turns out to be, how little self-censure he discovers in himself. Which may actually be a good sign.

Or which, on the other hand, could be an indication of his own monstrous lack of feeling these days, his drawing back from the flypaper stickiness of all surfaces around him, his liability to catch every cold and flu that goes around. His so-called deconstruction paper just hit at a lucky time, and it just happened to create a popular excuse for new experimentation at a time when budgets were big at DESY and CERN and SLAC. Now the only particles they're discovering are *virtual* particles, or simply "resonances," and he can't sift those polleny mathematical ghosts as enthusiastically as Pflugsk and the others, possessing so little aptitude for mathematics—for example having never felt good even about the application of SU(3) groups to the hadronic multiplets—having never even felt good about long division in grammar school. Because it has always been the rudiments that troubled him in life. Higher mathematics continues to seem like an immense coincidence, a kind of bridge in fog that others easily and confidently start to cross, while he alone has the cowardly foreboding that it's a pier rather than a bridge. He just *hates* Heisenberg, and everything that descended from Niels Bohr's unfair, tricky epistemology. He *hates* the smirk of a sleight-of-hand magician that creeps over every Heisenbergian's lips when they produce again the magical coincidence between "Uncertainty" and algebraic Lie matrices. It's unfair. It's the central unfairness of modern physics.

On the southbound freeway, the traffic has begun to grow dense, impatient; this is early rush hour. He should relax. He's a success. He is, by most people's standards, rich. And peculiarly famous. "Virtually" famous. In the period of publicity when his popularized book came out, media interviewers (so professionally deaf and brisk that they, while smiling, didn't listen at all) put him in the Einsteinian position of asking him about theological matters, exposing the scrawny ill-preparedness of his soul, while the cylindrical lens revolved unscrewingly toward him, indicating the camera angle was creeping slowly, intimately closer, moving in to kiss the pimple beside his ear. Did "God's" fingers pinch the slippery quark? Is the Gauge Field in time-space the fabric of "God's" "thought," so cleverly constructed as to wrap itself up in itself, including "everything," excluding only "nothing"?

The anxious metaphysical forlornness he feels is merely

an empty stomach. He's hungry, having glimpsed at the roadside the appetizing logo of the Jack-in-the-Box drive-in, reminded of their delicious cheap tacos in paper sleeves spotted translucent-amber by grease. The same banner—NOW HIRING—is there, taped in the window where it was a year ago when he first arrived in California. Its red letters have been bleached to violet under the storm of California photons, while presumably they keep hiring local teen-agers and then firing them rapidly enough to sustain a standing vacuum. Driving Roger's pizza place out of business, with efficiency and luck.

Mark *ought* to be hungry, he *deserves* to be hungry, having missed lunch when Roger's microwave failed to heat the Red Barons, and having forgotten to stop at the Body and Soul Together Deli when he left Berkeley.

The purple van coming up too fast behind him, then jerking to the left to pass, is of course Roger, who doesn't recognize Mark's car, probably merely despising anybody who travels at forty-five miles an hour in the right-hand lane. He passes over the next hill. And when Mark gets there, his van has disappeared ahead. As he coasts out of gear down the hill, Mark taps both soles against the rubber brake pedal symmetrically in their four zones of contact—toe, ball, instep, heel—and then the freeway exit slices away and pulls the car down to the frontage road, which veers away from the freeway and passes the entrance sign before Cobblestone Hearth Village Estates (with its newly added circular badge *Only a Few Left!*) marking the right turn onto Hearthstone Drive, into the crystallographically distributed clusters of cedar-shingled units on the hillside—bumping over the clanking heavy-iron lid (marked with illegible small numbers in blowtorch welts) that covers a new ditch in the pavement, swerving around a smashed jack-o'-lantern pumpkin in the middle of the road beside a pile of fresh rubble in a corral of striped sawhorses at the intersection of Marvin Gardens Boulevard leading to Phase I—past the sales office like a cute gazebo, with a California license plate still fastened to its side, where the elderly sexy iguana lady in her bronze silk paratrooper's suit of the many zippers will be pacing the floor alone, her footfall sounding of carpeted plywood on cinder blocks, with her small stack of "Here's To The Good Life!" brochures and her display model of the whole Cobblestone Hearth complex, like a board game on a billiard table—the unbuilt portion of Phase III modeled in transparent lucite prisms implying its, yet, Platonic ideality—and her flip book of floor plans to choose from. Mark's unit is an upgraded Mini-Deluxe, whatever that means. He doesn't remember. Roger would know.

In fact, Roger—who has probably already arrived at the carport to wait gregariously on the cement pad—will inevitably want to take Mark on a tour of his condominium, like a Cobblestone Hearth sales rep demonstrating the Gourmet Island Cooktop and the central vacuum system and rapping the optional ceramic tile counters to get the clink of solidity, and Mark will have to make admiring comments, as if he were being proven wrong about something.

The white gravy of construction work has stained the downhill gutters everywhere in Phase II, where five-year-warranty renovations are going on, and in the gathering dusk the flicker of color TV can be seen under the stapled-down polyethylene tarps that, late at night in the high winds, are heard to rattle and snap and bang. Between two early-model houses with long-established lawns, someone has erected a small picket fence, a knee-high fence only for ornamental purposes, which Mark takes a second look at as he passes, realizing it's only molded plastic, probably sold in rolls at PayLess garden department, and merely stuck into the turf. Maybe it's the kind of thing Roger could use to fend off Acquisition Systems—utterly useless as a barrier, merely the flimsy *idea* of a barrier, easily torn up from the hillock of lawn. Somehow it's erotic. Mark actually feels the slightest stirring of random sexual energy in the contemplation of pulling up the decorative fence. What a strange semiotic wilderness is the human mind. He's an incompletely evolved monster cruising these suburbs, a kind of incarnation of the notorious Night Walker, whose three, serial victims were discovered on Mount Tamalpais hiking trails a couple of years ago, and whose ubiquity caused padlock sales all over the county to quadruple, and whose rumor flew far and wide in feeding every citizen's appetite for feeling the shiver of blessedness. Beyond the next tier, in Phase III, abstract cages of two-by-fours define houses-to-be in air among fluorescent-tipped stakes in the mud where cable or sewer lines will be dug.

When he turns off Hearthwind onto Happyhearth, he finds Roger is not waiting in the carport, but rather fleeing around the corner toward his backyard, hopping over the plywood plank that bridges a dried-up mud puddle, a bundle of pennants over his shoulder—Oakland Raiders pennants—whose price must have been discounted indeed, because the Raiders moved to Los Angeles at least a year ago.

As he parks his car and gets out to quickly pop the hood and unhook his battery cables, he decides Roger must be inside neatening up his home for his tour. Mark will be able to run across the gap between the carport and the back door, and then, once inside his own house, he'll call Audrey to ask her whether she knows a more amenable lawyer. It will make a slightly embarrassing story to tell, his leaving work to build a "fence" with "Roger Hoberman" to ward off a threat so imaginary; but telling his wife every neatly interlocking detail will suppress, too, a certain sprained feeling in his chest, all day today. It isn't just his ten seconds of contact with Shubie—but rather a heightened sense, today, of contact with the usual thousands of unrealized worlds, as of *contamination,* by the millions of parallel possible universes supposedly reverberating immediately in overlapping clouds, the sheer waste of everything everywhere.

"Hey, good news," Roger comes jogging into the carport out of breath with a jingle of pocket change. "Good news. We got here before him. There isn't any sign of a stick or a post or anything. Because you know what I remembered? Do you remember a stake in the ground last year?"

"I'm sure I wouldn't have noticed." Mark lowers his car's hood.

"At the time, I just figured it was something the contractors left there by accident."

"Should I meet you out at the boundary, Roger? I'm going to go inside."

"Sure. Anyway, there's nothing there now, and we've got hours before midnight. So we can relax. Kick back."

"Excellent. I think I'll just go inside now, Roger."

"Okay, me too. Then you come over to my place. Sheesh, what's this?" He has noticed an old book on Mark's passenger seat, *Particle Immanence in Quantum Vacuum Space,* which he reaches through the open window to pick up, revealing beneath it a preprint from Carl Wanker at Columbia, "Deep Inelastic Scattering: Muon-Gluon Encounters." Roger says, "Whoa," starting to page through it, finding probably nothing but the most incomprehensible pictures, like Feynman diagrams and Lie matrices and daunting long integrals describing wave functions, while Mark gets out of the garage and strides up the walk, skipping to begin the octave of stairs leading to his door. "This is weird," he can hear Roger comment on his books, still standing by the car. At the back door, he connects the electricity at the fuse box and opens the emergency shut-off cock in the gas line. But before he can quite get in the door, Roger calls, "Hey, wait. Where's the thing you found?"

"The plaque? Oh yes. It's right over there." Actually, Mark can see it from where he's standing, in the dirt beyond the carport, its bronze still yellow, unweathered. "Go ahead. Check it out. I'm going in."

"What does it say?" Roger asks while looking around. "Permission to pass is forbidden? Revocable?"

"You'll see it. I'm going inside, Roger." He goes in and closes the door behind him, and he turns on the TV with the remote-control unit (first removing from it a yellow Post-it note reading *Change clothes now while you're thinking of it*), and he heads straight for the phone to dial Audrey's direct line at her firm, his finger ascending then descending the push-button rectangle's center row, then slanting up to the left, describing the routine shape of a hasty check mark, the counterfeit sign of normalcy which today will miraculously restore actual normalcy, virtual normalcy. And while her phone rings, he edges toward the kitchen window to view the backyard. From this side of the house, Roger's boundary isn't visible, only the Vietnamese family's yard to the east, its border against the vacant field marked by a toppled Safeway shopping cart and a discarded orange rubber traffic cone, themselves like markers of metes and bounds established by fairies, along with a small red plastic chain saw, which little two-year-old Hemingway Nguyen must have left there.

He leans on the counter and looks at the blank wall that is shared by Roger's adjacent Mini-Deluxe, the wall that, during the three weeks of their living here, has transmitted the sound of divorce, a silence, absorptive of Mark's and Audrey's married noises.

"Audrey Perdue," she answers the phone, using her married name, as implausible as a dashing girl detective's in Sunday comic strips. She sounds so intelligent and beautiful, he can scarcely believe what a whorl of warmth and beauty and efficiency his own life is tangential to. "Since when do you use your married name at the office?" he says, forgetting his purpose in calling, spun by contact with her.

"Where are you?" she says. A smile is audible in her voice. Sound waves from the larynx, when they hit the dental and labial barrier of the smile he knows so well, must be altered by something similar to the slot diffraction of light waves, and thus *audially* shine like polarization glare.

"I'm at home," he says. "Do you always sound this good at the office? Are you attractive around there?"

"Do I sound good? Of course I'm attractive."

"How long has this been going on, using your married name?" It seems dreamily almost a sort of treachery he has caught her in.

"Oh, I don't know. Why are you at home?"

He forgets why. "Oh, yes—because that Roger Hoberman called me at work. He claims someone is trying to take adverse possession of a little corner of our property. Do you know what that is?"

"Yes, I know what adverse possession is."

"It's absurd. This major corporation seems to be claiming about six feet of our property because of an ancient Mexican land grant. Or something. There's an old deed on file someplace."

"If it's six feet, let 'em have it. Besides, this is Cobblestone management's responsibility."

"But don't you think that all the intervening deeds of ownership would annul the old land grant?"

"I don't know. Are you asking me? Honey, I'm at work."

"But don't you think? Don't you think the ancient Mexican land grant is too old to mean anything?"

"Maybe not, if chain of title has been broken. Besides, if it's adverse possession, they only need to show color of title, which can be any little old document. Adverse possession is a whole process. It takes five or ten years in California, and you have to serve notice to everybody that you're taking the land. Are you talking about next-door Roger Hoberman? This does sound silly."

"What *is* color of title?"

"Color of title is anything. All it has to be is cause for belief or faith. Basically it's anything at all. Why is Roger involved?"

Mark sighs. This whole vacation from work seems inexcusable now. "He got this letter. Actually, we probably got one, too; I should check the mail. It says October 31st is the end of the five-year period. So *tonight* Roger wants to put up a fence. Like now." —The television has warmed up: On "Sesame Street," a black girl and a white boy are on a seesaw in an asphalt playground; then the white boy is kissing the black girl, and she rubs the kiss off her cheek with her wrist, looking off camera. She hates it. She hates the humorlessness of utopia, where a lady on a video crew makes her do these things, and she wants to go home, home to racism, to her family. "So," Mark resumes, realizing his mind has wandered, "I was thinking. Do you know a lawyer who can give off-the-top-of-the-head advice about adverse possession?"

"I wouldn't worry. Clearing title isn't our responsibility, it's Cobblestone Hearth Village Estates'."

"Well, then we don't have to bother with building a fence? I can tell Roger forget it?" With a dirty thrill, he realizes he's wheedling, adulterously, maneuvering toward freeing up the evening to meet Shubie. "We're supposed to believe there's a person named 'Big Adcox' who is going around patrolling the borders."

"All I know is, there's some ceremony they used to do, called the Livery of Cézanne, or something. They have to *use* the property. And they have to pay the property taxes on it, even if someone else is also paying at the same time. And they have to put everybody on notice that they're occupying it—the language is 'open, notorious, continuous, and hostile.' And all this has to go on for some fixed number of years. Anyway, if you can show you're still claiming it, you defeat the adverse claim. And you show you're still claiming it by a ceremonial thing called the Livery of Cézanne. Or something. It's a Celtic thing. It involves picking up a handful of dirt or a piece of turf and putting it in your pocket. Or dumping dirt on your head. Just do something with a handful of dirt, dear, and say any sort of legal mumbo jumbo. Are you still wearing your school clothes? I don't want you digging around in the yard in your good pants."

"What sort of mumbo jumbo?"

"Oh, Mark, I'm kidding. I'm talking about an archaic old custom. I'm not even pronouncing it right."

"Well, are you going to give me *any* legal advice?"

"Mark, if this person actually does show up . . . Is tonight supposed to be the last night of the five-year adverse tenancy?"

"Apparently."

"Just kick him off. Tell him, 'Thee do I expel and banish—a curse upon him who has no franchise, stay thee outside my boundaries, by the magic power of the Livery of

Cézanne . . .,' then dump a handful of dirt on your head.''

''Come on, Audrey. This might actually be something.''

''I think in old Anglo-Saxon law it helps if you're holding a padlock in your hand. Or the threshold stone. There's something to do with the threshold.''

''Do you want me to go get this letter? We probably have one in the mailbox.''

''Oh, Mark, I'm extremely busy. We have to catch the commuter to L.A. Did you remember? Tonight I won't be home?''

''Yes, I remembered.''

''Is that Roger Hoberman a wiener? He seems like such a wiener.''

''He's okay,'' says Mark, unexpectedly loyally. ''Although he does want to show me his kidney stones. I think he's got them around the house. Aren't they supposed to be big woolly disgusting things?''

''Sesame Street'' is now showing a fragment of a Mister Magoo cartoon: While Mister Magoo toddles squinting through a construction site, an anvil falls beside him; he turns to its crater and says, ''No, no thank you, I've already eaten.'' Moving along—mumbling ''How very kind!''—he raps a fire hydrant with his cane: ''Down, Boy!'' and then moves further along on wheellike feet, emboldened by his victory over the fire hydrant, while a steel girder slams to the ground in his path, which he walks over, remarking that it seems to be beginning to rain. His cane turns into an open umbrella, which the wind catches, carrying him fortunately over an open pit while he burbles happily.

Audrey said something he didn't catch.

''What?''

''Promise me you'll change out of your school clothes. Have you eaten anything? I made everything foolproof.''

''When will you be home?'' (She has indeed made everything foolproof. He sees now, a yellow Post-it note is stuck on the center of the TV screen, where it had been obstructing his view: *Salad in fridge,* it says in her firm handwriting.)

"Maybe later than I thought," she says. "The meeting is early, but the TV option is going to be trouble. The pope loves TV. Oh my god, I just realized. You'll get trick-or-treaters. Do you have any candy?"

"There're no kids in Phase III."

"You might get some."

"I'll be out back with Roger all night. I can't be answering the door every five minutes. Besides, there *are* no children any more. They're all 'Missing,' " he remarks illogically, his eye having come to rest on a milk carton whose back panel, headlined MISSING CHILDREN, advertises a photograph—beneath the words *Have You Seen Me*—of a cheery young girl who vanished from Elspeth, TX, on 6/12/84.

"Don't say lugubrious things."

"I'm not lugubrious."

"When you hang up, I want you to think of two things: eat and change clothes. Can you remember that? Hang on, I have to put you on hold. Wait." Her telephone system begins to play classical music in his ear. He's getting sleepy, empty-headed, beloved—staring into the open cupboard seeing granola, dietetic puffed-rice disks, Instant Breakfast, a strap-on flashlight for bicyclists, aspirin. Audrey (his wife!) has reached out her hand and stilled the restless, light-headed whirl, and for this moment the usual engine of impatience subsides in his heart. Sometimes marriage feels like a scam he lucked into, which he wonders how long he'll get away with. Maybe forever. He has *always* swum in belovedness, a spoiled boy, even before he was born, when his mother, before Kennedy's assassination, bought the first volume of the *Book of Knowledge* ency-clopedia at the supermarket—"A to Astronomy"—for two cents with any purchase of five dollars or more. He has always enjoyed imagining it, his mother standing before the cardboard display in the supermarket aisle, a virginal girl, immature looking, actually *younger* than today's silly promiscuous Berkeley students, but already clearing a place for her spoiled boy. "A to Astronomy" entered the house before *he* did. She went home and cleared a shelf.

Audrey comes back. "Oh God, sometimes I hate this job."

"Why?" he says, but not very sympathetically, fighting a sound of fatigue in her voice that seems to threaten their domestic arrangement.

"I get tired of being right all the time, and being so perfect. Sometimes you just want to relax, be wrong, be a slob."

"Like me."

"Okay, honey? I'll call you tonight. I think we'll be at the Century Plaza if you want me."

"Fine, but I'll be outside. Digging a hole with Roger. What a Neanderthal operation this is." Meanwhile he has opened the freezer, and his hand, wrist deep in the pouring smoke of the freezer compartment, alights on a bag of frozen peas, which he removes. Frozen peas make good sneaky eating, the chlorophyll green preserved cryogeni-cally, its magnesium atom held fast in ice.

"I'll call you at eight o'clock. Do you suppose you'll be building a fence at that time? Can you remember to be inside at eight o'clock?"

"I think he wants to build a big barricade, Audrey."

"Have fun," she sings in hanging up, cutting him off.

And immediately, with a betrayed feeling of abruptly halted momentum, he wants Shubie. He wants to have an affair. Alone again with the refrigerator hum, he wants to get out of here and go meet her at the nightclub and actually be brave like other men. Why? Because he's young. Because it's still possible. Because he's still too young to be home alone in the light of recessed fluorescent tubes reflected off drywall and linoleum, eating frozen peas. Audrey (Perdue!) would never find out. Shubie's bodily angles were so foreign and her mouth was so unexpectedly mobile that, at that moment in the woods in the chute of her embrace, he felt himself slipping away from the sun, its light strangled in the high church of eucalyptus boughs overhead, at last extinguished. How dark and chaotic the erotic is. And how impersonal. That's the horror of it, and the magnetism: the descent to anonymity in the flesh.

He can call her right now. The phone number of the physics office is easy to remember because it describes a shape on the phone dial like a benzene ring around the outer edge's numbers. She would still be at her desk at work. He actually puts his hand on the phone. If he calls her right now, without first thinking carefully, he won't have time enough to get nervous. He remembers the look of intrepid hope and risk in her eyes when he loosened his embrace and told her his wife would be out of town tonight, his throaty voice arriving from elsewhere, from behind a nearby tree. Her being, it turns out, so worldly and sophisticated makes a decent affair all the more possible. In being a mistress, a sophisticated girl like Shubie isn't necessarily cheated. Instead, she gets his better half. It's the wife who gets his allergies and his food preferences, his cowardice and stinginess and laziness and dullness and whining.

Through the window in the kitchen door, Roger Hoberman is visible crossing the zone of dirt that separates their back stoops. He walks with the gladness of a soldier preparing for a battle. He's coming over to knock on Mark's door.

Mark, having picked up the receiver, turns sideways and begins to talk fakily into the phone, against the loud dial tone, as if he were still deep in conversation with his wife, or perhaps his mistress. His mouth moves in agreement, in comment. Then he affects to be listening to her— while Roger, standing on the doorstep, makes blinders of his palms beside his eyes to peer through the reflective glass. "Is that what you think?" Mark says aloud into the receiver. "I don't know. Whatever you think, dear."

Roger sees him on the phone, grins like a scowl, makes a big scoop of the arm to invite him out, and turns to go back home. His big back, moving away, expresses ignorance and happiness.

Alone again, holding the breath-misted phone talking to a ghost compounded femininely of *two* women, he is an intruder in his own kitchen. He sets the receiver back in its cradle and lifts his fingertips away from its surface, where foggy prints shrink. On the whole, it's better that he wait to call her, until he's put some thought into what he'll say, what he'll be proposing exactly. Besides, she wouldn't be able to talk freely, she's at the office. Her home number is listed in the phone book. He can call her later tonight. Her flight leaves early tomorrow, so she'll have to pack before going out to the nightclub.

He gnaws off a corner of the tough plastic bag of peas with an ugly dip of the head. Eating a handful of peas as he goes, he walks outside by the back door. Peas always seem sweeter frozen, in their lace of crystals.

In opening, the back door's insulation strip makes a sticky ripping sound of newness. He has almost never opened this door. And he's sure he never once stepped off the concrete stoop onto the dirt. Doing so, now, feels strange. It's a long step. The ground hits the concrete at a low-tide mark. All of Phase III, which has no lawns, is pitched on earth contours yet unsculpted by landscapers. The cooler air outside stings the personal humidity of his body. Building a fence at the border with Roger will perhaps induce virtue. Or else, contrarily, provide some sort of entitlement to sin. In another half hour, Shubie will be at home and he'll look up her number. After all, she did say, *I'll be at the Art Club,* right after he told her his wife would be gone. There's fertile ground for misunderstanding. All about him in the dusk, Roger's battlefield lies waiting. Tractor treads are still frozen in the mud from the year of construction. Roger's back door is open. He comes around the corner dragging a large sack of lawn mulch through the back door, to drop it in the middle of the kitchen floor, where apparently he's going to leave it. It says *Ortho-Gro.* "Hey Buddy," Roger says, in the innocent, reasonable assumption that Mark would never be an adulterer.

"Hey Rodge."

"Come on in. Make yourself at home. Just a second, and we can go over to the playground. I'll show you the Dog Tooth Stone. You pace it out. Check my figures. You were right. That plaque over there is definitely new. I think they must have put it in yesterday. Because they wanted everything ready for midnight tonight . . ."

It's surprising—amazing, really—Roger's kitchen is a mess. There are *many* empty TV-dinner trays lying on the counter, ten or fifteen, all eaten—except for, in each, the stamped-foil compartment for vegetables, each containing its French-cut green beans or cauliflower or creamed corn, untouched, crusty. The empty boxes say *Chicken Cacciatore* and *Mexican Fiesta* and *DeLuxe Turkey Tetrazzini.* Behind the door is a collection of empty Gallo Hearty Burgundy bottles.

And further, in the living room and dining room, he sees no furniture at all. The whole place is empty. Mark glimpses—then averts his eyes from—a sleeping bag on the carpet of the den in a nest of old newspapers. Beside the sleeping bag on the floor is a Gallo bottle and a box of Lucky Charms cereal.

"Roger, how long have you lived here?"

"Yeah, I'm pretty sloppy. Do you want a beer?"

"Uh," says Mark, looking around. "Sure. Okay," he says, though he never drinks.

7
Have You Seen Me?

This rope'll be accurate enough. Goddamn True Value on Redwood Highway wants eighty dollars for a surveyor's chain," says Roger, crossing the street a few paces ahead of Mark, whipping a length of clothesline to take out the kinks, his voice too loud in the neighborhood in the sacred dimness of the dinner hour, the minute when solid and shadow are equal in the eye, among all those souls tardy and excluded who are not within the immediate glow of a refrigerator, a range, a television set. Suddenly Mark realizes in a moment of vanishing—stopping mid-street in the grip of dusk while

Roger walks ahead—that his wife promised to call him at eight o'clock from Los Angeles, which would be a certain guarantee that he and Shubie would be absolutely safe from discovery.

"Roger, how long will this take?"

"Will what take?" Roger is gathering his rope as he walks.

"This . . ." he swells against the whole inevitable entanglement, ". . . 'measurement.' "

"Well, okay, here's what I did," Roger shouts around him as he winds his rope. "I figure this clothesline is fifty feet when you stretch it tight, so this morning what I did was, I stretched it six times between the stone and the creek, which should be three hundred, right? You're the scientist."

There indeed, where Mark hadn't noticed them, around the corner of Happyhearth, are three flatbed trucks, one stacked with a pyramid of rolled turf; the other two carry small dense forests of leafless saplings, each trunk rooted in a burlap scrotum. The house, which until now has been like a raft adrift in the frozen mud, will be locked in by green turf. And the bagged saplings will be stuck in earth at regular intervals, as in the architect's original sketch, but with trunks cardboard-bandaged, supported by little staked guy wires. He almost would have preferred to go on as before, with the place ugly and unlandscaped; during the three weeks of their new tenancy, it always buoyed him every morning, to see the tossing mounds of dirt and construction debris outside the window as he makes coffee; there was something witty or sarcastic about it.

"At this point, I've got it memorized," Roger calls back over his shoulder. " '. . . Until an east-west line three hundred feet beyond Corte Madera Creek, which is marked forever by the Dog Tooth Stone.' So I figured we measure from the creek over in there. Now, see if you don't think that looks like a dog tooth.''

It's true, a rotten, unerodible canine, five feet tall, punctures the surface of the earth here in a sand pit among cast-concrete Flintstones dinosaurs, swings, a slide, and one of those child-repellent play structures of tires and railroad ties in the dark, lit by the signs of the stores in the minimall beyond: Marin Wine and Spirits, Mugs'n'Kisses, A Touch of Elegance, The Hair Experience. Two children in the sandbox, seeing the man stalking toward them with a bottle of beer and a rope, stop playing and stand up warily.

''Parallel is parallel,'' Roger shouts into the empty space ahead of him to bounce his words back at Mark. ''The other line I measured was down by the Vietnamese people. I figure the creek is mostly straight. Hi kids. I'm back again.''

The oldest child, a girl, comes out from behind a cement brontosaurus and, addressing Mark, chants with joy, ''I live right there, and my mother is home, and if you touch me I'm screaming''—having apparently decided that Mark is more menacing looking than Roger.

''Now what kind of talk is that?'' Roger says to the child, hopping the thigh-high wall around the playground. ''Did you kids see anything weird this afternoon? Like somebody snooping around?'' Following his lead, Mark steps— but more tentatively—over the short wall that makes him now a trespasser in their terrarium. ''We're safe males; we're good, we're nice,'' he tells the girl. ''I'm a teacher.'' It sounds like a lie. The tire-and-railroad-tie gym bears the usual familiar small sign: *This structure contains materials known to the State of California to be toxic.* The girl's younger friend, a boy, shouts happily at Mark, ''I'b screebig!''

''Shut up, Jason.''

"Now, you kids, be good," Roger says. He is tying the clothesline to a stake beside the Dog Tooth Stone. "See, this is basically perpendicular."

"Do you have a girlfriend?" the girl asks Mark as he is moving sideways to put a cement pterodactyl between himself and the children.

"Me? I'm married! I live right over there." Jason escapes from the sandbox and staggers toward Mark's knee. "Boo touch be, I'b screebig!" Delight constricts his throat so that he is already actually screaming as he embraces Mark's knee. Mark draws back, looking around in the twilight for witnesses. How blessed are he and Audrey, it strikes him, as the boy, Jason, closes his mouth on the crease of his pants—which, however, he feels legally powerless to resist. How blessed and efficient is their foresightful, and rather unique, childlessness, their freedom from the print of banana-sticky little palms. All the new parents he has known grow suddenly—however youthful—fuzzy and ill-defined around the edges, and their eye wanders. Whereas he and Audrey remain concentrated, sharply focused, retaining a crucial sovereignty.

"Sorry about these kids," says Roger.

"Ja-son, you homo," says Jason's older sister. He is trying to shinny up Mark's leg, pressing and pressing his wet nose against Mark's thigh like one of those glue bottles in grade school they called *mucilage* with a rubber slitted gland on top that kissed the construction paper, but Mark refrains from touching the child, and he totters unwilling to lean for balance on the poisonous gym. The girl turns to Roger, who is crouching beside the Dog Tooth Stone, and she pounds on his back, "Dad, Jason is *bothering* people." With the intention of clambering up Roger's backside, she hops to get a toehold in his belt.

"Are these *your* kids?"

"Whoa, you're popular," says Roger, standing up and shedding the little girl, having tied his clothesline to the stake. "Let's do this before it gets dark. I just want you to check my measurements."

"Roger, so these are your kids."

"Yeah, their mom lives on Baltic Avenue in Phase I. It's a weird situation."

The boy sets his chin on Mark's thigh and looks up, humming, *Heee heee heee*. Mark bends over to unpeel the grip of his little shrimp fingers. "We don't need to check your measurements, I *believe* it's five hundred feet." Jason's fingers are softly tenacious.

"It never hurts to double-check things," says Roger. "That's one thing I've learned."

"Daddy, Jason's *bothering* him," says the girl again. "Make him go home with mom and I can come over. Can I come over? But not Jason?"

Having mostly unlatched the boy, Mark gets back to the wall, on sand treacherous beneath his expensive leather heels. "All we need to do is check from the creek to our yard. Let's measure there, not here. Roger, it's getting dark."

"Do you really think so?"

The girl, who has been watching Mark, tells him, "My teacher is Mr. Warner. He lets me bring my rock collection."

There is no way to respond to that. "Let him *have* the playground, Roger. If he wants our yards, that's different. But let him have the playground. Besides, we should call whatever county office. They'll still be open. We can ask if there's a deed."

"Look!" says the boy, holding up an empty milk carton. He wants Mark to look at that same photo on the carton's side panel, of that same girl missing from Elspeth, Texas, who is now advertised on milk cartons all over the country. It's a school photo, judging by her just-brushed hair. She smiles, unprepared for the flashbulb of 1984, into the California dusk of 1992.

"I see," Mark tells the boy. "That's nice."

"Look!" he screams.

"He's got lizards in there," explains his sister. "He won't stop until you look."

"That's very nice," Mark says to Jason.

"You know what lizards have inside?" the girl asks Mark, with relish and disgust.

"Roger, it's getting dark."

Roger gives up, kneeling again to untie the clothesline. "Okay. Okay, but we gotta zoom and measure at the yard. We can do one measurement before it gets too dark. Can't we?"

—*Can't we?* Mark isn't able to focus on the question, morally weakened by the sense of quicksand around him. The usual sound of the rush-hour freeway seems, dreamily, to have vanished, in the acoustic low-spot of this sand pit. In the suck of a strange lull, the little boy tells Mark gravely, "You're in trouble."

To which Mark replies, "No I'm not." But with some hesitancy.

"What are you?" the girl demands.

"I'm a physicist. I live right over there."

"I'm a slut punk. Jason's a floating dead guy."

"Fine . . . Roger?"

Roger says, "Wait. The thing is stuck."

"I'm telling my mom," says the girl. "Come on, Jason. We have to say goodbye."

The boy tells Mark, "Mucus is my friend. And sometimes I have to say goodbye to my friends."

"C'mon Jase," the girl pulls on the shoulder of his jersey and they both run, she galloping, the boy lagging behind and then stopping to walk, as his pants have begun to slip down and inhibit his gait. He's carrying his milk carton, within which, if those lizards are still alive, they're deranged from rattling around.

"Roger, why don't we call the Civic Center and ask if Abraham really filed a deed. Let's. They'll still be open for inquiries."

Roger edges closer to grumble. " 'Slut punk'—can you believe it?" he says, with a jerk of his head toward his ex-wife's household right over there on Baltic Avenue. "They truly run wild. You know what one of her little friends at school is? A mass murderer. Or rather, he *wanted* to be a mass murderer but they wouldn't let him. You know the school district's new rule is that Halloween isn't allowed because it's satanist?"

Mark looks at Roger for a minute. "This kid wanted to *dress up* in a mass murderer *costume,*" Mark says, because it seems important to state a fact in the chilly evening air, as if there were invisible auditors in the gathering dark.

"He had a woman's wig and a white lab coat, and a scalpel and a Bible. You know? Like Altissima Brand?"

"Who's Altissima Brand?"

"Don't you remember? That famous doctor in Oklahoma, who circumcised everybody against their will? Circumcision isn't exactly murder, but—still it's pretty perverted."

"*Why?*"

"She thought they'd go to heaven automatically, even if mentally they were sinners. She read in the Bible, all you have to be is circumcised. I gather you don't follow the scandal sheets in the supermarket. Well, more power to you."

Mark puts his hands in his pockets, chilled perhaps by

his loss of control over events. "Roger, let's really not dally here. There's probably some law we're breaking. And you've got an open container."

"What, this? Here, would you hold it?" Roger passes his Budweiser bottle across the low concrete wall to Mark, and he starts using both hands to coil the rope. "And then Jason. He's been carrying lizards around since summer. It's his new thing. He's inseparable from his lizards."

"While you do this, I think I'll just go inside and try to call the Civic Center, wherever the official real estate records are kept." (Also, first of all, he wants to try reaching Shubie at home, where she'll be flying back and forth between closet and suitcase, skirts and blouses flowing in her embrace. Goodbye, farewell.) "The Civic Center ought to answer questions over the phone. Maybe they'll be able to say Abraham Garcia's claim is invalid. Who knows? Really! Maybe they can just punch it up on their computer."

"Go ahead," Roger says skeptically, and he goes on coiling his rope, failing to recognize a good idea.

Mark turns away to cross the street. "Maybe this whole thing could be settled right now, with one call. They might say, 'Abraham Garcia never existed, he's a figment of their imagination.' "

"I think you want the county recorder's office."

Mark crosses the street, carrying Roger's beer—able, with his free hand, to tweeze through the hole in the bag of frozen peas in his jacket pocket to pinch out another few. The street requires ten paces to cross, an octet on the asphalt, and a doublet on the concrete gutter. Roger, behind him, moving toward the flatbed trucks as he coils the rope, says, "Meanwhile, I'll just grab me a couple rolls of turf."

"Where's your phone book?"

"It's right there on the thing."

"What thing." He needs to invent a plausible pretext for calling Shubie, to keep their love accidental. Only accidents bring them together, never their intentions. Which is how any seduction would have to take place ultimately. Unintentional events can be kindled in the low-density spaces *between* human intentions, in this mist world mostly invaded by an interparticle vacuum where massive immanent particles hover to be born, shimmering between materiality and immateriality and stuffing all empty space full of infinite possibility for blooming "mass." One would almost rather live according to the old classical physics, where outer space pours in between every particle, a world simplified by the hygiene of isolation. She will be listed in the phone book as *S. Behejdi,* which could be anybody, the names of statistically unknowable strangers preceding and following hers in the book.

He passes the cold beer bottle to his other hand to put a chill in his right palm complementary to the chill in his left palm. The sidewalk takes two paces, the dirt four paces, and the concrete walkway will take sixteen short strides—or maybe an octet plus a quartet—to Roger's doormat. Which itself is a mincing doublet. He's glad to be sneaking away in the dusk from Roger's noisy theft of turf rolls—the truck's chains chinking audibly in the neighborhood as he hops up onto the truck bed. Meanwhile Mark Perdue, whistling a trill-disguised "Wish You Were Here," ducks into Roger Hoberman's kitchen—which is laid out exactly like his own, with the same eggnog-plastic light switches in the same places answering to his instinctive reach; the same linoleum pattern on the kitchen floor supposedly imitating terrazzo but more like a parcheesi board; the same talcum smell of new drywall and rubber baseboard strips of scuffed chocolate; the same clerestory windows cut from the same architect's template—which are purely decorative, therefore expensive, elements of the Mini-De-luxe package; even the same cupboard handles chosen by the architect's designer—so that, when he finds that the obvious thing holding the phone book is the small counter-top beside the refrigerator, he feels he'd already known in his bones that that was what Roger was referring to, since that's how he would have felt it in his own house. The heavy tissue of the phone book spurts easily from under his thumb and opens with perfect accuracy to the early *B* pages (urgency being a lubricant and a source of grace), and he discovers *Behejdi* in the gray columns—touching *Behavior* above and *Behelbub* below, in numb adjacency that makes her the perfect mistress. He sets the beer bottle on the counter, tapping the four glass crucifix points on the underside rim at up, down, left, and right. And he dials the number—a hopscotch pattern on the push buttons.

"Al Fabeda-Gam," says a man's voice, a Middle Eastern man's voice, with the slight sitar wobble of a muezzin, a waiter, a militant muslim Sikh, a gas-station proprietor, a convenience-store manager. She's got a boyfriend, an uncle, a brother. The scimitar of Islamic *morality* (which he had forgotten about until this moment) will separate them with its shining pure blade.

"I'm looking for Miss Behejdi," says Mark in the wrong language, bravely, resonantly—having of course the fall-back excuse of being her boss at work.

"Hello!" An older woman's voice interrupts. "I am here. Now you get off the phone, Ibra."

"Can I take the car?" says the man.

"No, your father needs it."

"I am rehearsing," he whines. "Is Firm Stool."

"They can rehearse without you. Who is this telephone?"

"Is for Shabar."

"Shabar is not *here*. You get off the phone please."

"Mama!" pleads the man, "Is Firm Stool!"

Roger runs in with a roll of turf in his embrace—it's obviously very heavy—and throws it at the floor. Crumbs of valuable dirt roll toward the baseboards.

Mark hangs up the phone.

"Okay," Roger puffs, back bent from the effort, but proud. "Check it out." Mark turns to face him with the shining face of a liar. With a toe, Roger starts kicking the roll of turf open to show its beautiful green grass, from the velvet soil of Wisconsin or some place, as tender as salad. It'll never thrive here in California's poison alkaline gravel. Maybe he'll have to go back to his house to call Shubie. He'll try again later, when Shubie herself might answer. It seems clear that the man who answered is not a boyfriend but a brother or cousin, which is something of a relief—but also this glimpse of her specific, hectic family mars the innocence of pure adultery.

"I'll just see if they're listed," Mark says.

"Who," says Roger, while he goes on kicking the swatch of turf on the floor.

"The county real estate office. Are you okay? You look like your back hurts."

"I've got a tricky back; I have to be careful of it."

Mark says goodbye to the pages of the *B* section—where resides the only local clue to the existence of the Behejdi household, whose entire dynastic "wave function" "expands" into nonexistence now, at the speed of light, as the page falls to cover it—and he wipes the fine pages across to the *A* section, where government offices are listed.

8
I Can't Read This, Sir

I can't read this, sir," says the woman at the county recorder, who sounds like she would like to get off the phone and close the office for the day.

"You mean you're not allowed to read it?" Mark says.

"No, I can't *read* it, it's all Spanish. And it's all that kind of writing where everything looks like an *f*."

"It's handwritten?"

"Sir, this is 1848."

"But it does say Abraham Gutierrez?" Mark looks at Roger. Roger is standing at the counter making humping motions that must relieve the pain in his back.

"The microfiche makes it harder, and the ink is written

right over, it looks like newsprint. Like the old kind of printing. But that's all there is under Gutierrez. After this, everything is his widow Hilaria Inez. But she can't speak English so it's under her lawyer Throckmorton. If you like we can fax it to you, but there's a fee per page. It's six dollars for the first page, and a dollar for every page thereafter . . ."

"Does it describe any land? Can you tell?"

"Everything in this office describes land, sir."

"Does it give locations?"

"I'm sorry—you'll have to come in. Or we can fax it to you, but it's six dollars for the first page, and a dollar for every page thereafter."

"Just tell me if you notice any specific place names? Do you see capitalized words?"

"I'm sorry, sir, but there are 256 pages of documents in this fiche, and the office is closed now. You'll have to come in tomorrow."

Mark says, "Okay, wait. Fax it to this number, will you?" Audrey's fax machine on the living room floor can receive and print it automatically; he doesn't have to be present. But then as he recites the number, he goes into a trance and the seven digits unlock a new problem: his house key is sitting in his kitchen, on the card table beside the phone. He has locked himself out of his own house. When he left, he pulled the back door shut firmly on its automatic lock. Audrey won't be home until two in the morning.

"I'll also need a major credit card for billing, sir. I need the expiration date and the account number."

Telling her his credit card number from memory, he feels he's lying, giving her a fraudulent number, sinking. He won't be able to get back into his house until Audrey comes back. The only alternative is to break a window.

Which will be necessary if he wants to change his clothes and go out to find Shubie in the dark nightclub.

"How many pages would you like me to send?" she asks.

"All of them."

"All of them?"

"Okay, just the important ones. Just send the one page with the original claim."

"Very good. That's six dollars."

"Thank you very much." The conversation seems to be over, and the receiver falls from his ear as he considers the bleak prospect of spending the night in a foxhole with Roger waiting for Audrey to come home and let him in.

Roger, who has been listening, turns away to rummage in the cupboard, saying, "I wish it wasn't October 31st."

Mark says, "Yeah?"

"Because if we mailed him a letter it wouldn't be dated till tomorrow, and tomorrow is past the deadline." He slaps aside cans and cereal boxes to get to the back of the shelf.

Mark hangs up the phone.

"So hey, I gather they said there actually is a document on file."

"Tell me, Roger. This Abraham was crazy? Who was he? This whole thing is really weird."

"He was an old man in the 1920s, so he must have been born in the nineteenth century. There used to be pictures of him on the wall in a bar in Sausalito."

"This woman said 1848."

"Well, there you are."

"Apparently he was married. He had a widow."

"He was mute," says Roger. "That's the story. Or else it's all bullshit. Do you want some?" He holds up a bottle of wine he found in the cupboard.

"Let's call them," Mark says, picking up the letter. Acquisition's number is at the bottom of the page.

"I tried. I told you."

Dialing the number, Mark says, "Yeah, but maybe."

"All they say is, *Mr. Adcox won't be in his office today. May I take a message?*"

The phone is picked up by a secretarial-sounding person, who says, "Public relations."

"I'm looking for Mr. Adcox."

"Mr. Adcox won't be in his office today. May I take a message?"

"I'm calling about a piece of property in Marin County. We got a letter from your office saying Acquisition is claiming possession of it . . ."

"Mr. Adcox is out on that property today."

"Well, yes. So are we. We need to notify your office that we—don't grant ownership—that we live here."

"I see. You should tell him that. That's the sort of thing he's out there for."

Roger is looking sharply at the conversation he can only hear half of, and Mark asks, on Roger's behalf, "Should we expect a . . . disagreement?"

"With Ad? No, he's very good with people. Why don't you give me your name and number, so I can tell him you called."

"He's out here today?"

"If you're there, you'll see him. You'll like him, Ad's great with people. You'll see. Would you like me to take a message?"

". . . No, I suppose not," says Mark, wanting to get off the phone now and feeling obscurely swindled by this exchange. "No, that's all right."

"Very good."

Mark hangs up and tells Roger, "He's around here now.

And he's not going to be confrontational. He's . . ."—*good with people*—". . . in public relations. The woman who picked up the phone said it was the public relations office."

"Well, fuck 'em. Are you sure you don't want some?" He's holding up his jug of wine.

Mark looks at him. "Maybe there isn't much we can do tonight, Roger. Just put in a symbolic little fence, before it gets completely dark. What do you say? Let's start being efficient."

"Hey, Mark! Hey! Your wife is a lawyer!"

"She's at work. By now she's probably gone, but I just talked to her less than an hour ago."

"You did? What did she say?"

"She said adverse possession is a legal reality . . ." He sits down on the big Ortho-Gro bag Roger left in the middle of the floor. "She said we should wait for Big Adnox tonight and say some sort of legalistic mumbo jumbo to scare him away."

Roger shakes his head, frowning down at his toe pressing a corner of the turf against the baseboard. "Fuckers."

Sitting on the bag of lawn mulch, Mark bows his head and presses his palms to his eyes, the heels of his palms sensuously gouging and crushing his eyeballs, discovering a sleepy itchiness. His body stands like a wick below his conscious soul. That insane Oklahoma pediatrician Altissima is somewhat logical in her ambition: maybe "God" could indeed be so niggling a tyrant—if your flesh has been circumcised, even against your conscious will, then you've entered into His covenant whether you meant to or not, though your thoughts may yet range free in sin and darkness. Mark lifts his face up, blinking, his hard-kneaded eyes fizzing in the bright kitchen light.

Roger shakes his head again thoughtfully, turning back to something he's doing at the counter—picking at his wine bottle's plastic seal. "I wouldn't marry a woman who's a lawyer," he says, and the non sequitur drives Mark to stand up and wander out of the room. "Well," he says, touching the passing doorpost, ". . . whatever."

His voice is hollowed by the acoustics of an empty room. Roger's unit is laid out in a floor plan exactly like his own next door, and the motions of his shoulders define the rooms around him as comfortably as if he lived here. It's his place exactly, except that someone has come and stolen the card table they eat dinner on, the two tubular alumi-num lawn chairs with plastic plaid bands plaited into a seat and back, the Record-a-Call machine on the floor in the corner, the framed Georgia O'Keeffe poster leaning against the wall by the door, its white iris implying an infinite collapse of inward space, like an astrophysicist's tunnel vortex dimpling time-space, where three dimensions fall inward into theoretically many. He doesn't like that poster, but he's respectful of it; it seems to provide a horn listening in on his new marriage.

The emptiness of Roger's living room invites an orbit. But he veers away from the direction of the sleeping-nest of newspapers and wine bottles in the den. On the floor before the front door is a roll of tar paper, and a roll of—he decides without too close an inspection—carpet remnant. It's tied with twine.

He avoids looking too closely into the sleeping den, but he can't help but notice a new, enamel-green power lawn mower. "Sears *Ultra*," it says on the metal skirt, so shiny it has obviously never yet been used. Big price tags and warranty cards still hang on it. But he turns away—setting a seal on a new category in his mind: things he will refrain from asking Roger about.

In Roger's dining room, as in his own, a light fixture—the same light fixture as everywhere, a mass-produced plastic halo—hangs low over nothing, over the empty area where a table should go. As in Mark's own dining room, it wards off entrance.

The marbleized fireplace—one of the most expensive options available at Cobblestone Hearth ("Optimism! That's the ticket!" Roger said)—has a mantle piece, on which several small glass bottles are lined up. They are identifiably Bayer aspirin bottles, the familiar small-shouldered shape, with the label scrubbed off, sparkling clean. Empty. No, not empty. At the bottom of each bottle rests a tiny speck or pebble.

"Oh my gosh, Roger, are these your kidney stones?"

After a pause, his voice comes from the kitchen. "Yeah, pretty perverted, huh?"

"You really do save them."

"Well, I don't usually have people in. It seems weird, I know. But you can't just throw them away." He comes in, carrying his wine bottle. "Once you get them, you can't exactly throw them away. I just put them there, it's not like they're supposed to be on display."

"Actually it's somewhat interesting." Mark holds up the first bottle, in which a sharp-edged diamond traps a soft light. Little grains that form in the kidney have only the penis as an exit. "They must be painful."

"Whff," Roger says, with a comic dilation of vision suggestive of pain-crossed eyes drawn to focus on his distant urinary canal.

"I think these are actually literally 'stones,' you know." At MIT, a friend of Mark's had a roommate who got kidney stones, who lay in bed for weeks waiting to piss into a tea strainer. In growing, a tetrahedral mineral lattice like calcium probably mounts into tiny pyramidal blades, or points, which would score the urethra in passing. Mark turns the bottle to reveal a facet in the gem, quartzlike, but clouded with rust: there may be actual iron oxide ingredients. It's an unmistakable color. The ions can be octahedrally arranged in a tetrahedral crystal. "I mean, they're minerals, right? Calcium and so on."

"Want some? I'm switching to wine."

"No. No. Thanks. I have my beer here." In fact, he's hungry; his fingers seek another handful of peas thawing in his jacket pocket.

"Typical . . . corporate . . . ," Roger says with disgust, nodding back toward the telephone.

Mark is holding the bottle up, and he taps it to make the stone hop like a tiny die, trying to bring up other facets. He is guilty of never having quite learned, in an undergraduate course on solids, about the molecular structure of crystals. It's possible that the lattice inside is densely crowded with creases and faults. He dimly recalls a textbook illustration, in a chapter he never reached, where a trellis of molecules is climbed by damaging cracks.

"So is your wife a feminist?" Roger is still diligently unpeeling the plastic sleeve over the cap of his wine bottle.

"Why, because she's a professional lawyer?"

"You know, a lot of this—" he stops unpeeling the plastic on the bottle, and he lowers his voice for emphasis, gesturing shruggingly about himself at the ubiquitous feminism ambient: "A lot of this has nothing to do with actual reality. You know what I mean? Like *actual* reality?"

As an encoded way of offering himself as a pal, the statement can't be rebuked, so Mark permits himself the sneaky hypocrisy of agreeing, "You can say that again, Rodge." In a way, it's almost generous of him, to risk proffering a barbarous bigotry.

He goes back to peeling the wine bottle. "I'm talking about, like, reality."

Mark holds the aspirin bottle up to the incandescent

light of the lamp, shadowing it from the fluorescent light penetrating from the kitchen, whose jumbled wavelength will jam in the crystal lattice of the stone. "Roger, do you happen to know the mineral involved?" As he shifts the bottle, snowflake-glint evidence of crystallization flickers in the pebble. "Your doctor might have happened to mention calcium? Like calcium oxalate? I know calcium is generally involved."

"I don't know anything about it. I'm thinking maybe we should start putting up the barricade. These Acquisition Systems people seem to be well organized, and maybe they'll send out a real asshole. Despite what they say. You know? We have to make sure we keep him off the property formally."

By holding the bottle up at eye height, it's possible to locate the gleam of a facet and then rotate it 360 degrees, slowly, to see whether a second gleam occurs at 120 degrees or 240 degrees, which might indicate that the crystal is indeed tetrahedral. ". . . There's certain kind of calcite that they call birefringent because it actually, like, *polarizes* light. You wouldn't happen to have a pair of sunglasses in the house, would you?"

"Sunglasses?"

"Polaroid lenses," Mark says, turning the bottle. "I could get some idea of how the light is traveling in there."

"No. No sunglasses. But listen, don't you think?" Going back into the kitchen with his wine bottle, he raises his voice to bounce it. "Do you think it's possible a corporation would send out some asshole who's willing to get crazy? If he's crazy, we have no defense. You don't have any defense against crazy people. Because then anything's possible. There aren't any rules. They win."

"I don't know, Roger. Maybe." He sets the bottle on the mantle and sets his chin on the mantle to fix his eye in the level ecliptic of the stone's rotation—thus closing his jaw on the whistling of "Wish You Were Here."

"Sane people are always at a disadvantage. I know you're a professor. You might not have that much experience of how weird things can get. We have to be exactly as weird as *they're* willing to be. What's the legal warning we're supposed to give Adcox? Your wife said?"

"I don't know. She called it the Livery of Season, or Cézanne. It's some *mis*pronounced French word. But she was talking about something archaic. It's an old ceremony." Unfortunately now his shadow has moved and the kitchen's fluorescent light is falling on the stone again and interfering with the cleaner wavelength from the ceiling lamp in the living room. He pours the stone out of the bottle into the palm of his hand. It definitely traps and confuses a soft light.

"Mm," says Roger. He is looking absentmindedly off toward the window, his wine bottle half raised. As if his mind had wandered to thinking in general of the hypocrisy and vanity of the modern world, he makes a little humorous cough of disgust. Then he refocuses his mind and takes a drink. "If you're not having any, I'll just be a slob and drink from the bottle. But anyway, what are we supposed to say, word for word?"

"I don't know, Roger. Like, 'Get off our property.' 'Oogah Woogah Boogah.' Whatever we want. She wasn't really serious."

They're remarkable, these stalagmites from inside Roger Hoberman's kidney, real rocks, but as foreign as meteorites. It strikes him that Roger cherishes them as trophies—after all, he does keep them on the mantle—and the trapped feeling comes back to flood the world, lifting him. He straightens up to regard, with some objectivity, Roger Hoberman, who has wandered over the empty floor to stand by the window and take a drink straight from his wine bottle, his back turned.

"You know?" Roger says, beginning to wax philosophical. "It's like, if you still believe in being honest? And having personal honor? And integrity? Simply being a normal average *guy?* Instead of . . . *fashionable?*"

"Come on, Roger," Mark says. "If we're gonna do this, let's do it." He drinks from his beer, finishing it off—immediately thinking of getting another from Roger's refrigerator, because the rest of the evening will be hostile to his better-educated nerves, and it's the kind of anesthesia ordinary people use. He'll help Roger build his fence outside in the dirt—or at least some kind of technical excuse for a fence. And later in the evening there may be time to just *visit* this dark nightclub full of—as he pictures it—slam-dancing punks randomly colliding with each other—where surely he would be out of place, staying clear at the periphery, because they really do bump into each other violently when they dance—but where, also, no one will ever notice him, all those kids are so isolated by their own narcissism, they never really notice other people, their self-gaze pooled on the mirror of nightclub darkness, where anything is possible. Something like *duty* seems to call him toward adultery, a duty to take one shot at eternity by a discreet indulgence in error.

Roger, still looking out the window with his wine bottle, says philosophically in wonderment, "You know?"

Mark heads for the kitchen. "Where's your rope?"

9
Oogah Woogah Boogah

Which is how Mark finds himself three hundred feet out in the dark territory of Big Adcox and the Night Walker, warily innocent and blind in a helmet of clinging light, his shoes sliding in the crumbly slope of a ravine, his face fearing attack by twigs, connected with Roger back in Cobblestone Hearth by his grip on the end of a clothesline: it's the diagrammed string of "gravity" from childhood textbooks, by which the earth, preposterously, was supposed to hold the moon from spinning away. It wasn't until his first lower-division courses at college that he learned how right he was, as a child, to doubt that stupid diagram. Fifty feet toward civilization, at the other end, after a long silence, Roger Hoberman's voice says, "Women these days, huh? Feminism." And Mark— momentarily grateful for Roger's partnership—makes an agreeable chuckle audible across the distance, his voice brave in the darkness. Guys like Roger, they're at liberty to say such things in the immense luxuriousness of ignorance and divorce.

After a minute he calls out into the dark: "Roger? How come you don't get some furniture?"

"Hey, did you move?"

"I didn't move, I'm holding it right here above the creek."

"Okay, I've got the stake in. You can come back."

He grips his end and climbs back up over the rim of the ravine, into the thin starlight over the field—or maybe it's indirect street-lamp light—which, now to his more absorptive retina, looks as bright as day, gleaming on the husks of grass seed. He probably seems, indeed, an academic nerd, lifting his chin away from the scratchy, allergenic weeds and wading like a child with a prance through the burrs and seeds; yet Shubie Behejdi discerns the sexy power of intellect in him, a secret but obvious intensity. Despite his rather slight build. And Audrey, too. He's a bigamist already, in spirit, stamping down the grasses.

Roger says, "Stop and wait when you get to that point." Meaning, to the stake. "See it?"

"Roger, why don't you have any furniture? I was just noticing."

He keeps pulling in and paying out the rope as he moves toward his yard, until at last he can't avoid answering. ". . . Well, you know—incomewise," he says. "The Olde Fashion is at a point where I have to be patient."

"But surely a few sticks of furniture—"

"Plus, the fact is, I'm not officially living here."

"You've been here for a year."

"Yeah, but I haven't been paying the mortgage. It's a long story."

"Didn't you make a down payment?"

"Yes, of course. Okay, years ago I used to have a Shakey's. The Shakey's failed. Shakey's International finally came across with my refund on the franchise. And *that* was the down payment on this place. But during the whole time before, I didn't have an address."

"You didn't have an address. Roger, you were a homeless person!"

"No, I just was sleeping outside, and I didn't have a job. I wasn't interested in all this."

"Where did you sleep?"

Having stretched the fifty-foot rope to its furthest extent, he turns away. "I have to find another stake. Stay right there until I can get this end staked down. Don't move."

"How long were you a homeless person? Roger."

"I wasn't a 'homeless person,' I was just going through something. It was about two years. It was nice. Beautiful country out there."

Another stick comes to Roger's hands, and he returns to grope on the ground for his end of the clothesline.

"Well, so . . . ?" Mark pulls up his own stake and approaches with the slackening rope. "I mean, you did pay a down payment—"

"Yeah. I got a lot of money when Shakey's International paid back what they owed me. Cobblestone Hearth is carrying the loan. Isn't that what you guys did? Twelve and a quarter fixed—that's hard to beat."

"So they want to kick you out. You haven't been making your monthly payments."

Roger gets down on one knee to adjust or retie the knot on his stake. Then he stands up. "People don't seem to be buying pizza right now. It's not just me, it's the whole industry. Shakey's, Domino's, Pizza Hut."

"Here." Mark hands him the torn-out stake, the rope tied to it, and Roger walks off toward the nearing line of semidetached units, lamp-lit within. This will be the third fifty-foot measurement.

"But I'm optimistic," Roger says. "They just have to have patience."

"How many months have you not paid the mortgage?"

"Twelve. My view is I'm behind in my payments, that's all. *Their* view, of course, is I'm a bum. We've sent a few letters back and forth. In fact, if you have a typewriter, maybe I could borrow it sometime. Handwritten letters always look . . . dorky."

"This is a hundred and fifty feet," Mark says. Roger steps on the stake to drive it into the ground. Mark pulls up his own stake and follows.

"I mean I fully intend to pay them back, with interest and penalties, but I have to wait for Shakey's International to come through with the other half of my refund, and I need to get the Olde Fashion cooking somehow. I need to make it a destination. That's the new strategy everybody says in *Pizza Today*. You want to be a destination. You need animatronics animals or puppet shows, or you need to install a virtual reality. Things like that are expensive."

"What's a 'virtual reality'?"

"Oh . . . some kind of shit."

"This'll be two hundred feet," says Mark, handing over his stake, with rope attached, which Roger carries away toward the ever-nearer line of semidetached houses. Across the remaining margin of the field, three living-room windows in separate houses are flickering with the blue explosions of television light. They're flickering in a synchronized erratic rhythm, peepholes on the same furnace: three total strangers are watching the same channel, their retinas dyed so completely by light that, if they came outside in the dark, they would be blind and vulnerable. Mark scans the pale field with all-seeing eyes.

Roger reaches a point where the rope is taut, and he kneels to stab his stake in.

"So you were a homeless person," Mark remarks faintly in amazement, really in admiration. He pulls up his own stake and walks in.

Roger shrugs. "It doesn't take much. No matter how normal you think you are. Anybody can take *one* blow. But you get two or three blows in a row, and it's hard to stay in the mainstream. It's funny, people have this *illusion*, as if they're in control. And anyway, being in the mainstream isn't so great."

"So what did you do? Did you, like, cook with Sterno? And sleep under bridges? If you don't mind my asking."

"Oh," says Roger dismissively, with a lift of one shoulder.

"Where did you *live?*"

"After a while I got that truck, where I could sleep. Around Marin, lots of people sleep in the Grange Territory."

"What's the Grange Territory?"

"You know. By the dump?"

"No."

"There's a lot of containerized-shipping boxes out there. Big metal boxes. You can run electricity and everything. Mostly rock bands practice in them. But me, when I got a van, I got out away, went north, kept on going. This is two hundred and fifty feet, right?" says Roger, accepting the stake and walking away. His odd remark, *It was nice; it's a beautiful country out there,* remains in memory, a statement of such vacancy that a kind of warm wind blows through it. Big valleys in summertime are bisected by a ribbon of shining highway. Clear heavy air floods desert floors where heat flows around you to grip you. An interstate freeway in the early morning is tinted violet by immense cool distances, immense stillnesses. He pictures an overpass through a dry gorge, beneath which Roger like a cowboy awakens in his sleeping bag in the glacier of silence in the canyon before the first traffic of the dawn begins to roll. Or in the rain, in a city like Portland or Los Angeles, in a doorway near a train station. Two years is a long time.

"Roger, if it's not too personal, what were your two or three big blows in a row?" Mark doesn't pull up his stake, though Roger has drawn his end of the rope taut and driven his stake in. "In your case."

"Who, me?" says Roger. "Come on, bring your end." Mark pulls up his stake and carries it to Roger. At last unable to avoid answering his question, Roger says, "Actually? Kidney stones, I guess. At first."

"Oh, that does make sense."

"It seems stupid, but kidney stones do tie you up a bit. And then you can't get reinsured for health insurance because you've got a preexisting condition. And my wife got the condominium, which didn't amount to much anyway. And blah blah blah."

"No, it makes sense," says Mark. "I knew a fellow at school with kidney stones, and he was always lying around in bed."

"But I don't believe in that, *blaming* things, blaming luck. Just hope for the best, plan for the worst, that's my motto."

"This'll be the whole three hundred feet," says Mark, passing the stake to Roger, who walks off with it.

"I *plan* my luck. I *take* responsibility. That's why the fucking Democrats are so popular around here: nobody takes responsibility any more. People lose their job and they stay home whining, *Somebody's gotta do something about me; I'm so pitiful. If I lived in Sweden, somebody'd do something about me.*"

"Well, I wouldn't get angry about it, Roger."

"It's *fine* to get angry. That's another thing that's out of fashion." He is standing in this empty field holding an end of clothesline. "Why is it not fashionable to get angry? It's fucking *okay* to get angry. Sometimes there are *things.* Okay? Sometimes there are just *things.*" With his arms he gestures around demonstratively, at "things."

"Roger. Okay." Mark's tone of voice—newly sharp—is a flashbulb on the yard, embarrassing Roger. With a glance over his shoulder, he begins to whisper across the fifty-foot gap, thrusting his face forward: "We're all supposed to be vegetarians or something. Like we're not even supposed to have real shit in our intestines. And like, be too pure for nuclear power." He draws one thigh across the other in a mincing knock-kneed dance, his fingers fluttering at his shoulders like tiny wings: *"Ooh, I'm too pure for nuclear power."*

"Is that the three-hundred-foot point?" says Mark, for Roger is standing on his own territory. Like football referees measuring for a first down, they have established the line right in the middle of Roger's property. Mark had meant to get him off his subject, but this new circumstance happens to collaborate with his anger. "See? See what I mean?" He throws down his stake. His arms rise antlerlike to embrace the air space of the yard around him. "Property is property. These people can have all the fancy lawyers they want, but property is property. Do you realize what's going on in the world? Like with people sleeping on the sidewalk? It's like Calcutta. I've personally seen it. And when it comes onto your own property, that's different."

He wipes his forehead and levels a finger toward the empty field. "Whoa, shit."

Where he's pointing, in the darkness at the border of the field, a dead child appears hovering above ground level, splashed with blood, dusted with white powder. Beside him, less immediately visible in dark clothing, is a tiny woman in a miniskirt. Her breasts are strangely distended. The woman says, in a small girl's voice, "I'm Slutpunk, the slut from hell."

The boy cries, "Gawick-oh-Gaweenie!"

The girl explains, "He can't say his *TR*'s yet."

"You guys," Roger says, "where's your mother? Is she letting you run around like this?"

"She's putting on her face. She said for us to go first. Besides, we already went. I got 'My Little Pony' stickers, and Jason got all stupid things. He got Good'n'Plenty and candy corn."

"Gawick-oh-Gaweenie!" shouts the floating dead guy, making his rigged-up costume tremble. "I like to keep myself clean! It's okay for me to touch myself! I can be free and natural with my penis!"

"Shut up, Jason, you gay," the girl says, then turns to explain to Mark. "My other dad gave that tape to him. He lives in Connecticut. He's not my real dad. He's a prick because he gave my mom bad credit, but my mom lucked out and got a MasterCard, so she's buying a house for us, but it's a surprise, and then we can get a *dog!*"

Mark had actually been frightened, slightly, by the appearance of the children in the field, and tiny shocked calories effervesce in his spine as he begins to move again, carrying his end of the clothesline in from the field. Roger says, "Come on, Mark, let's do this. Let's start digging. We've got to build something before midnight, if possible."

Mark crosses paths with Jason, who is trespassing happily on Roger's property, his costume cantilevered out in front of his stomach—a pair of sausage-stuffed white Levi's legs floating on a frame of coat-hanger wire, his actual legs obscured by darker pants. He crows again, louder, "I LIKE TO KEEP MYSELF CLEAN," addressing Mark. A fork is stuck into his skull.

"We don't have any candy," Mark says. If Audrey were here, she would have thought ahead and bought candy, but she is at this moment legitimately busy, making the way straight for the journey of the pope, aglow in his tall hat and his stiff gown. The little boy stops and stands with his wormy fingers wriggling on outstretched arms, and he says, "I feel good with my family. I'm proud of myself. I like to keep myself clean."

His sister, rolling her eyes, lifts her shoulders all the way to her ears and drops them. "My other dad brainwashed him. He lives in Connecticut, and he's got all these horses." The word *horses* is spoken with contempt, contempt probably borrowed from her mother.

"Mark, let's just say our property starts right there. Isn't that where you always assumed?"

"I guess I'll get a flashlight," Mark says, turning toward his back door.

He stops still: he has locked himself out of his house. At seven-thirty his cream chipped beef will automatically begin heating itself in the programmable microwave and then begin getting cold. He's so hungry now his stomach feels like a rag. Inside his dark house, the flicker of television light is evidence that he forgot to turn the set off. If he goes to the Art and Artifice Club, he'll have to wear the school clothes he's been wearing all day. Or else break a window to get in. And change into, say, jeans and a jacket.

He doesn't have anything that would fit in at a punk nightclub.

It will be awkward and troublesome later, sneaking to the other side of his house and discreetly breaking a small window: there's the barrier of a screen with an aluminum frame; and the windows all around the house are Thermopane glass (which he hates, its two layers at night reflecting his two selves uncomfortably.) At least their security-alarm system is disconnected, because he used to set off the alarm once a day, accidentally, until Audrey finally clipped the wires; since then, theirs has been the only unit in Phase III without a tiny lit ruby and emerald shining on a steel plate by the front door.

"Roger," he says, realizing he's on some sort of errand, "Where are your shovels?" He sets out, instead, toward Roger's open kitchen door.

"In the thing," Roger says. "There's charcoal briquets in there, too. Would you bring them, too?"

"Sure."

"Jennifer, can you be in charge of Jason? And make sure he doesn't touch things?"

The girl starts speaking again in tattling tones to her father, her voice receding as Mark goes into the utility closet, inside Roger's back door, to find a new shovel and a new posthole digger, both bearing Day-Glo orange price stickers on their blades. And a bag of Kingsford charcoal briquets. His only constant solace, traveling steadily at his side like the moon along a road, is the thought of Shubie, of his having risen to the secret prestige of adulterer, a thought that stirs in his groin a fragile yolk elongated by attraction. His hair, which had always flowed to one side to pile up above his left ear, has a good-looking new cut. In the new bedroom, he has a full-length mirror now, so he can check every morning that he hasn't, say, pulled a sock up over a pants leg or missed a belt loop, little mistakes that mar the dignity of a man whose paper created a sensation at the Rochester conference when he was only twenty-three years old, who was a VIP at the Aspen conference at the age of twenty-seven.—All of which, however, is invisible to Roger. As he carries the shovels and the charcoal bag out into the dark, Roger says, "Okay, do you want to start the fire? Or do you want to begin with the digging?"

"Whichever. Doesn't matter." Mark's tone, unfortunately, implies disinterest in both jobs.

"One thing I've learned," Roger says as he drops to his knees and takes a stab at the ground with his wooden stake. "You can make the best of a bad situation."

"Yup."

"So, you wanna dig?"

"It really doesn't matter."

"Okay, I'll get the lighter fluid. It's under the sink." Roger hops up and jogs toward the door with a large man's jingling alacrity. He's trying to be a nice guy. He says over his shoulder, "I have to be easy on my back. Carrying that roll of turf was stupid." Mark drops his arm load with a clank on the ground at the edge of the open field, and the little boy, his fake legs jiggling, tells him, "I can be free and natural with my penis."

"Good," says Mark. "So can I."

The boy points at the shovel and says, "Ell-menno."

"This? No, 'shovel.' This is shovel."

"Ell-menno." The boy points out into the vast darkness uphill across the field, toward Mount Tamalpais. "Peek? Peek cure?" It's got the intonation of a question, so interrogatory it makes the boy's eyes expand and his hands open, wriggling on the ends of his arms.

"No," says Mark. "Shovel," he points to the shovel.

Then he points out into the wilderness. *"Not*-shovel." Then again he points to the shovel—"Shovel"—and points out into the wilderness: *"Not*-shovel." It's the first lesson of life for us monstrous molecular humans, the first rule of logic, the Principle of Identity, the fundamental Aristotelian principle—which perhaps, at every nanosecond, in every grain of "space," is being shattered.

"Cure rest you." Jason turns and walks out into the dark field, crossing the ragged border where the weeds define a curtain of light, and he disappears, beginning to talk to himself in his own alien language. The sound fades as the boy gets further away into the dark, and Mark starts to look around for a likely place to begin digging: he lifts the posthole digger—a weird contraption like two big trowels joined in a scissoring pair—and he plunges its twin blades down to earth at the point where Roger had stabbed. But the digger only bounces, with a ring, from the hard mud.

"Hey, no," says Roger, returning. "You'll ruin the blades. Use the shovel to dig."

"Can I do it?" says the girl, following.

"On that, the tips'll get all bent in. Just use it for reaching down and pulling up stuff you've already loosened. Or else it looks like maybe we should have a pick. You know?" Roger's arms are full. As well as a tin can of Gulflite, he has a frying pan, a bottle of Lea & Perrins Worcestershire sauce, and two bars of hamburger meat shrink-wrapped in cellophane. When he drops the hamburger blocks in the frying pan, they sound like iron. They're frozen.

"Where's the boy?" he says. "Is that him I hear?" Jason's voice can be heard faintly in the darkness of the field. He seems to be having a conversation. He might have sat down in the tall weeds, because he can be heard but not seen.

His sister says in his defense, "It's perfectly healthy."

"This," Roger tells Mark, "is what happens when there's no father influence. Her second husband was a total dweeb. Where is he?"

Mark, feeling slightly responsible for the boy's having wandered away, says, "He's out there," and he picks up the shovel to try its effectiveness.

"Ever since I left, he's had an imaginary friend. At first when I moved out, I moved into the Bermuda Palms motel by the freeway—"

"Many children have a maginary friend," scolds the girl.

Roger lifts the bag of charcoal. "Go tell your brother to stop talking to his imaginary friend and come here."

"Okay." She's delighted. She runs into the dark. Roger turns away, and the tipped bag in his arms pours out too many charcoal briquets—half the bag—more than half the bag—in a big heap on the dry mud, which is probably as good a place as any to build a fire. Mark looks at him: the Bermuda Palms motel, in San Rafael, is distinguished by an immense neon palm tree, which however Mark has always seen dustily unlit, and he had assumed it's broken—had half-assumed, in fact, that the motel was extinct. Probably Roger lived there until his income ran out, while his first pizza place was dying. Meanwhile, his wife seems to have remarried and then redivorced.

"You and your wife lived around here? Before the divorce?"

"You should have seen." Roger stoops to recover far-rolled briquets. "We had a place in Marinwood on Sunstone, which is the good street. Like this but more so. *Four* bedroom. *Complete* clubhouse. With a package time-share in Lake Tahoe I never used anyway. I'm a workaholic. Or I was."

Beginning at the agreed-on spot on the ground where the tall weeds start—where somehow Mark's assumption, too, already defines an edge—he spears at the dirt with the shovel, making it rebound as the tip of the blade chips at the hard earth—only now remembering the insurmountable futility in all physical labor, the huge fact of life that scared him into academia—so that immediately he stops and leans on the shovel.

"But so now I come back and Jason is talking to imaginary people. Dot was married to this guy who's a total flake. A 'chiropractor,' right? Huh? And then she divorced him. And *he*'s been giving the kids these tapes to listen to—where there's soothing music, and this happy little voice says over and over again, *I love my mom and dad. I always wipe myself. I love to wipe myself. I do it every day.* Supposedly it's subliminal. You know what we're fighting, these days?" He straightens up, with sooty palms. "*Women* control everything these days. All this irrational shit. Like 'subliminal.' People take that seriously! What happened to rational? Women this, women that. Everything. Fuckin' candidates are elected by how they *look*. By how cute they are. What happened to men?" He drops back down and goes on rebuilding the briquet pyramid.

Mark stands there dinking at the earth with his shovel blade. "What did you do all the time out there?" he asks.

"Out there? You mean for two years? It was great. That is, it's not so great, too, but I definitely don't regret it. At first I was sick a lot. I kept passing kidney stones."

"Oh, of course. Yeah."

"But that didn't last long. In urban areas there's always free shelters. But you can always find work, even in the country. After I got my health, I just started to like the road. My mind got used to it. Your eyes get used to looking at longer spaces. You know, you only get a few years on this planet, in this life."

Mark keeps digging, if feebly. Roger probably sat on milk crates at the back of 7-Elevens, in the lee of the lavender brick wall where the angle of the building traps the sun's warmth, or even lay down, trying to pass a kidney stone; yet the whole picture is oddly cozy. That remark about getting used to looking at longer spaces makes Mark's own eyes feel suffocated. Maybe he lacks the physical frame, the robustness, to go out and live on his own and, say, sleep on the ground sometimes if necessary, but nevertheless, legs feel the desire to walk, eyes the thirst to see, and there's even something darkly appealing in the risk of being mortally ill in the middle of nowhere, like Roger. Everybody has to die sometime; it's possible almost to envy Roger his ability to take the chance of lying down in the cinders among windshield diamonds at the horizon between air and dust, where mystically the rib cage desires its gradual marriage to earth, its immersion in a dusty bath, which finally leaves only a rag at the surface to flip in the wind. Which is the end of us all, anyway, even the luckiest professor on the campus. Having dug more energetically for a minute, he gives the shovel a rest. "Why did you move in *here?*" It's only a natural question, but saying it now he begins to feel he's crossed over into being nosy. After only slight hesitation—in which he closes and rolls the lip of the briquet bag—Roger says plainly, "I want my wife. Again."

"Ah," Mark says abruptly, to end the conversation, and he starts digging with more purpose.

"I just faced this," he goes on.

"You know, Roger, that hamburger is frozen solid."

"That's okay. I've got a technique."

"See?" Jennifer's voice rises as she comes out of the

weeds with her brother. Fists on hips, she thrusts her enormous lightweight breasts out in air. "I'm the slut from hell."

Roger sets aside the charcoal bag. "No more precocious talk. Okay?"

"He was talking to his maginary friend."

Everybody stands around looking at Jason.

Roger gets down on one knee. "Tell me, Jase. What is your friend's name?" Jason lowers his eyes and grasps the two stuffed pants legs that stick out from his belly. Roger is trying to exert a fatherly influence.

Mark, feeling embarrassed on Jason's behalf, starts digging again. "Maybe we do need a pick," he says. Then he looks around for the wooden stake, to give it a try.

Roger asks again, "Jason?"

Jennifer answers for him: "His name is 'pff.' "

" 'Pff.' " Roger repeats the sound. "Is that his name?"

The boy only smiles at the ground. Mark keeps digging, for some reason embarrassed by this interrogation.

"Jason?" Roger insists, "Is that right? Is his name 'pff'? Can you say that? Let's hear you say his name."

Jason refuses to commit the blasphemy, and smiles as his eyes wander over the ground.

"Come on, Jason. Just say it once."

Jennifer rescues him again. "He never says it. Probably 'pff' isn't his real name. Probably 'pff' is just the name he calls him with *people*."

"Well, what does 'pff' *do* out there? Where does he live? In the trees?"

Roger's tone of jolly atheistic mockery excites the boy, who looks up and says, "Emenno!" wiggling his fingers at arm's length.

The meaningless word, in Mark's mind, now joins the indecipherable Berkeleyan sidewalk graffito *ARE est you* in

the sandy dictionary of possible jargon in the infinite number of logically possible universes. The sudden outward
fission of *possibility* everywhere chills him, as with the
slight breath of a house of cards collapsing all around, and
he returns to digging as his only reason for being here, the
stars above rushing away as the universe dissolves with
the instantaneity of a drop of ink in water. On his knees,
he raises the stake in both hands to stab it into the ground.
It's like concrete.

"Menno," says the boy in a new tone of doubtfulness.

Jennifer reaches for him. "Hold still. Your fork is falling
off."

Roger tells the boy as he stands and turns away, "Okay,
you can believe in any kind of people you want, that's *my*
view." And he picks up the can of Gulflite to—with a
ticktock popping of the inverted can—soak the charcoal
briquets, whose black soot pillows shimmer for an instant
while the cologne vanishes. The air is beginning to get a
little cold. A fire will be a welcome thing. "So your
mother's coming over?" Roger asks his daughter. The
daughter doesn't answer, absorbed by the spectacle of the
lighter fluid.

"Name's Dot," he tells Mark. "Maybe you've seen her
around, like at the Upper Class Club or somewhere."

"I never go there," says Mark.

"Neither do I. Neither does she, actually. Nobody does.
I think only kids do. And use the hot-tub jets to jerk off."

"Heh-heh," Mark says. He stabs the stake one last time
and sits up onto his heels, kneeling. "I'm not sure this is
worth so much trouble, Roger." He decides he'll finish
digging one hole, which is enough to excuse him from
further work, and then he'll break into his own house by
force. He'll break the bathroom window. A fog is coming
in from the dark mountain, the wick of his hair is collect-

ing it. Why is he wasting time here with Roger on this one lucky dark weightless night when the planets are so aligned that his "wife" is gone?

"Roger, what time do you think it is?"

"No, don't lose heart. Remember what the lawyer said."

"I just don't want to do it *tonight*."

"We have to. This is the last night of the five-year period. Just wait, I'll get the pennants and the bunting and stuff. At least we can put *it* up."

"Daddy, look!" says the little girl. "I'm gonna put this on." She is holding the can of Gulflite lighter fluid over the charcoal.

"No, wait, hon'," says Roger, reaching to take the can from his daughter.

Mark turns back to digging with an angry new resolve to be fast. "Okay, Roger, but I intend to be efficient. One or two posts won't take long. Right?"

"Look out," Roger says, kneeling with a lit match flaring in his fingers, prodding the underbelly of every little charcoal briquet, where slow flames start to stick. Jason and Jennifer come closer to the light—the delicate lilac of potassium tingeing the flames' base, rising to the usual mixed yellows of carbon and oxygen. Roger stands up to squirt more Gulflite on the fire and make it poof high. "Stand back, you guys."

"Your legs are burning," Jennifer tells the little boy. She pulls his fake legs back from the fire.

"Don't!" he screams.

"Keep your voice down," says Roger. He makes the fire boom with jets of Gulflite. "So!" he says to Mark, "You're a physicist. That must be interesting."

"Yeah." Mark's palms are already tender from the friction of digging. The hole is a few inches deep.

"Atoms," says Roger. "Protons . . ."

Mark doesn't reply. The stake bounces as he stabs the mud.

"I was always interested in that. Like what are things made of. You know? When you get down to it."

"Yup."

"What are they saying these days?"

"Yeah, really."

"No, I'm *asking*. Seriously, what is stuff made of these days?" Roger holds air slipping through his fingers indefinably. "When I went to school it was electrons, protons, and neutrons. But now you've got it down to even smaller things."

Every time he spears the earth, he nicks up a coin-sized chip of dust from the frozen mud. He stops to rest. "You don't want to know, Roger."—Everything is a rainbowlike standing column, a delusion. An optical phenomenon. Or, in reality, a semantic phenomenon.

"Like what is 'mass,' " Roger persists.

"There's no such thing," Mark says, feeling in his bones again the peculiar emotional fatigue of his job: there is more "mass" dwelling in the booming, bulging vacuum than in "matter," itself a mere insubstantial froth thrown out.

"I had one hell of a jerk for a physics teacher . . . Mr. Spry. I had to do a fucking science project for Accomplishment Week. Accomplishment Week was this *thing*. It's indescribable. And I thought I had a great idea: I taped pieces of hair on a posterboard, and I put different kinds of stuff on each bunch of hair. Like one bunch of hair had Coca-Cola on it, and another one had latex paint on it. And one had gasoline. And one had spit. It was supposed to be some kind of experiment. And I showed up in the gym for fucking Accomplishment Week with my stupid-looking posterboard with, you know, Scotch tape holding these locks of hair on . . . Shit . . . Like other kids made their own atom smashers.'' He sighs with happy self-pity.

''Daddy?''

His children, who had been quiet, watching the flames die down, stand up and move fearfully sideways toward their father to cling to his knees, both children looking out into the dark. ''What is that?'' says Jennifer.

''What.''

''Daddy, what *is* that?''

''What's *what?*''

''Something is out there,'' she says, frightened, her round face aflicker in the light like Roger's and Jason's. She hugs Roger's thigh and looks toward the dark mountain. Her brother, whimpering, makes motions of climbing Roger's leg. Mark, too, actually catches a little of the primitive shudder, his spine an arc in the circle excluding night, and he can't restrain himself from turning his back to the fire, but he sees nothing. His eyes have been washed by light.

Roger says, ''Honey, I can't see anything out there. What's out there?''

Not having an answer, she thinks for a minute. Then she says, ''A monster.''

''Bobser,'' Jason repeats.

''There's no monsters. How come you think there's a monster?''

''It's a ray gun,'' says the boy.

''Monsters don't have ray guns,'' Roger explains, using logic.

''I *saw* it, Daddy.'' Jennifer looks up at her father. She is so convinced herself that she's actually believable. She must have seen something. Maybe a distant headlight on a mountain road. Though there are no roads out there.

Plainly Roger's heart is clutched by love usually repressed. He gets down on one knee and says, into his daughter's hair, "I wouldn't let any monsters get you." His daughter, tickled but annoyed, writhes and shrugs and stuffs her hands in her armpits, throwing her head back against him.

"What color was the ray gun?" Roger whispers behind her ear. "Green?"

"Dad. It was red. Really."

"Monsters with red ray guns *never* eat little boys and girls. They only eat Space Food Sticks."

Jason, sensing levity, hops and sings out, "Bobser."

"Roger?" says a woman's voice behind them in the light—it's Roger's wife—flooding the scene with intelligence: the pile of smoldering charcoal on the dirt, Mark on his knees paleolithically with his wooden stake, the wine bottle, the six-pack of Budweiser, a second six-pack of Budweiser he hadn't noticed till now. ". . . Are you barbecuing?"

"Bob!" says Jason, meaning *Mom,* with another of his arm-flapping hops.

Mark feels a slight impulse to stand up politely. But instead her spectatorship encourages him—with a new self-sureness totally out of character—to simply lean aside and pull another beer from the six-pack.

10
Maybe You're Not Unscrupulous

My wife," Roger tells Mark.

"Roger, could you come over here?" Her wrist pushes her hair back.

"Hey, Dot. Sweetie, this is my good buddy Mark."

"Could you come over here for a minute?"

Mark can't make her out. Standing where she covers the radiance of Roger's kitchen door, she cleaves the light as she shifts her weight from one foot to the other. Her jeans are tight. They've been freshly ironed, a crease traveling down the front of each leg. Her hair is polished to a commercial sheen by shampoo and conditioner and blow-drying. In her arms she holds a platter and a carton of milk, objects of desire to the two children, who stagger toward the light to be near her. Jason strains upward whining, "Mine."

Roger tells Mark, "Just a second," and he sets down his wine bottle as a crutch to crawl up to a standing position. She withdraws further as he approaches, and again she bangs her hair with the back of her wrist, bowing her head and revealing the bright bulb in the kitchen doorway behind her. As in an eclipse, her figure is exceeded by spokes of light in the charcoal's smoke.

"You found us," says Roger. His hands lift and then drop.

"Roger, what is this?" she whispers, her fingers flicking discreetly toward Mark. Mark himself, reclining on his elbow in the dirt, raises his beer to salute her and takes a drink, newly loyal to Roger.

"Oh, honey, now don't be like that. Wait'll you hear." He reaches and almost touches her.

"You can't keep *doing* things." Her children plead for Jell-O, and she juggles her armload to free one hand and set it on the surface of the turbulence below.

"Come on, Dot, don't you want to meet my friend?"

"Your friend looks like a real gem." They think Mark can't hear.

"He's a physicist," Roger protests. "He's a physicist."

She sighs so quickly it's like a laugh, and she turns aside in frustration: the golden kitchen light dawns across a perfectly beautiful profile. It has always seemed to Mark that there's an elite class of people so beautiful that they're interchangeable, women for whom a man must be merely a rectangular dark presence at the elbow lacking particularity, and that such people keep getting married and divorced a lot, because they don't really notice each other very specifically, as if beauty were an analgesic radiance on the skin, a blinding dilation of the pupil. She tells Roger seriously, "You know Cobblestone management is really looking at you."

"Wait'll you hear. See, tonight is the deadline for this *ass*hole." He gestures out at the dark wilderness. "They're doing a thing called 'adverse possession.' Do you know what that is?"

"Why aren't you using the barbeque? People can *see* you."

"Hey, join us. I see you got some Jell-O."

"Actually, I was going to leave the kids with you. I'm going to a friend's house to study." With a lifting gesture, she implies the existence of the textbook now visible under her platter of Jell-O.

"You're going to study?" He crouches to see the book. "What is it?"

"Endocrinology," says Dot quickly and irritably, trying to put the idea away.

Roger turns back toward Mark and raises his voice to call across the distance, "Dot here is going to be an anesthesiologist. Isn't that great?"

Mark pretends to be caught distracted, as if he weren't eavesdropping. With a grin he raises his beer bottle. "Anesthesiology!" he calls back.

"Great having an anesthesiologist in the family," says Roger.

"Here's to anesthesiology."

"Think of the wild parties."

All of which makes Dot shift around impatiently trying to shrug off an awarded stole. Roger moves closer and, lowering his voice to a murmur that, however, is still audible, asks her, "You're going like that?" He's referring to her tight jeans.

"Oh, Roger."

"Is this study partner male or female—may I ask—"

Dot looks at him. "I happen to be very fond of Lucas, and he happens to be the lab assistant. It's a totally platonic relationship."

"Platonic." He puts his hands in his pockets.

"All right, Roger, I'll tell you the point I've reached now. Have you noticed nobody *else* ever has a little camp-out in the backyard like this?"

"Wait, don't change the subject. Besides, it's hardly a 'camp out.' " Neither of them has any idea that Mark can hear clearly, in the sharp night air whose close-packed molecules transmit compressional waves, their voices amplified theatrically by the wall at Roger's kitchen door. Motionless on the dirt, making faint scratches with his digging stick, he bows his head within the sensitive tympany of air. She says, "I'm not changing the subject, this *is* the subject." Her children are drifting discouraged back toward the fire, somber now in the sacred time of a fight. "The subject is, that I'm just *barely, barely*—" she says, inclining her head demonstratively back toward her own condo in Phase I, the oldest and most affordable part of Cobblestone Hearth. Mark understands: she's a single mother going back to school, and she's entering now a common desperation seldom experienced by the beautiful and the exempt. Mark is glad. The nerd in him takes a nasty satisfaction in life's revenge. She lowers her voice: "The subject is, the Cobblestone Hearth people have to eventually do something."

"They know I'm getting on my feet. They're cutting me some slack. Look, they haven't thrown me out tonight. It's the last day of the month, they should have come by now. They're letting me slide."

"Okay, Roger," she says. She hands across to him the

platter and the milk carton, ceremonially. Jennifer and Jason have sat down beside Mark, rather near to him, appointing him to the series of tall dark silhouettes that substitute for the Absent Father of California. Now in retrospect, her calling from the sandbox, *If you touch me I'll scream*, seems like a sad, wild sort of allurement.

Roger, disarmed now by having his hands full, says, "So you want me to baby-sit."

"I also want you to get inside. Everybody can see you."

"Dot, you don't know what this is."

"Yes I do. No more explanations, Roger. I've had it with explanations. It's time I told you something. Now don't get mad."

"What."

"I had to do this. I talked to the sheriff about taking out a restraining order on you, and I filed all the papers. Do you know what a restraining order is? I mean it, honey."

"Dot," Roger whines in disbelief.

She grasps her elbows, raises her shoulders, and looks at the ground.

Mark gets a new grip on his stick and starts digging faster, his ears scalded.

"I didn't want to do it. It's the lawyer's thing."

Roger whines, "A restraining order is for when a person is a real menace. I'm not a menace. What did I do?"

"I swear I'll never have to use it. It's only for the Bob divorce."

Roger looks around as if he wishes for an immediate place to set down the Jell-O and the milk carton, and then he gives up and turns back to her. "Honey. You don't need his money."

"Yeah, but *his* people will try to get away with everything. This is just for during the proceedings."

"And then you'll use this? In court?"

"They made me take out a restraining order on Bob, too, if that makes you feel better."

"What did I do, supposedly?"

"He's going to say you're a sort-of threat, and you hang around. But it's just for the Bob divorce, honey. It's just because you happen to be living here like this. He's going to say you're squatting, and that you were indigent, and you were in Vietnam. I'm sorry, but Roger, listen to me, please. It's the smart thing to do."

"I'm not squatting. I've got my whole down payment in this thing. Did you tell them that?"

"Come on, Roger, would you please just let me be practical, for once in my life?"

"A restraining order is for crazy people. What kind of 'threat' am I?"

"Honey."

"What kind of threat did I ever do?"

"Well, there were times when you were . . . physical?"

"I was never physical."

"Like you'd sort of grab my elbows?"

"Grab your elbows! Everybody does that. That's not physical. That's where I just wanted you to shut up and listen."

"It counts in court."

"And so you told them that?"

"Honey, please. I'm just trying to do the smart thing, for once." She looks at him.

Roger seems to think about it, then says, "You don't have to be an asshole to be smart."

"This is the law, Roger. This is the purpose of the law. The law is smart *for* you, so *you* can go on being nice."

Roger says, more softly, "I'm not squatting. Don't tell them I'm squatting."

"The Cobblestone Hearth management *has* the eviction notices on *file*. I mean, be realistic."

"They won't evict me."

"They changed the locks!"

"Yeah, and I changed 'em right back. They don't have any right to break into *my* house and change *my* locks. I should have had them arrested. That's what I should have done."

"They own it."

"No no no, I own it. That's what a mortgage is."

"In any case, it looks bad."

". . . This person you're supposedly studying with."

"Lucas is his name." She draws away impatiently. "Actually, I shouldn't stay."

"He's waiting," Roger realizes. "He's out front right now waiting in the car. Isn't he."

"He's okay, Roger. He's very interesting."

"This is the vegetarian. This is the guy who congratulates you for divorcing me because I was in the military."

"He's a different generation. Give him a break."

Roger draws a big breath and releases it, looking off into the night. Then he looks down at his hands. "This Jell-O is weird shaped."

"It's in the shape of a cell. I made it for my anatomy class party, but we never used it. All the stuff inside is the organelles."

Roger holds it up to the light of the kitchen doorway. "Organelles," he says sadly.

"DNA and stuff. The one is a body cell and the other one is an erythrocyte blood cell."

"Well, listen. One thing. I have to finish the tree house," Roger says. "The kids are expecting it."

"The tree house is out. The tree house is a violation of the restraining order." She grasps both elbows again.

"Honey, you always do these things, and then I'm the bad guy."

"What? What? Children need a tree house."

"I know, honey. Fine. But if you build a tree house, the whole legal proceeding falls apart. Don't you see? If I don't obey the terms strictly I'll lose my payments *and* the school support *and* the county assistance. *And* AFDC. *And* insurance for Jason and Jennifer . . . Are you aware? Just for the insurance alone, how would *I* come up with, like, four hundred dollars a month?"

"Isn't a 'restraining order' where I have to stay at least a hundred yards away from you at all times? And I can't even address you?"

"But it's very important, Roger. If I ever let you on the property, my whole legal case will fall apart." Her voice rises. "It's the smart thing to do. Shit, I don't even care about the money. I don't hate Bob that much. But *his* lawyers'll be unscrupulous. That's the thing. Maybe you're not unscrupulous, but you have to be ready for the other guy to be unscrupulous. That's how the system works."

The carton and platter in Roger's hands move out from him as he presents himself in his predicament. He lifts his face to the night sky. "Fucking *Bob*."

"Your friend can hear," Dot says.

"No he can't. Who cares. Do you go around saying I was 'indigent'? For Christ's sake. I worked when I was out there. I always take responsibility. And just because I drank some—or admittedly, too much—still I was drinking because I liked it. I wasn't an 'alcoholic.' And this thing about how I was 'physical' with you . . ."

"Roger?" she says softly, in a new tone of voice. It's a kind of plea. And it seems the one argument Roger can't answer. He stands defeated before it.

"Okay, well, listen. We'll talk about this later. I'll be

glad to baby-sit. Hell. Shit. But just remember." He weighingly hefts the milk carton and the Jell-O before her. They're supposed to symbolize something, like his steadfastness.

"I'll be back before eleven." Her hands at her waistband tuck in a blouse that's already taut, and she raises her voice to speak to Mark: "Nice to meet you." It comes out as a sort of jeer.

Mark looks up, as if surprised, and raises his digging stick in farewell. Jason, sensing that his mother is leaving, bobbles on his legs and complains, "Mucus is my friend."

"There you go," Roger says. "That's Bob. And his goddamn self-esteem tapes. I thought Jason wasn't going to listen to those any more."

"He isn't, but Bob had him for August."

"You know what I heard him say tonight? Dot? You know what he said? He said he can do anything he wants with his penis. Now, what kind of self-esteem tape is that?"

"I don't know, Roger. I don't know anything. I'm leaving now." Lofting her voice toward Jason, she says, "Bye, honey. Bye, Jenny." Then, though prevented by her jeans from fully kneeling, she descends and offers a collective harvesting embrace at child level. "C'm'ere, you kids." Jason and Jennifer trudge toward her to be enfolded. Mark goes on digging invisibly. "Mommy'll be back before eleven. Meanwhile, Daddy's going to clean up all his toys and go inside. And Daddy can put you to sleep inside if you get sleepy."

Roger says, "Wait a minute, would you explain something before you go? This *thing*—this what-do-you-call-it—?"

"Restraining order," says Dot, still hugging the children. She stands up and pats them back toward the fire.

"Does it prevent me from seeing *them?* This is pretty unusual, Dot."

Standing up, she plucks at her jeans' hips and thighs. "As I understand it, you still have 'visiting' and everything. The only important thing is that you can't come over to my house. The whole case falls apart if I ever let you in. I'm sorry, honey. I think they're worried *Bob's* lawyers will say you and I are back together. Now, I'll be back at eleven. I really have to go."

He watches her. "Honey, this divorce is too weird."

"I don't have to listen to your moral judgment. Things are at a point where I have to do the smart thing. *Rather* than the nice thing. Okay? All my life, I was nice."

She has begun to turn toward the street, but Roger stops her by touching the milk carton to her shoulder. With the platter drifting out in his other hand, he indicates his contested property. "Wait, I know this looks awkward, honey. Of course there'll always be awkward moments . . . Wait a minute, who's that? Is that him?"

Mark lifts his eyes from his digging to see a slender form standing at the corner of the house but backing away. It must be Lucas. "Dorothy?" Lucas says. "Are you all right?" His hair seems to be tied in a ponytail. He has a rock-and-roll musician's way of standing, as if hoofed.

"I'm coming, Lucas. Just wait in the car."

He takes another step backward and says, "He wasn't . . . detaining you?"

"Just wait in my car, Lucas."

As Lucas vanishes, Roger says, "What do you tell him about me? He seems to think I'm violent. Do I have a reputation for being physical now?"

"He's very spiritual, and he's an activist. There's a lot to admire about him. Now I really have to go."

In a stalling motion, Roger rejuggles the platter and the

milk carton in his arms, groaning. "So you'll be back when?"

But she has already, with a wriggle, escaped from the doorway light and then begun to pick her way warily, like a deer, over the dark uneven ground toward the street, two faint cuticles of illumination defining her dim, perfectly shaped figure in jeans. Roger, standing there outside the chute of light, with a plate and a milk carton, immediately swings on Mark with a jolly increase in the volume of his voice, "Dot can't stay. She has to do something she can't get out of."

"Ah," says Mark, simulating the airiest kind of disappointment, his stick stirring loose dirt in his shallow hole. The mystery of Roger Hoberman is somewhat cleared up: he was in the army. He was in Vietnam, where indeed the war had the virtue of being so distant, so exotic, so lustrous on network news, that the small country would finally never be anything more than a vermilion wasp on the far underside of the globe. He was in school at that time, above politics in general. He should have guessed; Roger is of that generation. And plainly, now, his wife is making a break for a better social class, going back to school, taking up with the sort of man who gets a military deferment and goes to graduate school. But Roger keeps clinging.

Out front on the street, her car—an expensive new white Corvette Sting Ray!—pulls out with a low rumble. She did refer to it as hers, rather than Lucas's.

"And look! You guys!" Roger bears down on his children. "Hey, listen up." He's the type who clambers noisily over the top of any unhappiness, and the wise children's skepticism is deepened. "Look what Mom brought us. Jell-O like skin cells and blood cells. Look." On the platter, clear Saran Wrap, stretched tight, squeezes down two trembling disks.

"Mine?" says Jason, reaching for the milk carton. He takes it but doesn't need to look inside; he is apparently assured by the rattle within that his lizards are there.

"Here you go." Roger sets the platter on the ground. "Don't let stuff get in."

Both the children look at the platter on the dirt.

"We need spoons," Jennifer complains.

"Use your hands. Did Mom already give you hot dogs?"

"Yes."

"Dot's a kick," Roger tells Mark, crouching at the fire and lifting the shovel to trowel a couple of rolled-out coals back up onto the heap, whose edges are now powdered with white ash, heating up. "Too bad she had a previous obligation. You'd like her."

"She seems nice."

"So anyway . . .," Roger says heartily, but inconclusively. He kneels before the fire again and falls into thought.

"How deep does this have to be?" asks Mark, referring to his pitiful hole.

Roger looks at him vacantly. Then he seems to wake up. "So anyway," he says, banging his fists on his knees, "Where we left off was: what are things really made of. I suppose it's something really bizarre. I suppose you think it's so bizarre an uneducated guy like me can't understand it. It'll just blow my mind." Despite Dot's having left, he seems to be performing for her still. "If there's no such thing as mass, then what's this?" He brandishes the iron pan.

Mark wishes he would put the pan down. It seems aggressive. "It's not that interesting. Not even physicists understand it." He, like Roger, is speaking in unnaturally loud, clear tones. This discussion is supposed to erase Dot's visit. "Do you really want to know?"

"Hell yes I want to know. I'm a human being." Roger aims behind him with a sweep of his frying pan at all the rest of Cobblestone Hearth, at all the other human beings.

"Well, let's see," Mark says, reaching deep to come up with some rescuing irrelevancies for Roger. "Actually, it's inaccurate to say there's no such thing as mass, because mass *is* something: it's a mathematical number. One way to think of it is, some people say mass is simply the result of the energy it takes for the universe to try to hold itself open."

"Mass is energy, like Einstein," Roger says rapidly disposing of the idea. He pokes at the hot coals, then starts tossing them like a salad with his shovel tip and his frying pan.

Jennifer's voice rises in complaint, "Daddy, Jason's in my *area*."

"Jason, stay in your own area," he says without looking up.

"For example," Mark says, "when you wind a clock and put energy in the spring, the clock gets *slightly* more massive."

Roger thinks. Then he says, "Like it weighs more."

"Yes. A wound clock on earth weighs slightly more than an unwound clock. Slightly. According to relativity theory. And then they tested it experimentally, and it turned out to be true."

Roger doesn't respond, but only flattens the pyramid of coals to settle the frying pan atop them. Then he softly marvels, "Hm!"

"Ordinarily, the universe ought to collapse, right? It ought to fall together into a blob. There's no apparent reason for it to do anything else. But it's possible that space is always getting *created* at the tiniest subatomic level. By foaming up from inside the vacuum. The structure of time-space is really a dense-packed structural foam. I mean, that's a present possibility." Mark's voice, blabbing on in the dark, seems to make their fire pathetic. Roger is wiggling the frying pan to flatten its spot atop the coals. And then, surprisingly, he shows signs of actually having comprehended: "Wouldn't people be able to *see* that? If the vacuum is full of mass, wouldn't you be able to look at empty space and *see* that?"

"Well, it's *potential* mass. And anyway, you can't 'see' anything. Even when you're looking at your own hand, you're not 'seeing' anything. You're not getting the immediate truth about anything. People seem to think 'seeing' means 'getting the truth.' For one thing, the signal is delayed by the speed of light, so you're not looking at 'your hand.' You're looking at 'information' from a second ago. Matter is information. Really everything is made of information. That's the big limit." Mark meanwhile keeps tapping his stake in his hole, where loose dirt pools. With the tip of his stake he flips a few grains of dirt out of the hole.

At last Roger heaves a big sigh and says, "You'll like this." He drops the frozen block of hamburger, with a clank, into the frying pan. "You just keep scraping off the cooked part. So every bite has a rare side and a well-done side."

It's disappointing. Mark had actually begun to enjoy confiding physics to Roger, but Roger's curiosity subsided before he got a feeling for how maddening matter is, how eternally unconsummated the mind's relation with matter is, indeed how erotic. He prods at the hamburger block and addresses the two children, "If you guys want some hamburger."

"We had hot dogs," says Jennifer. She is rubbing a handful of red Jell-O into her mouth.

"Pretty soon I'm putting you both to bed inside."

"Listen to this, Roger. The most recent evidence shows that matter acquires characteristics only by observation. In the last fifty years, physics has been taken over by these people."

Roger lifts the pan to check the coals. "Okay, I'm listening."

"The particle doesn't even have a *location* until the experimenter decides to look for it in a particular place. Until it's observed, the particle is a spread-out wave. The 'particle' is an idea. It's just an idea. Like, the basic unit things are made of. It's just an idea." Mark stops, hearing an imploring tone in his voice.

"I better just get these kids in bed," Roger says, and he stands up. "Come on you guys. No foolin'." He scoops up the limp boy and sets a hand on Jennifer's head to guide her and turn her toward the house. "Say goodnight to Mark."

"Goodnight," says Jennifer, looking over her shoulder at Mark with a genuine smile. He goes with the two children toward the kitchen door. They seem to be accustomed to this routine.

Mark sits alone by the fire and drinks some more beer, still excited by the lonely effort to explain. The goal of physics seems to him self-contradictory and mystical: to discover a fundamental particle so basic that it has no structure, no dimensions, no qualities: a "point." It seems an impossibility for humans to print their hallucinated, luminous diagram upon "space." And that very "impossibility" seems the source of human experience. When, this morning, a cylinder of water stood as a lucite baton on the floor of the kitchen sink, it was an apparition, a miracle, that stunned him for the rest of the day. All day his body has been a great dispersing cloud of particles too big for time reversal.

"No more wine tonight," Roger's voice surprises him nearby as he returns to the fire and bends to sit down. He picks up the wine bottle and sets it on the ground at a distance. "I'm not an alcoholic, but the last few months I've been cutting back."

Mark looks at him. He has a big face. As people get older, their faces get larger. But Roger probably has had a big face all his life. Roger reaches to tap the bottle with a knuckle, and he says, "Substance dependency," and winks.

The fire is beginning to get warm. Deep inside the cairn orange light and palpable heat have developed. A single cricket has been chirping somewhere out in the darkness of the field. But then it stops suddenly, as if strangled or stepped on, and it doesn't start again.

"Tell you. You know the thing about women? They don't know what they need. They think they want you to be reasonable. You be reasonable and you're already lost. People say they want 'reasonable,' but 'reasonable' is bullshit. You're lying to yourself."

The phone starts to ring in Mark's house. But he's locked out. It must be eight o'clock. Audrey is at the Century Plaza Hotel, holding a phone in the beige light of a lobby, standing by a corrugated wall of drapes. On the secret upside-down map of his palate, Mark's tongue is tapping a four-by-four grid of sixteen points in the silent intervals between the telephone's rings. Suddenly it seems possible that he *doesn't* want Shubie any more. Maybe hearing her absurd, warm, blurred family on the phone has lit her from new angles. Desire is such a dark, congested thing, and so impersonal. A single picture of a specific family can, with a flash, scare desire back into the dark.

Roger says, "Is that your phone?"

"What the heck," says Mark without moving.

"Tell you." With his spatula, Roger starts to knock the frozen puck of meat around in the frying pan, to keep it from sticking. "These days everybody's supposed to pretend they're reasonable and enlightened. Nobody takes responsibility for anything any more. All these phony guys. They're all fashionable."

Mark looks at Roger, trying to decide if, having been in Vietnam, he's indeed capable of violence. Mark's lucky cowardliness—his life as an academic physicist with his own reserved parking space—was predestined in his body, his small frame. Whereas Roger Hoberman was born with a great furnace of a body that would permit him to eat red meat, sleep out on the ground, be brave and foolish and loyal.

"So anyway, don't worry about me and wine," Roger says. The entire little speech seems to have been connected in his mind with his setting aside the wine bottle. "I've *been* through substance dependency. Once you acknowledge, yeah, sure, you *are* substance dependent, then you go on and figure out what's important, what's not. Like Dot's important." He pats the dirt beside him. "The alternative to substance dependency."

11
Substance Dependency

So, I'm saying even a *baseball* is a wave function, Roger. Even a baseball is a little bit fuzzed out by the Uncertainty Principle.''

''Are you digging?''

''I'm only stopping for a second. Although we might consider that maybe we don't even need a fence. After all, we're *here* if Big Adcox shows up. We're here. Here we are.''

''Possibly.''

''But just listen to this, Roger. This is interesting. Wait, is this the last beer? Oops. This isn't even considered avant-garde physics any more. Even a flying baseball, flying along, has no location or momentum until it's observed. Or that's what people think now. It's now theoretically necessary to say so. It's like, for example, it can't have *color* until a human looks at it. Right? The idea of color is something that happens only in the human eye and mind. Correct? Well, location and momentum are—or *seem* to be—a similar kind of thing. Do you realize what this means?'' It seems impossible to convey his ineffable feeling, of a baseball traveling along as a dazzling cloud of infinite possibility expanding like Krishna's ten billion manifestations or like Hiroshima, until—glimpsed, and thereby pricked by consciousness—the cloud collapses into a single baseball, floated and sustained on the wave of collective vision at the center of the stadium. "See, Roger. People go around thinking everything exists in a 'location.' We talk about point A and point B as if they didn't touch. As if they were two different places. We have this idea of 'locations.' We think we live in 'space.' "

"Here," says Roger, pointing at the bottle of Worcestershire sauce, which is within Mark's reach. Mark hands it to him. Roger flips the frozen bar of meat to reveal its cooked side, shakes Worcestershire sauce over it, and flips it back. Hunger, and love of his fellow man, gnaw on Mark's bones, and he leans in over his knees closer to the fire. The disulfide smell of garlic. Plus the burning meat's aldehydes.

"Can you imagine how this troubles scientists? Can you imagine?" He starts to drink from his beer, but doesn't. "It's subjective! Matrix algebra is for adding up quantities you'll never know! Roger! It means there's subjectivity in our experiments. Not only is there subjectivity, but it seems like subjectivity is the fundamental basis of everything. Because, here's an example: There's a number called 'spin.' It's a number that describes an attribute of a proton. Just say it's some quality of a proton. 'Spin' like a spinning top. Okay? Are you listening?''

"Okay," says Roger. "Spin."

"So if you take a pair of protons in the singlet state and shoot them off in opposite directions, they'll both have the same spin. If one is spin down, the other will be spin down. If one is spin up, the other will be . . .? Roger?''

". . . Spin *up*."

"Right. Excellent. So here's the amazing part. If one of the proton pair is measured *here* as spin down, the other one will automatically be spin down—no matter if you've waited till it's a million light-years away. As if it *knows*. As if it knows what just happened to the other proton in the pair. At a distance. The implication, Roger, is that reality is not local. Reality is not local. Widely separated locations are *contagious*. So when people talk about a place, or a location, that could possibly be nonsense. Possibly there's no such thing as 'location,' except in this one human light frame."

"What happens to the baseball when you put it in the locker?''

"What locker?"

"The locker in the locker room. If the baseball needs to be observed to exist, what happens when it's in the dark? I suppose it disappears whenever I stop looking at it.''

"No. Good question. No, the baseball is huge compared to a quantum particle. It's made up of millions of quantum wave functions, and they all interfere and superimpose. Molecules of horsehide and rubber and stuff are big huge things. So they persist statistically in time. Like *us*." He holds up his hand in space, a dependable apparition, the severed arm belonging to Shubie's uncle in Jerusalem. *"We* persist statistically in time.''

"Okay, here. Try this." Roger tears from the block of

hamburger a limp epidermis, shining moist on one side and hard-cooked to scabs on the other, and he offers it to Mark at the end of his spatula. It's still so hot it stings Mark's fingertips, satisfactorily, and he tosses it back and forth in his fingers a few times before putting it on his tongue, and then, choking on steam, gasps to chill it in his mouth. The stain of Worcestershire sauce on his palate is salty and garlicky. This is his first real food all day.

"Delicious!" he says despite the speech impediment of carrying it in his mouth. In the appetite-sharpening cold night air, the flavor seems to print through to his brain pan, and a happy new greed makes him move closer to the fire on his knees.

"See, you just keep flipping it, and scrape off the cooked part."

"You know what this is? This is gyros. Except with beef rather than lamb."

"I do this all the time," Roger brags. "I *live* like this."

He puts on more Worcestershire sauce, flips the tile of still-frozen meat, and tears off the charred skin to give half to Mark. Mark looks out into the dark, aware of the chill on his shoulders. "So tell me," he says, flipping the hot strip in his fingers, "how did you lose your first pizza franchise?"

"Location," he says, after a minute.

"Ah! Naturally! Location is everything. Where was it?"

"Same place as I have the Olde Fashion now."

"Really?" He isn't sure whether Roger is joking. "Roger! If the location was bad!"

Using his spatula edge with the sketching tap of a careful surgeon, Roger takes off a skin of cooked meat. "I tell you, Mark. Not everything in business is always perfectly clearly logical. Logic comes *later, after* instinct." He furrows his brow, trying to frame a profound thought. Mark looks down. That Roger is just as entitled to profundity as anybody is a rather pious realization—how little we all know of each other—and in the lull, empty-handed, Mark picks up his digging stick and rubs it idly under his thumb, contemplating its sharp tip in the firelight. Its point seems to define a fixed place in three dimensions, a mere human illusion. To strum its sharp "point" with a thumbnail is to pluck a harp of many unimaginable infinite threads intersecting in contagious space-time.

Roger says, "Part of it is, I *know* the Terra Linda area. I have a feeling for it. But also, I'll tell you something about pizza."

"Wait. You're almost out of wine, and I'm on the last beer."

Roger reaches behind him, where, on the ground beside the charcoal bag, he has an unopened six-pack. "See what a great host I am?"

"Here." In Mark's hand, the rim of the can slips easily from the six-cell plastic bracelet.

"Tell you about pizza." Roger flips the meat, and with his fingers he pinches off a bit of fresh-cooked skin. "Pizza isn't fast food. That's the mistake people make. A hamburger—that's fast food. French fries. Shit like that. Pizza is *slow* food. First of all, you don't just throw it out there. Did you ever stop to think what pizza stands for? Well, of course you wouldn't. Maybe you don't remember pizza." He flips the meat, finds the underside soft, and flips it back to cook some more. He eats his own ripped-off piece of scorched meat, which Mark is primitively jealous of. "Just like *I* never think about molecules much. And protons." With a hooked finger he digs behind a molar. "Takes all kinds."

"So what does pizza stand for."

"Pizza! Sheesh! Pizza goes way back. Pizza *used* to stand

for—I'm talking about when I was a kid—it stood for a whole different way of being in time. There was more time. You'd have a ball game in the park, or else you'd just be fucking around or something, and then you'd go get a pizza. I can't explain it in words. Everybody was equal."

"Equal," says Mark. The peculiar swerve of the idea, to Mark's also-drunken perceptions, makes a kind of straight line. "Like everybody got an equal-sized wedge," he suggests.

"I guess." He slides the block of meat to a different spot on the pan. "With pizza there wasn't all this bullshit." An extra ounce of personal meaning loads the word "bullshit," accompanied by a nudge of the head to one side: he seems to be referring to the freeway faintly audible in the distance. Which, in fact, perhaps would have been built within his lifetime.

Mark looks down and touches his lip to the rim of his beer can but doesn't drink—observing within the sneaky stronghold of his mind, that when you're in your early forties—as Roger must be—and your life is obviously adding up to be a failure, you must naturally start to see yourself as the last representative of older and better values: the whole society is wrong, not you. Probably if Mark himself hadn't had such good luck with his nomenclature essay, he would be—what would represent utter failure for a physics major?—maybe he would be unable to find work as a high school science instructor. And therefore he would be hanging around the Champaign-Urbana campus picking up part-time work around the edges of the computer-programming department. Or part-time work at the local high schools. A town nerd, on those shady, quiet streets of Midwestern summer, seen now only in the Viewmaster of nostalgia. "Maybe you should advertise," he says, having let his end of the conversation sag.

"Who, me? It's a franchise."

"Yes, but you can advertise, can't you?"

"No. Everything is according to the Olde Fashion corporate by-laws. Because *they* got sued by one guy who *did* advertise. It's a long story. It's how things are these days. You can't fight it."

"Surely you can do something."

"It all has to do with corporate liability. You can't 'do' anything any more. Of course, the first thing *I* would do is I'd stop selling shit like the Gummi Bear Polka. Who's going to eat a pizza called the Gummi Bear Polka? Nobody. But just try telling Atlanta that. If I took the Gummi Bear Polka off the menu, I'd be in violation of the contract and no longer entitled to the protections of franchise, blah blah blah. You have to do it by the book. Everybody's doing everything according to the book. And the only people getting rich are the people who *write* the books. Everybody *following* the books is in crash-and-burn, like me. Nobody trusts his own *self* any more. Everybody needs an expert or a book. My wife can't even have a marriage without checking in books to see if she's having fun and it's okay."

Mark drinks from his beer can, intending by the gesture to show fellow feeling. "At least, look at it this way, Roger: You've been out there. I'm not kidding. You always know you can survive. You've *been* out there." It's true, he envies Roger. If *he* had been more of a failure, he, too, might be free. The spatula comes across again, carrying the steaming cooked rind of hamburger, which Mark accepts on his palm pooled with the hot ink of its juice. Roger crabwalks sideways in the dust to the children's Jell-O and dips his scooping hand into the gel. "Want some?"

"Sure," says Mark, offering his free palm.

"Blood cell or flesh cell?"

"Doesn't matter."

"She's so funny," Roger says, as he sets a cool handful in Mark's grasp. "She's got carrot *shavings* in here—in just one little part."

"Well, they're supposed to be organelles, right? Carrot shavings are probably DNA. Are they in the nucleus part?"

"Nucleus, fuck." Roger scuttles back to the fire on one elbow, his free hand occupied by Jell-O. "I'm sticking with the blood cell."

"Or maybe mitochondria," says Mark, his eyes glazing over as he watches Roger flip the meat. A hazy little storm of grease fizz above the pan is backlit by the light of the kitchen door. "I forget what mitochondria are," he says—recalling only, in a high school microbiology film of living cells seemingly filled with glittering sand, freckles among the grains, identified by the narrator (and by the hovering arrow on the screen) as "mitochondria," along with the epithet, "teeming powerhouse of the cell," in the narrator's most resonant baritone, which, in the late fifties, seemed to identify mitochondria as—like the Hoover Dam or the space program—another of the achievements of American know-how. Science was patriotic in those days. Similarly nationalistic was the *Book of Knowledge* encyclopedia, at home above the TV. He can still recall the illustrations of better-than-Russian dams, wheat fields, spacecraft . . . Mark eats his Jell-O.

"I never paid attention," says Roger, referring to biology classes.

Mark is hungry. The frozen hamburger block in the pan will need to cook for a long time before it grows another tough skin to be stripped. He drinks his beer. He's guilty of being rich, in this more socialistic economy that Roger has set up by giving him all his beer and giving him the first cuts of meat. But what can you do about a man like Roger, who keeps setting up his pizza stands on the same cursed ground, who prefers to suffer his kidney stones out in the inclement weather?

"Roger, can I ask you something? Why did you stay out so long? You could have just gone to a hospital and lived on Medi-Cal and stuff. Couldn't you?" And, too, as an army veteran, he should have had medical coverage, but Mark refrains from mentioning his military past.

Thinking about it, Roger pinches off a bit of scarlet Jell-O and examines it in the firelight.

"You know what it was?" he says, his voice returning faintly from a long journey, and then sharpening in the present. "You know what it was? I had a leather jacket. In high school, right over the hill there at Terra Linda High, I had a really wonderful leather jacket. In a way, it kind of ruined my life," he begins to muse more distantly, losing focus, picking that same tooth again. "Because it was the perfect leather jacket. It kind of made sense out of everything. You know what I mean? I *added up,* when I had it on. This was my senior year. Sometimes I think I would have gone to college if I didn't have that jacket. I really wanted it. I had to work for it, and it was a hundred dollars. My mother let me buy it."

He reclines on the ground to reach behind him for the wine bottle, grabs it, and sits back up. One hand filled with Jell-O dyed red to imitate the oxygen-hemoglobin bond, he uses his teeth to pull the cork and spits it out into the dark. "I know it sounds completely ridiculous. Don't think I'm a dork. I think things like that happen to everybody, at a certain age. Remember how high school is?"

Mark pulls another can of beer from its plastic bracelet. Matching Roger in drunkenness seems a part of the economy of the campfire. "Tell you what," Mark says. "I think Acquisition Systems corporation has no valid claim. We're obviously *here.* We're *here.* Fuck 'em." He seems to be temporarily adopting Roger's language habits, simplistic and peeved. He stands up to go off into the weeds and take a leak, unzipping his pants.

"You know what I mean?" says Roger.

"About what? A jacket?" The air out here far from the campfire is cold. His stream of pee makes a folding small slap against the hard dirt between weed clumps. "I suppose I could probably remember a jacket I once wanted that bad." In Mark's case it was a red suede jacket with jangling strips of fringe that hung from the arms and from every seam, like the jacket worn by the lead guitarist of Blue Öyster Cult. He comes back to the fire zipping his pants. ". . . But my mom wouldn't let me buy it."

"Yeah, well, I got it," Roger says, staring bleakly into the fire.

12
The Livery of Cézanne

"S hit, what is that?"
It's gone now, but Mark saw it, too, a pencil
of red light in the field. Printed in a wink on the retina's
memory, it seems to have been a short segment of a ruby
beam, like a furlong of laser light in the foggy middle
distance—but fixing its position is impossible because, in
the dark, the sloping land mixes with the sky, rendering
distance and size meaningless in the vacuum of relativity,
where indeed a light beam can run either way, joining even
the most distant galaxies by its instant hyphen. Roger has
stood up to look into the dark and swim vaguely toward it.
"I'd be careful," Mark says.

"It's probably *them*." Roger seems to have gone back to Vietnam, emotionally. Mark is leaning away from the campfire light a few feet, to be less visible, whereas Roger, foolishly, is actually standing up straight in the light, fending off darkness with a forearm over his brow.

Mark says, "We don't need to be confrontational. Maybe we should leave them alone."

The beam lights up once more—this time much longer. "You see it?" Roger whispers. "What the hell is that?"

"I think that's the source there," says Mark, referring to a steady red coal at one end of the beam, further uphill. It begins to scan slowly to the right. A faint beeping comes from the direction of the light source. Then it's interrupted by an electronic *ding*, like the ding of the fasten-seat-belts sign in an airplane—upon which the beam disappears.

"I just want to talk to them," says Roger, still drifting outward. "Maybe Big Adcox is there."

"Well, don't *do* anything."

"I'm not going to *do* anything, I just want to talk." He keeps shifting and feinting to try to see through the fog, plainly a little nervous himself. "We have to, don't we? The whole point of this is to establish that we're here. Was there anything in particular your wife mentioned? That we should say?"

"What makes you think it's Big Adcox?"

"Don't worry. He's just got some kind of fancy fuckin' light."

"It's a laser," says Mark, with immediate certainty. "It's coherent light; I'd recognize it anywhere." The popsicle colors of the laser streams at MIT—the green of the argon-gas laser, the red of the ruby—had this same sweet Disney artificiality.

"Don't be ridiculous, Mark. What do you think they are, evil geniuses?" Roger drops to his haunches, trying to creep at shadow level below the horizon of the firelight. He grabs the shovel. "Just tell me what your wife said *exactly* about the Livery-Season thing."

"What's the shovel for?"

"Just for symbolic purposes, don't worry."

"Roger, she didn't really know. She said it was the Livery of Season, or Cézanne. It's probably just informing him it's your land. But you know, it's just an old Anglo-Saxon *thing*, Roger. It doesn't mean anything. We really don't have to go through with this."

"So I could just say, like, 'This is our land and you better get off.' Is that enough?"

Crouching, Roger reaches to knock the frying pan off the coals, which sends the precious hamburger into the dirt.

"Whoops," says Mark sadly, watching the meat roll.

Then, too, Roger pours beer from Mark's can onto the coals to douse them. A smell of sorrow and trouble rises in the steam as the firelight goes out. "We could call the police," Mark suggests. "So somebody would be here as a witness."

"No. No police. They just complicate everything. They already know me. The Cobblestone management calls them to evict me once a month."

"Really?"

"They'd probably just evict me again if we call them. I'd rather keep the police out of this."

"They *did* evict you?"

Out in the dark fog, a clink of metal equipment locates the intruder at an unexpected point far to the right. It's a clink that, too, pinpoints in Mark's mind the realization that this is a land survey: the light beam is supposed to define boundaries and measure distances. The sound was a lightweight, cushioned clink, like an aluminum tripod or some optical, electrical device. It's logical: the laser has replaced the rod and chain as a more accurate surveying tool. "They wouldn't be armed, would they? There's no necessity for that."

Roger rises with his shovel to call into the dark, and he clears his throat. *"Hello!"*

From the field comes the sound of a car door closing.

Roger calls more loudly, taking a step, *"This is our property."*

An engine starts. Then another car door slams. Whoever is out there wouldn't have heard Roger's voice. Through the fog, the headlights of a car—a jeeplike vehicle's headlights, high and close-set—appear and then swing. They establish, disorientingly, a new point in the terrain where Hearthstone ends in a cul-de-sac at the edge of the field, fifty feet to the right of the place where the laser source had been. The car turns in the cul-de-sac and drives away, its red taillights disappearing down Hearthstone Drive.

He and Roger watch it drive away, sharing, it seems to Mark, an odd feeling of being stood up. *I didn't notice him park there,* he thinks of remarking—though in fact he might have noticed it but without thinking it significant. Who knows, the jeep might have been parked there for hours— if the Hearthstone cul-de-sac provides the only local access to the Mount Tamalpais wilderness, and this surveyor needed to park here to cover the entire eastern border—*if* indeed that was a land survey—and *if* they were indeed from Acquisition Systems.

But who cares. Relief and disappointment together are coming over him, and the desolation of sitting before a cold fire of doused coals makes him hold his spine against the chill in the air, in the special spiritual isolation of the disloyal: Shubie never meant to meet him at the Art and

Artifice Club tonight. There was no lucky, efficient misunderstanding. That kiss was merely confused and polite. She walked off quickly, blushing. She is embarrassed by it. She's mortified. If she ever returns from the Middle East, she will certainly make a point of never showing her face in his physics office again. If he wants her, he'll have to carry out the impossible act of going out to find her, right now, right this minute. Her plane leaves tomorrow morning.

Roger says, "So—do you suppose they own the land now? Heh heh." He starts slapping the dust off his belly and knees.

Mark stares at the beer-soaked coals, their smell answering to a new turpentine in his stomach, a new sore throat. Only a few coals are still glowing around the edges.

Roger stands beside him to join him in looking down at the coals. He says, "They never even came near."

Mark stands up—to go inside, call it a night. His sitting position has pinched a nerve in his hip, and one leg is filled with ginger ale, as heavy as if it were on Jupiter. It's someone else's leg. Roger is suddenly loud, artificially. "Well!" he shouts. "Hey!" He claps Mark on the shoulder. "Mark buddy! We did good!"

"I'm sure they were using coherent light beams. They were defining boundaries." He rubs his hands and wrists and forearms to generate a little friction. "You know, I wouldn't have minded a little dirt in the hamburger." He bends down and, with his digging stick, chips the hamburger into the frying pan. It's hopeless. He sets the cold frying pan on the soaked coals.

"Hey, you two munchkins," Roger says, turning. His children are standing in the light of the kitchen doorway, Jennifer in a nightgown, Jason in pajamas, minus the harness that held his floating stuffed legs. Jason is still holding his milk carton. His hair is spiky from having washed his face.

"Why were you shouting?" asks Jennifer. They begin like candles to enter the battlefield. Apparently, Roger keeps pajamas around the house for them, indicating that this is not an infrequent occurrence; that Roger is *accustomed* to looking after the children while his wife goes out dressed for seduction carrying an endocrinology textbook. Mark doesn't have a watch, but it must be long after eleven, when Dot promised to return. Is the Art and Artifice Club still open? Or (as is more likely) does it just begin to liven up about now? It must be the sort of place that fills with customers only around midnight.

"Well, Rodge," he says. He turns away doing a small crippled jig to make a show of bestirring himself, limping with the old hernia of his mysterious grief, carrying the digging stake, his personal tool, in an effort to seem to be cleaning up. His semidetached unit looms dark and cold against the fog, its hollow plywood roof ledges launching a mausoleum's volume against the night sky. He's married now.

"Oh!" Roger cries, spinning to search the ground. "We have to put *something* up. Don't we?" He grabs one of the obsolete Oakland Raiders pennants sticking out from the crumple-necked paper bag, which apparently had been lying all night at the edge of their campsite. "The formal marking," he explains as he kneels before Mark's shallow hole to plant the pennant, holding it upright with one hand; with the other he sweeps loose dirt in around it. "The little flag of hope, heh heh."

It won't stand up, though he crushes dry pebbles of dirt down around it with all his weight. The pennant's heavy felt triangle keeps unbalancing it.

Mark turns away, unable to watch. "I'll just put this

away," he says, and what comes to hand is the shovel. Audrey might not be back from the airport for another couple of hours; he has to break a window.

". . . You never know." Roger goes on sweeping and patting a mound of soil around the base of the pennant, crushing it down with his knuckles. "Possibly a stupid little thing like this makes the whole legal difference."

"Daddy, look."

"Uh-oh, look. Mark." Roger rises to his knees. "It's in the front yard."

The red beam of light—like a frizzy yarn stretched taut steaming in the fog—is in front of the house, drawing its line between the house and the carport, right over the spot where the new "private property" plaque is embedded in earth, implying that in future he'll be able to park his car in the carport, and perhaps store his furniture there, but not to enter the house, because it will be somebody else's property. The light begins somewhere at the weedy end of Happyhearth, across from the playground, and then, flying away into the distance, it passes between Mark's unit and the Nguyens', where it disappears from sight in the fog. The miracle of an absolute null line, which, at the speed of light, can bunch space together like a purse string, renders vulgar all their measurements in the fluid dirt.

Roger stands up. "You kids get back in the house. Come on, Mark."

Actually, Mark would rather let Roger go out to talk to them, being himself not very good in situations where confrontation is a possibility, or even where self-certainty is necessary, certainty having always seemed the property of less thoughtful people. Roger's experience in the military equips him better for these things. The same beeping can be heard again as the beam scans for its target. This time the red crucible of the laser source is too far away to be visible, and too oblique. With the same *ding* tone as before, the beam shuts down, having apparently glimpsed its far-off reflective target. "Did you hear that? That's an electronic lock signal." In the fog, the amber street lights out front on Happyhearth Lane are muffled by haloes; and Roger's radiant kitchen windows, like Stonehenge, lay slabs of light on the ground, each the floor of a slanting hall of brightness. But the ground beyond is totally obscure.

Roger says, "Come on, Mark," moving ahead. And since the children also follow, pulled along by Roger's moving weight, Mark drifts after them all.

"Roger, Adcox is in the public relations department. Don't you think a public relations person is unlikely to be threatening? Or physical?"

"All we have to do," Roger explains as he walks, "is talk to them, and tell them we live here and we own this— which is basically what the Livery of Season *is*. Isn't it?"

"Daddy, they're by the old stump," Jennifer calls after him as she follows. "They're by the goalie marker."

"What's the goalie marker?" says Roger.

"You have to touch it when you're *It*."

As before, a car door slams—then another—there are two people out there.

Roger stops and stands still to raise his voice. *"Hey! Hey, could we talk for a minute?"*

"Daddy, don't shout."

"Are you Big?" Roger shouts. *"Are either of you Big?"*

But already the engine—discernibly the same engine as before—and then the illumination of the same close-set headlights—indicate that again nobody is listening. It's secretly gladdening to see the jeep pivot tightly in backing up, then in forward gear drive away down Happyhearth. While Mark and Roger hobble after the children toward the front yard, they can see—uphill on Happyhearth where the fog clears—that the Jeep is traveling calmly toward the main exit of Cobblestone Hearth Village Estates, to vanish from sight at the corner, beneath the benign astrological presence of the huge House of Omri sign above the horizon at the regional mall.

"There they go," says Roger.

The two men and the two children stand there. This defeat feels paradoxically like a victory. Mark looks around. ". . . I guess they think they own *my* house, too."

"There they go," Roger says again.

Mark goes to stand in his yard where the laser beam had been. "Do you suppose?" He wanders over the zone as if seeking a warm spot in air, his forearms afloat beside his shoulders like a wader as he crosses and recrosses the absent red string. "It's too bizarre, Roger."

Roger tells Jennifer, "Show us the goalie marker. Wait, I'll get a flashlight." He trots away toward the rear of the house.

Mark is left alone with the two children, and they both look at him.

"Daddy's going to get in trouble," Jennifer tells him with relish.

Mark doesn't answer, resisting the sticky feeling—of incompetence and responsibility—he always gets when he's alone with children. Both of them, lacking the gravitation of their father, seem to be drifting out to stand, like Mark, within the chapel of three dimensions on the small mound of his yard. The little boy's path gets hooked to move in circles around Mark with a sleepwalker's goose step, holding the lantern of his milk carton out before him at arm's length. HAVE YOU SEEN ME? asks the red printing on its panel. A child's wobbly orbit results from the balance of forces, widened by bravery and then constricted by fear of the dark. "Is that your house?" Jennifer says, reaching to tag his hip. He dodges. And then, having drifted to the corner of the carport, he steals a glance at the new bronze plaque, founded in earth right beside the path of the beam, legible in the darkness: "PRIVATE PROPERTY. Permission to Pass Revocable at Any Time."

"Okay, where's the goalie marker?" Roger returns with a flashlight. "You guys show us the goalie marker."

Jason knows where, and he gallops, leading the way across Roger's front yard into the harsh dirt beyond, where weeds that thrive by looking dead are getting a start. Twigs of bent rebar protrude from the bare earth churned up by the Phase III construction crew. A rubber traffic cone, bandaged by silver duct tape, lies on its side, broken by apparently having been run over by a tractor or something, its fresh aromatic-vinyl color immortal against rain or summer sun. The boy is running barefoot in his pajamas despite the jewels of peril in the postconstruction earth—until his sister catches up with him and hugs him to arrest him. He struggles and whimpers and finally cries, "No fair." She pulls the carton of lizards from him, which makes him break into a bloodcurdling scream of protest and he falls face forward on the ground.

"Jenny," Roger chides her, "You're older than your brother."

"It's right there," says Jennifer, and she points to a spot on the ground where a bronze hub is buried. While the boy screams, Mark goes ahead to kneel at the embedded marker. Plainly, the weeds around it have just been cut back in the last few minutes. The hacked stems are still juicy. The deeply installed marker is convex above ground, like a mostly buried bronze basketball. But it feels like it goes deeper than just a small sphere; it feels like it's probably set in a meteor-sized lode of sunken concrete. The marker itself is hard to make out without better light: a central core of brighter harder metal seems to run vertically down its central axis, appearing as a shining cap on its pole—probably titanium or vanadium steel or one of the colder metals. And on its polar top, where an east-west line meets a north-south line, an intersection is engraved: a crux.

"Here it is, Roger," he says, too quietly. Roger can't hear because he's trying to placate his children, the boy still crying even though he's hugging his carton of lizards again.

"Roger, can you bring the flashlight?" On the outer rim of the bronze circle, his fingertips seem to have found an engraved inscription.

"I think I might take these kids back to Dot's house and put 'em to bed."

"Dad!" Jennifer complains, raising her voice above Jason's.

"Come on," Roger says, gathering them both. "We can use your 'Miami Vice' sheets."

"Da-ad!"

"I'll let you watch the disaster video."

Mark moves to tenderly snatch the flashlight from Roger's hand—saying in apology, "Just for a sec', Rodge." Roger hoists the compliant boy up onto his hip, and he leads Jennifer by the hand. The girl says, "Can we watch the dead-people parts?" She's bargaining.

"No." He takes them down Happyhearth. "We turn it off at the tornadoes."

"Mom lets us watch."

"Dead people!" Jason exalts, pounding a fist on his father's head. "Ni'-night!" he calls back in Mark's direction.

"Dad, we didn't kiss him goodnight." But Roger doesn't answer and, as Mark gets down on his knees and elbows with the flashlight, the Hoberman family can be heard departing from the paving to walk downhill, toward the neighborhood of cheaper cedar-shingled construction in Phase I, where the developers had the bad idea, in probably the late sixties, of adopting the Parker Brothers Monopoly game as a theme, and all the streets are named after properties on the Monopoly game board. Baltic Avenue is the first street you hit below the Phase III hill, intersecting with Marvin Gardens. The girl's voice wanes in Mark's ear, reciting proof that she knows the dead-people parts well: "There's a part with a guy's hand in the refrigerator, and there's all these people floating around in a tidal wave . . ."

In the widening circle of silence as the sound sinks below the slope, Mark crawls on his knees in a half tour of the bronze disk to read the inscription carved around its rim:

To remove Lat 37°54'56" N Long 122°33'09" W Elev 63'08"
M.S.L. Bearing Hub unlawful to remove Azim. Mutil., Acquisition Systems Inc. Unlawful

The clonk of the flashlight touching the bronze disk discloses the sound of sunken permanency, as if this metal island were the tip of a *ton* of buried bronze, and Mark sits back defeated in the profane dirt. He shines the light on the inner core of bright steel, on which finer engraving appears, and he leans in close to read it. The words *Hewlett-Packard Land Data Systems* occupy a speedy-looking logo, off center. Three large holes around the center are identified by the words *RayDist mount*—which must be a trade name for the laser—and three smaller plugs are marked *I-R mount*—meaning, maybe, that infrared equipment is also used. Probably the equipment has prongs, and you lower it into the mountings. And probably the equipment has an internal programmable computer that already knows exactly where to scan for the next hub along the border. The laser must serve simultaneously as transit and theodolite, giving readings of distances and angles accurate to the wavelength.

He turns off the flashlight. A car is slowing by the curb in front of Roger's house, and Mark, looking up, immediately gets the accurate feeling that it's a police car.

Not that he can see the hazard lights on top. In fact, try as he might, he can't—it's too dark. But the configuration of square, wide headlights—and the quiet murmur of a big V-8 engine—and something about the tire-on-pavement crush, louder than usual—it's unmistakably a police car. He stays invisible by freezing, crouched in the weeds. He's hardly going to stand up and introduce himself.

Also like a police car, it stays unmoving at the curb after pulling over. They're sitting in there jotting on clipboards or something in the uranium glow of their dashboard. A fender-mounted spotlight flares up, and its beam begins to twitch over Roger's now sharp-shadowed yard, and then out across the field, where their headlights' burning talcum rests on distant weed tops. Mark sinks lower into the dark weeds with the gradualness of a setting planet. They'll never notice him. A second car arrives, a small pickup with the Cobblestone Hearth escutcheon on the door panel: this would be Bert, the security guard from the front gate. One relaxes somewhat, seeing Bert arrive on the scene, a retired gentleman so amiable that, wherever he goes, danger must not be anywhere near. On his truck door is painted the Cobblestone Hearth coat of arms: a clear shield of lawn green, connoting life's wide boring fairway, at its base an unscrolled empty ribbon, on which no motto is inscribed.

Bert parks his truck and gets out to approach the police cruiser, on his shoulder a felt badge embroidered "SECU-RITY." Two policemen, of different sizes, get out, stand, and tug readjustingly at their strapped-on weaponry. Mark crouches lower behind the bronze home-plate at the vertex of Big Adcox's territory, safe outside it; and he watches as the three men cross the zone of light under his view like moving targets, approaching Roger Hoberman's front door, unsuspecting that they are being watched—indeed walking with a casualness, almost a friendliness, that implies this visit is routine. The older, that is paunchier, of the two cops seems to have something like a cardboard Kleenex dispenser attached to his belt—from which he pulls out disposable rubber gloves for himself and his part-ner. The younger one, who is tall, rings the doorbell. While they wait, they pull the latex gloves with difficulty over their hands, making the macabre squeaky snaps of surgical rubber in the night. Bert hangs back on the sidewalk. If not for this errand, he would be reading a paperback on his collapsible chair at the main entrance's guard booth, the gate eternally raised.

Once their hands are gloved, the older cop passes out surgical masks, disposable paper bowls whose stapled elastic string passes around behind the head. They both put theirs on, over the nose and mouth, and go on waiting on the doorstep, embarrassed by their silly disguises. The younger cop rings the doorbell again. Of course there is no answer.

Mark decides he can stay right where he is. They'll leave eventually. It will take Roger a long time to put his children to bed. By the time he comes back, the police will be gone.

But the two policemen start to walk around the house toward the backyard.

Probably some neighbor complained of the noise of

Roger's shouting, and they are expecting to find both Roger and Mark out there. What they'll find instead is the evidence of their, as Dot called it, "camp out," looking more as if teenagers had been there—beer cans lying about, an Oakland Raiders pennant stuck in earth.

Bert stays behind on the front doorstep. He has some kind of tools, apparently screwdrivers. When he kneels before the doorknob, it's clear he's removing the lock. They've come to evict Roger again. Mark begins to move slowly, still crouching, away from the light, sneaking around to get a better view of the side of the house.

Before Bert can make much progress dismantling the lock, the front door opens from within. Inside is the younger cop, his white paper surgical mask pulled free and hanging loose—he naturally entered by the back door, which has been hanging open all night—and he must have stepped gingerly, bemused, over the bag of lawn mulch on the kitchen floor and the unrolled swatch of turf. Probably he wouldn't have noticed the five bottled gems on the mantle piece. Mark's own house next door is quietly dark, the blue TV light still aflicker in the kitchen, implying, within, the same innocent coma as everywhere else. He gets up on his feet and scoots in a crouch through the weeds in the far shadows, flanking the house at a distance to get around back.

"Roger?" a policeman's voice calls. "Roger, you around here?"

Mark slows and crouches lower again as the back yard comes into view. The older cop is standing over the beer-soaked charcoals, hands on hips. He makes a slow half revolution, pulls his paper mask down to hang loose on his chest, and calls into the dark: "Roger?"

The younger officer appears in the back door, and the

older one looks at him shrugging. "Just *was* here, seems like."

Pushed from behind, the younger cop is nudged outward by the old security guard, who is carrying a floor lamp and a small table. He sets them on the ground beside Roger's firewood pile, and, followed by the older cop, he and the younger one go inside again, this time to emerge with, between them, a huge chair—one of those heavy reclining chairs made of upholstered panels that separate and float apart horizontally at the turn of a lever. The older cop soon appears rolling and dragging a metal beer keg. All this must have been around the corner in the bedroom.

Bert manages to carry Roger's carpet remnant, dragging the shiny new lawn mower along behind himself to bump over the threshold. It takes both policemen to carry the roll of tar paper, like a heavy log. After that comes a rather expensive-looking television, which they set on the small table already standing there in the dirt. Another beer keg follows, but this one, judging by its ring and bounce, is empty. All of Roger's few furnishings are accumulating on the ground in the thickening fog. Bert comes back hugging an uncontainable bundle of clothes, including Roger's sleeping bag and wine bottle, and he bellies the whole armful with an exploding motion toward the reclining chair. Mark drops further down into the weeds' shadows and sits hugging his shins, his chin on his knee.

The two cops carry a big awkward appliance outside to set it upright on the dirt, which, when they stand back, turns out to be a beer dispenser—a floor-standing column with an ornate tap of brassy plastic. Then while the policemen stand around, Bert at last sets out two more big green plastic trash bags full of stuff. They seem to have finished their job. The two policemen cast glances about in the dark.

Bert pulls something out of his pocket—which turns out to be a new padlock, still vacuum-sealed to a cardboard backing. By tearing at it with his teeth, he succeeds in freeing it from its package, and he hooks it over a hasp that had already been fixed on Roger's door. The older policeman takes a few steps out into the darkness, unholsters his big silver flashlight, and flicks its beam around in the field. Mark is as safe as a jackrabbit, not moving.

"Roger?" the cop calls vainly.

"'S that you, Walter?"—It's Roger.

At that moment, he comes around the side of the house. Mark drops as low as he can in the shadows, and he stops his breath.

13
The Revival
of the Coals

The three officers hang their heads. Roger puts his fists on his hips, standing in their midst.

"Kinda late, Wally," he says.

"Well, we started here on a noise complaint"—across the weed tops, Mark can make out the policeman's voice, bounced out into the field by being gathered and focused in the angle of Roger's unit's back walls—". . . and we figured . . ." He goes on saying something Mark can't make out. Then he says, more distinctly, "Not if it was up to me."

Now all four men are hanging their heads and looking

at the ground. With a sigh, Roger says philosophically, "Wulp . . . law enforcement."

By their silence, everybody assents to the profundity of the remark. Everybody shifts position. Roger's fingertips, hanging now from his belt loops, make a generous tossing gesture into nowhere. It seems to imply that he forgives them. Then, with a drop of the head, he squints and says, "Rubber gloves?"

The older policeman lifts his hands. "The new thing. Nothing personal." He starts peeling off his gloves, and the younger cop does likewise. "Prophylactic masks, too." He taps the paper mask hanging under his chin. "It's all procedure now, with communicable diseases." With some squeaking and popping, they get their gloves off and stuff them away, as the older policeman, Wally, asks Roger, "You making any progress?"

In answer, Roger shrugs around at his obvious circumstances, and the shrug carries outward in concentric rings, making the three others, in the stripe of light from the kitchen doorway, shift their stance again. The suburban night seems peaceful. The crickets have fallen silent, and the only sound now is the lazy bend in the freeway to the east. An exciting smell in the air Mark identifies at last as frying meat. The coals, not quite extinguished by a splash of beer, are reviving by themselves, and the frying pan is sitting on them, with the meat. He can see the red glow in the center of the heap. It's possible that the police will leave soon, before the meat is overcooked.

Wally taps the younger cop, "This here is Jeff Tomlin. Married the Spivaks girl."

Roger looks at him and tells him, "Beverly."

Jeff nods, with a polite smile.

Wally explains to the rookie, "Bev used to work for Roger when he had the Shakey's."

"That's right," says Roger. And then another small silence grows among them. Mark feels free, invisible in the night all around their lit proscenium, camouflaged even by ambient noise. The sound of another truck on the freeway, amplified by the darkness all about him, would be unheard within the prism of light in the kitchen doorway.

"So anyway!" Roger raises his voice convivially too loud, pulling his hands from his pockets to throw them out, a feeble gesture like tossing money over his heaped possessions. In farewell, he says, ". . . Stop by for a slice some time."

"I have to tell you this, Roger," says Wally. "We got a new wrinkle. Cobblestone Hearth says this has gone on long enough, and they've sworn a complaint."

"And?"

"They're saying, no more kidding around."

"Aw, don't worry about it, Wally." Roger touches his knuckles softly to the cop's shoulder. "You just do whatever you have to do, and we'll go through the motions of this thing. *I'll* just swear out a complaint on *them*."

"No, they really mean it this time. See now, if they call me out again, they can make me arrest you. That's the difference."

"Just let me know," Roger says. "Just let me know." He stands aside amid his furniture, meaning it's time for them to leave.

Wally doesn't speak for a minute, then says, "Well, say hello to Dot." He shifts his big hippy police weight in the direction of the exit. The gun-belt leather creaks. "How's she doing?"

"Dot? She's doing great," Roger says, one hand afloat in a hostlike gesture of ushering them out. His three guests precede him through a sort of invisible door frame implied by the furniture. "Getting straight A's at College of Marin."

The last to leave, Wally turns back while the other two go on ahead. "Tell you, Roger," he explains with an inclination of the head toward Roger's possessions. "Cobblestone calls me about this, and I tell them, yeah, yeah, yeah, we're busy. But I figured, while we're out here. We already got a call because somebody was complaining about shouting."

"That was probably me. See, there's this *other* little real-estate war going on. I'm kind of fighting on two fronts right now."

Wally nods, meaning he doesn't need to hear about it. His thumbs hooked in his belt just like Roger's, he flips his fingers in farewell and turns to go, following the other two.

"Wally, c'mere, wait." Roger stops him, the two other officers having drifted ahead toward the street. "Listen, I want to ask you something."

Wally hangs his head again. His thumbs dig deeper into his belt, and then his hands hang dead. He seems to have spent this entire encounter looking only at the ground, his paper surgical mask caught between his chin and breast.

"Listen, has Dot come to you, with some kind of a thing?"

His little burp of a response—affirmative—is buried in his chin.

"What is that thing?"

"Restraining order," says Wally glancing up to Roger with narrowed lids. "She's got a legal right." His eyes dodge back to the ground. "She's a one, Dot. She always was."

Mark realizes they all went to school together, they all remember each other's innocence and mistakes. Roger's and Dot's love was once as pure as the drinking-fountain water at Terra Linda High School, and everybody was famous. Their divorce, and Roger's business failures, have been events within the tiny brilliant theater of refraction that is small-town local society. Everywhere you go, you find this local population of camouflaged natives who drive the roads more slowly, suffer the retardation of fidelity, resent the smarter intruders who move among them.

"Well, if she wants to enforce it, would you enforce it?"

"I'd have to, Roger. It's the law. Nothing I can do. My advice is, you just work things out with her. She's got the power." Wally turns to leave, passing by the open kitchen door to grasp its knob and pull it shut. "Gotta do this, Roger." His hand pauses, gripping the lock.

"Fine, sure, but tell me. What does this restraining order mean?"

Wally shuts the hasp on the kitchen door and, with a pinch of his big hand, closes the padlock. He says as he comes back to Roger, "Well, I don't know the terms of the divorce, but a restraining order means you have to stay away from her house. And she can keep you from talking to her. It wouldn't affect your relationship with Jason and Jennifer, I don't suppose."

Roger ducks to set his hand on the back of his neck. Wally makes a backward step and dabs Roger's upper arm. "Hey, seen anybody about the Better Safe Than Sorry Club? I know you got Jason coming along."

Roger scowls downward, rubbing the back of his neck. "Jason—he's not even three yet." Then he jerks his head to dismiss the policeman and conducts him out toward the street. Their two big backs subside from the light as the policeman begins to talk in cheery notes. Mark can't hear what he's telling Roger, but he can guess by the tone that he's changed the subject—to sports or property values or the Middle Eastern situation or something, applying the ointment of irrelevancy that in the end is life's only medicine. Alone now sitting on hard ground in the dark, Mark feels gradually saturated by a new kind of cold, a cold that arrives from the far corners of the wilderness. The coals under the pan are brighter than ever, and the smell of the salty meat makes him think half seriously of running in and snatching a piece of it. But of course he doesn't. They'll be gone in a minute. After he's sure they must have reached the front side of the house, he stirs from his hiding place and scrambles crouching along the raggedy border toward the other side of the house, to get a view of the street. By the time he gets there, Wally is lowering himself into his car. His young partner is waiting in the passenger seat. Old Bert has already left, in the Cobblestone Hearth Security pickup.

Roger stands by the car—he and Wally seem to be exchanging a few last words—and then the car pulls away while Wally, as a parting gesture, gives Roger the feeble encouragement of a thumbs-up sign from the car window.

Roger stands there for a minute. He ducks to scratch an ear. Then begins to shuffle back up toward the house and vanishes around the corner into the backyard. The police car's engine sound diminishes in the distance, relinquishing the neighborhood again to the possession of its secrets. An ordinary-looking neighborhood. Under the coppery suntan of sodium-vapor street lamps, parked cars of even the brightest hues are alchemically transformed to lead. The architects designed all the units in Phase III to look, postmodernly, like Parthenons and mausoleums dismantled and wittily recombined in various ways, painted in dinner-mint pastels. Mark considers simply going inside his own house now, forsaking Roger and his unfixable problems, his possessions all over the ground like a shipwreck. He sits up straighter and unbends the healthy kink in his lower back from crouching in the weeds for so long, his knees planted exactly astraddle the bronze hub in the ground.

Something large, as large as an alligator, moves in the weeds behind him. He is suddenly weightless with fear, perfectly still, his eyes dead with the effort to feel its movements behind him. Whatever it is, it's close enough to reach him with one good lunge. He spins and flies backward away from it and lands in a half crouch. It might be Big Adcox or one of his men.

It moves again—again alligator-like. Then it makes another motion, distinctively a human motion—the unmistakable shifting of an elbow. It's a man.

Mark says, in as authoritative a voice as possible, "All right."

The man doesn't rise from his hiding place. "I think that's our bearing hub," he says. He's dressed entirely in black, but he's wearing a pink, billed cap.

Mark is afraid. The man is holding something that might be a weapon. " *'Your'* bearing hub?"

"Whoa-whoa-wait," the man struggles up toward sitting and holds up his hands. "Nonviolent. Nonthreatening. Peace. I'm supposed to call in. If I don't, somebody'll come looking for me."

"This is 'nonthreatening'? Lurking around like this?"

"I'm not lurking. If anyone was lurking, you were." The man whips off his billed cap and runs a hand over his bald head as if there were hair there to press down. He's scared—a small, wiry man, about Mark's age.

"Are you Mr. Adcox?"

He looks around, takes a deep breath, and replaces his cap with a tug on the bill. "I'm with Acquisition Systems, but there's no necessity for being physical. Truly. We can resolve this to everybody's satisfaction. If you would please just stop adopting that aggressive body posture."

"This? What. This isn't aggressive." Mark's marionette shoulders have risen around his ears. He revises his way of standing.

"Maybe not explicitly aggressive, but you're sort of *looming,* as it were."

"Well, that—that *flashlight* looks like a, I don't know, a big stick or something."

"It's a flashlight. Look, it's a simple flashlight." He runs his hand over his shiny, tanned skull again and replaces the cap. "I'm sorry, I'm in public relations, and this is not my usual activity. If we could go inside and take it easy, I'll explain this. I'm sorry. You just jarred me. I'm not very good at . . . skulking around."

"Where in the world did you come from?"

"Across the field by the regional-mall parking lot. I have to walk the goddamned boundaries. As you seem to be aware, Acquisition Systems is reasserting an old claim."

"Well, come on, you should meet my neighbor. He's on the other side of the house."

But he stands away mistrustfully. "What was that police car doing here?"

"Nothing. They come by here once a month. That's something totally unrelated. Come on, we're around back behind the house."

"This is my job," he says. "It's nothing personal."

"I'm not being aggressive. Relax. Come and meet my neighbor."

"You're sure," he says. "About the police. I don't want to get into trouble."

"Take my word. The police weren't here looking for trouble. That was just something else."

"Wait," he bends over the bronze marker in the ground and turns his flashlight on it. "I need to make sure the surveyors were here. They're supposed to stamp a little seal in the metal . . ." While crouching, he takes a deep breath and recovers his confidence.

"They were here. You just missed them."

"My name is, yes, Adcox, that's right." He gets back to his feet. "I suppose you received one of our letters."

Mark reaches to shake his surprisingly small, pencilly hand. "I'm Mark Perdue. You're the 'Big' Adcox who signed it."

" 'Big' is for Beauregard, but people call me Ad. Call me Ad." Stepping forward, he reveals a frail collapsing, stirring motion in the hip. It looks like a congenital malformation of the bones. Mark goes ahead, turning his back on the intruder and thereby taking the risk that makes peace. "You're in public relations," Mark offers.

"You?" says Adcox.

"Me? What do I do? I'm a scientist. I'm at Berkeley."

"I'm sorry if I surprised you there. I saw the police car and I didn't know what to think." Big Adcox looks and behaves like a junior professor on the Berkeley campus, and in a way, Mark feels almost embarrassed to be bringing back to the fire such a small specimen, his feet—heel and toe—executing a symmetrical quartet of steps on the plywood plank that covers the dry mud puddle leading around the house. By his back door, Roger is bent over harvesting his miserable possessions.

"Roger?"

Without raising his head, Roger says, "Just a minute," making bailing motions, tossing rescued arm loads of clothes up onto the cement pad at the back door.

"I just had to check on something," Mark says in a filmy sort of explanation for his being gone. "Roger, this is Big Adcox."

Roger straightens up.

"Call me Ad. People call me Ad." In the light of the

kitchen window, he is revealed to have the plain good looks of, say, an athlete, but shoulderless, no taller than a boy. His hair at the sides is thick and black. You wouldn't know he was balding until he takes the billed cap off. His hips seem not to exist at all. It's like the effects of childhood polio, almost alarming. They seem to collapse inward and vanish.

The three of them are standing there without speaking, so Mark takes the responsibility of saying something—"So what's all this?"—referring to the furniture and clothes lying around, simply because it's too unusual a circumstance to ignore.

Roger looks about. "Oh. Visit from the Cobblestone Hearth management. As I predicted." He gives a little shake of one shoulder. "But it's no biggie." He distorts his mouth to smile, and then Mark understands: this eviction is a big setback for Roger. It's the first time Mark has ever seen Roger smile; in fact it looks like his first smile in years: his lips spread to bare his teeth, his eyes stray aside. "Nothing to write home about."

Adcox says, "Am I right? You guys are owners of these condominium units on the western edge? I think maybe Acquisition Systems owes explanations all round. And I'm their hired professional explainer." With a grin, on watery knees, he rubs his hands together. The speech has a prefab feeling, and he seems to be embarrassed by it.

"All right then!" says Mark with fake optimism. Roger is *his* responsibility, it feels like, and he edges in closer as if to intervene and moderate. "Explanations are definitely what we need. Right, Roger? Roger here is a businessman! He owns a restaurant! Isn't that right? So now tell me if you disagree, Roger—" he turns to Adcox. "The main question is, Does your corporation think it *owns* this property?"

Adcox holds up both palms in a stop sign, and he frowns, looking around. "Do you fellows suppose you have something I could drink? I spent all day at the Civic Center dealing with red tape, and now an hour clomping around in the dark. We meant to do this boundary walk during the daylight."

"Now wait, you have to understand, we physically live here and occupy this space. Isn't that right, Roger?"

"Ah!" Adcox holds up a merry promising finger and tells Roger, "We'll have a full discussion, Mr. Hoberman. I can see right away what your feeling about this whole pickle is, and it's perfectly understandable. Is it okay if I call you Roger and you call me Ad? Truly." He's such a slight, squirrel-chested man, his frailness itself is invulnerability, like a ventriloquist's doll folded on a forearm.

Roger is still dazed and querulous.

Adcox says, "Okay, I don't mean to beat around the bush, Mr. Hoberman. I'm going to answer your question very clearly. The simple answer—the *overly* simple answer—is, Yes, we do seem to own it, as far as anybody can tell right now. And you're now in the position of trespassers. But of course it's more complicated than that; we're not married to a principle of simply brutal conquest, we're reasonable and flexible, et cetera. But before we get into that, I want to relax and describe the whole situation. This can work out to everybody's benefit."

Roger checks behind him with a glance, and then says angrily to Mark, "Do you want one?" indicating the plastic oak stump on a pedestal, whose crown has a lever and a tap.

"I've got one already somewhere."

Adcox says, "I'm generally a teetotaler, but this is a special occasion."

Roger sizes him up, then turns away to knock around

among the cardboard boxes and Safeway bags for a glass his guest can use. 'Ad,' so-called, starts speaking to Mark. "All this Phase III was developed *after* we filed our adverse claim. See, I don't know anything about the law, I'm a PR man. You say you're a scientist, but do you ever read any philosophy?"

"Me? Philosophy?" Mark's simplistic contempt is borrowed from Roger.

"Spinoza says something. It's in his *Ethics,* and it's the credo of a good public relations man. Actually it sounds naive, but the point of it is, we can truly eliminate trouble from the world by the sheer power of understanding. Understanding. Clarity. Just getting a clear picture. If everybody gets a clear understanding of things, things don't bother them any more. People get the big picture." He stops talking, looks back and forth between Mark and Roger—who is at the beer dispenser—and, getting no response, he goes on, "I mean, a *good* public relations man is not a phony who simply tells lies for the corporation. A good public relations man has to be up-front with people—being in it for the long-term investment rather than the short-term fast profit. Do you see what I'm saying?"

"All right," Roger says, speaking downward into the glass while it—very slowly—fills. "What makes the Acquisition Systems corporation think it owns the property?" He sounds grim. He sighs.

Ad looks back and forth between them and then takes a big breath. "Well, it's complex. The company technically does have title. It's a long, boring, complicated story involving a lot of corporate mergers. See, Acquisition Systems is a limited partnership within North American Synico, which is the holding company for International Leisure. *I'm* actually employed by Leisure. We're on the stock exchange." He has obviously told this same story many times, so that now it begins to fall into a routine dactylic hexameter. *"So*—Acquisition Systems bought a local company called Miwok Oil. And Miwok Oil had absorbed the Tamalpais Land and Water Company in the 1930s. And *that* company had this deed on file. And there you have it. The county has been calling it common land for the last thirty years, but the borders have been crossed by encroachments over the years, like the mall parking lot over there, and you guys here. So now it's in our files, and we have to do something about it."

"Was it really the original claim of Abraham Gutierrez?"

"Yes, but actually his widow did the legal work that established title. Abraham Gutierrez was," he tosses his eyebrows, "rather a wild character. I actually have a photostat of the original claim, but I don't know Spanish." His hand dips in an inner jacket pocket to bring up a piece of paper. ". . . I was at the Civic Center all day . . ."

"I see," Mark says, just to leave his tag on the discussion as he edges away into the dark, trying to find his can of Budweiser out near the fire—where the coals have been glowing red and the hamburger is cooking fast by itself. If they don't eat it, it will soon be burnt, and lost.

". . . And, after all, it's not an extremely big piece of land, when you look at it. It only goes to that ridge up there. You can walk around it in less than an hour."

Mark can't leave the fire, his appetite sharpened by the smell. "Roger, let's eat this," he says.

Roger is holding the glass with beer. "The same Abraham who was the Sausalito Greeter?"

"Well, here," says Ad. "I have the original claim. I'm of course totally unable to read it, but it's definitely quaint looking."

Mark says, "This is going to burn up if we don't eat it."

"Yes, what does smell so good?" says Adcox.

The air is warmer next to the hot fire, and Mark's forehead and knuckles burn pleasantly as he kneels before it. The coals must have been wetted only superficially, because now it's a furnace. "Let's, Roger. Why not? It'll just burn up and go to waste. I haven't eaten much all day. There was another piece of meat around here. Here it is." —It's still cold, but it's thawed at the surface, and his fingernail starts digging at the juicy cellophane on its underside. "The other one got some dirt in, but dirt's okay."

"Dirt never hurt anybody," says Ad, rubbing his small fist in the socket of the opposite palm. He walks toward the fire, and the bad construction of his hip makes his feet seem oversized, lifted and dropped like a marionette's. Roger implies consent by coming out to the fire away from his heap of possessions.

"Can I see the deed?" says Mark. "This is the original claim?"

"Well—" Ad hands it to Roger rather than Mark. "Gutierrez's widow did a lot of the actual legal work later on. After 1848, suddenly land became very valuable around here. But this was what she based her claim on."

But Roger, who is moving groggily, merely glances at it, at both sides of the page, with contempt—and he hands it to Mark. In the firelight it appears as a bad photostat—of, however, quite legible handwriting—at the bottom of which are the English words "His Mark."

Venit Deus atque mihi dixit: Qui obtetitur limen erit.
Itaque hoc humum sanguine linguae emptum Deus mihi collocatus est.

Mark gives up and scans down the page, seeing one recognizable proper noun, "Rancho Saucelito."

"But listen, you guys, truly," Ad says. "Your quarrel isn't with us. This is between us and Cobblestone Hearth Village Estates. You guys can work this all out with *them*. He sits down on his folded ankles, in one graceless drop. "Hey, that one is still frozen."

"Roger's got a special technique. You keep flipping it. The raw side cooks and you scrape off the cooked part. Do you want some Jell-O?"

"Sure. I was supposed to be done with this boundary walk by dinner time." He reaches forward and pinches off a rather large bit of Jell-O. "Words fail to convey," he says, referring to his gratitude. He fills his mouth and then says something intelligible as: "Don't worry, the modern capitalist multinational corporation is a big softie. You'll see. It's not what you think."

Roger lowers the scepter of his spatula between Mark and Adcox. "Tell me." He continues to drop his eyes and scowl groggily. "Why is Acquisition Systems going to all this trouble? Why claim it by adverse possession over a five-year period? If they have the deed, why couldn't they just take it outright?"

"Because a bunch of people have encroached on the borders, over the years. And because there's a cloud on the title." Chewing, he looks at them both in turn. "The cloud on the title is that it originated in a hallucination. This fellow Gutierrez in the nineteenth century, as you may know, lived on Mount Tam and cut out his tongue and wandered in the streets. He was definitely a weird character. God 'told' him he could have the land, which is considered a delusion, so there's a cloud on the title. We can only show *color* of title."

"What *is* 'color of title'?"

"Who knows?" Adcox accepts the first cut of meat from Roger's spatula. He holds it gingerly in his fingertips and picks off first a crumb of meat to set on his tongue as he talks. "Color of title is defined as any cause for belief or faith. You have to *believe* you own something. It's a weak point in the mighty edifice of the law. I get the impression that if we wanted, we could have sketched out the boundaries and the deed of title on a cocktail napkin, almost, and called *that* color of title. As it is, we have Abraham Gutierrez's hallucination. Boy, I have to say, this tastes good. I didn't realize how hungry I was."

Mark looks at Roger, then back at Adcox. "If Abraham was mentally incompetent," he says, rattling the page in his hand, "doesn't that void his original claim? And void all subsequent claims?"

"I'm not a legal expert, but I personally think it holds together. If you ask me, I think *all* claims of property originate in a hallucination, if you go back far enough. He cut out his tongue with bolt cutters. Did you know that?"

"Abraham did? Why?"

Ad shrugs. "He was crazy."

"Yes, but why?"

"Don't ask me. He was crazy. But whether or not he was crazy doesn't matter. Acquisition is going to *contend* that his claim still establishes color of title, in law. What we've got going for us is that we've been carrying out the adverse possession procedure for five years, open notorious continuous and hostile."

At last Mark receives on his palm his full portion (one-third) of the meat that has been cooking by itself for the last fifteen minutes. It's so hot he has to toss it back and forth from hand to hand, gasping and blowing on it. Ad remarks in sympathy, "Hot!" which comes out of his occupied mouth, however, as "Ha!"

"Here," Roger says, to get their attention, and he demonstrates another technique of his: he pours a splash of his beer over his own meat, to cool it immediately.

"Good idea." Mark reaches for his beer.

"What's going on with this Jell-O?" says Adcox. His finger is sketching a figure eight in air over the ruined mounds.

"His wife made them," says Mark. "For biology class. The one is a muscle cell, the other one is a blood cell."

"I get it." Ad holds up a bit in the firelight to peer through its red prism.

Roger prods disconsolately at the remaining brick of meat in the pan, partly frozen at the core.

"Cooking fast," Mark observes.

Roger flips it. "Here, you take some," he says to Ad, making a scooping gesture of bestowal with his forearm, and he starts scraping at the meat.

"This is fascinating," says Adcox of the entire scene, with admiration.

Roger gives him a quick weighing glance. "Why did they send . . . *you?*"

"You mean a PR man? Because I can say anything I want. I'm not *legally* committing the company to anything. The legal staff is hiding out today, during this period."

Mark looks at him as he eats. "You're rather frank."

"I'll tell you something, you guys. Somebody as big as Leisure, over the long haul, has to keep everybody happy, because it's making an investment in the goodwill of generations to come. Truly. Nobody smart externalizes costs any more like they used to. Those days are gone."

"Thanks," says Mark as he accepts his hot flap of fresh-cooked hamburger. A cold ruby of juice runs down his wrist to his forearm, and he rubs it into his inner sleeve.

Ad takes another big bite and then goes on talking despite the revolving meat in his mouth, "I've been spending the whole week—I've been spending the whole week— trying to reassure people we won't put in a miniature golf course—or whatever their personal nightmare is. Maybe you want a wildlife preserve! Fine! So do I, maybe!" He chews. "But some people do want miniature golf courses. Humans need their habitat just like the wildlife. It's elitist to rule out a miniature golf course just 'cause *you* think it's tacky. You know what the dean of the Harvard Divinity School said once?"

The question is directed to Roger, but he doesn't say anything (and doesn't even seem to be listening, instead strumming the spatula edge idly over the hamburger's surface and then sighing), so Mark swallows and says, for him, "What?"

Adcox turns to Mark, "Something like, 'Take care in choosing your enemy; because if he isn't *you* already, he'll soon grow to be.' Or, 'You'll soon grow to be him.' Something like that. At the time he was talking about the Cold War. Castro and Kennedy." Adcox was a liberal arts major, Mark decides. Mark has always been defenseless against the glib.

Adcox gets no response, looking back and forth, so he goes on, "What I mean is, Acquisition Systems is inevitable here. It's inevitable, and you might as well get used to it. *But* it'll turn out to be a good thing. It *has* to. You know how capitalism works?" he asks Roger.

Roger looks at him, then looks down and flips the hamburger.

Ad says, "Of course. You're a businessman; you run a restaurant. All we do is allocate resources. To *serve* people. A good business isn't about power, it's about service. We want good relations with everybody in the neighborhood . . . Thanks . . ." Roger hands him another piece of meat. "So sue us. Recover your time and trouble. *And* sue Cobblestone Hearth for misrepresentation and court costs. This is what I'm telling people. You'll do fine. Acquisition will settle out of court. That's not a legal commitment, you understand. This is just what I'm *telling* people."

"Aren't you having any, Roger?" Mark says. It seems to him that Roger has been passing out the meat but taking very little for himself.

"Sure I'm having some." He picks off a bit and pops it in his mouth.

"This is great!" Ad toasts them both with his fresh flap of meat, juice on his knuckles. "I still have to go up to the next freeway exit. Can I get myself just a little more beer? Shit, I got Jell-O on my shirt."

"That's all right, I'll get it." Roger takes his empty glass from him and rises to his feet, but he just stands there staring into the fire, abstracted, and the two others look up at him. "I think I might get going soon. You guys can finish up. Have the rest."

"Where're you going?" says Mark.

Roger doesn't answer.

Ad, having sensed something in the lull, says, "In fact, I shouldn't stay. My car is parked by the freeway."

"Here," Roger hands Mark the spatula. "Don't forget to put the fire out."

"Where are you going, Roger?"

He turns away toward the house. "This stuff'll be okay," he says, referring to all his belongings.

"This was delicious," says Adcox, looking around now uncomfortably. He reaches into the pan, saying loudly, "I'll just take a last little bit." Then, as Roger has gone out of earshot to rummage among his belongings, he speaks low to Mark: "Did he just get kicked out?"

"Sort of. Also, his ex-wife." Mark's hand jiggles on a small ambiguous scales in air.

Adcox raises his voice to address Roger. "Great burgers, Roger. Many thanks." He rubs his palms on his knees and climbs up from the ground, his hip on its delicate pulley, and he starts looking around in the dark—for his flashlight. "And don't worry, you guys, have no fear. Reason will prevail. The law is reasonable. It's my job tonight to go around telling people they're trespassers—so consider yourselves told. But I *sincerely* want you to stay in touch with my office. Great *great* burgers." Roger isn't listening to Adcox's speech—nor is Adcox himself—both of them moving around beneath the drizzle of it, Adcox sucking his thumbs and fingers one by one as he looks around for his flashlight.

Mark—the only one sitting now—for the first time starts feeling trickily betrayed by this whole situation, and he stands up. "Well, wait a minute. I think maybe we ought to come out and state, too, that the property is ours and you're a trespasser . . ." As he speaks he finds himself addressing Roger. ". . . Isn't that right, Roger?"

"Why not." He isn't listening.

"Roger, shouldn't we formally tell him we don't grant any land?"

"Hey, Mark?" he says. "Maybe you could keep an eye on this stuff till tomorrow. Till like noon tomorrow."

"Yes, fine," Mark says, and then turns to Adcox. "Seriously," he tells him.

"Seriously?" says Adcox. "*Seriously*, I have to represent Acquisition as disagreeing with you. But as I said, *personally*, I don't think you guys have a care in the world. Truly."

"Well, but at any rate," Mark says, and then he asks

(though it would be embarrassing and undignified right now to bend over and scratch up a handful of dirt), "Have you ever heard of something called the Livery of Cézanne?"

"Cézanne? Like the artist?"

"It's an old legal way of claiming property."

"No. Can't say I have. Cézanne?" Adcox folds his arms over his flashlight.

"Something like Cézanne. It's archaic. You put a handful of dirt in your pocket, or a piece of turf."

"I see. How interesting."

"Or maybe a twig or something."

"You put a twig in your pocket?"

"Or something," Mark says, with almost an involuntary sneer.

"Maybe it's 'seizing,' " Adcox says, helpfully. "Maybe they mean Livery of—like—*seizing*." To demonstrate, his hands strangle empty air before him.

"Anyway, I think I'm just going to do that, right now," Mark says.

"What, the Livery?"

"This is probably stupid, but." He crouches to scratch up a handful of dirt from the spot where he had been digging all night. In a court of law maybe it would mean something." He stands up holding it.

Adcox says, "Are you going to put it in your pocket? I thought you said you're supposed to put it in your pocket."

"In any case"—Mark pours the dust into his pants' side pocket—"I hereby perform the Livery of Cezanne . . . on you."

Adcox watches. "Do you suppose that's all that's involved?" His arms still folded, he nudges an elbow toward Mark, smiling.

"Silly, isn't it." Mark rubs his dusty fingers together as if coins slipped through them, sifting the essential textural silliness of everything.

"I don't think there's so much as a single twig in all of Phase III, yet," says Adcox. He won't have noticed the forest of imported saplings crowded onto the truck parked on the street.

"So there you are," says Mark, concludingly, empty-handed again. He clasps his hands behind his back. He probably wouldn't have gone through with that if he were sober. Roger meanwhile seems to be rooting through his possessions. It would be nice to get Adcox off the property now. Adcox holds up his flashlight, which he flicks on testingly, saying, "You fellows have been very generous."

"Oh, are you leaving?" says Roger, while—unbuttoning his shirt with one hand—he slaps around the flaps of open cardboard boxes, looking for something.

"Got my flashlight, got my map." He's walking backward into the dark toward the street and waving a hand, mermaid-bodied from the waist down. "Truly, just call my office next week. Stay in touch on this. You've got my number. Thanks again, you guys."

Mark bends to get his beer and lifts it in farewell, then takes a drink after he's gone, standing there like a fool with a pocketful of dirt.

Roger is taking off his shirt, barefoot on the dirt, having left his muddy shoes on top of the TV. "What are you doing now, Roger?"

"Oh—" He tosses his shirt aside, and he kneels to peer into a plastic garbage bag full of clothes. One hand snakes deep into the bag, feeling for familiar fabric.

"Where are you going?"

"I think—indecision—is my present problem."

Mark watches him for a minute. "Well, what did you

think?'' he says at last. ''Do you think he was a phony?''

Roger gives up looking in the garbage bag and stands up bare chested, scanning around for another bag of clothes. Maybe everybody gets hair on their shoulders when they get past forty. It will even happen to Mark.

''Did you notice his legs? Didn't it look like the bones . . . weren't there?''

Roger pulls a shirt out of a bag and punches one arm through the armhole. ''You can stick around, Mark, if you want,'' he says, with a gesture toward the reclining chair, the TV, the beer dispenser. ''Have a nightcap.''

''Aw,'' says Mark, raising his shoulders.

Roger walks off in the dark, into the uncategorizable zone where it's permissible to urinate, near Mark's spot, and he unzips his pants to pee. Mark takes another drink from his beer, and then he stands there, wanting to go home but feeling tugged in several directions. At last he says, ''Where're you going, Rodge?''

''You have one more beer if you want. I just have something I have to do.'' He comes back and kneels before a cardboard box, pulls out a shoe, and then stands and starts to hop, putting it on his foot.

Mark looks away into the dark. ''It's pretty late.''

''No kidding, make yourself at home. Here!'' Roger slaps the reclining chair. ''Try this. This is living.''

He grabs Mark to guide him, backing him up until his calves hit the seat of the chair and he falls backward into it. ''Can't plug it in out here, so the massage won't work. But you'll get the general idea.''

''Yes, very nice.'' Mark elbows himself up.

''And then see?'' He turns to touch the plastic tree stump. On its front it says ''Brewmaster'' in script of Teutonic ribbons, on a plaque of polystyrene wood with regular staple marks molded in to imitate wood grain. ''But just wait . . . See, you got your beer . . . I need a fucking glass. Pull that handle down on the right-hand side. Down by your hand. It's got three positions."

"Actually, I should get inside pretty soon, too."

"Just hang on. Stay right there. I need a glass." Mark feels unable to interrupt as Roger stalks over his possessions, hands poised as if a glass were an elusive animal to be throttled. He finds one in a cardboard box where it was packed with some other kitchen objects—and he brings it back to the tap and releases the folding white flow of beer. "This is fuckin' great—you'll love this."

"Well, Roger, won't all this stuff get wet? It does look like rain. And that hasp there is just screwed in. You could easily unscrew it."

"Wait. This is great." Holding back the tap lever with one expert finger, he seems to be waiting for the foam to thin on the beer.

"Anyway," says Mark, with a sigh. "He had one good point. We could recover all our court costs, as part of any suit. If we do sue Acquisition. Don't you think?" Roger doesn't answer. It seems clear now that his wife will spend the night with her study partner. This pile of Roger's belongings is starting to feel like a trap; and Mark actually gets a physical stomach pain. Roger's free hand, while he fills the beer glass, is extended backward behind him to, from a distance, hold Mark pinned in the chair. "Okay, here," he says. "I once worked this out to six-point-three cents a glass." He turns around with his beer held like a rare potion between the pinch of thumb and finger at the rim. "You have to put the chair like this—" he bends over and wrenches the lever on the side, and the chair glides Mark out flat on his back, the headrest dropping away, the footrest rising to push his heels up.

"I see," he says with difficulty, his throat strangled as

he lifts his head against gravity, because if he lies back and looks up at the refrigerator-cold midnight sky, he feels uncomfortably like Roger's patient. Roger immobilizes him further by planting the beer glass on his breastbone, which Mark grasps with both hands to hold there upright like a taper.

Roger stands over him. "I *live* like this," he boasts, his arms spread embracing everything too big to hold, and he starts to revolve, "You've got your TV, you've got your beer, got your fuckin' . . . fuckin' home entertainment system—" he leaps to the TV and spins it on its table to face Mark. "Or fuck the TV. You can just sit there in peace and *meditate*—about *physics*," he says pointing at the stars. Then, dropping to his knees again, he begins to search through a plastic bag.

"About physics?" says Mark, surprised.

"At least you do something *real* for a living. Very few people do. I mean," he pauses to sit back and, for a second, hold empty air in his hands, "Physics!"

"Oh, it's all bullshit," Mark is about to say—but softly, more to himself, and therefore almost whisperingly, almost prayerfully—so he refrains from saying it. Because it might be the truth—like an admission that he doesn't want to go to work tomorrow or ever again.

"So drink up, don't go inside yet. Finish your beer. Where *is* your wife anyway?"

"She's on a business trip. She's supposed to get home—actually any minute now," he lies slightly. "Soon."

"Ah!" Roger has been limping around with only one foot shod, the other bare, and now at last he holds the shoe's mate, getting it onto his foot with a grinding motion. "Listen, I've got to do something." In farewell, he says, "It's been real."

"Where are you going?"

"Oh . . . nowhere."

"Hang on, Roger." Mark tries to thrash up out of the chair. His glass of beer spills all over him.

"Here, could you help with this?" Roger grasps a corner of the TV set. "I just want to get this one thing under an eave."

"Roger, it's pretty late." A cold sheet of beer saturates Mark's shirt. By rolling sideways he frees himself from the chair and stands up, and he slaps down his front to whip away the loose foam.

"Oop," says Roger, reaching for a piece of clothing or something to mop it up. "Here. Here's something."

"Are you just leaving all this stuff?" Already the furniture is covered by a sheen of fog.

"On second thought, the TV won't get hurt. So take care, buddy." He drifts backward toward the street. "We did good." He punches upward in air as he recedes. "We showed 'em."

"Is Dot at home with the kids?"

"Well, I fucking know where she is."

"Okay, wait. Wait. Roger just relax." He realizes he has grabbed Roger's elbow. They both look down at the point of snag, and Mark lets go. This is an uncharacteristically stupid impulse, getting involved this way, but he's had a lot to drink. And, too, some hot new feeling impels Mark into this, like the satisfaction of anger, like revenge, like friendship. "She's got that thing, Roger. That restraining order. I couldn't help but overhear."

"What. Just now?" Roger points a thumb over his shoulder. He, too, seems far from sober. Mark has to pee again, but won't right now.

"Listen to me for a second. You're already in enough trouble. If you go after her now and she calls the police, just think. Just think."

Roger stoops to pick up a mug of beer he left there. But he doesn't drink from it, he merely looks at it. Mark goes on, "Now, far be it from me. But do you want to know something frankly?"

"What."

"Frankly, she's—" his mind swerves from a plain insult—"probably a very attractive person in many ways. And I can see how you'd be attracted to her. But it just seems to me like—this whole situation could get you in trouble *worse*." He turns away. "Where's my glass?" He finds it on the ground beside Roger's stupid bear-trap Naugahyde chair. "Just think for a second," he says. He pulls the lever on the tree-stump tap causing the miracle of free beer to flow. It's a necessary ceremonial presumption, to go ahead and get beer for himself from Roger's supernatural tree stump, which at this moment feels like what they've been guarding from trespassers all night. He keeps an eye on his glass while, by tilting it under the flow, he makes the suds skid in a parabola down its inner wall. Thus he can prevent the glass from having any foamy head at all. The scummy golden oval mounts steadily. Roger says, quietly, "She's an attractive person."

"If you'll just think. You don't even know where she is." It's been years since he had too much to drink; tonight it provides the agility of recklessness. The glass, erect, at last fills with its golden piston, and he lifts it, now heavy, into the light of a distant street lamp, to see the thousands of evenly distributed bubbles rising, slow at the bottom, faster at the top, like the dissolution of galaxies in the expanding universe whose escaping stars gather speed outward at the edges to the point of vanishing.

Roger says, "I do know where she is." He half sits down, but doesn't quite, on the edge of the TV. It's as if he has just admitted that his life has been a thin joke and a self-delusion. Which is the truth. It has. That smile he gave Mark after the police left was nightmarish, a face decomposed like an exploded view of a puzzle.

"Okay, Roger, listen to me now," Mark begins, with an authoritativeness uncharacteristic of him. When, for a night, you let things spill forward out of control, you depend instead on a certain rescuing grace, provided by beer. He drinks a few big swallows' worth, necessary in setting the right tone. "Now listen, I want to give you some advice. Are you saying you actually know *specifically* where she is? *Specifically?*"

"She's at Rumplestiltskins."

"I don't know what that is. Is that a bar?"

"It's a bar in Novato."

"Well, Roger, listen. You have to acknowledge eventually that she's reached a certain point. She's being practical."

"Oh," Roger says. "You don't know Dot."

"Roger, she has a right to be practical. *People* have to . . ." He gestures around at Cobblestone Hearth, obvious architectural evidence of everybody's being practical, the conspiracy of practicality everywhere that defines the middle class, a class that Roger is doing his best now to be a part of. But, oddly, Mark's shoulders locked up a little on that last remark, on the axiomatic lovelessness of the world. He clears his throat, to loosen its tightening ring. "I'm making an effort to help you, here." He turns aside and takes a drink from his glass.

"Hey, Mark," Roger says, making a listless pawing motion in Mark's direction. He's still perched on the edge of the little table. "I think that's how you feel right now."

"No, wait, Roger, I'm trying to tell *you* something." Mark goes blind as he speaks. "I was able to pretty thoroughly observe your wife. Okay?" He stops talking to crush a belch in his throat. It takes a minute. He waves at Roger from the distance of his belch. "Just in that one little conversation. You can tell what kind of person people are. And I'm able to see: people don't get anything out of . . . *this*." He gestures out toward Rumplestiltskins, wherever that is. Toward the confrontation Roger seeks there.

But Roger is eyeing him with a rather insulting kindness. "Mark, you'll find you change from that. It's interesting. People don't change overnight, but maybe, you know, ten years from now, you'll feel different. I promise. It's the interesting thing about life, there's all these second chances going around."

"Okay. I tried." Mark discovers force in his voice. He had meant to preserve his calm. His eyes run all over the ground. A willed numbness and the old hump in his back will preserve intact his private luckiness. "I tried."

Roger points again toward the spot where his wife had stood. "They really don't know what they want. *You* have to take responsibility. It doesn't necessarily mean I'm wasting my time. See, the result isn't the point," Roger says, as happy as a Buddha sitting in the small waste of his life on cursed ground.

"Okay, for example, Roger," Mark lowers his voice calmly, turning back to face him. "Look at your pizza parlor, for example. Or look at *this* shitty situation."

"Mark, it doesn't matter. Do you get that?"

"Do you realize—" Mark says, but he stops himself and simply holds out his arms on either side, presenting the whole situation, its absurdity. What comes out of him is a series of exasperated sarcastic chuffs, nasally, not quite laughter. "You're telling *me?*"

Roger leans forward and reaches across to set a paw on Mark's wrist. "It's really okay."

"Roger, you're not listening."

Roger ducks his head, squints, grins, and punches Mark softly in the shoulder. "Hey, buddy." It's the chummy gesture of a Vietnam veteran, and suddenly Roger is reconstituted before his eyes: a Vietnam veteran, whose flesh therefore must lack certain crucial nerves. He is destined not to live in Cobblestone Hearth Village Estates. With remorse, Mark hoods his eyes.

"Hey, I've got to go," Roger says, standing up. "Really, Mark, thanks for your help on this. We definitely at least satisfied the legal conditions." He rakes over his pile of clothes to find a jacket or something. "These things will all be fine." In fact, the fog is condensing thicker and thicker all the time, looking more like rain. The aerosol droplets have a distinct vertical falling motion to their drift.

"Whatever you think," Mark says, unmoored as he separates himself among Roger's belongings now getting damp. He has his own house to return to like a dock twenty feet away. He looks down and pinches up the beer-soaked fabric of his thigh and shakes it, to encourage it to dry faster. Fortunately, most of the spill landed on his jacket, which is made of some sort of semi-water-repellent stuff, nylon-6,6 or some polyamide with not-too-long carbon chains.

"See you later," Roger says as he walks off toward the carport, pulling on a coat, leaving Mark there in the drenching mist alone with all his possessions.

Toward which Mark feels only the vaguest twinge of duty, easy to ignore.

"Take care," he says to Roger. One hand on the steady beer dispenser, he waits for Roger to be gone, and he picks up the glass of beer to take a drink.

The reclining chair faces the TV screen: it looks as if he's standing there waiting for his favorite show to come on. So he walks off toward the edge again, at last to pee, finding a third spot and standing still in the fumes of his own collared body heat while the hot cider piles up at his feet and starts seeking the ocean. The revving of the Kustom Kozy Kar's big engine bounces between the walls of neighboring units, and then its headlights scan dark walls and whirl across the far night. The V-8 roars and Roger is gone, the engine noise receding to leave only the sound, everywhere, of faint hissing as the fog alights. It's late. Mark comes back to the TV set, drinks quickly through the last ounces of beer in an effort to begin getting free of everything he's responsible for here, and he sets down the glass. He puts his hands in his jacket pockets—clutching the now-warm bag of frozen peas—and he faces the thought, the strange and unexpected thought, that going indoors at last is lonely.

He looks around at Roger's life tossed adrift.

His hand in his jacket pocket discovers the aspirin bottle from the mantle. He must have put it in his pocket without realizing it.

It's empty. He holds it up to the light of the street lamps out front. He rattles it to listen for the tink of the crystal pebble. The plastic cap is still on, but the stone is missing. He lost the stone.

14
Preventing the Spark from Passing

Maybe it's stupid but he feels responsible. It must be lying on the carpet inside, where he must have dropped it. So by an act of steely will he recovers his balance and sets sail toward Roger's back door, despite a certain slight disorientation from having thrown his head back to finish his beer. And in fact he is able nimbly to do two things at once: walk toward the door (a large, immobile target) *while* fishing in his pocket for a coin to unscrew the hasp. Anybody watching would think he was sober, the soles of his feet alternately holding down the steep earth with the firmness and casualness of perfect sobriety. The dime in his hand finds its way to the slotted head of the screw—his eye, for accuracy's sake, so near to it that he's almost bent into his microscope-aperture crouch—and he finds that, once the rim of the dime gets a grip in the slot, the screw wobbles like a loose peg. Apparently, the lock on the back door has already been unscrewed many times—or maybe even torn out violently. His hands don't want to grip. In all his muffled nervous system, the beer's millions of small ethanol molecules (simple hydrocarbons with one oxygen) are bathing every neuron and changing the voltage across the gap and preventing the spark from passing, so that he bumps and moves in Roger's doorway with the gentle clumsiness of a scuba diver breaking into a sunken hulk, gripping the steady jamb. The edge of the dime stays mostly in the slot, but the screw isn't rising at all from its seat, though he turns it and turns it. The head remains flush with the surface, its threads getting no purchase at all in the grain of the wood. He slips a fingernail under the screw head, and it levitates from the wood and drops into his palm. He's so clever. This won't take long. As soon as he puts the five stones back in order, everything else will start to fall back into place, on this peculiar, antigravity night when a unique configuration of the planets can carry a man's furniture outside onto the mud. Surely the missing stone will turn out to be lying on the carpet right in front of the fireplace. There's no other possibility.

The other screw is loose also. After just a half turn it falls out of its hole. It goes into his right-hand pants pocket, along with the first screw, and he makes a sober mental note of their location there, for future reference. When he opens the door and crosses the threshold, he starts to whistle louder, in an identifiable melody ("Wish You Were Here"), which sends before him into the empty house the announcement of his own innocence, the guilelessness and incompetence that can elevate a man to impunity all his life. Lift him to the Potts Chair in Theory. All the lights are still on. His first glimpse of the living room carpet gives him a foreboding that the stone isn't there. No immediate twinkle appears. The four other aspirin bottles are on the mantle, in their places. The police didn't remove them, or care about them. They probably didn't even notice them.

Holding his breath, he inspects the mantle closely but finds nothing.

So he gets down on his knees. He'll start in one corner, and crawl systematically in strips like a lawn mower. Actually, the excessive alcohol in his brain can *help* him to focus, by narrowing his vision and generally simplifying consciousness. He lowers himself and starts creeping along the wall examining a strip as wide as a bolt of fabric—Roger's carpet is all made of nylon polymers, like his own next-door, and has the same new-Mazda smell—until his head bumps the wall at the other end. To turn around, he backs and fills like a truck, and he begins to crawl along scanning the next strip, on already aching kneecaps. This is probably really ridiculous. But he will sleep more soundly knowing the stone is back in its bottle, without Roger's even suspecting it had been in danger. He is confident—despite the occasional logical pang of uncertainty—that this corporation's *prank* (and it is a prank) doesn't constitute adverse possession of their property. The expensive-looking bronze plug in the ground with its unintelligible inscription may indeed be slightly intimidating, but he and Roger are manifestly in possession of the parallelograms of dirt that appear on the maps in the portable sales office gazebo. And obviously Mark *lives* here. He *is* here. Here he is. Earnestly dog-paddling. A fact which Big Adcox's legal department could never dispute.

Not having found the stone in the second sweep of the carpet, he turns around at the wall and begins on the adjacent strip, with, now, a growing sense of futility familiar to a researcher. As he works his way farther out into the open space of the room, his chances of finding the stone shrink. As quantum mechanics has it, the probability density declines, farther from the fireplace. He reaches the wall at the end of his third swath, and still no stone is to be found. He sits up on his heels.

Out front on the street, a car door slams. It's Audrey.

He climbs to his feet and looks out the window. At the curb a smart blue van is parked, *Airport Express* on its side in big yellow letters. The driver is unlocking and lifting the rear hatch to take out luggage. Mark—immediately sober—stands just outside the frame of the window to watch, seeing his wife as sexier, more desirable, from this neighboring viewpoint. He can see the top of her head moving on the other side of the van. It must be two in the morning. Characteristically, she has the exact fee ready crumpled in her palm, which she hands across to the driver. Then she refuses the driver's offer to carry the suitcase, and she shoulders its strap herself. With a bob of the head, the driver turns back to his van.

She starts up the walk in her office suit with lovable seriousness and self-sufficiency. When she reaches the front step, Mark presses his greasy forehead against the pane to see her. She braces her purse on a thigh. She bows and rummages within it and finds the key. The fan of panes in the Palladian window above the door lights up as she enters the house, putting her key back in her purse. He can hear, faintly through the glass, the newscaster's voice on his own television, being broadcast out across the threshold. And he can hear, distantly, Audrey call his name up the stairwell in empty condominium space as cuboidal as the Parthenon's: *"Mark?"*

Summoned, he yet feels no necessity of obeying. Except

that there's nothing else to do. The prospect of facing Audrey seems to have wakened him, popped the pressure in his ears.

At the sound of a noise behind him, he turns. It's the pale little girl, wound up in a bed sheet. "Where did my Daddy go? His car drove away." She looks worried. Her little brother, behind her in the kitchen, begins, with a whimper, to cry, licensed now by the presence of an adult, having been brave so far. "How did you get here? You're supposed to be home in bed," Mark tells them, and the girl's face, too, swells toward crying, her eyes shrinking. She says, "Where'd Daddy go?"

"You children," says Mark with repellent authority, afraid he'll be called upon to embrace a sticky child. "You have to be quiet. You're supposed to be asleep."

"We're scared," says the girl, but the thought cheers her and she almost grins. Jason ventures in, wearing rubber galoshes whose unlatched buckles jingle. Audrey might come looking for him and discover him here on this unexplainable errand. "Okay, tell you what, you can sleep here tonight. How about that? Wouldn't that be great?" He skips around them to get to the back door, where, outside on the ground, the only possibility for bedding material that meets his eye is the tarp Roger has thrown over his firewood, a blue square of heavy-duty rubberized canvas— which will work fine.

He drags the tarp—not too roughly, trying to suppress the noise so Audrey won't hear—into the kitchen and then out onto the living-room carpet, where it crumples nicely into a semblance of a nest. A few oaken firewood splinters fall out. "Here you go. This is cozy." He kicks it into a corner.

The children are standing there looking at him.

"This is cozy. You'll be fine." He gives the tarp another

kick to plump it up and show how soft it is, and the two of them edge toward it as if it were a caldron.

"Don't worry, your father will come and get you," he lies. This is a purely local distortion of the universe's general ethical structure. "Come on, hurry."

Uncharacteristically graceful in his drunkenness, he gathers them both like a sheaf of wheat and lays them in the folds of blue plastic. "See? Just stay here. Everything is fine. Everything is wonderful." He draws the plastic over them and crushes it down around. "It's time to say night-night."

"You have to tell us a story."

"No stories. It's time to say night-night." He stumbles to his feet heroically. Maybe he has already decided *not* to tell Audrey he put the kids to bed here, because it's exactly the kind of efficient, inspired solution she considers irresponsible. Much of the day has been occupied with activities it will be easier not to tell her about. He will have to sober up and edit his account of the day. Outside, the fog seems to be lifting and a warm wind is coming from a new direction. Roger's belongings cluster and knock against the cement stoop. He closes the kitchen door behind him, closes the hasp, and presses the screws into place like thumbtacks.

He hops off the—rather high—stoop into the dark ground, just as the kitchen light is turned on inside his own house, flooding through the window, blinding him. All the kitchens in Phase III have these new high-tech halogen bulbs like art-gallery lighting, whose filaments capture some warm, brilliant section of the rainbow and concentrate it into an eye-piercing beam. The solid waves of mud are treacherous underfoot, and he drifts aslant toward his house, feeling uncharacteristically cut-loose in the crosscurrent of new warm air from the south, unable to sort out which events of the day he should leave unmentioned. His having actually kissed Shubie—and his having planned vainly to go and find her—has contaminated the entire day, and he feels himself treading among poisonous corals that would be invisible to Audrey, whose face appears in the kitchen door's small window, pressed close to scan the darkness. The back door opens, and she appears just as he reaches the plank of light on the ground—"Mark?" she says—and he swims up to her embrace.

15
House-to-House Fighting

What happened?'' says Audrey in his arms, her breath against his ear. ''Did we lose our property by adverse possession?''

Mark says, for a start, ''No, nothing happened, really,'' speaking to her dodging phantom as she turns out of his embrace and walks away. The night air on his skin excludes him from sincerity. On television, among dusty biblical streets, house-to-house fighting requires men to trot hunched-over along low stone walls.

''You've been drinking beer, yuck. How did you get your shoes so dirty?''

''There was a certain amount of digging.'' He is a little

breathless from his trespass, and vaporous on the skin—still just standing there in the doorway: is that a perfectly natural thing to do, or does it seem somehow suspicious and uncharacteristic?

". . . Not only did I drink Roger's beer, I spilled some on me."

"Poor baby, I want to hear about it. Anyway, the Vatican is insane." She's headed for the refrigerator to—as she always does when she gets home—open the door and stare into it while she talks. One careless hip is thrust high athwart the air as she stands, surprisingly sexy, and Mark feels again like the Night Walker, admitted to an unsuspecting woman's kitchen in a tract development. His hand in his jacket pocket discovers the frozen peas in their plastic bladder, now warm, and his fingers start to wriggle toward freeing a few peas. His other pants pocket is filled with dirt, which he won't mention.

"Can you imagine?" she says. "All we want is a preemptive merchandising registration. But he's got his own rules. Like he has extraterritorial immunity—which Mike later mispronounces as 'extraterrestrial.' Mike, from *Yale*. He goes, 'Even extraterrestrials have negative cash flow.' And this guy goes, like, 'Whuuh?' And Mike is like, 'You know, like the pope is an extraterrestrial.' "

She turns and asks, "Did you know that?" leaning on the open refrigerator door, catching him in the act of sorting four thawed peas, a quadrangle in his palm.

"What?" He impersonates her mild, tired husband.

"Did you know the Vatican is its own little deal? They have their own postal service and their own foreign policy and everything."

"No, how interesting."

She turns back to inspect the interior of the refrigerator.

She's so much smarter than he is. He puts the four peas on his tongue to roll them symmetrically to the four quarters of his mouth.

"—Anyway, the *pro nuncio*'s official position was that the church is simply indifferent to license poaching. But I think we got him in the end, because he's a realistic, practical person. I mean, he has the intelligence to see the church may not be worldly but they have to live in the world. A preemptive is so logical. It's only smart. It's like a prenuptial agreement, nobody likes it but you're stupid if you don't do it. All it is is *clarity*. It makes people be clear with each other, but also *with themselves! Inside themselves!*" She likes this observation and gloats for a minute as she scans the inner refrigerator. The thing Mark likes about their own prenuptial agreement, which Audrey herself wrote, is that it let him get away with postponing children. She says, without turning to look at him, "I knew there was no hope you'd change your pants. What did you boys do, anyway?"

Dirt has been scrubbed into the fabric of his knees. "We never even got much of a fence built." He sits down in the lawn chair, making its plastic plaiting creak. He wants to stretch out his arms to relax, to gather unto himself the air of his own rooms, but he doesn't. "It was dumb, that's all, it was dumb," he says summarily. He can just float on her assumptions and never mention specifics, the *un*-mentioned being the gripping, heavy invisible fluid all around us that holds us up, the *un*mentioned being what marries us.

"I see you ignored the cream chipped beef."

"Roger barbecued. I'm actually a little drunk."

"Why does he have all that furniture out on the lawn?" She closes the refrigerator, unbuttoning her clothes.

"Oh, it was a very complicated night. I'll tell you all about it. Roger probably won't be living there much longer. He has this *life*—revolving around his divorce."

"Where's the property line?"

"Well, a survey team did come by. And then a representative of the company came by. I'll show you the letter in the morning. They sent a guy around to walk the boundaries and talk to people, and he basically said—I suppose you'd call it a verbal commitment—that we wouldn't be pushed around too much by Acquisition Systems."

She doesn't know what Acquisition Systems is. "Right now I'm tired," she says. Her body crosses the field of his fixed gaze, as his mind flies away to sort out the adulterous elements of the day. In a minute, her voice arrives at his ear. "Anyway, tell me. Why does Roger Hobbleman have all his things outside on the lawn?"

"There *is* no lawn . . ."

"Won't the neighbors complain?" She goes up the stairs pulling a sweater over her head. "This seems like the kind of place where the neighbors complain."

Hands on knees, Mark pushes himself up from his chair, and he stands there. "We *are* 'the neighbors.' " It's a revelation, but a dull one. He seems to be getting away with going to bed while the whole world lies undone all around him—Roger's hasp loose, his children unminded, the stone lost, his own earthen property stolen abstractly from beneath him.

"Did you ever notice a bronze sign in the ground, by the carport?"

"I can't hear you," she calls from a distance. The weary song of her tone means that she doesn't really need to hear him, and therefore it's a kind of farewell. He crosses the kitchen floor stepping on the grey sections of the parcheesi terrazzo, and his left foot begins the ascent of the fourteen carpeted stairs—the top two of which routinely require a double step, to make sixteen. The bottoms of his feet fail to quite make solid contact with the frosty nap of the new carpet, like the foot soles of the floating pope, who is a kind of UFO. Everything is misted by the anticipation of its loss, preventing the *tangency* that humans think of as contact. In the bedroom, his wife appears to him in the big NIKE T-shirt she wears at night, saying "Twelve dollars now— for an airport shuttle." The remark is like a loose embrace. They'll sleep side by side again, separated by the interval of mattress that shifts like a shore between them all night.

"All that happened was," he begins, picking among the pieces in his mind, "we dug a hole that was supposed to be for a fence post. And Roger built a fire and cooked hamburger meat. And we talked to one of them."

"One of who?"

"The representatives of the company."

"Yes, you mentioned. You know, I tried to call you from the hotel."

"I was outside then. Anyway, it was interesting. Some kind of survey team came by. They've definitely got it mapped out. But their claim is based on the original claim of somebody who was mentally incompetent. Back in the nineteenth century." Every sentence he utters has the halo of a negative charge: it's *not* about Shubie Behejdi.

Audrey thinks while she's brushing her hair. "I'm told the five-year term of adverse possession is *additive*. If they've sent annual notices to the previous owners for the previous five years, they can sustain their claim."

"Well . . . ," Mark hangs his arms and shrugs backward, letting his jacket fall behind him. "In that case, I guess we're fucked. Have to live in the subway."

"Did you get the new script for *The Heart of Matter?*"

"I forgot it."

She looks at him and stops brushing her hair. "Where is it?"

He turns away. "It's in my mail slot at school. But, you know, they didn't take out that line. Where I have to say, 'There is truly no reality there.' "

"Can a janitor let you in? Mark? Is the campus locked up in the early morning?"

"I don't know." He occupies himself in bending over his sock drawer to rearrange the little soft grenades into hexagonal packing. "The fact is, Audrey, there *isn't* 'nothing' there. *Reality* is there."

"He's building a show theme, honey. It's not science, it's entertainment. They need you to say that."

"Yes, but it isn't true."

"Only a few *physicists* will know that. It's more or less true."

"No, that's the problem. Physicists think there's no reality, too, honey. I'm the only one left who thinks there is. Or tries to think there is. That's the problem."

"Mark, can you get into the building tomorrow morning to get to your mailbox? We have to be ready to shoot by ten o'clock."

". . . I don't know."

"Okay." She goes back to brushing her hair. "I'll have the studio courier it, first thing tomorrow morning."

Then fate enters the room: The finger of Mark's left hand is pricked by the stone, deep in the thready seam of his empty pants pocket. He's sure it's the stone. He again turns away from Audrey toward his sock drawer and, within the shelter of a shoulder, he looks down at the gleam revealed in the pinch of his fingers.

"Just be reasonable," says Audrey. "You're going to have to say what the script writers want. Anyway, when your second book comes back from the writers, there'll be *plenty* in there about the deconstruction of matter. It's your market position, honey."

He has no answer because she's probably right. And besides, he doesn't care any more, rescued now by the problem of how to dispose of the stone—which he carefully inserts again in the uttermost appendix of his pocket.

"By the way, the cover art for the book came. I sent it back. I'm going to ask the publisher to try another artist. It didn't look juicy enough."

"Juicy?" he says, not appearing to be the least bit sneaky or inebriated.

"Not novely enough. I'll show you."

He removes the two pennies from his pockets without spilling the handful of dirt in the one pocket or disturbing the stone in the depths of the other. Maybe he can simply leave it in his pants all night and wait till morning to return it; he sits on the edge of the bed to take them off, and he folds them. Then, on second thought, he rises and drags them across the floor to drop them—as if carelessly—on the pile of dirty clothes at the back of the closet. It will be easiest never to bother telling Audrey. Tomorrow he'll find a moment to sneak into Roger's place and put the crystal back in its bottle, and never think of it again. Half undressed, he sees himself in the mirror in his usual slouch as he sets the creamy blue worm of Colgate on the bristles of his toothbrush, and, with the hand not brushing his teeth, he unbuttons his shirt, as if this were an ordinary night, as if the two frightened children were not lying awake next door under a plastic tarp. Their father is in trouble somewhere.

He goes back into the room and says, "How was the flight?" Clearly Audrey is going to fall asleep fast. She's moving about with downcast eyes, efficient and sagging, groping toward bed against the snap of invisible webs. "It was fine," she says. "I'd like to look at that letter in the morning. I'm curious."

"Actually, I didn't check the mail."

"What Mike said made me wonder. About how adverse possession claims are additive." She crawls onto the mattress and pulls the quilt over herself, and she lies down diving away from him, her back turned, her shoulder defining an arc of exclusion.

He pulls off his socks, releasing the shower of a small cache of fresh-dug pebbly dirt, which falls on the carpet. "I'm sure it's nothing," he says. "The whole thing is stupid." He steps out of his ankle-entangling underwear and falls forward into bed, making the mattress jounce: her body's inert ballast on the wave indicates she's already swelling toward sleep.

"The whole thing is ridiculous if they're allowed to kick us off." He lies down.

Her falling asleep has made him wakeful, and his alertness is mischief. He can see he will lie here awake, as excited as a boy camping outside, feeling himself hardly denting the mattress; upon which Audrey, by contrast, is as heavy as an engine block. Her not suspecting anything makes her peacefully huge, an innocent giantess by contrast to him. Her breathing is growing regular.

As a test, he says softly, "Did you set the alarm? Audrey?" Her breathing flows on. Then, after a toss of her head on the pillow, a small sipping sound in her nostril joins the rhythm of breathing.

He lifts his head and rests it on the support of his elbow, regarding her objectively from above. Her eyelids, with their silver dandruff flakes, are already bruised and shiny in the depth of slumber. The allergic-looking red pinch above her Scandinavian nostrils—always sharper when she is fatigued—has grown more acute in the four years since he has lived with her. New also is the permanent parenthesis at the corner of her mouth, the rubbed look, the crease underneath that makes of her chin a knob. Her hair is drier and stiffer than Shubie's. When she's ninety, he alone will still see the girl she was, the moist-eyed, brave girl. Elegant fine wrinkles above her cheekbones—defining humor, defining beautiful skull structure—define also a peculiar softness that makes him want to move her unfairly to desire, and even though she's probably too sleepy, he sets a hand on her breast and cups its sad yolk against the pull of gravity. Through the fabric—through the neoprene imprint of the NIKE corporation's hasty orange *swoosh* trademark—the warmth of her breast communicates a sleepy reluctance to waken, until, with the strumming of his thumb, the nipple makes that old motion that feels like digging deeper for a purchase and then rising outward. It never fails to provoke the exact same waking in his penis, when he covers her breast with his hand and feels the nipple gather and push, alive, at the center of his palm. Maybe he shouldn't be doing this. She might come up from sleep irritably. But rather than stop, he slides closer, brings his breath into her hair, cups her turned-away body with his, and allows the weird alien ectoplasm of his penis to rest against the complicated crucifix cleft where the backs of her thighs meet. Seduction is a pleasure because a woman's life is so much more serious than a man's. The final involuntary eyelid flutter, the momentary panicky trustful grip, are her abdication of her greater seriousness to his mischief, for only a minute. His pleasure lies entirely in her loss of control as she is swung out, her eyes momentarily open in the amazement, the swallowing motion, his own gratitude in her trust in extremity.

She shifts a thigh. His hand moves to her hip—to that unbelievable cliff that forms between hip and waist when a woman is lying on her side. The vertebral column at the base of a female spine must be incredibly supple, the soft intervertebral Life Savers must be more resilient than any man-made material, where the spine attaches to the pelvis, whose hollow basin is capable of digging forward with such final violence. At that moment, Audrey's pelvis scoops backward toward him, implying that his penis, now so hard it feels shiny, is accepted, either because it's a necessary woman's courtesy or because somehow the ugly deep-rooted gristle could actually be considered interesting, if you're a woman. It's a washing motion, the motion of her body against him, the body that, beneath her usual stiff skirt, at the offices of Talman Courtney Ruben, must be an object of desire for all the male lawyers— perhaps just as dangerously as is the case at the physics department with Shubie Behejdi. Maybe Audrey has even, without mentioning it to him of course, allowed an occasional flirtation to get out of hand, to progress almost to the point of adultery. There was one handsome asshole, a junior partner Mark met once at a party, who seemed to possess the right routine superb egotism. The idea of her actually yielding is unimaginable, but the picture of her having *resisted* temptation, which is quite likely, makes her all the more desirable. And the idea makes her hand seem expert as it slips behind her. The primordial generous urgency makes him rise to, as a start, kiss the fold behind her ear (his tongue first tapping the final four spots of the sixteen-point grid on his inner palate).

"Oof," she says, arching her back.

His breath comes close to her ear.

"You're on my hair."

"Oops."

"You always do that." But the complaint, which had begun in a peeved tone, ends in a pout. She's his cute victim again, and she rolls toward him, into him. Looking for a forbidden moment into Audrey's intelligent eyes (wherein lies eroticism! the juncture of the soul with the flesh, the wise gaze with the moving hip), Mark slides a hand along her thigh, and he remembers—an asterisk of doubt marking the purity of the act—that this is the month when she's supposed to take a break from her birth-control pills, and that this morning she discarded the month's holy bandage, so that an early egg might be descending from the high inner shelf—but it's a thought he files away under "Forget" as she unfurls further toward him and magnetism wakens in their satin bones, and he ceases his soft, subvocal unwinding of "Wish You Were Here"—and at last the mouth that this morning touched Shubie Behejdi's lips, closes upon his wife's lips, which open up to disclose the empty space explored by tongue.

Her lips move. "Mark."

"Oops," he says. "I forgot."

"This'll be for a whole month. The last real pill ran out ten days ago."

"I forgot," he says.

"But wait." Her two hands glide down for that oddly mechanical lever, a gleam of promise in her eyes, succeeded by—when her hands encircle it—the old advertised expression of surprise and comfort. "There are other things."

And so lucky Mark Perdue resigns himself to pleasure. A kind of law of moral algebra, in life, would seem to demand that all this good fortune should eventually require a penalty. But there is none, none at all. Only children believe in such an economy. Life as a grown-up turns out to be strangely unresisting, a dreamlike experience of happy injustice. She descends with the ancient expression either feigned or genuine, of delight in finding leverage, and as she descends Mark rises—with almost disappointment—into the sovereign loneliness of having everything his way, which feels really like just another variety of being misunderstood.

16
Oops

He lies awake sleepless in the dark, amazed before his own stupidity. He simply wasn't thinking. He couldn't stop. The mattress was an isolated raft. This is how average people let their lives be taken over by circumstances—by giving up control for even just an innocent minute and letting blind chance decide their fate, which is fine for average people, who perhaps aren't already doing something more important than raising children, but certain others are entitled to retain control over their lives. Or even if Mark doesn't happen to be especially busy right now, it's his duty to keep his life free of premature encumbrances. The feeling, lying there, is like having been thrust downriver into a strangely quiet zone below the falls.

But Audrey herself deserves some, or more, of the blame, for allowing it—allowing him to blank out momentarily and press her down beneath him and rise against her and embrace her—and not cease to embrace her in the fateful spasm of his dull surprise. And now, as a consequence, his millions of white threads are thrashing toward—possibly!—a white pinpoint on the infinitely curved horizon within, where all the laws of physics curl up and vaporize, as on the rim of a space-distortion leading everywhere at once. Maybe actual pregnancy isn't a huge risk, statistically, but it's the principle of it, the irresponsibility of letting random statistical forces take over their lives, as if their own lives didn't matter. And yet Audrey is capable of actually falling asleep, as though nothing were wrong.

Which gives *him* the duty of worrying. He's not drunk any more. He's all too sober. From the taped-up window comes the soft regular tympanic thud of the black polyethylene tightening in the valley breeze, bandaged for warranty repairs like half the northeast master-bedroom windows all over Phase III because they were originally installed as single panes but were supposed to be Thermopane. By the time the Thermopane windows arrive, Audrey will perhaps be hugely pregnant, and their lives will have begun already to revolve toward the cruelty of children, the ruthlessness of their innocence, more absolute even than Mark's innocence. A pleasant morgue chill creeps against his bare chest, and he can't move, stranded, between remorse and gratitude, his eyes wandering on the Cobblestone Hearth ceiling, like a motel ceiling snowed with freeze-dried-looking sparkles. All the liquor in his system seems at last to have a coffeelike effect, which

makes his anxiety all the sharper. His tongue keeps marking a square sixteen-point grid on his palate. His back feels
arched. And then as he lies very still, he hears for sure—
what he had, till now, only suspected hearing—the sound
of the two children Jennifer and Jason, their voices outside. They're in the backyard. Maybe it's understandable;
they weren't too comfortable under that stiff tarp. They
somehow got out of Roger's padlocked unit—but they're
not going home. They're hanging around. It's a duty he
might as well face, going outside and taking care of them,
getting them back to their own house. He rolls to stand up.
By sheer fluidity of motion he doesn't jiggle the bed. The
cold air is quenching against his skin, as is the pleasure of
motion, and he walks naked over the creakless new
floor—guaranteed creakless for five years by the Cobblestone Hearth warranty—to the west window, which isn't
blinded by black plastic.

They're easy to see, sitting on the dirt around the now-
dead camp fire, in the squatting posture of refugees, butt
suspended between planted ankles. He goes across the silent floor into the closet and, pulling his pants on, he feels
for the lost grain, still in the pocket. Now is when he can
sneak it back onto Roger's mantle. And be done with it.

He needn't bother with shoes and socks. He'll go barefoot. Lacking a shirt, he puts a nylon parka on his bare
back, silky and cold. He seems to have disguised himself
as a bum, wearing only a down parka and his grimy pants,
no underwear, his guilty penis clapping loose in his pants
flaky with a donut-glaze, his bare chest probably smelling
of sex, his hair tousled. It's of course personally risky to get
involved in the lives of stupid people, yet a kind of dark,
subversive joy flows through him as he floods down the
stairs, his invisible reach emanating out in the darkness to
huge distances, grabbing the bannister on both sides alter-

nately and handing himself along spiderlike. He covers the carpet to the door in eight steps, and, toying with a panic as if he were escaping a burning house, he breaks out into the cool air outdoors.

The cement outside is cold underfoot. The children turn and stand up, and the little girl says loudly, "We couldn't sleep"—but rather proudly. They both start to come toward him among the obstacles of Roger's furniture.

"I think maybe your mother must be back by now," says Mark. He hops off the stoop. "You can go home and go to bed."

"We couldn't sleep," the girl says again. The boy collides with his knee and grasps a fistful of his pants fabric, and the girl reaches up to set both fists softly against his nylon jacket front, tilting her face up. "You have to tell us a story," she says in a quick transition to, almost, coquettishness, a bent-pin smile at the corner of her mouth.

"No stories," says Mark. He squats at their level to shed their embrace.

"You have to!"

"Keep your voices down. Did you guys watch the scary movie? Is that what scared you?"

Together, without hesitation, they nod their heads gravely.

"Don't you think your mother's home by now? Everybody's trying to sleep."

Something, maybe the thought of the scary video, makes Jason's features shrink toward self-pitying tears, and he begins to hum as a way of starting to cry.

"Jason, don't," says Jennifer, and she begins to beat her fist against his spine in rhythm, chanting—probably from a cartoon show or a children's record—"Nothing can go wron-go, I'm in the Con-go. Nothing can go wron-go, I'm in the Con-go." It must be Jason's usual medicine for fear, but it isn't doing much good, because his lip goes on jumping. "Okay, I'll take you home," says Mark, standing up. And he tells them loud and clear, as if aiming to be overheard by somebody. "You live on Baltic Avenue. You can show me where."

Jennifer goes on chanting, "Nothing can go wron-go, I'm in the Con-go. Nothing can go wron-go, I'm in the Con-go . . ." He picks up the boy, who stops whimpering. "Let's go." She grabs the hem of his parka and they set off around the house in the night air. Actually, it's not as cold as he'd expected. In these hours before dawn, a warm mass of air has moved in. Also, the fog is gone. He unzips his parka. He loves it out here. He loves air, the liquid atmosphere against his chest. Symmetry in footfalls is for some reason less important when he's unshod. Jason, in pajamas and galoshes, lays his head in the pit of Mark's neck. A toy he's holding is a decapitated Barbie. Out on Happyhearth Lane, the big hunchback centaur shadow cast by himself and the boy makes a sweep around him every time they pass beneath an amber street lamp.

"You ought not to have watched that disaster video," he says, loudly, for the benefit of an imagined eavesdropper.

"You have to tell us a story," Jennifer says.

"No stories. I have to go to sleep myself." They veer away from the road, and Jennifer takes his hand to pull him down the dirt slope toward Phase I, though Mark resists because he's barefoot. He sets the boy down and takes his hand, the boy being the only one of the three with shoes—but his unbuckled galoshes seem to have the effect of slowing him down. Planting his feet to keep from skidding on the slope, Mark hears his own voice as drifting unheard behind them—"Absolutely no bedtime stories . . ." Obviously their parents aren't firm enough with these children, so he repeats it with unmistakable adamancy, "Absolutely no bedtime stories."

17
Bedtime Stories

I want you to know," Mark tells the children as they descend into Phase I, messier than Phase III, with bikes in driveways, a single athletic shoe in another driveway, a smashed pumpkin on a doorstep, a broken laundry basket on a lawn, "I want you guys to know—that this is an *exceptional* situation. Not to be repeated. Usually, people show more respect for other people's sleep." On the downward slant, his toe bumps something, a white plastic pipe protruding from the raw earth, part of the unfinished sprinkler system, and he staggers forward and accidentally pulls the boy to the ground, where his face strikes first.

Jason, on his stomach, lifts his head and peers around and then, deciding to cry, launches into a full scream. It's probably three o'clock in the morning, and Mark is standing conspicuously on the slope as these children's abductor or abuser. He climbs back up the slope, temporarily, putting five or ten yards between himself and the children. He zips his parka to cover his bare chest. "No crying," he whispers across the distance. "I'm getting you guys home, and then that's that."

"You have to cuddle him," says Jennifer.

"You cuddle him—he's more familiar with you."

"He hates me. Adults have to cuddle him."

Jason, his whole body gone limp with the effort of crying, reaches the end of a long wail, takes in breath, and begins a louder one. Mark comes down the slope and bends to try to scoop him together, beginning at the shoulders, or at the hips, but the boy is so limp he keeps pouring out of Mark's embrace, so Mark tries shifting strategy and picks him up in the middle, which he folds over. It stops his crying for a minute. But as soon as he's able to hold him up against his chest, the boy can get his breath again, and cries all the louder. Mark starts down the hill. "Come on." To give the boy breathing space, he lets him drop away slightly. "Let's go," he tells Jennifer, tossing the boy lightly in his arms. "Let's get him in the house."

"You have to—" she makes crushing motions, "scrunch him."

"Come on." Mark is moving as fast as he can down the slope in a sort of groping gallop, which jostles the boy in a way that, it turns out, comforts him. Or at least worries him enough to make him shut up and look around. "Which one is yours?"

"Two Twenty-Three Baltic Avenue," she sings out. It's the same rehearsed tone in which she warned him this afternoon that she would scream if he molested her. She points to the end of the block, where, among cedar-shingled units unevenly distributed to simulate individuality, a front door is hanging wide open.

"Is that yours? Did you leave the door open?"

She doesn't answer. After thinking for a minute, she says, "Where did Daddy go?"

"He went to get your mother. Try to walk faster, he's going to start crying again."

"Daddy can come over and have sex and use a condom."

"You're going straight to bed."

"You have to read us a story."

"You're going straight to bed."

She skips to catch up and she hooks her fingers on his belt loop. Her shoulders press together, and she rises to walk on tiptoe.

"And no stories," he says, despising his fatherly, harrassed tone. Fathers are predefeated by circumstances, tied down by a million Lilliputian threads, and the futility of it is detectable in their voices when they try to command. It's the axiomatic mistake in having children: you're creating something greater than yourself, with, actually therefore, more authority than you. Jason, grasping Mark's neck with a slipping embrace that hurts like rope burn, cranes his neck to see where they're going.

"Is this it?" says Mark as they turn up the walk. "Is this your house?" A small stack of nested orange peels is on the step. The lawn is lush and well trimmed, which would be Roger's work. Lawn care must provide one of his many pretexts for showing up here despite his wife's efforts to stop him. On the top step in the light of the open doorway is a pair of large blue plastic dice, showing the easy three-four combination making seven, the statistical apex of the probability curve. Mark asks the girl, "Is anybody home?"

"We went past the tornadoes," says Jennifer gravely. It's a confession. She's referring to the disaster video.

"Hello?" Mark raises his voice and stands at the threshold. "Is anybody home? Roger?" The only sound from within is the loud rush of static on a television. They left it on. He unloads the boy.

The living room is dominated by the television, its empty screen ashimmer with the random specks of a completely information-free signal, filling the house with a white noise that, though not loud, smothers all sound. Jason—he's wearing flannel pajamas with some sort of cartoon characters pictured all over—runs ahead into the house and kicks off his jingling rubber boots. In the middle of the living room floor is a big clear Plexiglas hemisphere lying on its round back—a skylight, actually—as big as a tub. The children have filled it with water and thrown in a number of plastic toys, which float. Also afloat are a few knuckle-sized Baby Ruths and Butterfingers and Almond Joys.

"Was it all right with your mother to put water in this?"

Jason, at its rim, tips it toward himself to reach for a floating toy. "Here's my Transformer," he says. He rescues it from the water without spilling the whole skylight-full, and he brings it dripping to Mark, wanting Mark to play, to join him on the floor. It's a plastic toy of many moving parts, depicting a character who seems a kind of mechanical reptile or spacecraft. Mark makes an appreciative noise, for in fact it's interesting. The black-tinted observation windows in its nose are arranged in exactly the angular dispersion ratio that would reflect radiation in deep space and reduce envelope heat on reentry. The arms and legs swivel and fold inward into bays on the underside, ingeniously, so that the creature mimics a sort of hand grenade when folded up. And it has very plausible, if slightly sci-fi, vanes on its back, for heat distribution or aerodynamic guidance, which have exactly the curve that evolution, or good engineering, would provide, tapering according to asymptotic logarithms. It's really impressive. A scientist might have built it. Its cantilever-jointed spider legs seem designed to lower the center of gravity and maximize work leverage. Jason reaches up, his fist banging Mark's hip, while his easily ignored voice chants upward (he loves his family and he always cleans up his toys). Mark's thumb wanders over the spacecraft's forehead to press a hidden catch and discover a secret compartment inside—a control room with tiny video monitors and captain's and copilot's chairs and computers and a joystick to steer the craft—where Jason has deposited pieces of food: four marshmallow bits from Lucky Charms cereal. Maybe he took them from his father's Lucky Charms box beside his sleeping bag in the other house. Recognizably, they are the styrofoam-light dried marshmallows juggled by the leprechaun on the television commercial, one representative of each suit.

Jason strains on tiptoe for his toy and quotes a cartoon, "I am Vishnu! Shiva! Destroyer of Worlds!"

"Come on!"—Jennifer's voice in a far room is trying to summon them.

He asks Jason, "Do these things go back and forth as rudders?" One of the marshmallow bits drops out, but Mark catches it between his forearm and his hip. He rolls it to his palm and slips it back into the cockpit and closes up Vishnu's head with a secure click. Jason makes impatient hops, though Mark would just like to look at it a little longer. Since he was a child, they've developed new dyes for vacuum-molded polystyrene, and the surface of the toy is a persuasive deathly gunmetal pewter.

"Mine!" says Jason.

"Come on!" Jennifer's voice, in the far room, has the effect of making him drift toward the door, away from the pool of toys. "Mine!" Jason says again, more pitifully, and at last he passes the toy down to him at arm's length with the formality of resentment. "Here's your stupid toy."

"I'm ready! You guys!" His sister's tone is exasperated. In the adjoining room, she is lying on two couch cushions on the rug—all the rooms of the apartment are carpeted in fat caterpillar yarns of mixed lime, rust, and gold, the kind of deep shag carpet where granola gets permanently lost, and indeed a smell like old spilled food is everywhere, a housekeeping frizz on everything, the frizz of disappointment, of entropy. A rummage sale is the shifting shore dividing this life from chaos. A bed sheet is tacked up over the window rather than draperies. The living-room couch, of wide-wale blue corduroy, is a hide-a-bed; but its seat cushions are missing, exposing the canvas-and-spring mechanism. A witty Radio Shack telephone that must have been funny in the seventies, in the shape of big red plastic lips, has a peeling decal reading *World's Greatest Mom*.

"I'm ready," says Jennifer. "This is our favorite book."

She's in the unfurnished bedroom. Her bed is two couch cushions, blue corduroy wafers stolen from the living-room couch. Jason's bed is the third cushion, on the floor beside hers, with his milk carton full of lizards standing by. He leaps onto it. His body fits on a single cushion if he draws his knees up. The small crab of his hand clasps the blanket's frayed satin border and he pulls it over himself. Mark looks at them both in a psychopathic daze of trespassing.

"Okay. You guys'll be fine," he mumbles, lying, while

his eyes travel the room. "Your mother will be home soon." A chair in the corner is the torn-out bucket seat from an old Ford Mustang, horses galloping in a molded-plastic frieze on its seat panel, imitating tooled leather.

"You have to *read*." Jennifer lifts a book to slap it down on her blanket.

". . . Your father went to get her," he says. Standing in the doorway, he finds himself drawing in his shoulders against the lintiness of this place, but at the same time his incandescent spine is primitively drawn to light and warmth and frizz. On the bucket seat is a neat stack of freshly folded clothes, so obviously just-laundered that he can imagine the smell of warmth in the fabric.

"We'll go to sleep, but you have to read." She's got *The Cat in the Hat Comes Back* and some other book he doesn't recognize called *Where the Wild Things Are*. Having stepped forward and twisted his neck to see their titles, he steps back. "Your mom will be right back. I'm sure."

"Mom'll get a MasterCard, so she can get us a house," Jennifer says.

"You can't buy a house with a charge card," he says, but immediately it seems a cruel thing to say, and, to rise from having sunk to her level, he says, "Nevertheless, I'm sure your mother will buy a very nice house."

"Yes, but me and Jason have to be good."

He looks at both of them. Their eyes shine with the effort to hold still and be good. "Okay. One story. And then really, I'm not kidding."

"*Cat in the Hat,*" says Jason.

He comes over the threshold into the room, and they squirm up to be ready to pile onto him. It's hard to see how he should sit, or lie, to read to them, and in fact he could easily be mistaken for some sort of suburban pervert yielding to a fuzzy pleasure in a stranger's house. Yet he picks up *Where the Wild Things Are*. They've also, since he was a kid, started using new pigments for children's books. Everything is gloomy and dark and hairy-inked. The illustrations in *Where the Wild Things Are* are sunk in a grim twilight, in which ugly monsters with bodies of mastodons, bare feet of humans, beaks of parrots, cavort beneath palm trees on a shadowy island. It's stupid, there's no *reason* why the little boy in every picture would ever trust such monsters. Remembering how sweet is the logic of *The Cat in the Hat Comes Back*, he picks it up instead. "Okay, this one," he says with an elderly groan as he descends through an awkward curtsey and gets down cross-legged on the floor between the two children.

They scramble to climb over him on their couch cushions. Jason digs his heels into the carpet to push back into Mark's lap, and Jennifer lays her cheek on his thigh. The banana smell of children is morphine. For the first time, he considers the legal implications of his being here, alone without permission. All the grounds for suit, for the complete public ruination of his life, are here in the expansion of his heart, the comfort in his bones, sitting on the floor among strangers' children. "You guys better go to sleep fast," he warns them, stagily, his voice arising from some distant part of his body. Jason, his head against Mark's ribs, hangs on as if this is going to be a bumpy ride. The girl squirms against his thigh and prompts him, "The sun inna shine / It was too wet to play . . . ," so from the center of the little mammalian pile deep in somebody else's abode, he sends up his voice—first reading the cover, lacking the strength to open it and turn the pages: *"The Cat in the Hat Comes Back*—by Dr. Seuss." Jason's head is hot, a censer against his chest.

Then he reads, too, simply as a pretext for staying pleasantly immobile for a minute longer, the inscription on the small medallion stamped on the cover. "This says: 'Beginner Books: I Can Read It All by Myself.' '' Within the medallion, in cameo, is the celebrated Cat himself, in his melting top hat, chinless, his eyes closed in gloating, *deserving* to appear on his own specially minted coin.

Jennifer's elbow gouges his thigh. She reaches to open the cover for him. "The sun inna shine / It was too wet to play . . .''

Inside, the illustrations with their colors of carrot and lima bean and catsup, with their frondlike hands and feet, and the ropy, doughy tenderness they confer on solid mass—even the smell, like Play-Doh, of the book's opened pages—all have the effect of tranquilizing him, and justifying his being here. A pale, fearful boy and girl live in a shacky house on a tousled hillock with a single drooping tree. And their mother is always gone; her shapely calf and sexy ankle, exiting, are her only appearance in the book. The boy and girl are outside the house shoveling snow that looks as heavy as cement. It's an assignment their mother gave them in her absence. Then, exactly reconsituting Mark's memory in marzipan, the Cat in the Hat enters the property—and then the house—with the aplomb of a vandal, his furry toes drooping as he steps across the threshold, his hat and umbrella tipping askew, his eyes closed in complete happy insolence, objects in his vicinity tilting in the wake of trouble that follows him. Now, while Mother is gone, everything in the house can be turned upside down, every deck of cards can be scattered, every jar in the cupboard can be vengefully mixed, every chair can be knocked over. The children may try to voice objections, but only feebly, too congested by politeness. The Cat easily ignores them and heads for the bathroom, eyes still closed, and on the next page, spread out across *both* pages, he is sprawling in the bath tub and eating *pink cake*, the faucet gushing water into an already brimming tub that slings heavy splashes from its rim. Above him, the shower head, too, is pouring water, down upon the open umbrella balanced on his knees. His weird white-gloved hands, like dolphins on the tethering hoses of his arms, juggle the cake and a fork as he eats, his eyes eternally closed in his absolute calm confidence in his own psychokinetic control of chaos everywhere.

Mark remembers now: the *Oobleck:* the pink stain: when the cat's tub is drained, a pink ring is left on the porcelain, which stains everything it touches. If you use a towel to clean the tub, the towel is stained. If you whip the towel against the wall to clean it, the wall is stained. Whatever you do, the stain persists. Like an aromatic pigment, it has some photomagnetic properties, but in emulsion it doesn't alter the electronic structure of chemical bonds in the material. It's like an acrylic ester, nonbiodegradable, eternal. Most amazingly, it seems to *gain* in photomagnetism as it spreads. Even when diluted, it stays just as pink. Mother will soon be home, and the stain is contaminating everything in the house.

The Cat in the Hat, pretending helpfulness with his usual sarcasm, releases from his big doughy top hat twenty-six little Cats in Hats (one for each letter of the alphabet), and he directs them to help clean up the stain. They can't exactly be his "children," because of course the Cat in the Hat isn't married, but rather they are like small monsters counterfeited of his genes, and therefore lacking the nerves in their flesh for remorse or judgment. For instead of helping, they slap the spots into more, multiplying spots, joyfully. They sweep gobs of pink Oobleck into the whirling blades of a fan. When it hits the fan, a storm of pink jelly flies out through the window and onto the snow outside. Now all the neighborhood will see the poison.

> "All this does is make *more* spots!"
> We yelled at the cat.
> "Your cats are no good.
> Put them back in your hat.
> "Take your Little Cats G,
> F, E, D, C, B, A,"

pleads the little boy with scared poker-chip eyes standing knee deep in pink snow—reversing the alphabet, Mark realizes, as a kind of incantation to remove a spell,

> "Put them back in your hat
> And you take them away!"

> > "Oh, no!" said the cat.
> > "All they need is more help.
> > Help is all that they need.
> > So keep still and don't yelp."

Jennifer and Jason, against Mark's chest, are already solidly asleep, but he goes on reading anyway, locked in by the sweaty jigsaw puzzle of them. The word "Oobleck" still hasn't appeared, and he is beginning to think he may have been mistaken all these years: the Oobleck may have been in another Dr. Seuss book, a jelly not pink but green, associated with a tall, withered castle rather than this one-windowed house on a knoll. He feels betrayed; the "Oobleck" had furnished his first mental picture of a field theory, like a magnetic field or a gravity field, an influence occupying three-dimensional space which, supposedly, can have material effects without itself being material. It's such an obvious contradiction, the central, necessary mistake of physics, the idea that a blob of something purely nonphysical can have any contact or effect on something purely physical. Quantum field theory will never resolve the problem by simply calling everything a potential field, or by calling everything an accident of human consciousness. Mark looks down, through the prism of time-space, at his own Oobleck-constituted "hand" lying motionless on Dr. Seuss's page, and it looks inert. The human effort to "see" things, to print mental points on physical space, seems so futile that he doesn't care any more to lift his hand and turn the page, on which twenty-six tiny cats cavort in the pink snow, batting it with baseball bats, running lawn mowers through it, slapping it with flyswatters, having snowball fights at cross-purposes, swan diving into pink drifts. At which point the Cat—who has a debonair ability to stand with his ankles crossed and lean on thin air—produces the tiniest cat of all, the Z-cat, so small it can't be seen.

> "Look close! In my hand
> I have Little Cat V.
> On his head are Cats W,
> X, Y and Z,"

Dots of ink stand on the Cat's pinching fingers, which the two children examine, in awe and doubt. The next page is a huge close-up of the Cat's hand. On the fingertip of his weird two-fingered glove, radiating lines indicate the resonance where a microscopic cat stands, or so we are to believe.

> "Now here is the Z
> You can't see," said the Cat.
> "And I bet you can't guess
> What he has in his hat!
>
> "He has something called VOOM.
> Voom is so hard to get,

You never saw anything
Like it, I bet.
Why, Voom cleans up anything
Clean as can be!"
Then he yelled,
"Take your hat off now,
Little Cat Z!
Take the Voom off your head!
Make it clean up the snow!
Hurry! You Little Cat!
One! Two! Three! GO!"

The next page depicts an atomic blast, but pink, as pink as frosting. Spirals spin upward from ground zero. Impact waves shatter the air.

Then the Voom . . .
It went VOOM!
And, oh boy! What a VOOM!

Now don't ask me what Voom is.
I never will know.
But, boy! Let me tell you
It DOES clean up snow!

On the next page, the snow is all white and the walk is shoveled clean. The house looks as if nothing had ever disturbed it. All the tiny cats are gone. "Voom" is plainly a failure of Dr. Seuss's imagination, a lame ending, it was an obvious disappointment to Mark when he was a child, too. This is his ancient mistake, his resorting to books, his willingness to half-believe that a book will pertain somehow to the world, the impatience of his heart, the vanishing of everything he would hold. At last there is always the inevitable lonely moment of closing the page on the final words and looking up into the falling, silent world. When the children's mother returns—again only her calf appearing in the picture, so provocatively high-heel-shod for, supposedly, a mere ordinary shopping errand, that it's possible actually to feel a sexual stirring for her—the children are sitting disconsolately by the window again, pretending innocence.

Then our mother came in
And she said to us two,
"Did you have any fun?
Tell me. What did you do?"

And Sally and I did not know
What to say.
Should we tell her
The things that went on there that day?

Should we tell her about it?
Now, what would you do?
Well . . .
What would you do
If your mother asked you?

18
The Cat in the Hat Comes Back

He looks up. The house is quiet. There's no such thing as Voom. The only thing to do is go home, where he is married now. Jason and Jennifer are asleep, feverish cadavers, easily peeled from his chest. Their heads bounce unconscious as he lays them out on their separate blue biers, their mouths and noses misted by a paraffin sheen, like the glue sniffers that emerge from People's Park. Jason's arms rise in panic as he descends to the cushion, then slowly deflate.

Sewn into the seam of Jason's cushion is a big tough label, as big as a postcard, which reads, *ONLY THE RESIL-IENT FILLING MATERIALS IN THIS ARTICLE MEET THE*

*CALIFORNIA BUREAU OF HOME FURNISHINGS FLAMMA-
BILITY REQUIREMENTS,* and for some logical reason
(though it also reads, *Do Not Remove This Label*) he rips it off,
like a vandal, thereby protecting the children from the
premonition of house fire. He pushes himself up, with a
grunt, to stand at the altitude of an adult trespasser now in
the room. The rescuing "Wish You Were Here" tune begins again in a breeze behind his teeth, where he has a
unique talent for mouthing a private melody softly over his
tongue. In his pockets, the four fingernails of each hand
start to press on his palms in a symmetrical pattern. A
poster on the wall depicts a sunset with an inscription in
jotted nun handwriting, the kind of script that, on senti-
mental posters, carries some message cosmic and profound.

The static of the television still fills the house. This old
shag carpeting with its fat rust and lime yarns seems to run
throughout all the rooms, even into the bathroom. The
sheets tacked up over the front window in the living room
are children's sheets, printed with cartoon characters of the
same Vampire Bunnies that provide the theme for the
video game. This is the year of the Vampire Bunnies. They
appear on three-ring binders, T-shirts, video games, AIDS-
awareness pamphlets, their own television spin-offs.
They're a theme property Audrey's office would love to
have licensed. On the bed sheet, their images are fixed at
random polarities like constellations.

On the coffee table is a stack of textbooks. Dot apparently is an ambitious student. *Human Anatomy and Physiol-
ogy* has a cover illustration of a human silhouette,
acupuncturally sewn with a network of points, a map of
the nervous system or the lymphatic system or something.
The cover of *Algebra for Americans* depicts a discouraging
forest of foggy numerals; a phone bill is stuck in its pages

as a bookmark. *Sentence and Paragraph: Sixth Edition* looks boring. Is she, at her age, made to write topic sentences and supporting sentences and thesis statements?—There, too, is the empty case of the videocassette movie. "More Gruesome Disasters" is printed in trembling letters over a circular gun sight, whose cross hairs divide the field into four quadrants, each containing a still frame from the movie: a tornado churning shingles from a barn roof; corpses stacked behind a fence; a volcano; a man gazing miserably at the camera with, probably, some cause for misery like elephantiasis or leprosy or bereavement. It has the forbiddenness of pornography making the hand linger with disgust as he sets it back on the table and turns to move through the television static toward the bedroom. Within which, a king-size waterbed, in a giant glossy redwood frame, takes up all the floor area. He stops at the threshold. There's little to be seen—just litter on the carpet—a transcended pair of little boy's pajama bottoms, a spoon, a Marin County Yellow Pages, a brassiere at his feet. Within the brassiere's cup is a book of food stamps, and, never having seen food stamps before, he very gingerly picks them up. It's designed like a book of discount coupons—surprisingly cheap slips of paper, like Monopoly money, easy to counterfeit, in various colors of cheap ink, with presidents' pictures. "U.S. Department of Agriculture." He sets them back in the fabric cone of the brassiere just as he had found them. His feet are cemented in place. On the threshold before him is a randomly scattered deck of cards, whose faces show not the usual mosaics of royalty, but rather barnyard animals. What does the conjunction of a donkey and a double rooster signify? Or a milkmaid and a triple cow? Forbidden by the cards' paving, or by their unknowability, he turns back toward the living room, and, feeling all the entitlement and inconsequentiality of a small child as he explores, he goes under the cover of white noise toward the kitchen part of the living room, where the carpet gives way to green linoleum with a raised, embossed medallion on each tile. The formica countertop is printed with overlapping pastel boomerangs. A single raisin and a segment of spaghetti lie on the formica, dropped there from a saliva-slick chin. The stove top, the same avocado green as the floor, has week-old brown specks of, it looks like, tomato soup, and velvet dust around the rear burners, and in fact every surface makes him hold his elbows to his sides as if not to muss the bloom. The face of the refrigerator—avocado green—holds a *Marin Wine and Spirits* magnet clamping down the telephone number of the Poison Control Center.

He pulls open the refrigerator door with one crooked little finger that won't leave prints, and he bends, into its bologna smell, to explore its shelves in the cold light of the inner bulb. A margarine product is called I Can't Believe It's Not Butter! Low-fat milk. The old-fashioned faceted catsup bottle with a badge-shaped label. Carrot sticks in a glass of water. Diet Pepsi. A big squeeze bottle of the sort of cheap Toyota-yellow mustard you don't see any more. Similarly outmoded instant coffee: Taster's Choice. A laminated disk of Oscar Meyer Pimiento Loaf in a resealable package.

Leftover macaroni and cheese, glowing with inner ore, is in a bowl on the bottom shelf. The bowl is one of the Corning Ware bowls of his youth, blue with white etching. Exactly as in his childhood, it's overcooked, the curled tubes of macaroni embedded solid together, tough-crusted on top, and carved out by the curve of a spoon. He pulls free a single hard polyp from the top crust, which on the tongue, and beneath the molar, reveals the sweet vinyl salt of leftover macaroni.

He decides to be reckless and take some more, tucking the Cat in the Hat book under one arm to free up his other hand. Dehydration makes the paste shrink together, the slippery hydrogen bond replaced by a starch grip. But deeper in, deep beneath the carbohydrate molecular structure, there is no time, no decay. Particles abide in still, timeless depths; time and decay are a stormy surface far above. They are eternal in an instant. Free of time's directional arrow.

Yet somehow "story"—existence in "time"—enters the vast staticky sea of virtual particles in the quantum vacuum, and matter is born, wearing its cloak of space. To go from many dimensions to our "three" is truly a *fall*, like the biblical fall into sin, into specific story, into entropy. How amazing to think that, space and time being relative, the materials of this kitchen are the same materials that composed the moment almost three decades ago when his mother stood in the aisle of a supermarket and paused before the cardboard display offering "Volume One: A to Astronomy," for two cents with any purchase of five dollars or more—her mind free of any thought of having a specific child—himself!—thinking perhaps only that a home is incomplete without an encyclopedia. Here in the surrounding cloud of possible, overlapping universes reverberating in immediate space, that very moment is now eternally recurring. You could bring it back. Except for the webbing of lightbeams that trap material in "forward" time, you could reconstruct, out of these wave functions in this 1992 kitchen, that moment—in, perhaps, 1960—a time when supermarkets were a slightly dubious and garish new idea, when fluorescent bulbs were hung overhead in aluminum ice-tray grids, when the floor was made of wooden boards and the produce department provided small brown paper bags rather than plastic, when his mother was impossibly light and frivolous, a girl, pretty and selfish like modern girls. Cash registers were mechanical—beige steel—and they made a loud clank and ding and jingle as their drawer shot out. The encyclopedia would have been displayed in a cardboard shrine announcing, *Only 2¢ with purchase*. His parents still lived in an apartment then. But she went home and cleared a shelf. He can still remember being small enough to perch on the book's margin, the profound smell of ink on its pages, the creak of its opening, and falling through that encyclopedia for whole silent afternoons, a boy destined not to have the leather jacket he wanted.

He is aware that the front door is still hanging open, and that Roger or his wife could come in at any moment, but the macaroni is addictive, and nobody will really notice the theft later, so he stops merely nibbling and pulls the macaroni altogether off the shelf, and he sits down cross-legged to hug the cold bowl with one forearm and tweeze off and shake loose a bigger piece. It doesn't tear loose, so he finds it necessary to use his cupped fingers like a spoon to divide off good-sized segments. It's been many years since he sat on the floor before an open refrigerator in the flow of cold air that creeps along the tiles against the shins, in the bath of light dairy-reflected. His spine rounds over the bowl. Cleverly, he can tear off only indetectable pieces, which, by strategic choosing, will leave the general shape of the macaroni intact. No one will know he's been here.

The sandy swish of tires on pavement comes from outside—along with a sweep of headlights through the still-open front door—and he bounces to his feet wiping his fingers on his pants. That will be Dot. Through the front door he can see, in the driveway, a car fender—a low, white car.

There's a sliding-glass door, fortunately, at the rear of the kitchen, which leads out onto a patio.

It's easy to slide the bowl of macaroni silently back onto the second shelf. The refrigerator door's rubber lip, in closing, meets and sucks the white enamel just as Dot's footsteps arrive at the front porch. She's alone. Unfortunately the rear patio door is a heavy sliding-glass door of the old type, whose rollers will probably thump rhythmically as it slides. His sounds are still hidden under cover of the TV's white noise, so he lifts the catch and succeeds in sliding it a few inches to one side, very quietly. A partition still protects him from a full view of the living room.

"This darn—" says Dot's voice. She turns off the TV. Silence unites the rooms. Mark doesn't move. The opening in the doorway isn't big enough. And beyond the glass door is a second sliding door—a screen with a metal frame that will make a lot of rattling if he tries to move it.

But at his back is a closet. He slips inside it for temporary cover, its door slightly ajar. She'll never come in here; it's a broom closet, also containing a water heater. If necessary, he could hide here until she goes to bed. Or she'll go into the bathroom and close the door and he can make a break for it. He keeps rubbing his macaroni-greasy fingers on the fabric of his pants to take off every trace, the Cat in the Hat book tucked under his arm.

Her footsteps come nearer, then they diminish. Maybe, when she first entered, he should have walked out into the living room and presented himself nonchalantly. It is possible to brazen one's way through such unexplainable situations, by pretending nothing is unusual. Nothing unusual about putting the kids to bed, then having a little snack. But now it's too late. Now he's "hiding in the broom closet." He'll be arrested. His pockets are empty.

Except for the handful of dirt. And in the other pocket the stupid bit of quartz from Roger's kidney. He stands rigid breathing shallowly, his gaze resting on the water heater's EnergyKing logo, beneath which an aluminum plaque is riveted to the heater, engraved with the manufacturer's predictions of explosion and asphyxiation. Brisk, casual sounds come from the other room. She closes the front door. Phase I is the kind of place where all the doors are hollow core, except for the front doors, which are armored with metal.

The thump and roll of a shoe being kicked off. Then a second.

Then silence. She must be checking on the children, finding them asleep. The sound of a light door, closing softly. That would be the children's bedroom door. Then her feet cross the living room. A few *splash* and *plip* sounds indicate she's tossing some of the errant toys into the water in the upturned skylight.

Then she's in the kitchen. She turns on the overhead fluorescent lights, which, with a cellophane-crumpling sound, flicker into harsh brilliance, penetrating the thin vertical slice of air at his almost-closed door. His own nose looms pale. Dot's actual body passes across the slice of light in the door: in the vertical line of visibility, her three-dimensional form appears as a brief thermometer-column of color: she's dressed, fortunately. It hadn't, till now, occurred to him that she might be freely taking off her clothes as she goes about the house.

In a moment of silence, she stands still again. Mark stands in the dark, on his side of the door. He's supposed to be a university professor. He lives up the hill in Phase III. The idea of being discovered in the neighbor's closet, wearing only a parka and muddy pants, is so unthinkable that opening the door and walking irritably right out of this trap seems now almost fair, or possible, magically.

She moves again. She recrosses the slice of visible space, and the kitchen light goes off, returning Mark's closet to dimness. A living room light goes off, too. It's so dark now, he can't see anything at all. His eyes are plastic buttons. She lifts the phone and dials. It's two o'clock in the morning, who could she be calling?

"Hello," she says. And then her voice diminishes as she carries the phone on its long cord—this would be the plastic red-lips phone—around the partition into the living room, where it's hard to hear what she's saying. ". . . Two Twenty-Three Baltic Avenue in Cobblestone Hearth Village Estates. I have a trespasser here. I think I just saw him. Two Twenty-Three. Yes. Yes, I have an air horn . . ."

How did she know? What clues did he leave? In his closet, indecisive fear prevents him from moving. He could still make a break for it and run, noisily, ecstatically. But she's turned off all the lights. He would probably smash into something. He would have to grope.

At that moment, the sliding screen door moves outside: someone else is there.

Mark knows right away, it must be Roger. But apparently Dot has no idea. She seems to have run to the bedroom, judging by the sound of footsteps. Mark can only wait, the darkness teeming against his eyes. The glass door begins to rumble in gliding.

She's back. She's standing by the living-room partition. Roger is making chuffing sounds: he's carrying something heavy. Suddenly a deafening *honk*, like a train's horn, comes from Dot's hands, so loud it paralyzes Mark, transfixes his mind like a headache. The sound is so loud, it actually turns the darkness a certain indefinable color—

somewhere past reddish brown—and makes the sphere of darkness revolve. Or *try* to revolve, against stuckness. It's a very strange sensation. Then it stops. His inner ear aches sharply, especially the left ear, with a sort of *molten* ache that pours right in toward the core of his neck. In the subsequent silence, he swallows.

"Shit," says Roger's voice, audible through the swollen air. With a bang, something heavy drops on the kitchen floor. "Sheesh." He seems to be lying down on the cement outside, and he makes a small stifled groan of pain. Mark can't move. That horn sound was so loud, it seems to have temporarily taken away his will. His silhouette tingles in the strange noon.

Dot says, "Roger?"

"Shit," Roger's voice comes from outside, muffled.

"What the hell are you doing?" says Dot. "You scared the . . . bejesus out of me."

Mark's heart is beating so hard his throat and ears are making a rhythmic clicking noise in climax. He might almost black out. He puts a hand against the wall. Slowly—afloat in his parka, arms out to prevent its making a cushion-hiss sound—he slides down to rest on his haunches. He sets his head softly on the wall. He feels sick. Cool perspiration beads his hairline. The kitchen lights come on, and again his closet is dimly lit.

"Are you all right?" says Dot.

"What is that thing?" says Roger's voice, still outside. He sounds like he's lying face down.

"It's called a Siren Song. It's supposed to be harmless. Are you okay?"

Roger doesn't answer for a minute. "I can't *fucking* believe it."

"My God, Roger. Something terrible happened just now, at Rumplestiltskins."

"Just wait a second."

"Are you okay?" she says, going outside through the doorway. "It's supposed to be disorienting," she says, referring to her Siren Song. "I guess it works."

"I'm okay. It's just my back."

"I'm sorry, honey, but the most horrible thing happened."

"What happened?" Roger says, obviously in some pain.

"The bartender at Rumplestiltskins shot himself. Right in front of everybody."

"At Rumplestiltskins? When?"

"Just now. Just this minute. He was having an argument with his girlfriend behind the bar, and he grabbed her. Do you remember Kimberly Mannis?

"Kimberly Boccinelli."

"She's been cocktail waitressing there at Rumplestiltskins, and she's the bartender's girlfriend. Or she was."

"Who's the bartender?"

"Nobody knew him very well. His name was Glen and he was from Oregon and he played the oboe. That's all anybody ever knew. He was dating her for a few months. He did the saddest thing . . ."

Silence. Dot makes a sound of moving, and when she speaks again she's harder to hear. ". . . He did the saddest thing. Right before he shot himself, he told everybody, 'Don't worry.' He turned to everybody sitting around the bar, and he told us all not to worry."

"With a gun?"

"Yes. Yeah, from the cash register. He obviously never held a gun before, because he got it out of the drawer and at first he held it like, you know, like it was a turd. But he turned to everybody sitting at the bar, and he said, 'I'm sorry, don't worry.' And then he went partway into the kitchen, and he said don't worry *again*. And then he shot himself. It was really terrible, Roger."

"Why did he tell people not to worry?"

"Well, see, he had been fighting with Kimberly behind the bar, and they almost went at it. He almost lost his self-control. You could tell. He looked like he was going to strangle her. So he was apologizing, like."

"Kim Boccinelli!" Roger marvels. "An oboe player was dating Kim Boccinelli?"

"I know. She's still the same old coke whore."

"An oboe player doesn't seem like the type. For her, I mean."

Dot makes another sound of moving, going out toward the edge of the patio maybe. Her voice comes from farther off, "Gary Mannis was smart. He divorced her like you'd get out of a burning building."

"This was at Rumplestiltskins just *now?*"

". . . Oh . . .," Dot says, generally. Judging by the sounds, she seems to have been moving things around on a far corner of the patio. But now the sounds have stopped. "Anyway, Roger, what in the world were you *doing?*"

"The front door was closed and—as you know—I don't have a key."

"Well, you scared me, honey. You could have been anybody."

"I just," he mumbles, *"wanted* to drop off the tar paper and the carpet remnant."

"We just finished talking about that. I can't allow the tree house, Roger. I can't. If that tar paper comes on my property, my whole court case falls apart. You're not supposed to be here at all." She has come back near the door, to stand over him. "And anyway, it's what time of night? I've just had one of the most disturbing experiences of my life, tonight."

"I have to do it now. I'm cleaning up. I can't keep this stuff at my place any more . . . I think I'm going to be living in the van again for a while."

Dot doesn't say anything at first. There's no sound of any motion. Then she says, "Oh, Roger."

"It's only temporary."

Mark hears her get to her feet—apparently she'd been kneeling again—and the screen door rattles from her touch. "Are you just going to lay out here? In the dark?"

"Okay," says Roger.

"But you know you can't stay, honey."

"I know, I know." He grips his breath. He's going to come inside, and it's obviously painful. He wrenched something in the fall.

"It was terrible, Roger. Nobody knew what to do. And fucking Kim Mannis just walked out the door. Just went back and got her purse and walked right out. Like she was *mad* at him for killing himself. Can you imagine? . . . I'll just check on the kids, see if that thing woke them up." Dot passes into the living room, her body scissoring Mark's slice of light. Then the knee-thump and palm-slap of crawling—but slowly—comes across the linoleum floor, and at last Roger appears in Mark's narrow margin of vision, crawling on all fours. He sets his body gently on the kitchen floor face down. Mark—kneeling now in the dark, and staying very still—can sway to one side to bring Roger's head into view in the door crack. His face is expectant looking. His eyes open for a minute to crane wildly toward the doorway Dot went through, then they shut again hard.

"Is it your back?" says Dot, returning.

"Yeah. Just for a second." He winces as he shifts position. "What were they arguing about? The bartender and Kim."

"Shit, she probably wanted money for some lines. You could tell, he could have strangled her. Something came over him. He had one hand around her neck, and she was backed up against the wall."

Roger doesn't respond. Then, shifting position on the floor, he says, "An oboe player from Oregon. What do you do, if you're an oboe player? I guess you play in a symphony. And give music lessons."

Dot makes a shivering sound and says, "Oh, God." A minute goes past and then the kitchen tap runs. "Do you want a drink? I'm having water, that's all. I'm having water."

Roger opens his eyes, tries to follow her to see where she's gone, and then closes his eyes again. " 'It's always either a woman or a hat,' that's what the bouncer at Whango's used to say." He shifts again, trying to align his spine on the floor, experiencing little twinges. "I wouldn't want to be an oboe player from Oregon in love with Kimberly Boccinelli."

". . . You know what Lucas did? It was so embarrassing. Afterwards, before the police came, everybody moved away from the counter to be on the far side of the room. At first, they were scared from the gunshot, but then also they didn't want to sit there at the bar looking at this poor guy's feet sticking out the kitchen door. So everybody picked up their drink—like, the drink this bartender had just *mixed*— and they were across by the bandstand. So there's this big open space on the floor where nobody goes, and *Lucas* crosses it, to go to the bar—to get his tip back. We were just about to leave when this thing happened, so the tip was sitting there on the bar. And Lucas was the one guy to cross the open space. It took him forever, because it was all in little nickels and dimes, and he had to pick up each one separately. I actually thought I was going to throw up."

"Relax, honey," says Roger. "Take it easy."

"It was so terrible. It was one of those guns with a big bullet that doesn't just make a little hole. At least he did it in the kitchen. But still. It seemed like it was completely impulsive."

"Why don't you sit down, Dot. Sit down now. And have one of your cigarettes."

"The worst thing," she says, as she sits on one of the dinette chairs, making a creak, "was that he told everybody, 'Don't worry.' Even though he was scared to death. He was apologizing. He was being polite. Those were his last words. Nobody ever knew anything about him. And he says, 'I'm sorry. Don't worry.' "

"Dot, don't keep harping on it. Just forget it for now. How's the alternator?"

"On my car? The alternator on my car?" She takes a deep breath. ". . . It's been starting. I think my headlights were a little dim just now."

Roger sighs. "That's two hundred dollars right there." They seem to be picking up an old running discussion.

She sighs too, an echo of his.

She slides a cup or something. An ashtray on formica. A dinette chair is moved, with a scrape, and a jingle of its brassy tines. Then there's a creak as she moves in her chair.

"I don't know, Roger," she says, speaking generally.

She strikes a match, then inhales smoke with a smoker's characteristic irritable relief. Through his crack of vision, Mark can see Roger lift his face from the floor and turn his head away to rest the other cheek on the floor.

"I was looking for you tonight," he says.

"You were."

"I went to Rumplestiltskins. I was there, but I guess I left just before all the excitement."

"Oh?"

"I can see how things are—between you and Lucas."

Dot exhales smoke. "Roger, Lucas is fun. He's interesting."

"I could tell that. I was sitting at the end of the bar. I decided not to interrupt."

Dot sighs.

"I didn't mean to be spying on you. I didn't know you guys would be so . . . He looks like a rock star."

"Well, he's very smart, and very creative, and very sensitive. You have no basis for judging him."

"Just relax, Dot. I'm not trying to blame you about anything. Or start an argument or anything."

"Honey, you and I are divorced."

"I know."

Dot inhales again, and expels a stream of smoke across Mark's slice of vision, above Roger's head.

She says, "I'm taking care of my own self now, Roger. I suddenly had this realization: there's all the time in the world."

Roger opens his eyes to look at her feet, on the floor beside his head. Then he closes his eyes again and repeats her words. "There's all the time in the world."

"I don't want to have to *defend* myself tonight. I've been through a lot tonight. Okay?"

"All I want to say is, honey, I think you need me. I think you need me. At least in some things. Everything could be a lot better. I don't want to get you mad, I just wanted to say that, so you'll think about it."

She says at last, "Too much water under the bridge."

"No, baby, I don't care about these guys. Lucas, Bob, whatever. Even back to Pierre. I told you at that time. It's only bodies, bodies don't mean anything. It's all past."

The ashtray makes a sound as she slides it, and she

drinks from her water glass. "Bodies mean something." Roger doesn't reply. She shifts in her seat and says, "Roger, are your pants wet? Did you wet your pants? Honey!" She rises from her chair.

"Come on, Dot."

"You did!"

"Well?" says Roger. "Your little Siren-Song thing is frightening. All right? Sometimes this happens, with people. I've seen it happen a lot."

"Don't be embarrassed, Roger. Just a minute. Roll over."

"I can't. I'm stuck."

"What do you mean you're stuck?" She goes around to the other side of him.

"My back. I'll be okay in a second. Just let me lie here for a second. This back pain always gets better." He lifts his head again, to turn the other cheek against the floor. "Just let me lie here for a second."

"What do you mean you're stuck?"

"I can't move."

"Uh-oh, honey? I called 911."

"You did." His eyes open and scan around toward her ankles, then close again.

"Let me just change you. You can't go around wet."

"Ouch. Don't. You called 911."

"Just before you came in. I'm *trying* to roll you over."

"So the cops'll arrive. And I'll go down on their records for sneaking around here and terrorizing you, I suppose. And then I suppose they'll use *that* in court."

"You *know* you're not supposed to be here. I *told* you about the restraining order."

"Dot, all that has nothing to do with us."

After a pause, she says, "Just stop complaining and turn over."

"I can't turn over," he says—but in pain—for she is indeed pushing him over onto his back, it's clear from the sound of her straining. As his head rolls on the floor, his eyes open wildly. Then he squeezes them shut again. "Don't. I'm not kidding, leave me alone. I'll feel okay in a minute and then I'll go."

The clinking of a belt buckle makes him slap at his stomach. "God damn it, don't."

"Stop fussing," she says. "Besides, honey, the restraining order is for the Bob divorce. It doesn't affect you."

Roger's gaze drifts over the ceiling. People these days think you're some kind of loser if you're *not* scheming and selfish. What you call 'smart.' "

The sound of sliding cloth. The tinkle of a loose belt buckle. "Roger, you'll never change."

"Am I going to have no pants on when the cops arrive?"

"Just wait, let me get a face cloth."

"It'll probably be Wally. Remember Wally Weibel? The masturbator in Mr. Dank's homeroom? He's the cop on duty tonight. He and his partner are the ones that did the eviction tonight. I'd better not be lying here with no pants when they come."

"I'll get you dressed again before they get here. Just hold still. You always tie these double knots."

"Dressed in what? One of your pantsuits?"

"Lift your foot . . . We'll think of something. I have jogging pants."

Roger's eyes focus bleakly *through* the ceiling, seeing these pants. He says, *"Pink* jogging pants."

"No, they're white, they're perfectly masculine. Plenty of men wear jogging pants these days."

"Yeah. Men like Lucas."

"You don't know anything about Lucas."

Roger goes on staring at the ceiling.

"What does he do?"

"Come on, Roger. Don't start."

"Really, what does he do?"

"He does a number of things. He's a very talented song-writer. And he's a teaching assistant at the College of Marin. Actually, he's getting a master's degree at San Francisco State University."

Roger thinks about this information, closing his eyes. All that can be heard is Dot's nurselike motions. She says, "We'll have you out of here in a jiffy."

"Anyway, Dot. The reason I came. I didn't even think you'd be here. I just wanted to drop off the carpet and leave you a note. Because all my stuff is outside in the backyard, and you should go over and take anything you want. There's some perfectly good stuff."

"Roger, I don't want you sleeping in your van."

"Don't worry."

"Why not stay on Jeff and Dianne's couch? They'd be happy."

"No."

"They'd be delighted."

"Dot, I'm forty-three years old."

The whispering whip and click of shoelaces being un-tied.

The creak of leather.

Dot says. "How will I be able to get in touch with you?"

"Don't worry, I'll be in touch . . ." Roger's mouth is strangely compressed, his vision distant. "I'm still your man. You know that."

After a pause, she says, but with reluctance, "Yes, I know that."

"Just take whatever you want. I'll haul away whatever's

left. There's a better TV than the one you have, and there's my Barcalounger, and that lawn mower. I'll go by tomorrow and take away anything you don't want."

"There. We'll have you out of here *long* before they come. They say it always takes them forever to come."

Roger heaves a big sigh and says, irrelevantly, "So anyway."

"Can you lift up your bottom?"

"Dot? When you said you realized there's all the time in the world, what did you mean?"

"Just now?" She stands up and turns on the water at the sink. "I guess I realize mistakes don't matter. You can do whatever you want. Nothing is forever."

Roger doesn't respond. She lets the water run for a while, probably getting it warm to dampen a rag. Then she turns it off, returns, and kneels. Roger says, without opening his eyes, "I don't know, Dot. I think maybe there *isn't* all the time in the world."

She doesn't know how to answer that. Denim cloth slides on the floor, as she moves his pants to one side. "Yes, I know, baby. Sometimes people just have to be patient."

She stands up to run water at the sink again.

"Nothing *isn't* forever," says Roger. "I mean, everything is forever. You know?"

She turns off the water and goes on standing at the sink. She expels breath, in the evening's added-up fatigue. Something in Roger's remark has affected her emotionally. "No, honey," she says.

"Dot, I know you're trying to get out of Terra Linda, but you can't. You are *in* Terra Linda. And where are you gonna go? Hollywood? Dot, you're forty-three years old. And I'm here. *I'm* here. That's something."

No sound comes from Dot's direction. Then she says, "I know, baby, but the real world, out there, isn't like that. Only Terra Linda is like that."

The front door is rapped by a knuckle, in a merry rhythm.

"Great," says Roger.

"That's them." Something softly hits the sink basin. "I'll get rid of them."

Roger's eyes follow her as she leaves the room, her body crossing the door crack in Mark's closet. Mark can't imagine how he would explain himself if the police discovered him hiding here. Maybe they routinely check all closets. All he can do is hold his breath and make himself still. Desperation reduces him to a sort of fairy-tale logic: a strong-enough wish to be invisible can make him *truly* invisible. Whatever may be going on at the front door, it can't be heard. Dot must be whispering. Roger pillows his head on his hands.

But then footsteps approach, and a man's voice says, "Your husband!"

"Lucas, wait," says Dot.

"What does he want? What's he doing?" Lucas's shoes, sounding like enamel-hard leather boots, arrive at the kitchen floor. He says, "Oh." Obviously he has found Roger lying on the floor with no pants on.

"You don't understand," says Dot.

"I wet my pants," Roger tells him. His face doesn't change expression. He keeps his eyes fixed on the ceiling.

Dot tells Lucas, "His back is hurt, so he can't move. I used that self-defense siren. When he first came in I thought he was an intruder."

"Dorothy, are you all right?"

"It's okay, Luke. Everything's fine."

"Are you sure?"

"Roger just had a little problem. He twisted his back in a fall. But he'll be leaving soon."

"Are you absolutely certain? Was he abusive? If you like, I could call the police, just to be sure."

"No, don't bother, I already called them."

"Oh! Oh!"

"Lucas, everything's fine. You're misunderstanding all this."

"Really?"

"Really."

"Well, do you want me to stay? . . . Maybe I'd better go."

"Maybe you should. I'll see you at school."

"Really? Okay," Lucas says. But there is no sound of his moving. "I guess I'll just be going."

"Everything's fine," says Dot. "Roger was just going to leave. Weren't you, Roger?"

"Dorothy, I'm not sure I feel right about leaving you like this. Maybe I should just stay until the police come."

"No, he's fine, Luke. You're misunderstanding the whole thing. He wasn't abusive."

"Well, something must have happened. I'm sorry, Dorothy, but *somehow* he wrenched his back. *Somehow* you had to use the Siren Song. I understand that the wife in these situations wants to cover up and make everything seem okay. That's perfectly natural. But Dorothy, he doesn't deserve your protection, not if he was showing any abusive behavior. Or even mentally. I'd be remiss if I ignored the obvious signs."

Roger at last speaks. "I'm leaving," he says, his eyes closed.

Lucas, after a pause, addresses Roger. "I'm sorry, Mr.

Hoberman. Roger. I would never want to interfere in any-body's . . . situation. But it seems incumbent on me. Given the obvious situation."

"Lucas, really," says Dot.

"Just until the police come. Okay? Then I'll go. *I'll* feel better."

Dot gives up, leaving the room. "Roger, hang on. I'll go get you some pants." She's headed for the bedroom.

Lucas clears his throat. He and Roger have been left alone in the kitchen—though, as far as Mark can tell, Lucas is lingering half out of the room, hovering at the border of the partition to avert looking at Roger's naked-ness. His voice seems to come from some further distance as he says, "I just want to see you out the door, Roger. I'm sorry, but it seems the right thing to do. I understand that you've experienced some . . . problems. You've been adapting. But this is like a textbook example of a domestic . . . problem. All the signs are here. I would feel remiss if I left."

Roger says at last, "I understand. You don't need to keep talking."

Dot speaks from the bedroom, "Lucas? This *is* a more complicated situation."

"I have to do the right thing, Dorothy. It would be obvi-ous to any observer."

"Do the right thing," Roger says, with contempt, and he coughs with a chuckle of pain like a bum.

Lucas, now offended, tells him, his voice softening to-ward mercy, "Mr. Hoberman, there are government agen-cies you could take advantage of, to help you. Especially for Vietnam veterans. To help them readjust. People want to help you. Society wants to help you."

Dot returns from the bedroom. She says, "Here you go."

She crosses Mark's vertical slot of vision, and the sweat-pants she's carrying appear as a swift falling shuttle in the slot. "Not pink," she says. "White. See?"

"Dot?" says Roger.

"Give me your foot. These'll go on easy."

"Dot? All this shit—all this restraining order—has nothing to do with us. You know that."

There's anger in Roger's voice. It makes Lucas shift his stance around. He says, "Dorothy, I think he clearly *would* be abusive if he could stand up. How long ago did you call them? You might have told them it was a Vietnam veteran. They'd probably come faster if they knew there's a history."

Roger whines, still addressing Dot, "What is this? Why does this keep coming back? I wasn't even in battle. I was a fucking pot-walloper. I was making meat loaf in Manila, half the war."

"Roger, lift your butt. Can you move?"

Roger looks at her, confused. "God damn it."

"Okay, just lay there," she says, standing up. "Just lay there till the cops come. Let 'em find you like that." She crosses the floor, and again she lights a cigarette. The only sound is the scratch-scratch of one of those disposable butane lighters. Nobody says anything.

"Really, Mr. Hoberman," says Lucas. ". . . Roger." And then gently, "Things change. People have to change and grow. You've got some issues to deal with."

Roger squeezes his eyes shut. Then he begins to tip the hull of his body around to lie on his face, rolling out of Mark's limited angle of vision. After he rolls, he lets out a breath. He reaches forward to draw a light chair toward himself—one of the brassy dinette chairs comes into view—and he uses it to climb on and pull himself up.

Then, kneeling outside Mark's angle of vision, he must

be pulling his pants up. His body comes into view briefly: he is indeed wearing white jogging pants. They're too small, stretched high above his ankles. He stands, his shoulders pinned high in air. Carrying himself stiffly like a stenciled outline of a man, he limps out of Mark's line of vision. The sound of the front door—heavy, armored— closes upon silence again in the condominium.

19
Mark's Escape

He's alone now with Dot and her boyfriend, and at this point it seems reasonable that they might open the closet door. For a broom? Or a mop? He tries again to picture himself making a break for it, getting across the floor and out the back door before they have a chance to respond.

"Well!" says Lucas.

Not getting any response from Dot, he adds, "Strange night!"

Dot enters Mark's line of light. She sets the dinette chair back in place.

Part of Lucas comes into view, setting a steady hand on

Dot's shoulder as they both move on out of sight. He says, "The poor guy."

Dot doesn't respond.

"He's his own worst enemy. He's only hurting himself."

"I think maybe you should go, Lucas," says Dot. "I'm not in the mood any more."

"Oh, understandably, understandably. This has been two traumas in one night." He is following her as she moves. "But isn't that an ironic revelation? That the big war hero was actually a cook? The whole time? He never even held a gun? Obviously he's compensating for *that*."

"Mm-m," says Dot, two faint notes.

"All that machismo is undoubtedly to compensate for being a wimp in the army. For not living up to the male expectation of brutality."

They've moved into the living room area. Dot says vaguely, "I didn't see his car out front." She must be drifting to look out the window.

"It's really amazing. Society used to do that to people. Give them these rigid *roles*."

Dot doesn't answer. Then Lucas's voice, bounced off the front windowpane, says, "There he goes."

A toy plops into the water of the upside-down skylight. Dot is tidying up.

Lucas muses, his voice still bounced off the window glass, "How can you help a guy like that? You can't. I see somebody like that, and I always think, 'There but for the grace of God goes me.'" . . . Then, turning, he says, "Okay, but listen. Lock all your doors, Dorothy. I don't think he'll be back, but we'll both sleep more soundly. Do you want me to wait here until the police come? This is the *second* shake-up in one night. If I were you I'd feel slightly frazzled."

"No, I'm fine."

"Oh, God, I think you did get some on you . . ."

"Where? No, that's not blood. It's salsa."

"Are you sure? You know, it was amazing how the blood flew out in the opposite direction. And the guy beside you—"

"I'm sure it's salsa."

"You know, Dot—" Mark can tell from his tone of voice that he is starting to embrace her. "It's not just for your sake that I want to stay here tonight. It's for mine, too. I'm a little traumatized myself."

". . . Still," Dot says, inarguably.

"You're sure. You don't think he might come back."

"No, Luke. Really. You can just leave. I really appreciate it, but you can just leave now."

The front door opens. Lucas starts saying something in a low voice, outside on the front porch.

They're gone, and Mark seizes his chance. He presses with a knuckle to open the closet door a few inches, discovers no one in sight, and runs to the wide-open back door, flickering barefoot across the interval of linoleum so fast that no weight touches the floor. Escaping a shiver, he passes through the open rectangle of the patio door and feels himself vanishing in the darkness of the tender lawn, dew between his toes. The great boom of silence outdoors envelops him. At the edge of the yard, he stops running and, moving more slowly in the dark, comes around the corner of the house to crouch in the shadow.

He can see Dot's front porch. They're both standing there on the steps, completely unaware that he was ever in the house. Dot stands on the top step haloed by the light of the porch lamp. Lucas is facing her, but two stairs below. His head is tilted back to look up at her. Then she speaks, and he bows his head. She gestures out toward the street, and they both look at Roger—who is already distant on the sidewalk—reeling away oddly sideways as if hung from one armpit. His hands are lifted before him like paws.

Mark can stay safe where he is, behind the bushes at the corner of the house. Lucas does indeed have a ponytail—and heeled boots. On his chin is a very small, pointy Errol Flynn beard. In farewell, he drops back to set one foot behind him on a deeper stair, and he reaches up to clasp Dot's offered hand in both of his—then turns and trots down the sidewalk and, with a salute, pulls open his car door. It's a Volkswagen Bug. Dot's palm rises to make a circular erasing motion, and Lucas ducks into his car, her faithful knight. He manages to make his VW engine, in starting, sound jaunty, a cough and a roar. As soon as all three parties have dispersed in different directions, Mark will appear, he'll get onto the sidewalk, like a citizen, and walk straight home to his house, where his refrigerator always hums and sends a hot breath along the terrazzo floor, and the little plastic clock ticks at the bedside, its second hand screwing a spiral clockwise through time. And he'll crawl up onto the bed, where his wife's animal warmth will revive him and drive out of his body the drowned clamminess of having gone through this dream. In which the only casualty was Glen the bartender, an oboe player from Oregon. Lucas's car pulls away, and Dot turns to go in, shutting her door softly. Mark is the last spectator. In the driveway stands Dot's heavy white Corvette.

Roger—his figure grown smaller in the distance—seems to be walking in the wrong direction. Before reaching the intersection of Marvin Gardens, he limps across Baltic Avenue on the diagonal and he climbs the embankment toward Phase III. But the bias of his climb is not toward his own condominium but *away* from home. His van is nowhere to be seen: he seems to have brought his tar paper to

Dot's house on foot. All of which will have to remain one more mystery unsolved—and that will be just fine.

Lucas isn't quite gone: his car does a U-turn and runs past again, making a roaring sound from the 1960s, the rattling Volkswagen engine valves' distinctive tambourine jingle. Mark waits a minute longer to watch Roger mount the top of the slope and then keep on tacking diagonally, limping on the level ground above, sinking perspectivally. At last he disappears, his head dropping beneath the dirt horizon.

Then Mark comes out from the shadow and walks straight to the sidewalk, where he turns an abrupt angle (the crucial angle, the crucial comical turn, where lying stops and normal reality begins again) and sets a course toward home and stays in motion, his shadow unraveling beside him. The sound of Lucas's engine, after he rounded the corner onto Boardwalk, has quickly vanished altogether. The circle of peacefulness widens in the neighborhood. No police cars are in evidence.

On the sidewalk, he's a citizen again. Rather than taking the shortcut up the embankment, he'll stick to the pavement to get home. The street curves gently, and he begins at last to put a safe distance between himself and Dot's house. He feels athletic, light. After a night of too much drinking and too little rest, there is almost a clear space of philosophical lucidity, elation, a happiness perhaps enjoyed by criminals. His slippery red leg muscles are glad to be moving, unnaturally wakeful in their fatigue: he's an upright cadaver like one of the skinless braided homunculi that must be pictured in Dot's anatomy book, as he walks the grounds of Cobblestone Hearth Village Estates among the dark volumes. The earth underfoot swells and subsides and Baltic Avenue rises on the curve toward the hilltop, and as the land melts around him he gets one last look at

Dot's house—glancing burglarlike over his shoulder—to see that no police cars have yet arrived. He's free. He's nonexistent, from Dot's point of view. According to the von Neumann interpretation of quantum mechanics, his *non*existence expands in outward waves at the moment he rounds the corner and vanishes from Dot's universe. It's very quiet. The strange neighborhood rotates past him in midnight's photo. At Marvin Gardens, he turns uphill, toward Hearthstone, into Phase III, passing the sales office's white chapel in the moonlight. The old Phase I sidewalks are cured, browned, sunken in turf. But ahead in Phase III, he can see, all the sidewalks are so new they seem lightly powdered like sticks of fresh-unwrapped gum, and they still lift up above the ground as it drains away. When he reaches them, their grooved texture is sharper under his bare feet. Somewhere in the urban glow on the horizon, the neon sign of the Art and Artifice Club may still shine in the night.

Behind him, tonight, are probably several mistakes, but one thing he knows about life is that you can never finally tell the difference between a mistake and a success, fate being a tapestry with more than one side. Ascending through night air, it occurs to him that our oversimplified three-dimensional space-time is a sort of fossil. In higher real multidimensions, wondrous exploding unimaginable events are constantly being fossilized anew in our slow-motion hallucination of "existence." Actual reality is a constant firestorm in many dimensions, of which our 3-D world is an ashen cinder. When all he could see of Dot's kitchen was a vertical line, her passage back and forth appeared as only a winking line—or rather as line segments—shuttling up and down in the thermometer of his view. A leg, or an arm, could be *inferred* only by the blip it created in scissoring across his slot of light.

Which would be how extradimensional events appear in our collapsed, fallen world: unimaginable shapes in multidimensions swim *through* us like dolphins. And in passing through our plane, ripe spheres appear only as flat hoops expanding and shrinking; a slicing wand appears only as a speck that glides; entire worlds touch us only as momentary smudges of tangency. Dolphins and whales, bulging and tapering, slip through us. Or rather, they *sift* through the sieve of space-time, making the visible sequin-shimmer of "solid matter"—which we think we touch, locally—so that a particle has physical existence in our world only by our forgetting its origins among such brilliant angels of other dimensions. Dot, in Mark's limited visual plane, seemed only an occasional vertical cursor flashing, though to Roger in his kitchen she was a dove of mercy, circling and circling.

In a way, Roger Hoberman's inevitable eviction from Phase III, where he never belonged, will be a sort of relief. He keeps everybody around him guilty of not being as bighearted as he is. His weird remark, hours ago beside the camp fire—that he has to have Dot because she's "the alternative to substance abuse"—is actually slightly scary. Such romanticism is not what you imagine in a next-door neighbor. Reaching his own cul-de-sac, Mark starts lifting into a jog, out-of-breath, climbing the hill, chastened with every passing second.

He stops. He can see Roger—his figure in the distance—walking up Hearthstone Drive toward the exit gate. He must have parked outside the gate. Maybe the guard wouldn't let him in, under new orders from management. Mark probably isn't conspicuously visible, standing still where he is—but nevertheless he drifts forward into the zone of shadow between streetlights.

He's still shambling with his hands held up circus-bear-like, which must help his shoulders keep a grip on his wounded spine. If he's headed for the front gate, he is taking a peculiar path: when the Hearthstone Drive sidewalk curves to the right, he keeps going in a straight line, on some azimuth of his own, sustaining the same gait though the paving veers from beneath him. Maybe he knows a shortcut to another place along the border, where he parked his van.

Mark puts his hands in his pockets and, in case he should be glimpsed, sets out quickly to cross the street into darkness, looking preoccupied, looking like somebody else besides himself, if that's possible. Once across the street, he risks a glance backward: Roger is just vanishing through the weedy curtain where the street lamp light gives up. Mark's fingers sift the handful of dirt in his pocket. And then he realizes he has locked himself out. Again. He's absolutely sure: when he closed the back door, it clicked with a sound of certainty, a sound his ear now still holds in accurate echo.

He stops and stands indecisively—somewhat angrily now, really—on the unpaved area before his own dark house. In his hand is a Cat-in-the-Hat book. He's an amnesiac. He has no money. His pockets are empty, except for the gemstone still in his pocket—which you could never "spend," which you couldn't take down to the 24-hour Denny's by the freeway and pass across the counter in exchange for a cup of coffee and a roll. He has been truly stupid, all night, to feel he had some duty to restore it to its jar. Maybe he'll never have to give it back now, he thinks, holding it in his palm.

He won't even try the front door. It always locks automatically. He goes around to the back door just to give the knob a try. Roger's possessions are still there. He trots to hop up on his own stoop and try the door.

Of course, just as he had thought, it's locked. Shaken, it doesn't budge or even make the slightest sound, held fast in its frame by the fresh rubber insulation strip. If he rings the bell to wake Audrey, he'll have to go into the whole story. He gives up on the door and turns out toward the dark land that falls away behind the house, his bare toes gripping the edge of the concrete as on a diving board. It's possible to imagine that the sky is getting pale. At the moment of jumping down off the stoop, he glimpses the light of an airplane departing on the horizon, sinking in the east as slowly as a declining planet, which might be Shubie's plane, an object for his farewell. Actually, it's probably too early to be Shubie's plane; but he can choose it as the necessary symbol, he can *think of* it as her plane, to accomplish the, as Bloom might say, necessary efficient misunderstanding that will let his life go on.

Going around the side of the house toward the bathroom window, he is so impatient, or even urgent, that he senses himself to be, though singly, *aswarm* about the house, as he looks for a vulnerable spot. The bathroom window is the only place, so, without pausing to let in fear or reasonableness, he punches his fist directly through the two layers of glass and withdraws his arm so fast that he doesn't get cut—though he does create a pile of broken glass on the floor which will have to be explained to Audrey in the morning. There's no avoiding that now. Each detail is connected to all the other details, so that the whole story will have to come out, hard to explain though it may all be.

The inner crank is easy to reach, through the hole, and he cranks the window all the way open and hops to wriggle upward and be born in reverse, entering the walled silence within that makes the outside air seem, by comparison, a deafening ocean. His palms first touch the tile floor. Looming, glassy sound-reflection tells him that the porcelain toilet is right next to his ear. And then his feet land. His bare toe gets a painful scrape on the window frame, a bone-deep bang. But he deserves at least a little pain, considering the night's follies. He climbs up from the broken glass to stand on two feet and limps out into the living room and up the stairs quickly on tiptoe, a wounded satyr pulling off his parka before he enters the bedroom, so that its nylon whispering won't awaken Audrey.

He arrives at her bed bare chested. But his hand—having dipped habitually into the parka pockets—is holding the tough tag, legible in the faint light: *ONLY THE RESILIENT FILLING MATERIALS IN THIS ARTICLE MEET THE CALIFORNIA BUREAU OF HOME FURNISHINGS FLAMMABILITY REQUIREMENTS,* and he tucks it into the book. Forget it. Audrey makes a noise, and he stops halfway through taking off his pants. She starts snoring loudly. Naked over the bed, he stands still, to try to halt the momentum that brought him here. His own vapors rise off him. It was a long, fast climb uphill. The clock beside the bed makes its regular click. Outside the window, a star, unfastened from the firmament, is drifting, falling. It's another airplane, which, too, could serve as the object of his farewell to Shubie. As could any departing plane from this moment on. Goodbye, goodbye. Prayer needs a physical object, to fly toward. Reality is a network of the most efficient misunderstandings.

He's so anxious, hovering, he finds he could almost touch Audrey and wake her, to tell her what's been happening, everything, to ground this voltage in her body. He'll be too excited to sleep. Yet, having recovered his breath now, he begins the elaborate slithering process of getting between the sheets beside the healing warmth of her T-shirt-clad body. It's easy. He slips into a marsupial groove. A completely indiscriminate forgiveness radiates from his wife. The pace of her snoring doesn't change. Maybe the truth is, he'll be saved not by her, but only by his wanting it badly enough. Only hours of skin-to-skin contact will warm his chilled bones like that warmth of being buried in hot children.

And yet, as he lies there, a thought strikes him: that the Most Efficient Misunderstanding—or The Luckiest Misunderstanding—is a sort of organizing principle, a *general* principle. It's the rule by which an electron chooses its path (as Feynman pointed out), but it's also the rule by which consciousness (impossibly) enters matter. At a *point*. The whole fabulous idea of a *"point"*—a "location without dimension," as defined in high school geometry— is the fundamental mistake that makes physics possible. That makes "space" possible. Any "point," however succinct, will at last admit the needle of any schoolboy's mind and open up into a vortex through which all the universe may flood.

And so science is pinned down to fictitious "locations." You can blame Euclid for defining it originally, innocently. Or you can blame your high school teachers. Or you can blame *yourself* for not trusting yourself, not feeling the native authority to contradict your high school teachers. The entire dream of space is piled up from sandy nonexistent points. The invention of the integral calculus doesn't solve the problem, because mythic "points" still hide beneath the integral functions. Slowly, he peels back the sheet and he rolls to creep off the bed—just for a minute to jot down these words on his computer. "Defining point as 'location without dimension': luckiest, most efficient misunderstanding." An idea still very vague.

It isn't even exactly Arnold Bloom's idea. He must admit it's his own idea. Naked, he betrays his wife just for a minute more, creeping away from the bed. The door to

the other room is already slightly open. He doesn't turn on
the light but—stepping over the hazard of Audrey's skis on
the floor—he turns on the computer in the corner, whose
screen floods his face with radiation. "The most efficient
misunderstanding," he whispers aloud to himself. "The
luckiest misunderstanding." Or—ha!—he might type
nothing more than just a *period* in the center of the screen:
a point. And let that alone be the object of his contemplation tomorrow.

The effort of physics has always been to explain what
presence is. And the "point" is the human mark of *presence*. Yet, being dimensionless, it's supposed to be also, at
the same time, *absent*. And that contradiction licenses the
entire specious dream castle of geometry. It licenses all
space—as well as time. For the *instant* (of time) and the
point *both* are the motes from which experience is built, the
faith that there are fixed places.

Guilty again of being anointed—undeservedly, inexpli-
cably—he sits down, the wood cold on his butt, his face in
the screen-glow an idol glowering, a pre-Cambrian deity
moving over the emptiness of light, and he brings up a
fresh new file on the computer. Again he's attacking the
venerable Niels Bohr, the priestly Karlheinz Pflugsk. But
somebody has to take this step off a cliff, and it might as
well be him, he's expendable, he's been promoted to irrelevancy, it's the nearest cliff to step off of. Tonight he only
wants to get down the words, "most efficient, or luckiest,
misunderstanding"—and tomorrow morning develop the
specific implications—how to begin thinking of a universe
in which every "point" is a perfect misunderstanding. He
decides that, as a matter of fact, he will indeed type only a
single period onto the screen, wittily, a succinct ovum to be
enlarged in the morning—because, for one thing, he
doesn't want to kill the idea by phrasing it, yet.

The computer's software program interrupts him at the tap of the key, asking, ''DO YOU WANT TO SAVE THIS DOCUMENT?''

He taps the Enter key—affirmative.

''PLEASE CHOOSE A TITLE,'' the machine advises him. And (as the computer makes a digestive inner crunching noise of inscription on its storage disk, the sound of a thought actually being cut by beams of light into the disk surface's delicate magnetic bloom) he enters, as a provisional title, a word he might as well go ahead and be bold and use openly: ''Meta-''

A sound—Audrey's querying voice—comes from the other room. She's awake. Now he can tell her the whole story, and he turns toward her voice.

''Mark? Where were you? Where are you?''

''Here I am,'' he says. ''I'm right here.''

About the Author

Louis B. Jones is a graduate of the M.F.A. program at the University of California at Irvine and the author of *Ordinary Money*. He lives with his family in Mill Valley, California.